Men of Whiskey Row Series

SWEET

Obsession

D.A. YOUNG

Sweet Obsession
Copyright © November 2015 D.A. Young

This book is a work of fiction and intended for mature audiences aged 18+ only.

ISBN: 978-0-692-10878-9

Cover Design and Interior Formatting—T. E. Black Designs; www.teblackdesigns.com

Editing—Little Pear Editing Services/ littlepearediting@gmail.com Copyright © March 2016

Proofing—Ideality- Consulting / latrisa@ideality-lity.com/ Copyright © April 2018

PLAYLIST

EVERYTHING HAS CHANGED – TAYLOR SWIFT FT. ED SHEERAN

LET HER GO – PASSENGER

EASY TO LUV U –STACIE ORRICO

FOOL OF ME – MESHELL NDEGEOCELLO

COUNTDOWN – BEYONCÉ

LOVE ME LIKE YOU DO – ELLIE GOULDING

RIPTIDE – VANCE JOY

CHANDELIER - SIA

(SITTIN' ON) THE DOCK OF THE BAY – OTIS REDDING

FIRE – THE POINTER SISTERS

COME WITH ME NOW – THE KONGOS

I BELIEVE IN YOU AND ME – WHITNEY HOUSTON

ALL SUMMER LONG – KID ROCK

LOSE YOURSELF – EMINEM

STAY WITH ME – SAM SMITH

B* DON'T KILL MY VIBE – KENDRICK LAMAR

INVINCIBLE – KELLY CLARKSON

CRASH MY PARTY – LUKE BRYAN

HELLO – BEYONCÉ

This book is for you.

For believing in me and the adventures.

For being just as excited to dive into a new escapade as I am to share it with you.

For loving the Men of Whiskey Row and their women as much as I do.

Thank you very much.

"It's better to cross the line and suffer the consequences, than to just stare at it, wondering for the rest of your life."

-Unknown

PROLOGUE

1992
WHISKEY ROW, TENNESSEE

*T*HE TURNOUT FOR THE FUNERAL service atop a high hill, just outside of town, was sparse. The only attendees were Reverend Melton, Jeb the undertaker, a handful of drunken men, and three boys. The boys listened stoically as the man of God struggled to find decent things to say about the deceased. Eventually, he stopped trying when he noticed the second oldest boy sneering at him. He glared at the lad and quickly finished his brief speech before letting the other men speak. They bemoaned the death of their drinking partner, blathering on about how much liquor he'd been able to consume in one sitting. When they finally walked away, they patted the shoulder of each boy, slurring their condolences. Still, the young trio remained silent.

Standing next to the grave, the boys watched dirt slowly fill the hole and cover the casket. It had been a depressing affair, nothing like the glorious service held a week earlier in the cemetery where the entire town came to pay their respects as the angelic voices of the church choir filled the sky. On that day, the townspeople wailed and cried, feeling the tragic loss of one of their own. The many dishes of food brought to the Sullivan doorstep would feed the boys for at least two months. Yes, this turnout was different. But it was one the boys wouldn't have missed for the world.

Reverend Melton stopped next to the group. He studied each of their identical stone-faced expressions, searching for a sign of compassion. None would be forthcoming. Like their parents, the boys were incredibly good-looking. Jackson was the eldest, and resembled his dear mother the most, down to his calm personality. Standing tall at five-feet-ten inches, he sported short black hair and a solemn pair of hazel eyes. Already, he appeared wise beyond his thirteen years as he assumed the now available role of the family patriarch.

Eleven-year-old Darby was the second eldest, and unfortunately, resembled their bastard of a father. A strapping lad, he had thick, reddish-brown hair that fell to his shoulders in thick sheets with a pair of dark, stormy green eyes. Many a blistering lecture had been given to him because of his constant mischief, but he shrugged it all off with the Sullivan 'devil-may-care' attitude and a shit-eating grin.

And then there was Casey, the baby of the family, at eight years old. He inherited his dark blonde hair from his paternal great-grandfather, and it was cut in a bowl shape that framed his delicate face. Being small in stature, due to a fever at birth, had earned him the unpleasant title of 'Little Shit' from their father. His bright hazel eyes filled with tears as he, too, stared at the gravesite.

Clearing his throat, the reverend began somberly, "Boys, I'm sorry for your loss. It's bad enough to lose your mother, but to also lose your father–"

"We didn't lose our mother. She was taken from us, Reverend!" Darby interjected scathingly.

Casey clutched his thigh, sniffling quietly, and Darby ruffled his hair reassuringly. Reverend Melton shot the redhead a censorious frown as he bent down to console Casey. The lad twisted away from them and launched himself at his eldest brother. Jack picked him up with an easy familiarity and rubbed his back, comforting Casey as sobs shook his tiny body. Helpless, the man of God could only watch as the inconsolable little boy cried harder.

Addressing Reverend Melton, Jack nodded his head and spoke for the first time that morning. "Thank you for your time today, sir. We appreciate you comin' out in this weather to assist us with this matter. Drive safely back to town, okay?"

Realizing he'd been dismissed and by a thirteen-year-old lad no less, Reverend Melton simply nodded and made his way down the hill, saying prayers for them the entire way. The grave was now a quarter of the way filled. Jeb was working fast because the University of Tennessee was playing against Vanderbilt in less than an hour and he didn't plan to miss that football game. Jack and Darby exchanged a meaningful look before Jack spoke up.

"Hey, Jeb, why don't you go on ahead and get outta here. Darby and I can finish up."

"Awww hell! I can't leave you two to bury your pappy. It ain't the Christian thing to do." Jeb protested while discreetly sneaking a peek at his watch.

Darby's contemptuous snort made the old man stiffen with indignation. "Old man, please! You're as much a Christian as the Devil is an angel."

Jack hid a smile as Jeb scowled at his younger brother. Darby didn't cower, meeting the older man's glare head on.

"One of these days, Darby Sullivan. One of these days..." Jeb threatened, taking a step toward the little

11

bastard, who instead of retreating, fisted up and puffed his chest out, a challenging smirk on his face.

Jack stepped between them, giving Jeb a hard look. "But today ain't that day, Jeb. Thank you kindly for your time. We can take it from here."

The old man shrugged. What did he care? He would still be paid regardless.

"Suit yourself, youngin'."

He dropped the shovel, and tipped his hat, murmuring, "My condolences to your family."

Then he took off running down the hill to his truck, hoping like hell the boys had saved him a seat at the bar.

It was a cool afternoon, the sky overhead was clear, but in the distance, dark, ominous clouds promised a whopping thunderstorm and rain showers that would last a couple of days. The boys had carefully studied the Weather Channel's ten-day forecast last week after burying their mother and specifically picked this day. Soon, it would be time, but for now, they settled down to wait.

Jack walked over to the large backpack he'd packed earlier this morning and took out some sandwiches and sodas. Darby pulled the blanket out, and they all sat down to eat in silence, lost in their individual thoughts. Full off a half-eaten peanut butter and jelly sandwich, Casey soon drifted to sleep in Darby's lap.

"So, what's the plan, Jack?" Darby mumbled around a mouthful of bologna, mustard, and wheat. His older brother was the only person in the world he would listen to and follow blindly. His back bore the marks of his father's belt buckle for his outright defiance, and his ears had often been scorched by his mama's lectures, but all Jack had to do was look at him, and Darby would cut all bullshit aside.

Jack looked up at the sky, the black clouds were closer, resembling an oil slick spreading their way. Soon, *he thought, fissions of anticipation spreading along his skin. "I spoke to Aunt Kelly in Memphis. She's willin' to take us in."*

He didn't mention that in exchange for room and board, he would give his money-hungry aunt some of the money his mother had secretly saved for them. Aside from his brothers, Jack wanted nothing more to do with anyone named Sullivan, let alone live with a complete stranger, but he needed to make sure they didn't get separated. "The goal is for us to stay together, no matter what. It's what Ma would have wanted."

Thunder rumbled angrily, and the clouds were now directly over them, ready to impart their fury. "Come on, Darby. It's time."

They rose to their feet, leaving Casey to sleep restlessly on the blanket. Darby reached into the backpack and pulled out a can of lighter fluid before following Jack to the open grave. When they suggested the deceased be buried out of town, no one had put up much of a protest. Patrick Sullivan was truly an evil man, and the town was relieved to be rid of him. The only protest had come from lazy, old Jeb when they requested that a deeper than normal grave be dug.

Without looking at each other, the brothers swiftly unzipped their pants and relieved themselves into the ditch of Patrick's perpetual resting place. Once finished, Darby contemptibly spat into the hole then shook lighter fluid down into it. When the can was empty, he held it up for his brother to see, then threw it into the hole.

Jack reached into his pocket and produced a lighter. He flicked it open and a blue flame shot out, almost hypnotizing him with its sway. As he spoke, his voice took on the Irish lilt that only surfaced when the boys were emotional.

"We do this to honor our ma, Moira Sullivan. A kind and beautiful lady she was. May she finally rest in peace

without having to look over 'er shoulder for yer' sorry arse. She was a true angel, loved by everyone who knew 'er, especially 'er boys. I know she's happy now to be rid o' the likes o' ya as we are. Yer' gone but will never be forgotten, Ma. May ye rot in hell for all eternity, Patrick Sullivan, and even then t'would be too short a time for ya in our opinion."

Darby nodded his agreement. Jack then dropped the flame into the pit of hell with his eyes burning with unshed tears of rage and sorrow for the unfairness of it all.

Quickly, the flames consumed the casket in a crackling fury, almost reaching the top of the grave. As the fire blazed, Jack and Darby looked on serenely. It climbed higher just as the sky split open and unleashed the rain. They gave the burning pit the one-fingered salute before quickly gathering up their trash and throwing it into the flames. Darby pulled their raincoats out before strapping on the backpack while Jack wrapped Casey in the blanket then a raincoat, making sure that he was protected from the downpour. They started down the hill, and Casey stirred sleepily, revealing troubled hazel eyes.

"Is he truly gone, Jackie?" Casey whispered, as if afraid to believe it.

Jack held him closer. "Dinna fash yerself, Case. He'll not be botherin' ya' again. Get some rest now."

And Casey went back to sleep, a peaceful smile on his face.

The rain turned into a torrential downpour. By the time they reached the bottom of the hill, they were exhausted. The trek back to town would be grueling in this weather. Simultaneously, Jack and Darby noticed the black town car parked on the side of the dirt road. Two men, underneath umbrellas, stood beside it. They appeared to be waiting for the boys.

The dark-haired one sported a full beard and wore his hair slicked back in a ponytail. He was a muscular man who stood six-feet-six-inches tall and wore a lumberjack plaid shirt and well-worn jeans with work boots. Jack recognized him as Alexei Romankov, the town's richest businessman. The boys nodded respectfully to him, and he returned the gesture.

The other man wore a tailored dark suit, and his long, pale blonde hair was pulled back from his angular tanned face. His expression was intense as he surveyed them through narrowed, eyes. He was a stranger, and that was completely unacceptable to the boys as it was synonymous with danger. Swiftly, Darby pulled his trusty switchblade from his front shirt pocket and placed himself in front of his brothers. The blade in his hand gleamed with deadly intent, matching the promise of violence in his green eyes.

"Who the fuck are you?!" Darby demanded, waving the knife menacingly.

Alexei suppressed a smile, while the incredulous blonde stranger raised his eyebrows. Calmly, they approached the threesome.

"Young man, if you don't wish for me to give you the proper ass kicking you rightly deserve, you will put that knife away. NOW!" he spoke sharply, in a gentrified tone. To Jack's surprise, Darby obeyed immediately. Nodding a greeting at Jack, he continued, "My name is Ian Rusnik, and I knew your mother. In the event that something happened to her, I was to come immediately for you. Unfortunately, I did not hear of her passing until this morning," he added sorrowfully. "My condolences to you, gentlemen."

"How do we know you are who you say you are?" Jack inquired suspiciously. He was unaware his ma had any friends other than the ones his father had allowed her to have, including Alexei's wife, Vivienne. She was not allowed to be friends with or interact with any man. Suddenly, Jack was very tired. His arms were heavy from carrying Casey, and it hurt too much to think. He just wanted to get out of the cold and rain and be alone to gather his thoughts.

At that question, Darby's blade flicked out again. As Jack glared at the stranger defiantly, he could feel Alexei's astute gaze on him. He dared not look his way because then he would be reminded of his mother's close friendship with the man's wife. For sure, he would lose it. He needed to be strong for his brothers, not bawling like a stupid baby. Thanks to his bastard da, he was now the head of the Sullivan family.

Ian gave Darby a disapproving look. To Jack, he calmly stated, "Loose wall in the pantry."

Jack froze, remembering his last conversation with his mother as she furiously whispered to him while his father screamed on the other side of the locked bedroom door.

GRABBING HIS SHOULDERS, MOIRA LOOKED him in the eye. "Looks like we've been found out, boyo. I want ye to take yer' brothers far from here. Yer' now in charge, Jackie. Go to the McNally residence; they'll know what to do. Stay off the main road! When this all settles down, the money I've saved for us is in the loose wall in the pantry. Remember that! Loose wall in the pantry. You boys are my greatest loves. Always remember that and be happy."

She kissed and hugged each of them fiercely. They sobbed quietly as their father's roars filled the house. "Now go, Jackie! I'm counting on ya'. Go!"

With tears in her eyes, Moira shoved the bedroom window open for them. Jack knew in his heavy heart that this would be the last time he saw her alive. Grabbing *her hand, he pleaded, "Come with us, Ma!"*

Moira Sullivan touched her eldest son's face and offered a smile mixed with sorrow, love, and regret. "Jackie, I'm giving you and yer' brothers a chance to be free of this hellhole I've created. I wish things could have been different, but they can't. Be happy, a stór."

Straightening up, she coolly commanded, "Now as yer' ma, I order ya' to leave this house and not look back! Never look back, my love."

And with that, she shoved him halfway out the window. He jumped the short fall to the ground and ran with his brothers toward the woods as they heard the bedroom door burst open.

Screams of fury and agony filled the night air. Twice Jack had to wrestle Darby back as his younger brother tried to return to the house, tears of rage streaming down his face. Casey's cries of terror were shrill, giving Jack a headache, but he forged ahead to their closest neighbor's home, not once looking back.

"JACK?" THE SOUND OF DARBY'S worried voice shook him from his reverie. "Jack... what should we do?"

"We should go with this man." Ian smiled slightly and reached for Casey.

Darby stepped forward. "I'm watchin' ya'. Try anythin' stupid and you'll not live through the night. Do ya' ken?"

Plucking Casey up gently from Jack's arms, he tsked Darby while Alexei rumbled with laughter. "Young man, you are entirely too bloodthirsty for your age. Perhaps a stint in the military academy will straighten you out."

"Like hell that's happenin'," Jack disputed, placing a hand on an agitated Darby's shoulder to calm him. "We

stay together, Ian."

His tone was like an arctic wind, his eyes far wiser than his years. Alexei bellowed with laughter and Jack sensed his approval. With a snort, Ian calmly replied, "Of course, Jackson. Please, let's leave now and get out of this dreadful weather."

As he walked past Ian to the car, Darby muttered under his breath, "City girl."

"Go on, boys. I'll take care of this," Alexei urged in his heavily accented English. His gaze approving as he looked up the mountain to the flames burning furiously despite the rain.

Jack started to follow his brother to the car, but Ian stopped him.

"Want to tell me what happened up there?" he queried, eyeing his new ward speculatively. Jack could see the reflection of the fire in his eyes.

"Bonfire party," he murmured, not looking back as he stepped into the safety of the warm vehicle and his new life.

CHAPTER

One

New York City, New York

THE DOOR TO THE STUDY flew open, startling the man who was just about to knock on it. Immediately, he stepped out of the way as a ball of fury with a mutinous expression stormed by him, leaving an aromatic cloud of orange blossom and white gardenia in her wake. The scent instantly aroused him just as it had for the last four years whenever he encountered it. He watched as her long legs carried her swiftly toward the front doors, a butler with a bland expression, already holding one open for her departure.

"Get back here, Noelle! We are not finished! Noelle! Noelle!!" The older black gentleman shouted furiously from behind his desk where he stood, waiting for his command to be obeyed.

He'll be waiting awhile, Jack thought. "She's gone, Ronald."

He managed to contain his amusement as the normally personable senator, now annoyed, threw himself back into his chair like a petulant child pitching a fit.

"Anything I can help you with?"

Jack was curious as to what would make the ordinarily shy, quiet woman break character and rise like a stormy phoenix. The transformation had been magnificent, he mused, thinking of the fire in her eyes and elevated color to her face. Her movements reminded him of an electric storm back home in Tennessee.

Ronald sighed impatiently. "Noelle's asking me to release some of her money from the trust fund my parents left her so that she and her girlfriend can start that damn event planning business! I don't think it's a good idea. There are already too many companies like that in this city. They'll get swallowed whole by all the bigwigs, and then she'll be out of that money! I tried to explain that to her and what do I get for my troubles? Ungratefulness and a temper that rivals her mother's to boot!"

Jack inwardly cursed the older man for his assumptions. Didn't he know that doubt, not failure, was the biggest killer of dreams? Of course not. Ronald Kramer didn't have a clue. He and his wife, Alicia, came from old money. From birth, he'd been groomed to be a successful politician like his father, grandfather, and great-grandfather before him. His idea of struggling would be whether to wear a crimson tie or a burgundy one.

"How much was she asking for?" Jack asked casually, hoping his tone conveyed just the right amount of nonchalance. "By the way, here's the list of charity events that I thought you and Alicia might want to look into sponsoring. I highlighted the ones that are close to the First Lady's heart."

Ronald eagerly accepted the papers. "Thanks. I'll go over these with Alicia tonight when she gets in from Florida. Noelle wanted a two-hundred-thousand-dollar advance."

Jack frowned. This was Alicia Kramer's third trip to Florida this month. "What's going on in Florida?"

"We're looking into having a home built there, and she's been scouting properties," Ronald replied, flipping through the pages. "I see a couple of events already that I know she'll want in on, thank you."

Alicia Kramer, with her coolly unflappable personality, embodied class and manners. Secretly, her staff called her 'The Robot' as she appeared devoid of emotion. This statement wasn't entirely true, though, because she did have two passions: meddling in her family's lives, with tons of unsolicited advice and Michelle Obama, including her wardrobe.

It was stipulated in the Kramers revised contract with R.R. & S Relations that Alicia, if possible, was present at every event that Mrs. Obama attended. Jack had to also add his own clause that the Kramers would be on their own if they were deemed a stalking threat due to Alicia's extreme 'fondness' for Mrs. O. Normally, Ronald indulged his wife to her heart's desire, but even he had to draw the line at spending Christmas in Hawaii, so they could 'accidentally' run into the First Family.

When it came to her passions, Alicia was nuttier than a squirrel's den before winter. It was one of the main reasons that made Jack hesitant to jump into her crosshairs regarding a certain beauty. Not that he'd had much of an opportunity to, considering she avoided him like he had lice whenever they happened to be in the same vicinity.

"Well, let me know what she likes, and we'll see

about getting her in. I'm gonna take off now. Call if you need anything."

Jack waited until he got into his matte black Range Rover Sport to make the call. The phone rang twice before it was picked up on the other end. A raspy voice with a heavy Long Island accent answered, "Hello?"

"Ira, it's Jack. How you doin'?" he greeted his longtime friend and client.

"Jack, my boy! I can't complain. Business is booming, but the wife wants me to turn in my reigns, retire, and leave the daily grind to our boys. But, I says to myself, 'If I do that then I might as well give my company away for free, ya know?"

Before Jack could answer, Ira sighed despondently. "Those two knuckleheads don't got the business sense God gave a sloth! And on top of that, they fight like freakin' cats and dogs! All your hard work into establishing our reputation would go down the toilet if I even *thought* of retiring, Jack."

"I'm sorry to hear that, Ira. Perhaps I have a solution that will work for both of us."

Already aware of the turmoil at Rothman Investments, Jack had intended to speak to Ira about his spoiled-ass sons. The situation with Noelle Kramer was only accelerating the process.

"I'm listening," Ira urged. "I love making money, but Maureen won't wait on me forever to give her time. Got to do it while I'm young, ya know?"

Jack smiled into the phone. Ira was sixty-five years old and hated the thought of retiring. He would probably die at his desk because he wouldn't make time to go to the hospital.

"I have a friend with a sound business plan. All that's needed is the funding to make it happen...."

CHAPTER
Two

$\mathcal{S}$ TRAWBERRY-RHUBARB. CHERRY-LEMON CURD. *Sweet Potato-Praline.*

Pie flavors invaded Noelle Kramer's thoughts while waiting alone in the oversized conference room. She couldn't help it because baking relaxed her, and she'd just recently discovered a love for pie making.

Chocolate Crème Brûlée. Coconut Key Lime Cream. Bananas Foster. Why had she let Sidra talk her into this? Noelle Kramer asked herself anxiously for the hundredth time. *Lattice. Crimped. Graham.* She'd moved on to crusts now as her mind replayed that conversation.

"Girl, call Jack! He's a fixer. He'll know what to do," Sidra Barton, one of her two best friends, urged. *"All the bigwigs use him as a consultant when their image needs polishing. His ideas are brilliant, and he's damn good at what he does! I mean, he does a great job for your dad, right? Jack is a virtual genius and nice too, unlike that asshole baby brother of his! Besides, he's so damn forgiving on the eyes. I totally feel like I should pay him just for the view whenever I'm in his company."*

Sidra finished with her signature husky laugh, and

Noelle joined in with a weak one of her own. No one, not even her closest friends, Sidra and Avery Monroe, her other bestie, knew how she felt about Jack Sullivan. And they'd been tight; sworn to countless secrets since the second week of first grade at Vistmore Prep Academy!

"I just feel so angry and humiliated, not to mention terrified about how this will affect my family," Noelle confided. Inwardly, she cringed at the backlash that would undoubtedly ensue and how her well-respected family would weather it. The Kramer name would forever be tarnished. God, and her mother's reaction... Noelle shuddered at the thought of being on the receiving end of Alicia Kramer's sharp tongue. Last but not least...what would Jack think??

Noelle nervously paced the conference room floor, her stomach swirling with butterflies as she waited breathlessly for Jackson Sullivan, P.R. Extraordinaire, a.k.a. 'The Fixer'. A man who walked into a room and commanded everyone's attention without saying a word. His gorgeous, rugged looks took Noelle's breath away, and his swag vibrated at the highest possible frequency. The intensity of his hazel eyes touched her to the very depths of her soul.

Over the years, Jack had barely said more than a handful of sentences to her, but it was enough to make her heart race, just the same. Nothing sexual, just simple shit like *'Hi, how are you?'* But he possessed a deep, slow, southern drawl that was insanely sexy and made country crooner Sam Hunt's voice sound like Pee Wee Herman. Whenever Jack spoke, all she heard was *'I want to make you scream with my tongue'.* So, perhaps there was a bit of a 'lost in translation' problem, which usually resulted in her gaping at him like an idiot. And that was the reason she tended to avoid him whenever possible.

Whenever they were at the same functions, Noelle

could hardly look at Jack. She was afraid that everyone would see her ill-concealed yearning for him. Her nights, though, were filled with visions of his brawny, muscular body totally dominating hers, and often, she'd awake, having to finish off what was started in her wild fantasies.

Not that those dreams would ever turn into reality. In Jack's presence, all Noelle ever felt from him was pity. Since her parents were his clients and her godfather was one of his business partners, Jack was often exposed to various stages of "Operation Fix Noelle". Interventions staged to 'save' her by her overly-caring and too nosy for their own damn good family. As he stared at her with those unreadable hazel eyes, Noelle could feel Jack's disgust at how pathetic she was rolling off of him in waves. He would excuse himself as if he could hardly stand to be in the same room with someone as pitiful as her, and she wanted to die a thousand deaths from embarrassment.

The run-ins weren't as bad now that Noelle rarely saw Jack since she'd finally moved out of the Kramers fortress. Against her parent's protests, she decided to move forward with her business plans after receiving a pre-approved loan offer in the mail. The letter was almost too good to be true as it outlined plans for helping small business owners to achieve their dreams, but Noelle knew she had to try. Much to her surprise, her request for a loan was approved, and the owner of the investment firm, Mr. Rothman, had worked closely with her and her business partner/best friend, Avery, to ensure they were prepped for success.

The event planning company, On a Whim, which they co-owned was off to a promising start with a steady stream of small businesses with scheduled events. Just two weeks ago, they were asked by an aristocratic polo player to plan his birthday party without even proposing a bid. It had the potential to be the highlight of the season and would definitely open doors for On a Whim. The ladies could hardly contain themselves.

Since they were little, the ladies had dreamed of organizing something on this scale. Avery would cut flowers from the Kramer garden and make pretty arrangements for their tea parties, while Noelle baked scones and prepared sandwiches. Sidra provided the music with the mixed tapes she'd created and beatboxing until it was time to eat. Now, they were all grown up, turning their dreams into reality. Noelle was in charge of menu planning and catering. Avery was in charge of entertainment and decor. Currently, they were working out of their homes to save money for an office space. Sidra was still deejaying but worked for Jack's firm as well.

The growing enterprise was a good thing because it afforded Noelle less time to think about the one man she couldn't have. But now, she needed his help and would resort to begging, if needed. The door slowly opened, and she steeled herself in anticipation of seeing the man she'd been desperately in love with since she was twenty-one years old walk through it.

JACK, WITH HIS PHONE GLUED to his ear, hurried through the elevator doors of the tenth-floor office suites of his business, R.R. & S. Public Relations. The crisis he was presently handling involved the current Miss World Beauty, Inez Gaines, and her now-ex drug-dealing boyfriend, Jimmy Vasquez, who'd supplied copious amounts of drugs to two of the three judges on the panel in exchange for her winning the title. The truth was discovered this morning when, during a heated lover's quarrel, he decided to throw it in her face that she would not have the title if it weren't for him. After blackening his eye, Inez promptly informed Jack and the authorities of his illegal activities. Jimmy and the judges were quickly arrested and awaiting a bail hearing.

Jack knew that as soon as Jimmy got out, he would stop at nothing to slander Inez's image and that of the pageant. A buddy of his in the NYPD had tipped him that Jimmy was already screaming from jail that the bitch had used him just to win the title. He needed every piece of information on the little fucker that he could get his hands on, but for now, he had to concentrate on making sure both of his clients came out on top.

"I want it leaked to the press that Inez and the douchebag have been separated for a while because she suspected something illegal had transpired and that she's been working with authorities to get a full confession from him. I don't want her portrayed as a victim! That's not who she is," Jack barked the orders to his first assistant, Eli Weinberg.

"Inez Gaines is a strong woman who knows right from wrong! She hit him in self-defense because he tried to physically assault her. Get me the list of charity functions that she has lined up. She is going to attend each event and will be handheld through them all. Under no circumstances is she to be left unattended with an audience or have access to social media! Call Darby and make sure he tightened her security detail already and knows she is not to speak to the press! Her volatile personality makes Donald Trump look predictable, and I'll be damned if her ex's lawyer will get to paint an image of him being a victim of domestic violence."

Jack fired off more orders as he walked through the sliding office doors and waved at Margo Helkam, his personal assistant. She followed him into his office. Sensing that she wanted a word with him, he lowered his voice, ending the call with, "And please remind my brother that Ms. Gaines is a client and to be treated as such. Translation: *We. Don't. Fuck. Our. Clients.* He's a goddamn lawsuit waiting to happen."

Just thinking of his hellion of a brother made Jack wince. Women loved Darby Sullivan, and he reciprocated their feelings until they wanted something permanent. He faced his personal assistant with a charming smile.

"Good morning, Margo. I like your new haircut, and isn't that the scarf I gave you for your birthday two weeks ago?" Although she was almost fifty-eight and a happily married grandmother, Margo blushed, taking in her boss's gorgeous face. *Merciful heavens, he was a good-looking man.* One that had women acting like all types of fools. They attempted to sneak past her into his office and called all hours of her shift, trying to reach him. All of them wanted to be Mrs. Jack Sullivan, and who could blame them?

He was movie star handsome with his thick, curling black hair, straight nose, sculpted cheekbones, and chiseled jaw. His tall, muscular body filled out the tailor-made suits he wore to perfection. His mama, Margo surmised, had raised him right. Jack believed in treating people fairly, and he worked tirelessly. He employed forty people directly under him and made it a point to touch base with all of them during the workweek. He was as kind as he was smart. That wasn't to say that he didn't have a temper if you crossed him. Margo winced thinking about those who had challenged him.

Now, what was he saying? Ah yes, the scarf and her hair, which she self-consciously touched. Her Albert hadn't been crazy about the sassy, pixie look, but she thought it was time to retire the salt and pepper chignon style she'd worn for the last ten years. Her bright smile was stunning against her walnut complexion. "It is indeed, sir, and thank you."

Jack flashed a quick smile. "Looks nice. Excuse my language, but we've got a real shit storm heading our way. It takes precedence over anything else we're working on. Eli will be contacting you shortly with the details for a press release to write up. Postpone everything else. Today's lunch will be a mandatory in-house affair for everyone while we brainstorm in the main conference room. Order from Ruth's Deli for a delivery around one this afternoon. Field any calls for me from Viv and Ian, got it?" he asked, sorting through the stack of memos she'd placed on his desk.

His two partners were blowing his phone up because they'd been adamant about not taking Miss World Beauty on as a client, especially when the gorgeous, but temperamental, Inez Gaines won the title. He loved and respected them dearly, as they had shown him the ropes of this business, but his gut insisted that they get Inez, and Jack always went with his gut.

Margo nodded agreeably and turned to leave. Then she remembered something and delicately cleared her throat. Jack glanced up curiously. "Sir, what should I tell the young lady in the conference room? She's been waiting for you for over an hour? She doesn't have an appointment but insisted on seeing you. Very pretty girl, if you don't mind my saying."

"Get rid of her. No one gets in without an appointment, especially today with this circus going on," Jack replied tersely.

"Very good, sir. I will let Ms. Kramer know that you are unavailable and will attempt to schedule her at a later date. I do apologize–"

"*Kramer?* As in Noelle Kramer?" Jack interrupted sharply. "*Noelle Kramer is here?* In my conference room?" At Margo's nod, he swiftly moved around his desk and headed for the door. Pausing in the doorway, Jack turned back to his bemused assistant. "*This* takes precedence on my schedule now. Hold all my calls and meetings today until further notice. You and Eli need to partner up on the Miss World Beauty fiasco until I'm done with my meeting with Ms. Kramer."

Jack hurried to the conference room. *Noelle Kramer was in his place of business.* Anticipation and desire made his heart race and groin tighten at the thought of seeing the young beauty again. He paused outside the conference room door, watching through the window as she paced up and down the room like a sleek panther. Once again, he marveled at her loveliness, pleasure sweeping through him at being able to observe her at his leisure. Usually, he had to make sure his gaze didn't linger on her too long, lest he draw attention to himself. His attraction to Noelle was even more intense than it had been the first time he laid eyes on her at her twenty-first birthday party four years ago.

The night his life changed forever.

———————————

FOUR YEARS AGO

IT WAS AN EXTRAVAGANT AFFAIR with all the 'who's who' of New York in attendance. Normally, Jack didn't go for pretentious crap like this but decided to make an exception because it was business. So, he donned a black tux, gelled his hair back, and showed up. Within ten minutes, he'd known that his being there was a mistake. Anxious to get away from the snobbery of the mega-wealthy assholes surrounding him, Jack slipped into the family library undetected. Only after he settled into a leather club chair in the far corner, shrouded in darkness, did he give a sigh of relief. He would stay another thirty minutes out of courtesy to the family and then make his getaway.

Although Jack knew the Kramers well, the birthday girl was somewhat of a mystery. Apparently, Noelle had been attending culinary school in Paris, and her return happened to coincide with her twenty-first birthday. Her mother, never one to miss an opportunity to show out and be seen, used the event as a way to reintroduce Noelle into the elite society. Jack had just pulled out his phone to check emails when the door quickly opened and then slammed shut again.

He couldn't see anything in the darkness, but he could hear them breathing. Jack scented her before he saw her. An aromatic fusion of something flowery seduced his nostrils. Then the sconce next to the door was turned on, and he forgot to breathe as he took in the alluring vision before him, illuminated by the light.

She was leaning against the closed door. Jack estimated her to be about five-feet-eight-inches tall with skin the color of brown sugar. Her hair was pulled away from her finely sculpted oval face, showcasing her perfect forehead. Elegantly arched eyebrows over large eyes that were narrowed, as if in concentration. Later, he would discover that they were a dark gray, the same color the sky turned before a storm in the Smoky Mountains of Tennessee. Her nose was cute, with a slight tilt at the end and framed by cheekbones sharp enough to cut butter. She would have been mainstream pretty if it wasn't for her lips. Oh yes, that mouth was a game changer. Her red-glossed lips were a true gift from the gods and looked pillow soft. So full and lush, they made Angelina Jolie's lips resemble straight lines.

Jack was hard and heavy as a lead pipe between his legs, imagining their voluptuousness wrapped around his cock while he pumped in and out of them. Jesus. She was fucking incredible. The inspiration for every love song ever written. The kind of woman you went to war for, and if you lost the battle, in no way were you defeated with her by your side. She was also young. An obvious fact that Jack's straining cock was willing to overlook.

"Shit! Shit! Shit!" she muttered in a soft but frustrated voice, rubbing her temples with both hands. In a burst of energy, she paced rapidly in front of the door. Jack used the opportunity to admire her slender but curvy body encased in a strapless, frothy, lavender concoction that swirled and whirled around her as she moved. Her shoulders gleamed like satin, and he ached to push her bodice down and fill his palms with her breasts. Jack had to force himself to pay attention to her one-sided conversation.

"Why did I let her talk me into coming back?! I should have just stayed where I was. No one would have missed me," she moaned, flailing her hands about. "Fuck!! Come on Noelle. Girl, you can do this! Get it together. It's just for one night then you can take off." A quick glance at her gold watch made her gasp in alarm, reminding an amused Jack of the white rabbit from "Alice in Wonderland". "Late again! Mother is going to kill me! But first..."

He couldn't remember the last time he'd enjoyed himself this much in a female's prescence. Noelle Kramer was doing what no other woman had been capable of doing and in such a short time – captivating him. Jack's mouth went dry as she dipped her hand between the succulent mounds of her breasts. *Oh, sweetheart, let me do that for you,* he thought, trousers painfully tight. *Christ, he really needed to adjust himself,* surprised that he was this hard for a beautiful stranger. Unfortunately, any movement would give away his hiding spot and bring attention to him. To Jack's surprise, Noelle pulled a small bottle of liquor out of her bosom.

"Good thing I tucked this in my bag before exiting the plane," she crowed with delight, unscrewing the lid and downing the tiny bottle's contents in one gulp.

"Here goes nothing."

Noelle set the empty bottle on the console, adjusted her bodice, then slipped out of the room, quietly shutting the door behind her. Jack shot to his feet, groaning in agony as he adjusted himself. *So, that was the birthday girl,* he mused, walking to the door. His phone vibrated, and he pulled it out to read the text.

RUNNING LATE! YOU MUST BE BORED TO TEARS. HAVE YOU STARTED PLANNING YOUR EXIT STRATEGY YET? IF SO, SHALL I CATCH UP WITH YOU LATER THEN?

Jack reached the door and picked up the empty bottle. Her perfume lingered in the air, seducing him further. He pressed the gloss covered top to his lips, where hers had been seconds ago and licked it. *Tequila.* Noelle had downed the fiery liquid without flinching. A sense of admiration filled Jack. She was beautiful, entertaining, and could drink hard liquor like it was water. She was also his client's daughter...and young, dammit. He needed to walk away. Jack stared at his phone for five minutes, deliberating pros and cons, then weighing consequences. Finally, he replied to the text.

CHANGE OF PLANS. I'M STAYING.

33

THAT WAS FOUR YEARS AGO, and Jack was no closer to Noelle now than he'd been the first time he laid eyes on her, though, it wasn't for lack of trying on his part. Whenever she saw him, Noelle politely smiled, offered a greeting, and then disappeared. Jack couldn't really say that he blamed her. Being the youngest in a family such as hers, she stuck out like a sore thumb between her two siblings. Her older brother and middle child, Darren, was a surgeon married to a Boston socialite, and her sister, Sloane, the eldest, was married to a famous Greek playwright and owned a successful art gallery in Soho. Between both siblings, there were five grandchildren. Meanwhile, Noelle had no marriage prospects known to her parents on the horizon.

It was definitely a bone of contention between Noelle and her parents, Senator Ronald Kramer and his old money, socialite wife Alicia Kramer. They felt she wasn't utilizing her potential and never hesitated to point out to her how accomplished her siblings were, which, in turn, made her siblings lecture her during family gatherings. These moments always reminded Jack of the 'Festivus' episode on "Seinfeld".

As they derided her degree, which amounted to a glorified fry cook in their eyes, Jack, from his end of the dinner table, willed her to tell them to fuck off, but she never did. Noelle just sat there in her pretty Kate Spade or Ann Taylor attire with a polite smile on her tension-lined face. In the end, Jack needed to excuse himself for fear that he would suggest one of his firm's oldest clients eat a fat dick and chase it down with a tall glass of 'shut the fuck up'.

The few times that Jack did see Noelle relaxed were when he entered the house through the kitchen. Noelle would be happily conversing in French with their chef and assisting with meal preparation, that is until she'd catch sight of him. It made his stomach turn, seeing the anxiety in her eyes, conjuring up dark memories of his Ma trying to anticipate Patrick's next unpleasant move. So, Jack simply nodded his acknowledgment and kept it moving.

During dinner, Noelle, stole looks at him whenever the family complimented a particular dish. Observing her reactions, Jack realized the dishes she worked on were the recipients of the rave reviews from her unknowing family. Amidst the lavish compliments bestowed on the chef, he'd raise an eyebrow at Noelle as they heaped praise on the red-faced little bastard, daring her to come clean and her wide eyes silently begged him to keep her secret, which he did.

Finally, unable to take any more of her parents' stifling attitude, Noelle relocated to Park Slope in Brooklyn four months ago. Grinning to himself, Jack wondered what Alicia Kramer would say if she could see her youngest child right now.

Gone was the sleek bun and "Stepford Wife" attire that made Noelle a clone of her mother and sister. In its place was a bohemian goddess. Her hair was a riotous mass of lustrous black curls. No makeup covered her flawless brown skin except the clear gloss on her sexy mouth. Her long, flowy dress with spaghetti straps was a vivid cobalt blue with large orange and white flowers splashed all over it. The deep v neckline exposed her sexy cleavage. Numerous white bangles adorned each sleek arm and she'd donned a pair of delicate strappy white sandals. Her skin gleamed like silk, and Jack wanted to reach out and see if it was as sumptuous as it looked.

Lust rolled through Jack like a freight train. Mentally, he pictured himself bending Noelle over the table, lifting the lower layers of her dress, and sinking into her from behind as his hands slid around to cup her breasts and hold her in place. Fuck, he needed to get a grip, but it really couldn't be helped. His dick just knew what it wanted, and it loved some Noelle Kramer. Jack had been with many women, but none had ever affected him the way she did. It was a scary fact, considering they'd never even kissed. Shaking his head, he took a deep breath, slowly opening the door.

Noelle whirled around to face him, the long skirt of her dress opening, allowing him an all too brief view to admire toned legs before they were concealed again. Disappointed, Jack raised his gaze to hers, drowning in luminous gray eyes fringed with long curling lashes. Her sexy lips parted in a nervous smile as she greeted him in her soft modulated voice.

"Hi, Jack. Sorry to drop in on you like this, but I have an issue." Noelle nervously raked a well-manicured hand through her curls. Taking a deep breath, she exhaled a soft whoosh. "And it's something I believe only you can help me with."

CHAPTER
Three

*N*OELLE WAS BEING BLACKMAILED.

There were nude pictures of her. *With another man.* An ex-boyfriend by the name of Remy Dumont. Now the asshole was threatening to make the pictures go viral, knowing the damage it could do to her family name. In exchange for his silence, Remy wanted Noelle to marry him so that he could become a U.S. citizen *OR* give him three million dollars to make the photos disappear. She had a week before he would take action.

Rage, white-hot and consuming, filled Jack as he tried to focus on Noelle's nervous prattling. *Another man had dared to touch what he considered to be his,* he seethed, watching her luscious lips form the words that he was struggling to process. *Another man had been with the woman he obsessed about. Been inside of the body he fantasized about.* Jack, tapping his pen against the table, tried to appear calm and collected as he shifted in his chair and adjusted the knot in his tie.

Tap. Tap. Tap.

How he wished it was a knife gauging the son of a bitch's eyeballs out. Remy Dumont; what a pussy name!

"I haven't seen Remy in four and a half years. Our

relationship kind of ran its course by the time I left to come home. I thought we parted as friends," Noelle explained warily.

Jack realized she was watching his right hand make stabbing motions with the pen he was holding. *Relax. Wooosaaaa. Focus, Sullivan,* he lectured himself. It wasn't about him anymore. Noelle was now his client and as such, needed him to be at his best, whether he liked it or not.

"I need to ask you some questions," Jack coolly informed her, pulling out a notepad. He waited for consent, and she nodded agreeably.

"What's his full name and age?"

"Remy Alain Dumont. He's twenty-five, just like me."

"How did you meet?"

"Hemmingway's, a bar close to the university."

"How long did the relationship last?"

"On and off? Three and a half years. We kept breaking up because he thought getting high on whatever drugs he could find was more important than getting his education."

"Before last week, when was the last time you spoke to him?"

"Two weeks before I left Paris."

"So, no correspondence at all? Emails, social media, letters? Any mutual friends pertaining to any of those things?"

"None."

"Does your family know about him?"

"Only my sister and that's because she was going through the pics from my time abroad. I downplayed the relationship, though."

"What was the exact nature of your relationship that he was able to take such personal pictures of you?" Jack asked dispassionately through gritted teeth.

Even though he already knew the answer, and it was fucking killing him, he needed her to say it. *Wooosaaa! You didn't even know she existed back then. Wooosaaa!* Noelle squirmed under his intense scrutiny.

"We, um...dated." At the skeptical look on Jack's face, Noelle clarified, "We were lovers for a while. Nothing serious, though. It just kind of happened and turned into a relationship of convenience. It wasn't even that great, just something to pass time," she lamely finished, watching Jack's eyebrows practically shoot to his hairline.

Damn, I'm rambling again. Noelle, rubbed her forehead tiredly, wishing for the thousandth time that she'd never dropped her panties for such a piece of shit. At the time, she'd thought it was a sign. She was in Paris, studying to become a chef when she'd met a Remy, just like the Disney movie Ratatouille. Maybe too much. Boy, had he turned out to be a big fucking rat, all right.

"So, you weren't in love with him?" Jack demanded harshly. "You were just fucking him? Is that something that you do often?" he snarled, finally losing his cool, watching as Noelle gaped with mortification. The room was flooded with strained silence before she regally rose to her full height and looked down at him, her beautiful gray eyes turbulent at his insinuations.

"Contrary to what you and my family seem to believe, I'm an adult! You know, someone who is capable of making logical decisions? No, I do not take sexual relationships lightly. Gawd, cut me some slack! I had the whole sexual health history talk and used protection like everyone else. Remy never came off as being this...*sleazy*. Never did I dream that I would have to worry about him betraying my trust. He was always so easygoing." Noelle shook her head in disbelief.

"He didn't seem like that type of guy, but I also

think I was drugged. I...I've never done two of the sexual acts depicted in those photos before. It was something that Remy and I constantly argued about. I just think that I would have remembered doing that stuff. Anyway, I came to you because I didn't know who else to turn to, and Sidra insisted that you'd be able to help me. But maybe this wasn't such a good idea? All I hear in your tone is judgment. Hell, I might as well have been talking to my parents. I think I'll be going now because I'll be damned if I sit up here and let you shame me."

Jack winced at the well-deserved dressing down, but Noelle was too busy rummaging in her oversized white purse to notice. Finally, she withdrew a letter-sized manila envelope and tossed it on the table in front of him.

"Here are copies of the pics I made for you. I'll let you decide if I can continue pursuing my current career or if I should just make a career change right now and give Jenna Jameson a run for her money," Noelle spat sarcastically before walking out the door and slamming it behind her. Jack watched as she stormed down the hall and out of his sight.

Well, well, well.

Who knew all that sass was overflowing underneath her shy exterior?

And she was funny too. Jenna Jameson, the porn star? *Like hell,* Jack snorted. He eyed the envelope. Inside were pics of a naked Noelle. He needed to open the packet but was torn. Professionally, Jack needed to see what kind of damage control was required, but personally, he knew that if he saw the body he'd been fantasizing about for years, he wouldn't be able to sleep until he'd bedded her.

With a sigh of resignation, Jack snatched up the envelope and pulled the pics out, trying to view them objectively. Just as he thought, they were inflammatory. In the first pic, Noelle was naked and on her back with her eyes closed. Her arms were thrown over her head, and there was a wiry built black man with braids nestled between her legs. In the next pic, the same man's naked backside was in full view with Noelle's behind in front of him. Her face was turned away and covered by her hair with arms spread out in front of her. The last pic showed the front of the man, naked and kneeling on the bed as an equally naked Noelle covered his lower area with her head. The man gripped her hair and she appeared to be giving him a blow job while he was in the throes of ecstasy.

Jack tried to view them objectively, but it was hard not to notice Noelle's toned body with full breasts topped by large, perfectly shaped chocolate nipples. Her ass was also full and firm-looking. Her skin was flawless. *Holy Hell.* The image of her naked was now forever embedded in his mind. Cursing in frustration, Jack's hand drifted to his crotch, and he adjusted himself, instead of finding scissors, cutting out Dumont, and jacking off to Noelle's image. *Jesus, he was a sick fuck.* The poor girl had come to him for help, and here he was, getting off on her impending scandal.

Instinct told Jack the photos were staged, taken without her consent. Noelle had mentioned that she might have been drugged. He studied her expression in the first pic again. She might as well have been a mannequin. A woman receiving oral would have some sort of expression to indicate whether it was good or bad. Her eyes were closed and so was her mouth. Her face devoid of any emotion. Her nipples were unaroused, and her hands just lay above her head, palms open, not clenching anything. Even in the other shots, she wasn't gripping the sheets or the douchebag's thighs. There were only three options at this point: A) This guy was the worst lover in the world B) Noelle was a lesbian, or C) she had been drugged.

Jack was going to go with option C and pray like hell that B wasn't even on the radar. Option A was a non-motherfucking factor because, by the time he was done with Remy Dumont, he'd be lucky if he was able to even *eye-fuck* anyone.

THE CONSULTATION WITH TARIK OWENS was taking longer than expected. Although Noelle had come prepared with menu proposals, the hot playboy extraordinaire was far too busy flirting with her to glance at her recommendations for his birthday bash. A talented polo player of Algerian and British descent, he had deep olive skin, tousled sun-bleached hair, almond-shaped blue eyes, and a sexy smile that kept the ladies throwing their panties at him on and off the field. He was extremely put out that Noelle appeared immune to his charms. This was their third meeting, and she'd already decided that if he slid over one more inch to close the gap between them, there would not be a fourth.

"Oh, do lighten up, babe! You know what they say about all work and no play," Tarik oozed in his charming British accent, giving her a sexy wink.

Noelle ground her teeth in frustration. It wasn't that she didn't like Tarik, but frankly, he was wasting her time thinking she should be delighted to bask in his fuckboy glory. And when you wasted her time, you fucked with her coins. On a Whim couldn't pay bills on insincere flattery and sexy smiles, no matter how good looking the source. Noelle briefly closed her eyes and counted to ten for patience yet was unsuccessful.

Opening them she surveyed Niko's, an upscale eatery in Manhattan that served authentic Greek and Italian fare. All around her, other diners were having a great time, enjoying the wonderful cuisines. Meanwhile, she had long since lost her appetite for the plate of moussaka in front of her, fending off Tarik's advances. Not that she'd had much of an appetite since leaving Jack's office three days ago. Every time she thought of his words and disgusted looks, Noelle wanted to crawl under a rock and hide forever. Unfortunately, she had a business to run, so any feelings of embarrassment would have to wait.

"I have four menus here, Mr. Owens. Please pick one," Noelle firmly instructed, ignoring his comment. She refused to entertain him a second longer. "Your birthday is in four weeks, and you've revised the guest list six times! This has caused a delay in sending out the invitations. We have yet to visit any of the venues I had lined up for your approval because you keep traveling off to God-knows-where with the latest supermodel! The only reason we are having this meeting is because my friend, Sidra, is friends with your best friend, who happened to mention that you would be here today for lunch, and I *conveniently* ran into you outside," Noelle growled.

Tarik's eyes widened, and he opened his mouth to speak, but Noelle held up her hand to silence him. She took a deep breath because it just about killed her to say what she had to next. "I really don't feel that my company is meeting your needs, thus making us incompatible. At this time, I'm going to exercise my withdrawal clause from the contract and refund your fifteen-thousand-dollar deposit."

At first, Tarik just stared at her, his mouth agape in shock. Then he threw back his head and howled with laughter, drawing the attention of the other patrons. His laughter was rich and melodic, and Noelle could see everyone becoming enamored with him, which irritated her further. Finally, realizing she wasn't joking, he stopped laughing to gaze somberly at her.

"Noelle, I apologize for my boorish behavior. You should have told me of your displeasure with the supermodels...there is no need for jealousy. I am more than enough man for all of you birds," Tarik finished teasingly, finally closing the space between them as he put his arm around the back of the booth they shared.

Aaand now, they were done.

Noelle and Avery really needed his business to establish the company but not his bullshit. "Tarik, we are now having what is called a *'Bye Felicia'* moment. Your check will be returned in the mail, but lunch is on you."

Amidst his protesting, Noelle grabbed her papers, stuffed them into her leather attaché and grabbed her purse. She slid out of the booth, and promptly collided with a large black wall.

Strong arms reached out to encircle Noelle as she lost her balance. She grasped at them, feeling the well-muscled arms beneath the suit as she inhaled the tantalizing cologne the 'wall' was wearing. "Oh, my goodness, thank you! I am so sorry about that," she spoke with a smile only to freeze as she looked up into the angry hazel gaze of her rescuer. Her genuine smile of contrition turned into a fake one.

"Hello, Jack."

JACK WAS JUST ENTERING NIKO'S when he heard the familiar laugh of Tarik Owens, one of his firm's clients. At first, he hadn't liked the young man, deeming him too cocky. Vivienne and Ian had disagreed, however.

"There's nothing wrong with loving and appreciating life. We should all take a page out of his book," Ian suggested, aiming a pointed look at Jack.

Vivienne simply added, "That man is so fine, I'd let him get away with slapping my mama."

As Jack came to know Tarik, he begrudgingly came to the conclusion that perhaps, the other man wasn't that bad after all. Tarik had a great work ethic and was professional at all times during his media events. He figured he'd walk over and say hi while waiting for his lunch companion to arrive.

Headed toward the intimate booth at the back of the restaurant, Jack realized who Tarik's date was and found himself hating the egotistical jackass all over again as he stood next to the table, glaring down at Noelle's bent head. Too busy gathering her things and attempting to beat a hasty retreat, she didn't even notice Jack until she slammed into him.

The moment Noelle's body collided with his, and he was engulfed in her unique scent, Tarik was forgotten as he stared into her hostile eyes, following her small pink tongue as it darted out to lick her succulent, glossed lips. Suddenly, Jack was aware they had an audience. Reluctantly he stepped back from Noelle, glancing at Tarik who was staring at them curiously.

"Hey, Jack! Good to see you." Tarik offered a friendly smile, standing to his feet to shake Jack's hand. Jack automatically shook hands, even though he wanted to punch the other man in the throat for looking at Noelle like she was all of his favorite desserts combined into one dish.

"Tarik. Noelle. Am I interrupting something?" Jack asked smoothly, observing the unfinished meal and partially-full wine glasses.

Noelle shifted, adjusting her belongings and Jack used the opportunity to take in her appearance. Black blazer, white V-neck silk camisole, skinny black jeans, and black peep-toe flats completed her business casual attire. She'd accessorized with layered, thin, sterling silver chains and bangles, and diamond stud earrings, and her curls were pulled back in a low ponytail. He allowed his gaze to rest on her cute toes for a moment, thinking the vibrant fuchsia color really complimented her skin. *Fuchsia?* Since when did he think of fuchsia? They were just pink, dammit! Shit, she had him really fucked up.

Fuchsia.

Noelle gave him a hard look. "Not at all. I was just leaving. Goodbye, gentlemen."

She walked away despite Tarik's objections and pleas. Noelle could feel Jack's scorching gaze on her the entire time. It was just as she got to the door that she felt the light grip on her elbow and looked over her shoulder into Jack's steely gaze. Even through her jacket, her arm felt singed by his touch, and she tried to jerk away. Jack only tightened his hold, escorting Noelle out of the restaurant onto the busy sidewalk.

"Do you mind?" she asked with a pointed look at his hand. He gave her a smile that didn't quite reach his eyes, continuing to hold on to her, although he did loosen his grip slightly. Jack didn't seem the least bit concerned with the irritated looks he received, delaying the steady flowing hustle of New York pedestrians in a hurry, by keeping them in the middle of the sidewalk.

"What's going on with you and Tarik?" Jack demanded, ignoring her question and still pissed at finding them together, all cozy and shit. From a P.R.'s standpoint, he could reluctantly admit that the two of them looked good together, but jealousy reared its ugly head. Jack wanted to throw Noelle down on the table and fuck her in front of the entire restaurant so that everyone would know whom she belonged to, especially her. Noelle winced, and he realized his grip had intensified. Reluctantly he released her. "Sorry. Now, again, what's going on between you two?"

"Why? Are you worried that I'm going to get my oversexed claws into him?" Noelle jeered, giving him a dirty look while he continued to glower at her, jaw clenched. She sighed irrationally.

"What do you mean what's going on with him?! There's *nothing* going on with him, okay? Nothing. Nada. Zip! Tarik was supposed to be our first big break, but I can't even get him to focus on planning his own stupid event! All he wants to do is try to figure out different ways to get into my panties! Now, I have to go back and tell Avery that I walked away from our biggest client to date because if I didn't, I would have stabbed him to death with my butter knife!"

Jack smiled slightly at her outburst, and she pursed her lips with frustration, barely resisting the urge to stamp her foot like a spoiled child.

"I'm so glad I could amuse you, Jack. It's certainly a step up from the disdain you were projecting the last time we met," Noelle added snidely. His smile disappeared, and he appeared troubled, his gaze focused on something over her shoulder.

"We'll talk later. Don't worry about Tarik. I'm sure he'll realize you mean business and straighten up. Now, unless you're interested in joining me and your mother for lunch, I'd start walking away if I were you."

Jack laughed quietly at the look of abject horror on Noelle's face. She shot past him without another word. He stared at the formidable dragon marching his way and grimaced, wishing he could follow Noelle.

CHAPTER *Four*

"ICE WATER WITH LEMON AND I'm also ready to order. I'll have the Cioppino with the grilled artichoke salad, hold the dressing," Alicia Kramer stated imperiously, handing her menu back to their server just as Jack slid into the seat across from her. He could tell from the tic of her right eye that she was annoyed at being kept waiting for ten minutes, but it couldn't be helped. Jack needed to make a certain polo player understand that the only relationship he would have with Noelle would be a professional one – and that it would be in his best interests to straighten up.

"Excellent choice, madam." Their server turned to Jack. "And for you, sir?"

"I'll have the fire roasted lamb chops and mint orzo with an iced tea, and please bring sugar with it, thank you." Jack smiled politely, handing over his menu while Alicia seemed amused. He raised an eyebrow questioningly, and she shook her head knowingly.

"Sweet tea. You can take the boy out of the south, but the south remains tried and true," Alicia murmured, picking up her fork and knife. Jack wasn't foolish enough to think that was a compliment, watching her inspect the silverware with a slight frown on her perfectly made-up face.

At the age of fifty-nine, Alicia Kramer was still an attractive woman. There was no gray in her hair, thanks to the discreet coloring skills of an expensive hairstylist. She maintained her size six figure with the help of personal trainers and a strict eating regimen. The fine structure of her face hinted at delicacy, but Jack knew she was more Rottweiler than Teacup Poodle. Alicia Kramer ran her home and family with a polite, yet unyielding force. She was Ronald Kramer's right hand, and he never made a decision without consulting her first. Jack recalled something Ian had once confided to him.

"My God, the airs that woman puts on! When we were in college, Alicia was the queen of Cracker Barrel! She knew where every one of them was located and their hours of operation too!" Ian snorted derisively as they watched the Kramer matriarch nibble demurely on a watercress stalk as though it was the best thing she'd ever eaten.

Jack didn't bother addressing her comment. He was focused on the frown marring Alicia Kramer's lovely features, in public no less. He happened to know that she spent an astronomical amount of time and money to maintain a wrinkle-free, youthful appearance. That frown was a telling sign that she was deeply disturbed by something, making him wonder if she knew the real reason for their meeting today.

"Was that the famous polo player everyone's been talking about?" Alicia inquired with interest. "I read somewhere that his father was some kind of European royalty."

"Yes, that was him. Sorry about keeping you waiting," Jack apologized, not really caring to be reminded of the good-looking younger man who appeared spellbound by Noelle. An interest that hopefully, he wouldn't be stupid enough to act on now that Jack had set him straight.

He grabbed his briefcase and pulled out the Kramers' agenda for the following month. "Here are all the political events scheduled for June. The lists are separated by Democratic functions, Kramer fundraisers, and First Lady events."

"Oh goody! I'm especially interested in knowing where we can raise money for Ronald." Alicia took the packet Jack had prepared and slipped on her reading glasses. For the next fifteen minutes, they discussed the pros and cons of each event, until their food arrived. Jack dug into his meal with relish, enjoying the tender lamb combined with the cool mint in the orzo. He watched in amusement while Alicia picked delicately at her food. She sipped most of the broth from her seafood stew and ate only the artichokes from her salad.

"Is the food not to your liking, Alicia?" Jack inquired mildly.

"It's a little spicier than I would have liked," she admitted, delicately wiping her mouth with the napkin and staring at his damn near empty plate. Alicia shuddered slightly as though the thought of consuming a full meal brought her nightmares, and then suddenly, her face brightened, instantly putting Jack on high alert. "I think it would be a great idea for us to get involved with the "Let's Move" campaign! Would you please reach out and see if it would be possible? Perhaps they need an ambassador of sorts?"

The hairs on Jack's neck stirred, and he knew he wasn't going to like where this conversation would lead next. "What did you have in mind, Alicia?" he asked slowly. "Your commitment to this project would have to be high priority. Are you prepared to step away from your other projects to dedicate to this?"

Alicia waved her hand dismissively. "Oh please, Jack! I'm way too occupied to take this on. I was thinking that Noelle could do it. I don't know if you're aware, but Noelle used to attend camp for kids of a 'larger stature.'" Alicia raised her eyebrows, making a subtle widening motion with her hands. "She has experience in this sort of thing. It will give her something meaningful to do. I'd rather she do this, than run all over Manhattan attempting to solicit herself like a prostitute with this party planning nonsense."

Cold fury roared through Jack, every other noise in the restaurant dulling to white noise while he listened to this shallow bitch dismiss *his* beautiful Noelle.

"From what I understand, her business has repeat clientele. That's not bad, considering she's been in operation for only five months," Jack replied abruptly. "That would be an indication that she's definitely doing something right. Wouldn't you agree?"

Alicia rolled her eyes. "Well, who are her clients? They must be desperate and willing to hire anybody. I don't think they're anyone that we would want to be associated with. Don't get me wrong, Jack. I love my daughter, but I find her taste to be slightly...questionable. For instance, take that outfit she was wearing today," she said, looking him directly in the eye. "It was trendy and vulgar, nothing a real lady would ever be caught dead in. Too bad she took off before I could tell her."

Ah-Ha.

Alicia had seen her daughter and was pissed that Noelle had, with his help, managed to avoid her. "I think your daughter has a good head on her shoulders and an exceptional mind for business. Today, she closed a deal on a major event that most of the city will be dying to attend. Noelle's far too busy to be involved in your charity work at this crucial time in her career. I think Darren would be a better fit. He is a heart surgeon after all," Jack returned smoothly, realizing that he'd deliberately put himself in Alicia's crosshairs. That was fine with him because, at this point, he was all out of fucks to give when dealing with her high-handed ass.

Alicia surveyed him coolly. "I disagree. Noelle is a much more suitable candidate; besides, Darren is busy saving lives. You're rather passionate about my daughter's life, Jack. Why is that exactly?"

"I'm interested because she's got the skills to make it to the top. Obviously, I haven't known Noelle as long as you have, but from what I've seen, she is an excellent chef. Why do you think those dinners at your home were so wonderful? Tell me, have they been the same since she left? That chef you hired severely embellished his culinary skills. He got lucky when he discovered Noelle's passion for cooking and degree. When you hired him four and a half years ago, we strongly advised your husband against it. He didn't listen to us because *you* just had to have a Michelin star chef. Did you know that on the weekends, Noelle used to give him cooking lessons?"

Jack took a sip of his doctored sweet tea, watching Alicia's face flush with embarrassment. He realized at that moment that she had not been aware of the goings-on in her own household. Alicia's expression was now a mask of ice. *Oh, you're pissed, lady? Well, fuck you! I am too!* Jack thought, prepared to go the distance for Noelle.

"Again, what is your interest in my daughter?" Alicia asked, her tone now colder than a nun's bed. A man with smaller balls would have dove under the table. Jack Sullivan was not that man, and he was far too busy having a 'nobody puts Baby in the corner' moment to tread lightly.

Jack reached back into his briefcase and pulled another folder out. "I'm only speaking my opinion. I'm sure your concern for your daughter is...genuine. I'm not a parent, but I'd like to think your feelings come from a good place. At this time, I need you to let me do my job in the best way that I can. Stalking the First Lady is not a priority for Vivienne, Ian, or myself. This is a service we will no longer provide for you. So, I suggest you get yourself moving on that "Let's Move" campaign and prepare to break a sweat," Jack continued as if he wasn't aware that Alicia's mouth was flapping like a fish out of water.

"What *is* our main priority as stipulated in the contracts that we sign with our clients is ensuring that they always look impeccable and are portrayed in the most positive light. To make sure that they are never associated with negativity and eliminate any threats that could tarnish their image, correct?" Jack held the folder out to a furious Alicia.

"Correct," Alicia snapped, snatching the folder from him. *How dare this hillbilly talk to her like this?* she fumed, thinking that it was time to remind him who he worked for. As Alicia opened the folder, she promptly froze upon seeing the pictures inside.

Jack sat silently, watching the blood drain from her face while Alicia hurriedly flipped through its contents. It didn't give him any pleasure to do this, but it was his job to protect his clients. Alicia and Ronald were his clients, but Noelle was his heart, and he'd do everything in his power to protect her, even if it meant being a bastard to said clients. Alicia's eyes rose to meet his, and they were filled with trepidation as she anticipated his next words.

"Alicia Kramer, *you* are now the threat to your family. My job is to eliminate threats, and I'm damn good at it. I've got a couple of options as to how I can proceed with that information, but we need to get a few things straight first. Do you understand me when I say that you have no more time to meddle in Noelle's life? Or block her business efforts? You are now at a pivotal point in your life where you realize it would be in your best interest to just let her experience life and be there to support her along the way, you feel me?" Jack asked in his charming southern accent that Alicia was realizing, too late, was tempered with steel. He held up his hand and their server appeared with the dessert menu. Jack smiled his appreciation, keeping his laser-like stare on Alicia as she nodded her head to indicate she was listening.

"We're going to need a minute to decide, sir." He waited until the server left, leaned in, and whispered across the table. "Good. Now, I don't know about you, but I could really go for some dessert while we focus on how to discreetly extract you from the problems you've created down in Florida."

Brooklyn, New York

ACCORDING TO THE PRIVATE INVESTIGATOR that Jack hired four months ago, Noelle was well- liked in the community and participated in numerous neighborhood events. He knew he was going overboard and being stalker-ish, but what other choice did he have since she no longer lived at home? How else was he supposed to know she was okay? The report also stated that Noelle wasn't romantically involved. He could have just as easily asked his brother Darby to obtain that info, but the thought of that infamous hound dog anywhere near Noelle made his blood boil.

It took Jack two days to compile most of the information he needed on her ex. Remy Dumont was born in Marseille, France to wealthy Ghanaian parents. They sent him to study at a university in Paris, but he dropped out two years after enrolling. Furious, his parents cut him off and told him to work for a living. Instead, he supported himself by running numbers and living off of rich, older women. Recently, he'd fallen in with an unscrupulous crowd and was looking to disappear. Jack was simply waiting for a call from his youngest brother, Casey, an attorney in Washington D.C., who had contacts in Paris to confirm what he already knew. There were several ways this could play out, but he was trying to choose the right one that would alleviate Noelle's worry *and* work in his favor. Jack felt a stab of guilt about manipulating her, but he was too far gone with possessing her to think about that now. Knowing that there had been someone before him made Jack even more adamant that there was no one *after* him. He was going to be it for Noelle.

So, here he was, on a Thursday afternoon, parked directly across from her brownstone, impatiently waiting to get a glimpse of her when he should be working. Jack's intent was to relay the information he'd gathered and discuss what their next move should be. From his vantage point, he could see the entire block.

About a dozen kids were playing in the street, and moms were speed-walking with their strollers. Across the street in the park, a yoga class was being one with nature, while enticing aromas drifted from the various food trucks parked along the curb. Suddenly, he saw her jogging toward her brownstone. Noelle's satiny skin was glistening with perspiration, her sweat dampened tank top and shorts clinging to her curves. Sighing, Jack glanced down at his dick, which now resided in a permanent state of hardness anytime he saw her. He was going to have to do something about it and soon.

Jack watched as a group of elementary school kids ran up to her. They busted out singing and beatboxing while one of the boys started breakdancing. He was pop-locking and made a motion to pass it on to Noelle. To his surprise, she bust out a few intricate moves of her own and passed it back to the kid. Jack chuckled to himself as the other kids laughed at their buddy's stunned expression. Noelle hugged the boy then they all high-fived her and ran off down the street, leaving her to continue on her way.

Suddenly, Noelle broke into a full sprint, and the next thing Jack knew, she was launching herself into the arms of a tall, curly-haired blonde guy whom he hadn't even noticed was now standing by her brownstone steps because he was so intently focused on Noelle. Body tensing, Jack sat up straight, a growl reverberating at the back of his throat. Fury and possessiveness tore through him as the asshole caught her, twirling her around before soundly kissing her on that gorgeous, laughing mouth. The veins pulsed on Jack's forehead and his fingers flexed so forcefully his knuckles cracked. *Who the fuck was this clown???* Trying unsuccessfully to clear his vision of the haze of rage, Jack had one thought: he was going to *decimate* that sorry ass investigator after he got done with this bitch-ass Goldilocks motherfucker.

Somehow Jack managed to refrain from getting

out of his car, crossing the street, and beating the shit out of this stranger for daring to touch Noelle. But swift action was needed, and he was suddenly clear on which course to take. He flung his car door open, then his cell phone rang. Glancing down at the number, he quickly answered it.

"Talk to me, Casey."

CHAPTER

Five

"THEO!" NOELLE LAUGHED AS THE beautiful man before her swung her around in his strong arms. His scruffy chin found her neck, and she squealed her happiness at seeing her friend. "When did you get back from Sedona?"

It was good to see Theo Adams, a close friend from her Paris days. He was the former boyfriend of one of her classmates, Evie, at culinary and they'd socialized many times as a group. They'd broken up and when he relocated to New York City from his hometown of London, he'd looked Noelle up. An artist, Theo not only supplied the art world with his one-of-a-kind masterpieces, but he'd also supplied her with some of the best weed she'd ever smoked. Noelle discovered how talented he truly was one night as they were puffing away at his place and insisted on seeing some of his work. Thoroughly impressed, she hooked him up with her sister, Sloane, who demanded he sign with her on the spot.

Theo's career instantly took off. In return, he kept Noelle supplied with weed for practically nothing. Smoking was her way of relieving the tension caused by her family's interference. Funny, she hadn't needed to smoke a joint, pop a Tylenol, or down a cocktail or two, for that matter, just to get through a family dinner in the four months since moving out of her parents' home.

The taste of freedom was intoxicating, and Noelle was drunk on liberation. Gone were the prissy outfits her mother insisted she wear. She now shopped in vintage thrift shops and loved showing a little skin. Noelle embraced her natural hair and only made it to the beauty shop if she knew a family event was scheduled. Just the thought of her parents' horrified expressions if they ever discovered their meek-as-fuck, well-mannered daughter was an occasional pot-smoking, borderline hippy. *Quelle horreur!*

But that was nothing in comparison to how the family would lose their shit if those pics were publicized. Hopefully, Jack would have a solution. Noelle was beginning to worry since she hadn't seen or heard from him since running into him at Niko's two days ago. Sidra had tried reassuring her.

"Girl, just 'cause you can't see things happening doesn't mean he's not making them happen. Trust that he knows what he's doing."

Noelle really hoped that was the case. Otherwise, she would need to have a sit-down with her parents' soon and prepare for the backlash because there was no way in hell she was going to pay Remy's drugged up, conniving ass one cent.

"I got in last night, beautiful. I've already placed a delivery order for Aurelio's meat lovers' pizza and wings. Plus, I brought a lil' of the good shit." Theo slyly patted his shirt pocket. "Tried something new in Sedona that will blow your mind."

"Ooooh, good stuff! Please tell me you made the pie a large, or I will go all kinds of "Hunger Games" on your ass," Noelle warned half-jokingly.

Theo threw his head back and howled with amusement, causing women on the street to give him approving glances as he picked up his case of paints. Noelle took a moment to study her friend. Standing at six-feet-two-inches, he looked more like a model than an artist with his long, lean build, and shoulder-length, dark blonde curls. With eyes the color of the ocean and a sensuous mouth, women flocked to him like bees to honey. Theo was an irresistible Casanova. Rarely was he ever found with the same woman twice.

Noelle almost wished she were in love with Theo because that would be a walk in the park for her. Instead, she was in love with a devastatingly handsome, judgmental asshole. She was kicking herself for even going to him with her dilemma. Somehow, she just thought Jack would be different. She remembered the first time she saw him....

PAST

IT WAS NOELLE'S TWENTY-FIRST BIRTHDAY, and her mother had planned this obscenely large debut to introduce her to New York society. Flustered by the number of people who were pushing into her personal space, she'd gone off to sneak a quick drink. God, why hadn't she stayed in Paris? Europeans kept shit real, unlike Americans, who smiled at you while calculating the value of your outfit, determining whether you were worth talking to in the span of five seconds. Her jaw ached from gritting her teeth and smiling so damned much. She could feel her mother's eagle eyes, ensuring she didn't fuck up, tracking her every move like a heat-seeking missile.

"Noelle, please keep in mind that tonight, you should be looking to make a match. There aren't that many available suitors of our stature, and you aren't getting any younger, dear," Alicia sweetly reminded her for the hundredth time while adjusting Noelle's bodice.

Translation: Beggars can't be choosers.

Noelle had just declined another dance when a man's melodious voice whispered in her ear, "Please tell me you won't disappear at midnight and leave a slipper behind. My dear, you've been gone long enough, and I refuse to fly to another continent just to have conversations like we used to."

Noelle whirled in delight to see her godfather standing there, grinning with outstretched arms. Ian Rusnik was her late Uncle Harvey's companion of over twenty years. Normally one to uphold tradition, Alicia Kramer had chucked it in the 'fuck it' bucket and named him Noelle's godfather to please her brother, much to the dismay of her snotty, homophobic parents. Harvey was her only sibling, and she refused to turn her back on him as their parents had for being out and proud.

"Uncle Ian!" Noelle squealed loudly, causing people to stare, much to her mother's consternation. He enveloped her in a hug, and she closed her eyes, inhaling the familiar scent of his cigars, cologne, and the special godfather scent that was uniquely his. "I've missed you! I'm so glad you made it."

"Come dance with me and allow me to save you from "Mommy Dearest"," Ian whispered conspiratorially. Without hesitation, she stepped into his arms, and they began to waltz.

"You're the best, Uncle Ian. Thank you," Noelle laughed joyfully, and he joined in.

"No need to thank me; I recognized that hungry look on Alicia's face. It's the same one she'd get when Harvey and I would cook in our tiny apartment. Poor thing was so busy trying to seduce your father that she refused to eat real food until he put a ring on it," Ian clucked with mock sympathy, referencing Beyoncé with a roguish wag of his brows.

"Oh, shit. For real?" The concept of her immaculate mother actually being hungry for food was surreal. Even at dinner time, Chef precisely calculated her meals with measuring cups and now did the same thing for her miserable sister-in-law, Annamiya. Unlike them, Noelle refused to fall in line with that policy. No sir. She loved food way too much.

"Mmmhmm. She was like that tiny chicken hawk on the "Loony Tunes", and we were hiding Foghorn Leghorn from her." Ian's eyes glowed with satisfaction as Noelle struggled to contain her mirth. It was nice to see his goddaughter smiling on her birthday. He felt a pang of nostalgia.

Oh, Harvey, you would be so proud of our girl, he thought wistfully, desperately longing for his partner who'd died of pancreatic cancer six years ago.

While they loved all of the Kramer children, Noelle was the one who tugged at their heartstrings. Lacking the confidence of her older siblings, she deliberately lagged behind, hating to bring attention to herself. Smart, funny, and pretty, Noelle was often overshadowed by her sister's dance recitals or brother's basketball and lacrosse achievements. Oftentimes, she could be found in the library reading a book or in the kitchen helping to prepare meals.

It frustrated Alicia to no end, and fearing that their daughter would be an underachiever, the Kramers took Noelle to see a psychologist. The shrink's diagnosis: she's a kid, leave her alone. When that didn't work, Alicia, in disguise, of course, took Noelle to Queens to visit a woman who claimed to be a psychic that she heard about from one of her maids. Madame Deon took one *look at the fidgeting, anxious, little girl then addressed Alicia bluntly.*

"There's nothing wrong with your daughter. Nothing that a little love and care on your part won't fix. A word of warning: if you continue at the rate you are going, you WILL lose her."

Dislike for this uppity bitch oozed through every word. Her heart went out to the poor angel who was stuck with her. Nose in the air, Alicia Kramer sarcastically thanked her for her time, and they promptly left with her muttering about charlatans.

After that, Noelle was put into dance, sports, and singing, all of which she enjoyed but won no accolades. Needless to say, her parents streak of disappointment grew tremendously. It was only when Harvey suggested culinary school that Noelle found her passion. She loved working in the kitchen and challenging her mind with recipes. She won awards for her amazing dishes in county fairs, and how did Alicia reward her? By sticking her in a 'fat' camp for kids to make Noelle aware of the dangers of overeating. Harvey and Ian were furious as they watched the light in Noelle's eyes dim. Ian was tempted to tie Alicia to a chair and force-feed her bread and sugar for a week. It was only when Harvey put his foot down or rather, inserted it up his sister's controlling ass did Alicia relent.

"Uncle Ian, you are so out of control!"

As they whirled around the ballroom floor, Noelle felt a prickle of awareness go through her. It felt like she was being watched. She glanced around the ballroom, noticing nothing out of the ordinary until her eyes clashed with a pair of molten hazel ones across the room, and time stood still. Leaning against the entryway, with a slinky blonde whispering in his ear, trying to get his attention, was a tall man whose muscular build was fitted into a black tux that was clearly tailored just for him; he wore it like a second skin.

He was perfection, standing at about six-feet-four-inches tall with short black hair that had a slight curl to it. Thick, slashing dark brows framed his extraordinary eyes. His sharp cheekbones, firm lips, straight nose, and square jaw were utterly masculine, making all the other men in the room fade away. And he was watching her, Noelle Kramer. His eyes leisurely roved over her from head to toe, a perusal so torturously slow, that she knew he was mentally undressing her. Noelle could feel her body responding to him, her heart galloping while her breathing slowed to shallow puffs as if she were a newborn baby, and she involuntarily shivered in Ian's arms, stunned that a complete stranger could pull such a reaction from her.

"Are you okay, dear?" Ian asked concernedly, taking in Noelle's flushed cheeks, dilated pupils, and parted lips. Her attention was focused over his right shoulder.

"Who is that man? I don't believe I've ever seen him before," Noelle whispered, afraid anything louder than that would break the spell she was under. Her gaze still focused on the dazzling stranger, prompting Ian to look. Immediately he knew whom she was talking about, and from his vantage point, the gentleman in question couldn't take his eyes off of her either. For an instant, his mind flashed to another beautiful, young woman years ago who caught the eye of a dashing man. Unaware of the danger until it was too late, Ian hadn't been able to rescue her, and that relationship had ended in tragedy. But this man was more like his angelic mother than his demonic father, Ian assured himself. Only good would come of it; he was certain.

This time, Ian would get it right.

"Allow me to introduce you, my dear..."

ALL THAT WAS LEFT OF their meal was a pizza box with grease stains and a few rogue toppings and an empty wine bottle. They had smoked two joints on the rooftop, and now, it was time to get down to the business of posing and painting. Noelle watched as Theo arranged his brushes then adjusted his canvas in her living room to capture the best light. Dressed only in a men's white dress shirt and her boy shorts, Noelle waited restlessly on the chaise lounge for Theo to start immortalizing her. Suddenly, he looked at her with those piercing blue eyes and grinned.

"Relax. I spent some serious cash on that weed to lighten the vibe and loosen you up. You're not going to freak out now and change your mind, are you?" Theo asked worriedly. Noelle shook her head no. In exchange for negotiating the low rental price of the brownstone with his cousin for her, Theo had asked if he could paint her.

"I see so many elements in you, Noelle! You're complex like magic bars and seven-layer dip," he joked half-seriously. "I'm fucking dying to see if I can catch all of them."

"Just chill. I want you to lie back and let me do my thing," his British accent soothed her.

The marijuana should have been working its magic. Instead, Noelle was even more wound up than before she'd smoked it. Ever since her meeting with Jack, she'd been agitated. Noelle felt like she was going to crawl out of her skin. Her sense of awareness was heightened – from the sound of his deep, bourbon-soaked baritone to that irresistible, seductive smile. She had been aroused simply by his large hands controlling the pen. His fingers were long and thick but calloused, which was a contradiction to the rest of his appearance. That struck her as odd, considering any time she had ever seen him, he was in business attire.

What exactly did he do in his spare time to have calluses? It was unnerving to have intense feelings for someone you really knew nothing about.

Noelle's attempts at inquiry were met with suspicion from her mother and a knowing smile from Uncle Ian. Everything she knew about Jack was from Google and Page Six. She knew he was from Tennessee and the eldest of three brothers. A graduate of Harvard Business School, he'd started his PR firm with her godfather Ian Rusnik and their other partner, Vivienne Romankov. The firm had an eclectic clientele and represented everyone from politicians, musicians, and authors, to athletes, models and T.V. personalities. Her father, Senator Ronald Kramer, had been with the firm since its inception.

Jack, to his credit, tried to keep a low profile, but when you were the poster boy for success, sex, and money, it was damn near impossible to be incognito. The gossip column Page Six had dubbed him the city's most elusive bachelor since John F. Kennedy Junior. Noelle sighed glumly, thinking of all the glamorous women constantly vying for his attention. She didn't stand a chance, but that didn't stop her from dreaming about or longing for him from a distance.

During her father's last campaign, Noelle volunteered at home base and saw Jack on a daily basis. Tongue-tied, she always made it a point to make sure they were surrounded by other people and that there was no direct interaction between them. Every time he saw her, he was cordial, and she would mumble a hello before slithering away. Why couldn't she be more like her friends? Sidra had an easy camaraderie with Jack and always chatted with him whenever she came to the campaign office. Avery did as well, and it frustrated Noelle to no end that she didn't even have enough gumption to pull off a simple conversation with him.

At her father's victory party, Noelle managed to snap the perfect picture of Jack as he stood in the background, listening to her father with a thoughtful expression. As soon as she moved into her home, she'd had it developed and framed. She'd never admit it aloud, but sometimes Noelle practiced talking to it. Ugh, she was such a dork!

"Wanna tell me about it, babe? I'm a good listener," Theo's cajoling voice interrupted her thoughts, and she smiled wanly.

"No, just trying to figure some things out. How's it going over there, Picass-ho?" Noelle teased. "Hang out of any windows lately?"

Theo's bedroom exploits were legendary in his circle of friends and had almost gotten him shot. Hired by a wealthy socialite's husband to paint her portrait, he'd quickly taken on the additional task of pleasing the woman between the sheets as well. One night, when her husband was supposed to be out of town, he'd come home unexpectedly. The woman liked to have adventurous sex and had insisted Theo 'do' her in her husband's study. Having nowhere to hide, Theo had jumped from the second story window, landing in the bed of roses below.

"Jealous much? You know, if you'd let me, I could help you unwind," Theo replied slyly, with an exaggerated wink.

"Boy, please! You know I'd have you crying for your mama." Noelle joked and turned her head away dismissively, missing the speculative look Theo gave her.

"Most women like a man that's in touch with his emotions," Theo murmured, adding more color to the canvas. Noelle smiled, studying his paintbrush moving in bold sweeping strokes. "How's your business going?"

"It's doing really well. Everything is a learning process. With every client being different, we just have to learn to anticipate their needs. We've had clients since day one, which was a pleasant surprise considering we only used social media in the beginning to advertise. Ian, my godfather, has been giving us pointers. At first, he wanted to do our publicity for free, but I declined." Noelle laughed at Theo's incredulous look. "I know, stupid, right? I thought Avery would never talk to me again, but if we're going to make it, I don't want it to be with anyone's charity."

"Yeah, I get what you're saying," Theo concurred. My parents were furious that I decided to study art instead of following them into the world of medicine, but I just couldn't stomach being around blood and sick people all day."

He shrugged carelessly at her startled look. "Sorry if I'm missing a sensitivity chip, but I'd rather someone get a caring and compassionate doctor than a total wanker like me. Angle your chin toward the light."

"Yeah, me too," Noelle teased as she complied. Her thoughts turned to her parents and their profound disappointment in her decisions. "Do your parents support your work?"

He snorted derisively. "Not at first, but that changed when they found out that the Surgeon General bought one of my first paintings. Ever since that happened, it's been nothing but love."

Noelle grimaced. "Well, I'm glad they came around. I could offer to do my father's next political event for free, and they would still decline."

"Don't worry, luv. They'll come around. Let's make a deal," Theo suggested. "If I'm right, and your parents do come around, you birds will cater my next showing for free, eh? If they don't, and by the way, I'm really hoping that they do, I'll auction off one of my paintings, and the proceeds will go to the charity of your choice. Deal?" Theo looked at her expectantly, holding his hand out to her.

Grinning, Noelle shook it enthusiastically. "It'll never happen but deal. Are we going to be much longer? Not trying to be rude, but I've got an early morning meeting with a couple of food vendors in Long Island."

Theo stood up, gathering his supplies. "Yep, I'm done here for tonight. Still have to go home and shower. Got a late night rendezvous that I'm not trying to miss. She's a yoga instructor." The last part was said with such reverence that Noelle rolled her eyes at him. Sliding her arm through his, she walked him to the door and gave his cheek a quick kiss.

"One day, you'll find a woman who won't put up with any of your nonsense."

Theo looked at her with an intensity that was gone in the blink of an eye, leaving Noelle wondering if she'd imagined it.

"When that day comes, I hope she's ready. *Ciao*," he murmured, opening the door where they promptly came face-to-face with a seriously pissed-off-looking Jack Sullivan.

CHAPTER

Six

PAST

WHISKEY ROW, TENNESSEE

"*WHAT THE FUCK WERE YA doin' with Vlad this morning, Moira? Ya looked like his whore lettin' him grope you in front of everybody! Have ya no shame?!*" *Patrick Sullivan roared.*

This line of questioning was followed by the resounding sound of a slap and Moira's muffled cry of pain. At the sound, Jack ground his teeth and quietly left his bed. He and his brother had been in bed for an hour before their Pa came stumbling through the door. Darby was fast asleep, but Jack was old enough to recognize the signs that had been leading up to this event all day.

This morning, a heavily pregnant Moira took them to do some shopping in town at the General Mill Store. They'd run into their mother's good friend, Vivienne Romankov. Jack thought that next to his mother, Vivienne was the second prettiest woman in the world. She had the smoothest honey tinted skin and slanted, molasses-colored eyes. Her raven black hair hung in waves down her slender back.

Vivienne was newly married to Alexei Romankov. The Romankovs were one of the richest families in Tennessee, and the two women had met at their mutual OB/GYN several months ago. A friendship was formed instantly. Vivienne was bright, funny, outspoken, and opinionated. Moira was also all of those things – as long as Patrick was not around. He didn't care for Vivienne or her strong personality. He also didn't approve of the mixing of races and considered minorities to be beneath him.

On this particular morning, Vivienne and his mother were discussing morning sickness, when Vlad Olafsson walked by. Vivienne placed a gentle hand on his arm and expressed condolences for his wife's sudden passing in her sleep. Moira did the same, and he gratefully hugged both women before continuing on his way. It was a brief and simple interaction and shouldn't have been considered problematic. But Jack noticed his father standing in the doorway of the market across the street, studying them. His ma was no fool and had quickly finished her shopping and they headed home. All day, she was tense, jumping at the slightest sounds she heard outside. Dinner was served at five, and Moira had urged them to eat quickly. Afterward, they were to take a quick shower then on to bed.

"I wasna doing naught but comforting him, Patrick Sullivan! Fer God's sake, the man just lost his wife. I offered condolences from both of us and said we'd help with the kids if he needed! Do ya ken me? Tis all!" Moira stated defiantly.

"And what about yer consortin' with the likes of the communist's nigger bitch? I done told ya to keep my boys away from the spics, niggers, and chinks! This damn town's overrun with them! They're the reasons I cannot find work!" Patrick snarled. As he crept down the hallway, Jack could hear scuffling and his mother's *inaudible cries. With caution, he peeked around the corner and saw his mother bent over the sofa while his father's pale ass, clenching as he moved behind her. His hands were on the back of her neck, keeping her immobile, while he was grunted like a frenzied pig. Jack wanted to throw up. Helplessly, he wished for the millionth time that he could overtake his father. Defeated, he moved to go back down the hallway when his bastard father's words stopped him cold.*

"Yer mine, Moira. I will never let you go..."

JACK TOOK IN NOELLE'S DISHEVELED state. She wore a man's white dress shirt and barely there shorts. Her slender thighs, long, shapely brown legs, and tiny feet with red-colored toenails were on full display.

"Am I interrupting something?" Jack demanded icily, continuing to survey pretty boy. According to the private investigator he'd reamed thoroughly, Theo Adams was a friend of Noelle's from overseas. He was a new hotshot on the artistic scene, and judging from the belligerent expression on his face, his interest in the gorgeous girl standing next to him was anything but platonic.

"Jack..." Noelle breathed, shocked to see him on *her* doorstep of all places. At eight-thirty in the evening, he was still immaculate in his navy Hugo Boss suit and tie. His expression indicated that he was seriously annoyed, and she really hoped he wasn't going to be the bearer of more bad news.

Jack inclined his head curtly. "I wanted to discuss a few things with you. If now is not a good time..."

Noelle quickly stepped back and held the door open. "No, please come in! Theo was just leaving."

Theo stepped aside quickly as he risked being run over by the larger man, who gave the impression that such an idea would please him. Jack stepped past them, and Noelle closed her eyes, deeply breathing in his cologne as he headed down the hall. *Lord, he smells good,* she thought dreamily.

"Really, Noelle? *That guy?*" Theo's disgusted tone brought her back to reality. She opened her eyes to his annoyed expression. "That's the guy that has you moping all over the place? He's *way* out of your–"

Shooting him a look of irritation, Noelle opened the door wider. "Good night, Theo."

Not giving him a chance to say anything else, she shoved him out and shut the door in his hurt face. She pressed her face against the wood, trying to sustain the hurt his words caused her. She didn't need any reminders. Noelle was well aware that she didn't have a snowball's chance in hell of being with Jack Sullivan. Taking a deep breath, she locked the door, put the chain on it, and walked down the hall where Jack stood in the middle of the living room, observing her space.

She wondered what he was thinking. Noelle's brownstone was a far cry from the refined palatial elegance of her parents' estate. Her childhood home was filled with tons of breakable antiques and no-touch rules. It had a very museum-like feel to it, and growing up in that cold, stoic household, she treasured the welcoming normalcy of her school friends' and uncles' homes.

Although she was raised in subdued elegance, Noelle's taste was wildly eclectic. Her style ranged across bohemian, vintage, rustic, and industrial. You could see it reflected in her decor with the tarnished crystal chandelier, printed velvet pillows, and navy leather-tufted sofa. Floral vases with eccentric patterns were overflowing with various plant life. Her favorite pieces were the large reclaimed wood coffee table and bookshelf her godfather Ian had given her. They were replicas of the pieces in his home, and when he saw how much she loved them, he had them commissioned for her as a surprise housewarming gift.

When she'd moved into the large three-bedroom dwelling, Noelle had painted all the rooms in varying shades of neutral colors. There were floor-to-ceiling windows in every room, therefore tons of light offset the rich taupe and grays. The wood floors were an aged walnut covered with multi-colored Kilim rugs. White subway tile and recycled wood cabinets complimented the kitchen and bathrooms. Gold framed pics of her loved ones were scattered throughout the place. Since the kitchen was where she spent most of her time, she'd designed it to hold up to ten people, about the usual size of her dinner parties. It also boasted a huge dining table and was filled with state of the art appliances.

"So, what brings you to Brooklyn, Mr. Manhattan?" Noelle inquired sarcastically, watching as he bent to admire her table. Jack straightened to examine her, taking in her clothing or lack of it with a disapproving frown.

"Who's the guy, Noelle?" Jack asked coolly, although he already knew. He just wanted to hear her confirm that nothing was going on between them. Jack was actually proud of his controlled tone because internally, a raging mass of jealous fury was brewing, and he was dying to chase the asshole down and give Theo Adams a southern-style ass- whuppin' that he wouldn't soon forget.

"Theo is an old friend of mine. Would you like something to drink?"

The look in Jack's eyes made her think of a predator stalking its prey, and she took a step back, watching with relief as his gaze lost some of its power.

"No, thank you. I actually came by to let you know that we've reached out to Mr. Dumont." Jack gestured to her sofa. "Do you mind if I sit down?"

"Oh, my goodness, sorry! Yes, please sit down," Noelle urged and with her permission, he settled his large frame with ease into her leather couch. Amidst all the feminine floral and velvet touches, as masculine as he was, Jack should have looked out of place with his suit and tie, but instead, he looked absolutely perfect. *Like he belonged in her space,* Noelle thought with enormous satisfaction as she took the seat across from him on the velvet chaise. "Well, what's the word, Sullivan? Am I going to have to change my identity or what?" she asked flippantly, trying to hide her nervousness.

Jack grunted but didn't answer. He was busy drinking in Noelle's bronze skin gleaming under the soft lighting and her seemingly endless legs. He was certain the artist hadn't missed any of those details. "Do you always run around damn near naked when entertaining men?" Jack demanded, a bite to his normal even tone, enraged once more as he imagined her all hugged up with punk-ass Theo. *Damn!* He really needed to get his shit together.

The temperature in the room hiked up another fifty degrees with his provocative question. Suddenly, they were both aware that they were alone, away from her nosy family and the hustle and bustle of his office. Just the two of them. Noelle sucked her teeth, rolling her eyes at his implication.

"First of all, I am nowhere near naked, and even if I was, this is my damn home, and none of your damned business! If I'd known that the great Jack Sullivan was going to grace me with his presence tonight, I would have dressed in my finest silks and rolled the red carpet out for your arrival," she snapped at him.

Despite his anger, Jack grinned. He was seriously feeling this fiery side of Noelle far more than the passive one she usually exuded. He suppressed his laugh when she huffed her indignation, tucking her legs underneath that luscious bottom. All of a sudden, Jack felt the tension he'd been carrying for the last couple of days drain from his body. It was nice being here with her alone, and he planned to have many more moments like this by proceeding with his plan.

Time to get to work.

"Dumont wasn't bluffing about blackmailing you. He made some bad gambling investments, and now it's time for him to pay up. But that's only going to happen if you give in to his blackmail and pay the money. Otherwise, he needs to get out of Europe, and you're his only solution. Dumont knows that if he marries into a well-known political family, he'll be somewhat protected."

"These people he did business with like keeping a low profile in their country, and your ex is the type who would make a lot of noise if he felt threatened. Your pics would come out either way, and this could have lasting negative effects on your father's career," Jack finished bluntly, allowing the realization of how huge a scandal they were trying to contain to dawn on Noelle. Her hands were wringing the bottom of her shirt tightly while she processed everything.

When problem-solving in his business, Jack was adamant about informing the client of the enormity of potential damage that could be done. He gave them a moment to feel the fear before alleviating it with a rescue plan. It was what he'd fondly coined 'tough love', and it enabled him to do his job smoothly.

"What can we do to fix this?" Noelle was determined not to let Remy win. She owed it not only to herself but her family as well. They shouldn't have to suffer for her poor choices. "If it was just me, I wouldn't give that asshole one fucking penny. But it's *my family*..." she shuddered. "Oh my God, Jack! *My mother*!!"

Jumping up, she paced the room, her hand over her mouth as if to contain a scream. Jack enjoyed the alluring view she unknowingly presented: hair whipping, hips switching, and ass swaying. *Focus Sullivan,* he reminded himself, willing his growing erection to stay down. No such luck. *Shocker.*

"Alicia would not be happy with pics of her baby girl in her birthday suit floating around, that's for sure," Jack added, wincing for good measure. That was the understatement of the year. Although he'd put a considerable dent in her armor, and she'd reluctantly agreed to back off, the Kramer matriarch was still no one to fuck with. Heads would certainly roll, starting with the beauty's in front of him if the pics were made public. Fortunately for Noelle, Jack liked her head attached to that delectable body. "Now, I'm going to do what's best for my clients in a way that allows them to focus on their priorities as I make their problems disappear. Lucky for you, I have an easy solution to your problem."

"You have a plan??" Noelle whirled to face him, hope illuminating her lovely face. "Well, don't keep me in suspense! What's the plan?"

Jack watched her carefully before dropping his bomb. Could she see the triumph he was trying so hard to conceal? He'd struggled with utilizing the plan. Until he saw that British turd sniffing around her. *Noelle was his and no one else's.* Jack was done beating around the bush.

"We get married."

PAST

NOELLE'S HEART POUNDED FURIOUSLY AS *Ian escorted her across the ballroom to where 'Tall, Dark, and Fine as Hell' stood, watching their approach. His hazel eyes gleamed with frank, masculine appreciation as they thoroughly inspected her. Goosebumps spread over her skin; she was short of breath and unable to look away from him. He'd completely ensnared her without even trying. Mortification filled her with that understanding.*

"Are you okay, my dear?"

Noelle reluctantly dragged her gaze away from the specimen of male perfection ahead of them to look into her godfather's amused eyes.

"I don't blame you for staring, my dear. He really is quite dazzling. Hell, you should see his brothers'. AND he's considered 'the ugly one'. Their parents were also quite the lookers," Ian finished with a tinge of bitterness.

"He has brothers? Who are better looking? Good Lord, there should be a crime against that much fineness in one concentrated area."

Ian laughed as they reached the beautiful man, and Noelle realized he was even better looking up close as he gave them a heart-stopping, devastating smile. His skin was smooth and supple-looking with a faint hint of a five o'clock shadow.

"Jack, good to see you," Ian greeted warmly, releasing Noelle's arm to give the other man an affectionate hug. Turning back to Noelle, he explained, "Jackson is one my business partners in our public relations firm. Jack Sullivan, this is the birthday girl, Noelle Kramer. She's also my goddaughter," Ian added with a warning look at the younger man. Noelle blushed when Jack winked at her.

Be still her beating heart...

"Ms. Noelle, it's a pleasure to meet you. Happy Birthday. I hope you don't mind my attending your party. Ian invited me. Are you enjoying yourself?"

His voice was deep and velvety with a southern drawl. Noelle wanted to throw her panties at him right then and there. With a voice like that, she didn't care if he described his bowel movements as long as he never stopped talking. Belatedly, she realized both men were staring at her with curiosity, waiting for her to say something.

"It's nice to meet you too. You can crash my party anytime," she finally answered, breathlessly. Whaaat? Who said that?? At his amused expression and Ian's raised eyebrow, Noelle flushed. Clearing her throat, she corrected herself. "I meant, it's an absolute pleasure to have you here. I..uh..hope you're enjoying yourself."

"Oh, I definitely am. Would you like to dance?"

That deep baritone with the charming accent made her bones melt. Jack held his hand out. Still dazed, she nodded and placed her hand in his much larger one. It was electrifying, and awareness ran through her in currents. Jack studied her intensely and judging from the way his hand tightened around hers, she knew he felt it too. And in that instant, Noelle knew, with this one meeting, everything had changed for her. She knew that all other men would be compared to this one and that they would fall severely short.

But all too soon the moment was broken by her mother's cool, commanding voice as she glided up behind her daughter and gently pulled her away. Noelle frowned at her, annoyed that she was no longer touching Jack, who also looked irritated by the interruption.

"Please excuse us, gentlemen," Alicia trilled, smiling brilliantly. "Noelle, darling, I've been looking for you everywhere! You simply must come with me! Geneva Winters middle son is home for a brief stay. You remember Charles, don't you? He's an investment banker now. Anyhow, he recently ended his engagement to Tabitha Lodge and is available! There's no time to lose as you're not getting any younger. Posture in place and smile agreeably to whatever he says. Let's go, dear," Alicia ordered briskly, whisking Noelle away before she could decline her mother's opportunistic offer.

Mortified, Noelle helplessly looked back and found Jack expressionless with his hands shoved in his pants pockets, watching their departure. Ian wore a disapproving frown, an indication that he would have blunt words for Alicia later. Pissed off at being treated like a child, Noelle pulled out of her mother's grasp.

"'Smile agreeably to whatever'? Really, Mother?" Noelle shook her head in disgust, horribly embarrassed at her mother's treatment in front of Jack Sullivan and Ian. "Thanks for setting us back fifty years. Gloria Steinman should definitely ask you to speak at her next rally on women's liberation."

"Oh relax, Noelle! I'm only looking out for your best interests. Charles Winters is a good match for you. If you're not going to have a lucrative career, then you should at least have a lucrative marriage. Or both! Look at your sister. She's beautiful, successful, and has a wonderful marriage. You just have to want these things for yourself. I don't know where your lack of ambition

comes from." Alicia shook her head in disappointment, clearly traumatized by her youngest daughter's life choices.

"Well, never mind, here we are. Charles! Hellooo!! You remember Noelle, don't you?" Alicia simpered, shoving Noelle forward to meet the studious-looking man who offered his hand and held hers limply. Just to be sure it wasn't her, Noelle squeezed his hand with more vigor, and he frowned. Nope, nothing. Releasing it, she glanced across the ballroom. Jack was still watching her, and for a moment, it felt like they were the only two people in the room. Even from afar, this thing between them was tangible, like an electric wire.

The moment was soon broken by the return of the beautiful blonde from earlier. She pulled him onto the dance floor, and Noelle hated to admit it, but they made a striking couple. They appeared to be having the time of their lives, laughing and talking to each other, she thought, blatantly staring with envy. The woman radiated confidence, and Noelle knew with certainty, would never have allowed anyone to treat her like she was a five-year-old.

There was no way someone as sophisticated as Jack would ever be interested in someone as gauche as me, Noelle thought despondently only half-heartedly listening to whatever the hell Charles and her mother were conversing about. From that moment on, she made it a point to avoid being alone with Jack Sullivan so as not to embarrass herself further.

CHAPTER

Seven

NOELLE WAS SILENTLY SHAKING AND clutching at her stomach as tears rolled down her cheeks because she just couldn't stop...*laughing.* Jack watched in silent bemusement as it went on endlessly. Out of all the reactions he'd expected her to have, this wasn't one of them., It left him feeling slightly offended. Typically, women fell all over him and laughed with him – not at him. Five minutes passed. Ten minutes passed. Finally, she stopped, wiping her eyes with the backs of her hands.

"Ooooh boy! Thanks, Jack. I needed that." Tension broken, Noelle sighed in relaxation, giving him an expectant glance. "Now what are we really going to do?"

Was she for real?

"We are going to get married, Noelle. I wasn't joking," Jack restated firmly. She opened her mouth in protest, but he ignored her. "The kind of people your ex is mixed up with are the worst kind of greedy lowlifes. If you give in to Dumont's blackmail, they will eventually come after you and everyone you love, ruining your family's good name in the process. Are you willing to risk that?" Jack interrogated her sharply, prompting her to slowly shake her head in the negative, eyebrows furrowed in concentration.

"I didn't think so. In his culture, there is a mafia-like syndicate that ensures everyone falls in line and doesn't bring dishonor or attention to them. I know a guy that can make all of the shit he has on you disappear, but I have to show him that we are legally married. It's disrespectful to make advances on another man's wife in general, but from where his family originates, they take it to the *umpteenth* power. All your problems will disappear. Unless you've told anyone other than your closest friends about this, no one needs to know," Jack finished smoothly, watching her expression grow pensive.

Jack knew it was a long shot that Noelle would tie herself to him because frankly, he wasn't even sure if she liked him. She avoided him like the plague, always careful to make sure they weren't alone. He felt like a pathetic fool hopefully waiting for her to come to the obvious conclusion as she digested the information. There was a prolonged moment of silence before Noelle finally spoke.

"Would you like some pie?"

Pie? The hell??

And because he'd been raised to be a gentleman, he politely said, "Yes, please. I would love some."

Noelle beamed at him and took off toward the kitchen, leaving him alone in the living room. *Pie.* Jack shook his head in bewilderment. Why couldn't pie be code for *sex*? Fuck yeah, he'd love a big helping of sex with her. He stood up peeking as she walked down the long hallway to the kitchen. Again, her ass teased him from underneath the long shirt she wore. The urge to bury his hardness in her, balls deep, was excruciating. He wanted to fuck her like an animal marking its territory so that everyone would know whom she belonged to. And that was the part of him that scared him the most. Noelle brought feelings out in him that, until they met, Jack didn't know he possessed or was capable of feeling.

Women passed through his bed and remaining cool and detached with them had never been an issue. It was like a business deal; each party walked away mutually satisfied – until Jack was alone. His thoughts turned to the insanely stunning girl in the kitchen. He longed to make her his and felt the need to destroy any man that looked her way. Older than her, Jack knew he had no right to want her like he did. It was pure madness. An image of his father flashed before his eyes, and he rubbed his face trying to clear it.

You are nothing like that psychotic bastard.

Jack wandered around her living room, attempting to clear his head from that negative bullshit. Taking in all the framed pictures of friends and family she had, one frame, in particular, was hidden behind all the others but immediately caught his eye. Jack was amazed but even more perplexed to see that it was a picture of him taken at one of her father's events two years ago. *Why did Noelle have a picture of him?* Discreetly he put the frame back as Noelle re-entered the living room with a tray that held two slices of pie and two glasses of milk and set it on the coffee table. Jack couldn't even remember the last time he drank straight milk. *That's how goddamn sweet she is; don't corrupt her*

"This is a new recipe of mine, peach-blueberry-basil. I hope you like it." Smiling shyly, Noelle handed him a plate.

"It smells delicious," Jack replied truthfully, moving back to his seat across from her. Aware that Noelle was watching him, he cut a piece of the golden-crusted pie and put it into his mouth. The flavors of the fruit, basil, and cinnamon layered his tongue, making him hungry for more. It was delicious, reminding him of his mother baking on Sunday mornings before church.

"Damn, Noelle, this pie is amazing."

Quickly, he shoved another bite into his mouth. The crust was buttery and light, making him groan in sheer pleasure. All too soon, his plate was empty, and he looked so forlorn that Noelle laughed and went and cut him another piece. The musical sound played in his ears repeatedly, making Jack realize how badly he wanted to be the only one who made her laugh and smile.

"Did you get Tarik to straighten up?" Jack queried, licking his fork clean. Noelle watched his tongue swirl around the fork prongs, with an inward groan, imagining it on her nipples.

Lawd, have mercy.

"Actually, he called me yesterday to apologize," she beamed, remembering how surprised she'd been to hear from him. "We have a meeting tomorrow afternoon at four. My goal is to get everything finalized by the end of the meeting. Avery is coming with me to make sure he stays on task."

Jack nodded his head. "Good plan. Another way to achieve that goal is by making sure the environment is business-oriented. I find that meeting my clients who are prone to distractions in boring places makes them focus on the task at hand. They're eager to do what I need them to do in order to get out of there. If you'd like, you guys are more than welcome to use my conference room," he volunteered. That way, he could keep an eye on Tarik as well.

"That's great advice, and we actually did rent a meeting room. If the non-refundable deposit didn't already clear, I would have totally taken you up on your generous offer."

They continued to eat and talk about work, avoiding the topic of marriage altogether. When the plates and glasses were empty, Jack gathered them up and took them to the kitchen, despite her protests. Noelle lay back, thinking again how well he fit in her space.

Jack had discarded his jacket and loosened the pinstripe tie. Damn, he was so freakin' sexy, and just looking at him was arousing her, which was nothing new. It seemed to be the constant state Noelle was in whenever she was in his company. It pissed her off how much of her emotions were invested in a man who before this week, barely knew she was alive. She thought he would address the topic of marriage again, but instead, he was examining her table.

"Don't you just love it? It was a gift from Uncle Ian, along with the bookcase." Noelle pointed to the corner where the beautifully carved bookcase stood. Jack turned to look as she continued. "I've been in love with some of the pieces of furniture at his house for a couple of years now. On the day that I moved in here, he surprised me with them. The craftsmanship on both pieces is stunningly unique. From what I understand, the carpenter works on commissioned items only and is in very high demand. I don't even want to think about what Uncle Ian paid for them," she finished with a mock shudder.

Jack smiled enigmatically. "They're really nice and compliment your space, which suits you perfectly."

Noelle blushed and murmured, "Thank you." She realized by his patient look that he was waiting for her to bring up the subject of marriage again.

"Okay, Jack, how would this work? I mean, do you really think we could pull this off?"

Jack answered carefully. "Monday, we go down to the courthouse and have a quick ceremony. Afterward, we'll send the certificate to my contact, so he can put things in motion overseas. In the meantime, to give our relationship some validity, I think it would be best if we were seen in public together as frequently as possible. I can spin a credible story for those who know us, but honestly, the less we say about our relationship to family and friends the better. That way, the chances of us getting caught in a lie will be slim to none. We would need to stay married at least six months. I know a really good lawyer who can draw up a prenuptial agreement to protect our investments."

"Six months is a long time. Won't this cramp your social life with your revolving door of women? I don't think there's a stick big enough to beat off your hundreds of admirers with." Noelle's saccharinely sweet smile quickly turned into a frown when he grinned smugly in response.

"This is actually a situation that would be beneficial to me as well. In my line of work, my job is to fix things for our clients so that their lives are interruption free and they are seen in the most positive light. I frequently encounter women who see me as a knight-in-shining-armor type and concoct ridiculous situations where I'm left wishing someone would just rescue *me* instead. If I were taken off the market, I wouldn't have those problems anymore and could just focus on doing my damn job," Jack said simply. He gave her a woeful look. "Won't you help a poor lil' country boy out and say yes?"

She gave an unladylike snort. "Maaan, please! Don't give me that crap. You think being married would stop these thirsty chicks from pressing up on you? Your voice alone could convince women to drink your bath water," Noelle imitated him by deepening her voice and adding a country twang. "This here dirty-ass bathwater is the best you'll ever taste. Why, the dirt bubbles just melt on your tongue, darlin'."

Jack howled with laughter, and Noelle joined in, enjoying the way the deep booming sound filled her home and did crazy things to her tummy.

"Marriage might make some of them go away, but I doubt it," she mused, looking at her hands, particularly her empty left ring finger.

"Does this mean you're considering my offer, Noelle?" He was still chuckling over her teasing. It was the kind of shit he took and gave to his brothers. Add 'funny' to the growing list of traits he discovered that he liked about her.

"Possibly… and when the coast is clear, the marriage will be annulled, correct?"

Noelle knew the deal and resented him for it. Jack's firm went above and beyond to protect their clients, and the Kramers were excellent clients. *Of course, he's going to get rid of you as soon as possible! Why would someone like HIM go for YOU?* her inner voice taunted her. Gritting her teeth, she did her best to ignore it. At his raised eyebrow, she carried on dryly, "Silly me. Of course, we'd get an annulment! I mean look at *us*. It's not exactly like we're each other types." Noelle waved her hands between them to indicate their different styles.

But Jack interpreted something more. He sat up straight, all traces of humor gone and fire blazing from his hazel eyes as a slow flush was crept up his face. With crisp preciseness, he retorted, "Oh yeah? What am I, Noelle? What, *white*? Or is it because your family comes from money? What exactly is it, Noelle??"

She recoiled as if he'd slapped her, and Jack felt a pang of remorse. The thought that she might be color struck and averse to having an interracial relationship had never entered his mind. A sharp pain ripped through his chest. Fuck that shit! He *would* fight for them to have a chance and overcome any objections she might have if that was her concern. Although they lived in the most diverse city in the world, he was well aware that racism still existed. He'd grown up with an animal that deliberately exposed his family to its ugliness on a daily basis.

Noelle shot to her feet. "How dare you imply I'm some sort of snobby, racist bitch? It just gets better and better with you, doesn't it? First, I was a whore and now, this shit! Fuck you and your offer, Jack Sullivan!!"

Jack also stood up and got in her space. "Well, what the fuck did you mean exactly? Besides, I wouldn't know if you were a ho or a racist because you always run away like you're afraid of your own shadow whenever I come around, Noelle," he rebutted harshly. She opened her mouth to retort in anger but opted to take a deep breath instead before continuing in a more reasonable tone.

"I didn't mean it like that. I just meant that you're this great-looking, successful guy whose career is on track. And well there's....*me*. The Kramer screw-up destined to wind up living with a hundred cats if my mother doesn't get her way. Why would *you* want to tie yourself to someone that?" Noelle quizzed bitterly.

Jack felt his heart start to calm down, but his anger remained. This time, it was directed at her mother. "Someone like *you*? You're fucking joking, right? Someone who's funny, smart, and gorgeous? Someone so kind that she lets an incompetent chef take credit for her amazing meals?" He shook his head in disbelief. "Don't sell yourself short, Noelle. You most certainly are a catch. Just ask your artist friend," he finished irritably. Yeah, he was still mad as hell behind that shit.

"And in regard to an annulment, if it's still an option, maybe you'll be able to get one," Jack murmured, staring at her sexy lips before raising his smoldering gaze to meet hers, allowing her to see the unguarded lust in his eyes. "Or just maybe you'll like being married to me too much to consider one."

SEXUAL TENSION CRACKLED BETWEEN THEM, and Noelle wheezed with the comprehension of his words. *Holy. Sheep. Balls.* Jack Sullivan wanted her. The realization made her panties virtually flood. She looked down and even the dark fabric of his slacks couldn't conceal the massive erection he made no attempt to hide. Confidence mixed with elation surged through her, which made her feel higher than any 'good shit' Theo had ever given her. Yeah, she was definitely going to have to throw these panties away because they were beyond ruined.

"I'd expect you to be faithful," she blurted out, flushing sheepishly at his raised brow. "If ...*if* we did do this, I certainly wouldn't want to be blindsided by any indiscretions and made a fool of."

"That's not a problem for me, and I'd expect no less from you. There will be no other men. Are we clear?" Jack wondered what Noelle would say if he told her that from the day they met, other women had ceased to exist for him. As far as other men were concerned, when it came to her, his mind was in a "Game of Thrones" state where all threats needed to be eliminated. "Another thing I should clarify is that while there won't be any other women; I certainly will not live like a monk. Do you understand what I'm saying?"

He wanted them to sleep together. She would get Jack as her husband and get to sleep with him. Noelle looked around wildly for an unseen fairy godmother. Licking her lips, huskily she replied, "I understand, but can you even hear how *crazy* this sounds? We barely know each other and would be fooling nobody! What about our likes and dislikes? We might not be compatible..."

Swiftly, Jack closed the distance between them, pulling her soft curves into his hard planes, his large hands framing her face. He watched her gray eyes widen in awareness as his erection pressed against her stomach aggressively.

"Let me show you what I like. Okay, Noelle? I can show you better than tell you," he urged thickly, mouth hovering above hers, waiting for permission. His warm breath tickled her face, and she clutched at his shirt, dizzy with yearning for him.

In her family's eyes, she might be a loser, but this was a chance to be with the guy of her dreams. She would not screw this moment up. The lyrics to Eminem's "Lose Yourself" started running through her head, but unlike Rabbit, she wouldn't toss her cookies. They were on her turf now and suddenly, she could see everything crystal clear. All she would ever want was on the other side of her fears. *It was now or never.* She yanked his head down and his lips met hers in a searing kiss.

CHAPTER

Eight

ER LIPS, SO SOFT AND full, were addicting and his favorite part of her body. Jack gently coaxed her mouth open, sliding his tongue in to meet hers. *Heavenly*. Noelle tasted spicy-sweet and her tongue was like satin sliding against his in an erotic tango. The kiss deepened, and Jack pressed her body closer to him as she wound her arms around his neck. Noelle broke the kiss to nibble greedily at his lips, and her shaking hands lowered, swiftly undoing his tie and unbuttoning his shirt. Jack sucked on her bottom lip, sliding his hands under her shirt and cupping the smooth full globes of her ass. She moaned softly into his mouth as those magical fingers caressed her.

Jack swallowed every sound she uttered, continuing to devour her mouth hungrily. Scratch the decision about her lips being the best, it was her sexy derriere that was perfection...or was it her lush breasts pressing into his chest? No, it was her flawless, silky brown skin. Okay, it was just *her*. Period. Every fucking single thing about Noelle was perfect.

The fire between them morphed into an inferno as Jack hoisted her up into his arms and she wrapped her legs around his waist, grinding her center against the stone-like hardness in his pants. The friction between her thighs increased tenfold, and Noelle threw her head back, allowing Jack access to lick the sensitive nerves on the exposed column of her slender throat. Wrapping an arm around her waist, he moved with her, pressing his straining cock against her aching core.

"You like that don't you, baby? You're so fucking wet. I can feel you through my pants," Jack whispered gravelly against Noelle's ear as she clung to him weakly. Breathing sharply, he inhaled her womanly scent and knew he wouldn't be able to leave her untouched tonight. Jack walked over to the velvet chaise and placed Noelle on it, kneeling in front of her. He yanked her shorts and panties off. Her tantalizing scent wafted up to him, making him animalistic with need. "Scoot up, love, bend your knee, and open up. I want to see your pretty pussy," he ordered harshly, desire thickening his voice and making his southern drawl even more pronounced.

Noelle shivered in anticipation and did as she was told, leaning up on her elbows. She watched as Jack sat back, stroking his dick through the fabric of his pants. *Why were they still on??* Expression unguarded and stark with wild hunger, Jack's scorching gaze was centered on her exposed pussy, and again, Noelle marveled at his flawlessness.

His tan skin was smooth, and through his shirt opening, she could see his six-pack. While in his arms, she'd felt all muscle from the strength of his carrying her to the firmness of his thighs and butt. Noelle bit her lip, stifling a whimper as she watched him move his hand over what promised to be a good time. Restlessly, she shifted in anticipation of his next move. *Damn, she needed Jack in her!* Whether it was her pussy or her mouth, which she'd never tried, despite what those pics showed. She just wanted to *feel* him moving in her! *Filling her.* His breathing was labored as if he was struggling himself, and she stared lustfully through heavy-lidded eyes as the bulge in his pants grew impossibly bigger. But Noelle didn't want him composed. She wanted him to be wild as fuck and out of control, as she was.

Sliding her fingers down between her thighs to her glistening, puffy nether lips, opening her legs wide, she gave Jack a show. His eyes flew to hers, and she held contact as she masturbated in front of him. His face was stark with desire — for *her*, Noelle Kramer. A heady sense of power filled her, knowing that she was solely responsible for his lack of control. Stroking up and down in a languorous rhythm and tracing her tender clit with the barest flicker of her nails, Noelle's eyes drifted shut as arching her back, she channeled the goddess of decadence. Brazen purrs escaped her lips, feeling her sex spasm in anticipation before sliding her shaking fingers inside, touching herself the way she did whenever she thought about him.

The room was quiet except for the sounds of their panting and the juicy sounds coming from her pussy. Then she heard the sweetest sound – him unbuckling his pants. Noelle's eyes flew open to watch him extract himself from his underwear. A strangled sound, a combination of a wheeze-moan, squeaked from her throat. Jack's dick was the stuff of women's dreams everywhere – lengthy with a satisfying girth, guaranteed to have her bow-legged. The head was an angry flush glistening with his excitement.

Jack knelt in front of her and pulled her drenched fingers out of her core. Noelle watched as he took them, coated in her essence, into his mouth and sucked every, milky drop, driving her crazy with his warm, skilled tongue. Eyes closed, groans of pleasure spilled from his throat. "Jesus, you taste good! Taste yourself, baby."

He leaned down and kissed her, and Noelle drew on his tongue, tasting the sweet tanginess of her arousal. She loved the way his lips felt as he expertly owned her mouth. Jack thrust one of his long, thick fingers into her wetness, stealing Noelle's soft scream, and proceeded to fingerfuck her, slowly at first, then faster as he added another digit. Noelle moaned her encouragement into his mouth, thrusting her hips up to meet them while his other hand plucked at her turgid nipples through her shirt.

"Unbutton this, Noelle," Jack commanded against her swollen lips. Weakly, she followed his orders, having no will to defy him. She was pliant, vulnerable, and exactly where she wanted to be – at Jack's mercy. He continued kissing her as his fingers masterfully fucked her. Jack broke the kiss off to stare at the most perfect pair of breasts he'd ever seen. They were much better than the pictures. Plump and high with dark brown nipples that were begging for his attention. Bending his head, Jack captured a tip in his mouth, swirling the hard nub with his tongue, grazing it with his teeth. Noelle shuddered, gushing even more around his fingers. She protested loudly when they left her pussy, but it quickly turned into a wail of ecstasy as Jack slid down to replace his fingers with his tongue.

Never had Noelle felt anything like this before. Her nerves were vibrating throughout her body. She became more aroused with each stroke and twirl of his long tongue as he tunneled through her wetness. Jack's fingers gave exquisite pleasure to the gem between her nether lips, and Noelle thought she would pass out as she thrashed frantically against his face.

"Baby, baby, baby, you taste so damn good," he

crooned. *Fuck, he couldn't get enough of her!* Sweet, beautiful, deceptively dangerous Noelle. She was bathing his tongue with her cream, driving Jack insane with her delectable taste, and corrupting him with her decadent pussy. Out of control, he fed with a savage yet torturously slow ferocity that made tears of ecstasy seep from the corners of Noelle's eyes.

Noelle could feel her impending orgasm building when he suddenly switched up and latched onto her clit while his fingers dove in and expertly stroked her g-spot.

"Don't...stop, Jack. I'm gonna...aaagh!!"

A pleasure so sublime that it felt supernatural, detonated, spiraling like a cyclone, sweeping through her body. As it wracked her body, Jack hungrily lapped up all of her sweetness.

NOELLE LAY SPENT, STRAINING TO catch her breath. She was a boneless mass as Jack rose tall and majestic before her. He hastily shucked off his pants and boxers and Noelle felt her body come back to life as she watched him stroke his manhood. She couldn't take her eyes off of it, standing so erect with a curve that promised to heighten her sexual experience. Large and swollen, the prominent head glistened with the pearl-colored liquid of his excitement. Noelle licked her lips eager for a taste of him, which shocked the hell out of her because giving head was something that she'd never done nor ever had a desire to do. Her eyes flew to Jack's and found him watching her through heavy-lidded, hazel eyes burning with satisfaction.

"Since we've already covered one of the sex acts that you'd never indulged in, we might as well kill two birds with one stone."

Noelle sat up and his shaft became level with her face. *Was it strange to think it was beautiful?* Noelle wondered, reaching out to touch it. Although she could feel the veins underneath the skin, it felt like warm, velvet covered-steel in her hands. Jack groaned as she tentatively stroked him from the base all the way to the tip. Taking it as a sign that he liked what she was doing, she continued but with more confidence. More pre-cum appeared at the tip. Noelle looked up at Jack to find him watching her.

"Taste me, Noelle," Jack ordered hoarsely, holding his breath in anticipation as he watched her luscious lips, waiting to feel them surrounding him.

Obediently, she opened her mouth, tonguing his essence from the bulbous head. It was sticky, salty, and absolutely delicious to her. Noelle opened her mouth and took in as much of him that was possible. Jack swore harshly as the feeling of her lips and tongue suctioning him almost brought him to his knees. He mentally counted backward, starting from one hundred as she took him deeper still. Instinctively, his hands lifted, gently gripping her head to guide her. What she couldn't fit into her mouth, Noelle stroked up and down with her hands. More of his nectar flowed, and she eagerly swallowed, swirling her tongue rapidly around him as if she were licking a lollipop.

"Fuck, darlin', just like that! Take more of me. Open up! Shit! Your mouth is like velvet, Noelle," Jack hissed, dropping his head back with a savage growl and flexing his hips forward, gripping her head tighter and guiding her. She hollowed her cheeks, drawing her mouth up and down on him, making Jack feel like his skin was a livewire.

"Mmmmm...."

Jack damn near lost it as the sound of her ecstasy

vibrated around his dick. He felt a tightening in his balls and blood roaring through his ears. *Don't cum, don't cum,* he chanted in his head. The sight of her sucking his dick was the sexiest fucking thing he'd ever seen. Her eyes were closed, and her expression was pure bliss as if giving him a blow job was exactly what she wanted to be doing tonight. All of his senses were on overload, and he needed to feel her pussy wrapped around his cock right *now*. He pulled her back by her hair gently and stepped away when her lips released him with a wet *pop*.

Jack dropped back to his knees, in front of her, and yanked the shirt from her body. He gripped her waist and dragged her down so that Noelle was now in his lap, legs draped over his thighs. Her saturated pussy rubbed against his hardness, scorching him with her heat. Jack bit her nipple and eased the sting away with his tongue. Noelle thrashed her head wildly while he enjoyed the view of her naked beauty.

"I can't be gentle right now, darlin'," he warned starkly. "Are you sure you want this?" Dazedly, Noelle nodded her head, her eyes stormy with need. "Then hold on tight." She sat up and wrapped her arms around him, licking his ear and sending a jolt of desire shooting up his spine.

Groaning, Jack gripped Noelle's head, feeding her hungry kisses while reaching between them to angle his cock at her ready opening. He stopped kissing her long enough to look down between them. *Beautiful.* The sight of their skin melding together, hers a dark bronze and his paler hue was so erotic to Jack that it made his cock pulsate with his need to be in her. He plunged into her beautiful brown body and nothing had ever felt as perfect as her dripping tightness suctioning around him.

"Jesus, Noelle!" Jack breathed raggedly. Not an

overly religious man, he prayed ardently for control. "Your pussy's fucking *golden*. Are you sure you can take this?"

Jack wasn't being cocky. His desire was an unleashed beast that couldn't be reined in. There was none of the cool, calm, and collected lover that he was with other women. Noelle had officially ruined him for anyone else. He belonged to her and she to him as it should be.

Noelle sighed her pleasure into his mouth as her body adjusted to the heavy fullness throbbing inside of her. "More, Jack. I want more," she pleaded, aching to be fucked by him.

Knowing he wouldn't be able to last long in this position, he pulled out and turned Noelle over onto her knees to lie across the chaise. Turning her head back to look at him, she beseeched, "Take me, Jack. Please! Fuck me now!"

"Hold onto the other side and spread your knees wider," Jack instructed urgently, shrugging his shirt off watching her sexy behind sway and dip. Waiting until Noelle did as instructed, Jack grabbed her hips, angled his cock and thrust into her. Going balls deep, pent-up need unleashed, he fucked her mercilessly.

The purring symphony Noelle intoned, escalated as she threw her ass back to meet every powerful thrust, liquid pleasure running down her thighs. Sweat glistened on their bodies as they came together over and over again. Jack was working Noelle over in a methodic, yet possessed manner, leaving no doubt that he owned her pussy. Their guttural sounds of gratification filled the room, and the air was permeated with the musky scent of their lovemaking.

Jack leaned over her to grip the chaise, bracing himself as he moved deeper and deeper into her. He ran his tongue down her skin licking the beads of moisture from her back. *So. Good.* Grabbing her damp curls, he turned Noelle's head to access her mouth sinking his teeth into her plump bottom lip slowly sucking on it. His other hand slid between her slick legs to capture her hypersensitive clit between his fingers, stroking it in time to his thrusts. Noelle broke the kiss, crying aloud at the unbearable bliss she was receiving, shuddering as tiny ripples started in her toes and spread up and through her body.

"Does my baby need more?" Jack crooned in her ear, rotating between forking and tugging gently on her clit and smacking it lightly. The orgasmic waves were tsunami-like as they crashed over her body and swept her away to an all-consuming climax. Noelle was drowning in sensation as her orgasm went on and on, causing her to jerk back against him uncontrollably. Being with Jack was unlike anything she'd ever imagined, far exceeding her wildest fantasies. The pleasure-pain her throbbing pussy was receiving from him was an exquisitely addictive torture that she was now dependent on. Jack handled her body as if he'd always known it.

Every plunge through her swollen tissues rubbed her against the sumptuous velvet of the chaise, stimulating her achy nipples and the rest of her already oversexed body. Jack's kisses were heady, and Noelle couldn't get enough of them. And his dick. *Lord, his dick.* It was her fucking absolute kryptonite. She held on even tighter to the chaise as another orgasm swept her away. Jack's large hands moved to clutch her hips as he, too, caught the wave. With one last surge, he stiffened, spilling himself deep inside of her womb, before collapsing over her.

WHEN THEY FINALLY RECOVERED, JACK carried Noelle into the master bath and drew a bubble bath in her gigantic claw-foot tub. She lit Seda France candles then lay back against his muscled chest. Cradled between his powerful thighs, Noelle was content to let the warm water soothe her deliciously aching body parts.

"Middle name?" Drowsily, she traced circles along his strong thighs that were covered with fine dark hair.

"Conall. Yours?" he whispered against her ear, pressing a kiss to her lobe. Noelle shivered, feeling her nipples harden as he traced the delicate shell with his tongue.

"Lynette. Birthday?" She could feel him hardening against her lower back. Anticipation was making her girly parts kick into overdrive again. *Oh dear.*

"May 15th. Yours is January 18th."

So, his birthday had just passed, and he was a Taurus.

"Ooooh! Happy Belated Birthday! Favorite food?"

"A dish my ma would make. I've yet to find anyone who cooked it as perfectly as she did. Every Sunday after church, she'd make it. My brothers and I would just inhale it. I haven't had it like that in forever..." he trailed off.

Hmmm. Traditional and loyal; good to know.

"Is that her name tattooed on your arm?"

Adorning his left arm was a beautifully drawn tattoo. It was the name "Moira" with angel wings on either side and a Celtic flag flying behind it. Across his back, she'd discovered another tattoo that read 'Ní neart go cur le chéile'. Noelle certainly hoped it was his mother's name because jealousy's fangs were deeply embedded in her upon discovering the artwork and refused to let go, even though everyone was entitled to a past.

Please say yes! Please, please...

"Aye."

And the way his deep voice took on an Irish lilt was too hot for words, she thought, smiling as the green-eyed monster disappeared. His firm lips were now trailing soft kisses down the delicate curve of her neck. Noelle tilted her head to the side, giving him better access, and Jack rewarded her with a bite to the spot where her neck and shoulder connected then licked it languidly, causing Noelle to grip his thighs while goosebumps appeared on her flesh.

"And the...one on...your back?" His lips were wreaking havoc on her weak spots.

Jack paused his gentle assault to slide his hand in between her tender nether lips. His fingers caressing her sensuously, jacking her pulse rate up to an alarming rate. "Strength in Unity."

"F-Favorite color? Mine is j-jade g-g-green," she stuttered, finding it hard to catch her breath and form a coherent sentence. His mouth was back to working overtime on her neck, with one hand cupping her heavy breast, teasing the peak by squeezing and pinching it while his other hand...*God bless his multitasking skills.*

"I like brown, darlin'. Not just any shade of brown either. Nope. My favorite brown is the color of your skin, all rich and shimmery like brown sugar. You've got me wantin' to taste every inch of it."

His words sent Noelle over the edge as his motions increased tenfold, and head thrown back on his shoulder, Noelle rode his fingers, her hands gripping his thighs for stability. Water sloshed over the edge of the tub as she succumbed to the powerful orgasm, bucking uncontrollably and gasping his name.

Was it possible to die from pleasure?

Noelle fell back against him, relaxed and sated.

Jack laughed silently, aware of the effect he was having on her. Judging by his rock-hard penis that felt like a sharp knife trying to pierce her back, the feeling was mutual.

"Stand up, love. We're not done yet," he urged, shifting her forward.

Though she was tired, Noelle stood because her body was no longer hers to command. She felt something cool slide down her back, and the scent of her favorite lavender and citrus bath wash filled the air. She cooed her delight as Jack nibbled on her booty while bathing her. When he rinsed her, Noelle tried to turn and face him, but Jack stopped her by holding her hips firmly.

"Noelle, do you trust me?" She didn't hesitate, nodding her head eagerly. "Brace yourself against the wall and spread your legs slightly, darlin'." Jack trailed a finger between her full cheeks, causing her core to clench as she assumed the position. "I wanna taste you again. Will you let me, sweet Noelle?"

His southern voice was like dark thunder threaded in desire. Cupping her bottom, Jack spread her cheeks, blowing cool air on her most intimate areas and she shivered helplessly, her sex quivering in response. "Can I, Noelle?"

And just like that, the girl who'd once been accused of being an uptight prude was deliciously rimmed by Jack Sullivan's masterful tongue. Noelle found herself bending over until she was gripping the sides of the tub with her shaky legs spread as far as they could go while he finger-fucked her pussy and Frenched her star. The sinful debauchery of the taboo act and his superb skills brought her to an earth-shattering climax that left her quaking and reveling in disarrayed delight. With an arm around her waist to steady her, Jack rose and helped her out of the tub.

Noelle sat drunkenly on the closed toilet seat while he dried her. Throughout the entire process, she couldn't take her eyes off of his dick that had her hypnotized as it bobbed with every move Jack made. It looked painfully flushed in its aroused state, and she felt a surge of empowerment knowing that she was the cause. Jack caught her looking and gave her a sexy wink.

Noelle blushed but wasn't ashamed to be caught looking. Slyly, she said, "I think my new favorite color is red."

Jack's shoulders shook with amusement at her comment, but he didn't reply. Verbal foreplay would lead to the real deal, then her delectable body contorted in positions she was nowhere near ready for. When he was finished drying her, Noelle returned the favor, taking her time to trail kisses down Jack's spine, giddily laughing when she bit one of his firm buttocks and he clenched them in response. She ran her hands, sans towel, all over his heavily muscled body, licking up droplets of water everywhere, but he refused to let her touch him *there*.

"You're gonna be the death of me, sugar, if you put those sexy lips on me again." Jack kissed away her pout and led her to the queen size bed, tucking her in. Leaning down, he gave her a heart-stopping smile, gently kissed her forehead, and dressed under her admiring eyes.

"Jack, wait! I just realized we didn't use any protection." Panicked, Noelle sat up in bed. *How dumb could she be?!* A wave of horrified embarrassment mixed with shame swept through her. "I'm on the pill, and my last OB/GYN appointment was three weeks ago. I got tested, and I swear I'm clean."

Jack gave her a serious look. "That's good to know. I've never had unprotected sex before tonight, but if it will reassure you, I can get tested."

He didn't add that it wasn't important because once they were married, he planned to stay married, so protection wasn't a big deal to him. The sooner he could knock Noelle up, the better.

Asshole! His conscience screamed, but Jack shoved it to the back of his mind.

"Jack, have you ever been in an interracial relationship?" Noelle's eyes dropped to the sky-blue eyelet duvet cover as she plucked at the pattern nervously. "I mean, I know you want to help me out and trust me, I appreciate you doing it, but are you sure that this is the right course–"

"Look at me."

Noelle's head snapped up at Jack's hard tone. The savageness in his hazel eyes made her want to draw the sheet around her protectively. "If someone expresses their opinion to you about *us*, a matter that doesn't concern them anyway, please bring it to my attention immediately. Do you understand?"

Jack's tone implied that he would welcome anyone stupid enough to try. Speechless, Noelle blinked her acquiescence and he continued. "I will never let anyone hurt you or come between us, Noelle! As my wife, you will be shown the utmost respect. I know we live in a world that likes to think it's far more progressive than it actually is, and yes racism unfortunately still exists, but you need to understand my background to know the color of your beautiful skin matters to me only because I can't get enough of seeing and touching *you*."

Noelle blushed at his words. "That's good to know and thank you for the compliment. I just had to know. When you're a person of color, the world *does* see you differently. Hell, even as well-liked and popular as Daddy is, the ton of racist hate mail he receives is mind-blowing. It certainly makes me hyper-aware of how unkind the world can be."

You should try being the son of Patrick Sullivan, Jack thought bleakly, even while giving her a reassuring smile. Stiffening slightly, he replied, "I'm not worried in the least. Are you? About being affiliated with a white guy?"

Noelle heard the challenge in his tone and threw him a speculative look. "I'm more worried about being tied to someone so good-looking and all the drama it will bring from the ladies than his being white."

Jack's smile dropped. "Let that be the least of your worries, darlin'. As long as I want you, whoever wants me isn't even a factor. It's time for me to go. I hope tonight showed you how compatible we are. I've told you I want to pursue all aspects of marriage, but I give you my word that we won't sleep together unless you come to me and say that's what you want too. I do want to warn you that I won't stop touching you unless you tell me to stop."

His hooded gaze ran over like a caress and her nipples pebbled underneath the covers in response. "I promise you won't regret marrying me. Meet me at City Hall Monday morning at eight sharp. I'll lock up behind me. Sweet dreams, Noelle."

After he left, Noelle slid under the covers, exhausted and bemused. Aloud, she contemplated, "I can't really marry him, can I? It's such a crazy idea! I'll tell Jack no tomorrow."

Noelle yawned, drifting off to sleep, knowing full well she wouldn't tell him no.

Damn Jackson Conall Sullivan and his Svengali-like hold.

CHAPTER
Nine

*F*RIDAY AFTERNOON, NOELLE WAITED PATIENTLY for her two closest friends to arrive at the Crabby Shack in Brooklyn. It was one of their favorite spots to eat because the food was simple, delicious, and fresh. Since she arrived first, she placed their usual order of Alaskan snow crab legs and spicy steamed shrimp with corn and potatoes for sides.

While waiting, her thoughts drifted back to her evening with Jack. The intensity of their lovemaking and how out of control they'd burned made her want to experience it all over again. And again, and again. Noelle was so lost in her reverie that she didn't notice the tall, dark beauty heading her way. She gave a surprised shriek when Sidra Barton plopped down in front of her, causing her friend to give her a quizzical stare.

"Hey, babe! Everything ok? You were really zoning out there for a minute."

Sidra's voice sounded a lot like Alicia Keys' and always had the opposite sex hanging on her every word even when she was telling them to kiss her ass. It worked well with her striking looks. Skin the color of milk chocolate complimented her perfectly symmetrical features in an oval face that was framed by a shoulder-length bob of jet black curls laced with indigo and dark purple streaks. She had wide whiskey-colored eyes with short, thick lashes. Her eyebrows and cheeks were high, delicate arches, and her mouth was a perfect full bow. A soft, pointed chin rounded out her ethereal appearance. Sidra's body was lean and lightly muscled. Already standing at five feet nine inches, she absolutely adored high heels and dressed like she just stepped off of a rocker-chic runway.

Women envied her, and men wanted to be with her, but behind the vibrant personality and looks was one of the sharpest minds and tongues Noelle knew. Sidra was their high school valedictorian and graduated Summa Cum Laude from Cornell University. Although she currently worked with R.R. & S. Public Relations in what she called the 'Wining and Dining' department, Sidra was making a name for herself in the world of deejaying, a skill that she honed to perfection in college to pay for her living expenses. Unlike Avery and Noelle, she didn't come from money but was offered a full ride to the colleges she'd applied to.

"No, just thinking about some things going on at work. What's up with you, babe?" Noelle gave her friend an admiring smile. Today, Sidra was wearing acid washed skinny jeans paired with a white muscle t-shirt with the words 'Wild Child' scribbled across the front in red font. Her hair was in huge rolled curls and oversized black sunglasses pushed them away from her face while red and black bangles adorned her wrists. Noelle glanced under the table to appreciate the four-inch red Jimmy Choo stilettos on Sidra's feet.

"Well, the firm just took on two more clients. One of them is Dominick Harris. You know, the lead singer of that indie rock group Bison Blue? The one with all the tattoos? I met him the other day, and the man is sexy as all get out in person, girl. I invited him to attend a firm event in D.C. next week with one of my other bosses, Vivienne Romankov. He looks like the kind of guy who'd show you a good time. Want me to hook you up? I know it's been a minute on your maintenance, mama," Sidra offered with a devilish smile on her fire-engine red lips as she reached for her glass of iced lemonade.

Noelle coughed, feeling color creeping up her cheeks. Seeing it, Sidra set the glass down with a thud, causing a little bit of the tart beverage to splash onto the table. "Oh. Hell. No. You look just like Sylvester when he swallows Tweety Bird! You got some, didn't you?"

"Got some of what?" a polished voice behind Noelle inquired.

Saved by the bell. Swiveling her head, she found their other bestie, Avery Monroe, standing by the table. She smacked Sidra lightly with her oversized flower printed clutch and received a snarl in return before Sidra scooted over. Avery slid in and kissed her cheek while grabbing Noelle's hand and giving it a warm squeeze.

"Sorry, doll. You know I love you, but the thought of sitting across from you as you inhale food like its air and not gain a pound is depressing, especially to someone who only has to *think* about food and five pounds appears on *each* hip," Avery kidded with a warm smile, ignoring the censorious frowns she received from her friends.

Standing at five-feet-two inches tall, Avery was the smallest in height of the group but not in size. She was a size fourteen in a figure that many men likened to a 'brick mansion'. With curves for days, she made

Nicki Minaj look like Popeye's girl, Olive Oyl.

In high school and college, Avery was obsessed with reduction surgeries, and she'd only worn oversized clothes that made her look dumpy as to not draw attention to her body. Eventually, she started to accept her body shape and embraced a very feminine, classic modern look with full midi skirts and dresses. While her friends were model striking, Avery was pretty in the classic sense and became more so the longer you were in her company.

If you weren't initially distracted by Avery's body, then it was her smile that drew you in. She had a wide, generous mouth, and her entire face lit up when she blessed you with that dazzling smile. It made you notice how her large dark brown eyes sparkled with gold flecks and high cheekbones glinted in her upside-down triangle-shaped face. Her copper skin glowed and was only enhanced by her long, dark brown wavy tresses. She was a genuinely friendly, kind, and caring person without a mean bone in her body.

Men usually missed all of these wonderful attributes since they were too busy trying to get to know her from the neck down. By the time it dawned on them that there was more to her than just a sexy body, her hand was in their face before she graced them with a complimentary view of her thick backside, gliding away.

Although Avery had grown resigned to the fact that her curves weren't going anywhere, she tried to keep them under control. While Noelle liked to run and do Pilates and Sidra liked kickboxing, Avery *hated* to exercise. So, she dieted instead. *Obsessively*. She'd tried them all and was always on the lookout for the latest fad.

"Well, dish, honey. Don't leave us hanging," Avery urged. "I wasn't aware you met anyone new."

Noelle cleared her throat nervously. "Nothing's going on, and no, I haven't met anyone new." *Technically, that wasn't a lie.* "How's Pierce doing? Does he like his new job, Ave?"

She was referring to Pierce Wesley, Avery's boyfriend. There was silence at the table, both of her friends staring at her as if she'd grown a third eye.

Suddenly, Sidra pointed the crab leg she was trying to crack open dangerously close to Noelle's face, causing her to jerk back defensively. "Uh-uh! See that right there? Humph! That's the kind of shit that lets us know you're holding out. Avery knows we don't give two shits about her stick-up-his-ass, name-droppin', social-climbin'–"

Avery interrupted her warm up before Sidra really went in.

"*Wow.* Really?! That's how you guys feel about the first guy that's *not* trying to get in my pants?" She was pissed and on the defensive. "Pierce is a very sweet guy who happens to be a complete gentleman. I like the fact that when we're together, it doesn't feel like I'm wrestling an octopus all damn night!" she hissed at Sidra, who simply rolled her eyes in response.

Noelle attempted to soothe her ruffled feathers. "Calm down, Avery. We didn't *say* that we disliked him."

Although if she were honest with herself, she did find Pierce Wesley to be very shallow. He seemed more interested in the fact that Avery's family name could practically be traced back to the Mayflower than Avery herself.

Sidra snorted rudely, turning in the booth to give Avery a hard stare. "Well, I'm saying it! I don't like him, and I think you can do way better. Since I'm already going there, you need to get over this obsession with your body and eat some damn food! Look at your plate! You have three 'scrimps' and a child-size serving of corn and potatoes. Last I checked, this place didn't serve kids meals and *you* sure ain't a damn kid! You are a fine, full-figured, bodacious woman who needs to accept it. Move on from Pierce and find a real man who will work you over so good in bed that you won't need to worry about dieting. Or you can just take your big apple bottom ass to the gym with me and Noelle."

With suspended breath, Noelle watched Avery's hands clench and unclench and her left eyebrow twitch. Sidra was the type to bust your balls and call it a day. Noelle just went with the flow until she could no longer. But Avery, although well-mannered and ladylike, had a *terrible* temper. Slowly, she turned to face the expectant Sidra and took a deep breath.

"Why don't you save the ball-busting for the men who are interested in you? You know, the ones you go all 'Solange in an elevator' with if you feel like there's a chance you might like them? How about you give someone a chance to know your beautiful, kind heart? *Oh, I know why!* It's because deep down inside you know you're scared of being rejected," Avery countered. "Please don't act like I'm the only person in this booth with scars and kindly Shut. It."

Sidra looked like she was going to stab Avery with the crab claw she was death-gripping in her hand. Avery raised an eyebrow as if to say, 'I wish you would'. The restaurant grew quiet, and the manager nervously had her hand on her phone ready to dial 9-1-1. Noelle knew they didn't know that Sidra and Avery loved each other fiercely and would turn on them in a heartbeat if they tried to jump in and assist. But the topics being discussed were too close to their hearts for hurt feelings not to be involved. So, she did the only thing she could do to distract them...

"Guess what? I slept with Jack Sullivan and we're

getting married. Surprise!" Noelle announced brightly, taking in their shocked open-mouthed expressions as they turned back to her.

Well, at least they weren't arguing anymore...

CHAPTER
Ten

$\mathcal{J}$ ACK STOOD BEFORE THE FLOOR to ceiling window of his office, not seeing the perfect, cloudless blue sky. Normally, he could appreciate the view of the Manhattan skyline, but not today. Today, he couldn't function because victory was within his grasp. He'd had a taste of Noelle, and the reality was so much better than his fantasies, changing everything Jack thought he knew about sex.

He wasn't a prude, but Jack didn't partake in pussy-eating with every female he slept with either. Except with Noelle, he couldn't get enough of her taste and wanted to stay buried between those silky thighs forever. He'd almost cum just from her exploding in his mouth. Then the feel of those velvety lips inhaling him, and her silken tightness clenching around his cock...*Jesus*. All he could think about was her touch, taste, and the way she looked when he fucked her. So, yes, the reality surpassed the fantasy, but it was also worse because he couldn't think of anything but her. Nothing was getting accomplished today.

The ring of his cell phone shook Jack out of his reverie. He pulled it out of his pocket, glancing down to see it was his middle brother, Darby, returning his call. Earlier, he'd called and had to leave a message on his new sarcastic voicemail.

"You've reached Jackson Sullivan's Pussy Delivering Service. If you are a damsel currently associated with my big brother and in distress, please leave your name, phone number, and address so that I may drop whatever the hell it is that I'm doin' to come assist you and take you wherever you need to go. That's right folks. Damn how important my shit is, I am here for YOU. Y'all have a nice day now, ya hear?"

He pressed the accept button with a smile, southern accent emerging in full effect. It always happened when he conversed with his brothers and friends from his hometown of Whiskey Row. "Still got your panties in a bunch, lil bro?"

There was a slight pause before Darby gave a low chuckle. "I don't, but pretty, little Ms. Inez does. She was lookin' to blow off a little steam from the pageant scandal and was pissed that yours truly couldn't oblige due to your "No Involvement with Clients" policy, which, to me, totally contradicts the "Keep Them Happy" policy. It's a fine line to walk, ya know? I mean, I'd hate to be the one to put your firm's spotless reputation at risk because of a *dissatisfied* client...."

Jack clenched the phone but remained silent, refusing to take the bait. Growing up, Darby loved to push peoples' limits. He was pretty good at it, but Jack refused to be pushed. All he had to do was remain silent, and Darby would eventually tip his hand. The silence stretched into two minutes. While waiting, Jack picked up the framed picture on his desk of him, Darby, and Casey, taken the last time he was home. Just looking at it made him smile. He and his brothers were as close as could be and would die for each other. If shit went down, they would always have each other's backs.

Jack also knew that on the other end of the phone, Darby would be wearing that maddening grin while he waited for him to respond. Casey and Darby were like oil and water, and it took very little for Case to fly off the handle with him. But not Jack. By the time he was four, he'd perfected the waiting game, hiding quietly for hours if Patrick was on one of his drunken rampages. Three more minutes passed and after seeing he wouldn't be getting the rise out of his older brother that he was looking for, Darby gave a long sigh.

"Well, lucky for you I found a solution where your firm and client came to a... *ahem*...mutually satisfyin' solution."

"And what, pray tell, was that?" Jack's overtly polite tone was the only indication that he was not as calm as he would have his brother think. Darby chuckled again, and this time, it had a little evil twist to it that raised a red flag for his older brother.

"Nothin', Jackie," Darby reassured him, using his childhood nickname. "We had a nice drive down to Baymoor, Maryland. That town is really pretty, almost puttin' ours to shame. It was real quiet though, so I had to find ways to keep myself busy until Eli got there." That last part was said innocently. *Too innocently*, Jack thought. "Anyhow, enough about me. What's goin' on?"

Still suspicious of Darby's seemingly guiltless remarks, Jack decided to give Inez a call later and do some backup damage control because he knew his brother and his slick ways too damn well.

"Darby Liam Sullivan! I know ya ate the brownies for the church picnic. You've still got the chocolate smeared around yer mouth!" Moira scolded furiously, hurriedly wiping his face clean.

"It wasn't me, Ma! I swear it!" Darby insisted dramatically. The lie earned him a plucking from his mother. "Ow! What was that for?" he whined, rubbing

his injured ear while Jack and Casey struggled to hold in their laughter.

"Oh, ya swear now, do ye? Fer shame, looking me in the eye and lying right to me face! Yer never going to get to Heaven's pearly gates being full of blarney, Darby Liam Sullivan! Jackie, help yer brother to get cleaned up. I see Father Vincenzo talking to yer Da. Oh, Lord...be quick about it!"

Jack blinked away the memory. "I called because I need you and Casey to come to New York. I'm gettin' married, and I'd like for you guys to stand up with me," he informed him nonchalantly. His statement was met with silence. For once, the smart-ass was rendered speechless. "Darby? You still there, bro?"

"Hold up just a damn minute!! Did I just hear you say married?!" Darby finally shouted incredulously.

Jack smiled, pleased to finally get a rise out of him. "Yes, I'm gettin' married to Ms. Noelle Kramer on Monday so–"

Darby interrupted him. "Wait a minute! Isn't that Ian's goddaughter?" Before Jack could answer, he continued on. "Does he know about that? Isn't she that fine-ass filly with the pretty gray eyes and bangin' body? Ooohwee! I ain't mad atcha, brother! Seen a pic last time I was in Ian's office and thought about takin' it along on one of my breaks to the bath–"

"Careful, Darby. That's my soon-to-be wife that you're talkin' about," Jack interrupted in a tone that promised deadly repercussions for his brother if he didn't shut his big mouth.

"It's like that, huh? Well, lemme hurry up and catch the next flight out. I can't wait to greet my new sister-in-law all nice and proper like," Darby said lasciviously.

"Piece by piece I'm gonna take you apart, Darby," Jack vowed solemnly while on the other end, his brother hooted with laughter as he hung up. Jack called Casey next and left him a message regarding weekend plans before replaying the voicemail Noelle had left for him earlier.

"*Hey, it's Noelle. Soooo... remember that thing about keeping this private for our friends? Well I kind of let it slip to Sidra and Avery, and to make a long story short, they want us to celebrate with them tomorrow. I just don't think I'm going to be able to keep them away from City Hall either. I figured tomorrow is as good a start as any for us to be seen in public, right? We're doing the charity fundraiser at the Blue River Country Club, and I would love it if you could make it. Sorry for the super short notice. Starts at seven p.m. Don't leave a girl hanging, okay? Bye.*"

Just the sound of her voice got him primed to fuck. Of course, he would make it. Nothing and no one was going to keep him away from her.

HE WASN'T GOING TO SHOW, Noelle thought despondently.

It was now seven forty-five in the evening, and the fundraiser to raise awareness for hungry children in America was in full swing. According to the chairwoman of the foundation, On a Whim had done a fabulous job with the 'Take Me to Thailand' theme, and she couldn't thank them enough. As soon as she walked away, Noelle and Avery did a discreet fist bump, which was their ladylike version of 'Yassss, hunty! Yasss!'.

They'd transformed the club into a lush, tropical paradise filled with various types of floral arrangements that included orchids, hibiscus, lilies, bougainvillea, and the country's national flower,

Ratchaphruek. Candles were placed in the middle of huge lily pads that floated in the enormous pool. Two large golden Buddha statues were placed at each end of the pool, a perfect complement to the sleek, white modern furniture. The servers were dressed in authentic *Chut Thai*, the formal national Thai costume, and the soft background music was a mixture of *Bong Lang*, the traditional northeastern music of Thailand and *Luktung*, Thai country music. As a thank-you gift, guests in attendance would receive paper lanterns to write messages or sentiments on that would be released into the air at the end of the night.

"Stop with the sad face," Sidra ordered crisply. "You are looking way too good to be sitting on the sidelines! That man should be horsewhipped for standing you up."

Noelle winced and rolled her eyes before turning to smile at her friend who was on point per usual in a tropical print fuchsia Diane Von Furstenberg wrap dress. Her hair was blown out in a full bob, and the silver strappy stilettos on her feet were a sexy contrast to her chocolate skin. "Nobody's sad, doll. Just maybe a...little disappointed. Besides, it was a last-minute invitation anyway."

Sidra rolled her eyes at Noelle's lame excuse.

"Noelle, you can't fool me," she said bluntly. "Besides, I'm still mad at you for dropping that little bomb yesterday! *Are you sure about this?* I mean, you can't even rely on him to be here for this event," Sidra shook her head doubtfully. "Don't get me wrong, I like Jack. He's cool and a great boss, but you're my girl, and I hate the fact that you're here looking like a million bucks but feeling like someone just died!"

Noelle flushed self-consciously. It was true; she *had* dressed with Jack in mind. The navy blue satin crop top she wore was sleeveless, with a plunging neckline that showed a tasteful yet teasing amount of cleavage that just came in under ladylike. Her full, knee-length skirt was white with an intricate pattern of fuchsia, navy, and light blue feathers splashed throughout. White heels completed the look. She wore diamond studs in her ears, a delicate silver chain rested against her collarbone, and a silver and diamond cuff on one wrist. Her hair was a heavy curtain of black waves flowing around her shoulders.

She was about to deny Sidra's claim, but a movement over her friend's shoulder caught her eye. Any protest she planned on voicing died in her throat. Jack had just entered the pool area and was busy scanning the area while nodding and shaking hands with people he knew. Noelle noticed the entire time he conversed with those around him, he never stopped looking around. *For her,* she realized with satisfaction. His eyes finally met hers, and Jack offered a private smile that made Noelle's heart do somersaults as she returned it.

Sidra glanced over her shoulder. "Well, I guess I'll just cross him off of my shit list. Damn! That man looks at you the way I look at bacon. How the hell did I ever miss that?"

She turned to look at Noelle, who was still staring at Jack with a goofy smile. "Guuurl, you are *sooo* far gone. Just keep in mind that you have to think of relationships in terms of shopping for cosmetics. Is he the kind of man who'll have you running to Sephora to replace your lip gloss? Or is he a jerk that'll have you replacing your mascara, instead?"

Noelle watched Jack's confident swagger as he cut through the crowd, people scrambling to get out of his way. She noticed plenty of women, and even a few men, were feeling him, but he only had eyes for *her*. It was hard to do but she pulled herself away from his hypnotic stare to glance at Sidra. They smiled at each other before simultaneously agreeing: "Lip gloss."

Jack reached them, eyes still focused on Noelle. He bypassed Sidra, only acknowledging her presence with a murmured "Hey, Sid" and pulled Noelle into his arms, his mouth slanting across hers assertively. The kiss was brief but sweet with a tease of tongue action. Nonetheless, it had Noelle clinging to his jacket lapels, craving more of him. They broke apart reluctantly, but his eyes gleamed with promise as he pressed his forehead to hers.

"Sorry, I'm late. My brothers decided to fly in tonight, and they insisted on coming with me." Jack brought his lips down to Noelle's again, and she opened up, allowing him to explore her mouth as she pressed her body into his, desperately needing the intimacy. The hardness pressing into her midsection let her know Jack was just as affected as she was. Reluctantly, he stepped back but kept an arm around her waist possessively. "Forgive me?"

"Of course. Where are they? I'm dying to meet them." Noelle wanted to ask him how much they knew about their arrangement but now wasn't the time.

Beside them, Sidra interrupted sarcastically. "Ummm...hi, Jack. Nice to see you too. How am I doing? Why I'm doing just fine and you?"

Jack gave her an apologetic grin and opened his mouth to apologize, but Sidra's gaze sharpened, and she threw her hand up at him.

"Wait a minute! Did you just say that your brothers are here? *As in plural?*" she interrogated him suspiciously.

Grinning, Jack winked at her. "Yes, *both* are here. Please play nice with Casey. I think maybe you guys just got off on the wrong foot. I'm sure he'd love the chance to smooth things over with you."

Noelle looked behind a groaning Sidra and saw two extremely handsome men coming their way and drawing a great deal of attention in the process. Both were equally good-looking but complete opposites of each other. The broader and taller of the two had dark, wavy auburn hair. His strong jawline was covered with a neatly-trimmed beard. With dark green eyes, a straight nose, and sensually full lips, he looked like a bottle of sin served straight up. He stood at about six feet-eight inches, and Noelle could tell that underneath his well-cut suit, he was heavily muscled. Although the suit was supposed to make him look gentrified, she could feel his wildness itching to get out. No one had to tell her he was an untamable heartbreaker; the wink he gave her confirmed it.

The other man was leaner and about six-feet-four inches, and... well...*beautiful*. There really was no other way to describe him. His dirty blonde hair was short on the sides but longer on top. It was tousled as if some lucky woman had the pleasure of running her fingers through it, tumbling onto his forehead. Thick, straight, dark brows framed his sleepy-looking hazel eyes with long dark lashes that curled at the tips. His model looks boasted high cheekbones and square jaw faintly covered in stubble, and his mouth was full, soft looking and kissable. Where the other man was pure testosterone, this one was angelic.

Noelle gave her friend a warning look to hopefully stop what she suspected was coming next, but per usual, Sidra was off and running.

"I sincerely doubt that, Jack. Don't get me wrong. Darby is cool as hell, but that other one? I like dealing with him as much as I like dealing with the stomach flu. I know he's your family and all, but he walks around like he's got one of my Louboutin's stuck up his repressed ass."

At that, the bigger of the two men threw his head back and gave a resounding laugh, causing Sidra to jump and whirl around. The other one's eyes were disdainful icicles as he glared at her. To her credit, Sidra didn't flinch. She just smiled sweetly at him before addressing Jack.

"Add *sneaky* to my list."

"Oh, Ms. Sidra, it's always a pleasure to see you. Gimme some sugar, darlin'."

The laughing giant got himself under control long enough to open his arms, which Sidra went willingly into with a genuine smile. She completely ignored the other man whose baleful stare remained lasered on her. Finally, he spoke to the back of Sidra's head as she remained cuddled in Darby's embrace.

"Sidra, don't you look like the epitome of class? Pity the illusion is ruined when you open your mouth," he disparaged in a biting drawl.

Noelle gasped, and Jack stepped forward with a frown on his face. The other man holding Sidra gave him a dirty look. "I think your mama raised you to have better manners than that, Casey. I suggest you try again."

"You're right, man." Casey turned a dazzling smile on Noelle. "Ms. Noelle, I'm Casey Sullivan. I'm absolutely delighted to make your acquaintance. Please forgive me for pointing out that your friend is classless."

Before Jack and Darby could jump on him further, Sidra stepped out of Darby's arms to meet Casey's glare, dead in the eye. "Casey, what an unpleasant surprise. I wasn't expecting to see you tonight. Love your suit. It complements the blackness of your soul."

She dismissed him without another glance. "I'll catch up with everyone but *him* later. Darby, we have to kick it before you leave okay, boo? Deuces."

Leaving them to watch her fierce strut, she soon disappeared into the crowd. Casey's jaw was clenched, and his cheeks were stained red with his anger. He looked like a beautiful avenging angel ready to smite the path that Sidra had taken.

Darby continued to be amused while Noelle and Jack looked at each other in bemusement. They both knew Sidra never backed down from a confrontation, and Jack was secretly amused because Casey *never* had problems with the opposite sex. This was a first for both of them.

Clearing her throat, Noelle addressed both gentlemen. "Hi, I'm Noelle Kramer. It's very nice to meet you both." Jack squeezed her waist, giving her an expectant look, complete with a raised eyebrow. "I'm also your brother's fiancée."

She felt heat creep up her face as the brothers smirked knowingly at Jack's territorial hold.

"Damn, you've got it bad, Jackie! Well, Ms. Noelle, I'm Darby Sullivan, and it is an absolute pleasure to make your acquaintance. Now, don't just stand there! Let me give you a proper greetin' to welcome you into the family." Darby opened his arms again with a friendly smile. But when Noelle moved to hug him, she found herself bound to Jack's side, his arm a band of steel around her waist.

She gave him a look that said '*Seriously?*' But he was too busy glaring at Darby. "Piece by piece," he promised his brother, who smiled back innocently at him.

"Christ, Darby! You know you're bad when your own brother won't trust you with his woman. Ms. Noelle, welcome to the family," Casey finished smoothly, giving her a warm smile. Unlike his brother, he didn't attempt to touch her, especially when Jack had that strange, crazed look in his eye.

"Thank you both very much. Why don't we go mingle and enjoy ourselves?" Noelle suggested. She muttered to Jack under her breath, "I know I could really use a stiff drink."

It was going to be a very *looong* weekend if the drama between Sidra and Casey escalated. Before they could leave, Avery rushed up to them, a vision in a coral colored maxi dress that skimmed her voluptuous curves. Her hair was piled atop her head in a chic topknot, and around her neck, complementing her generous cleavage, was a gold multi-layered necklace with tiny gemstones weaved throughout.

"Hey, guys! What's wrong with Sidra?" Her expression concerned, she reached up to kiss both Jack and Noelle's cheeks. "I said hi to her, and she walked right passed me! One of her exes didn't show up, did they? I triple-checked that list myself. If that's the case, keep her away from the utensils and anything flammable."

Suddenly, Avery became aware of the two strangers standing there — two *very attractive* strangers. "Oh my! Sorry, I didn't mean to interrupt."

Casey gave her a slow smile that caused her to blink owlishly at him while Darby simply nodded politely. Jack raised an eyebrow as he caught his loud-mouthed, shit-stirring, smooth-talking brother's eye. There wasn't enough money in the world to *pay* Darby to be quiet about anything. That he was strangely silent in the presence of a woman was unheard of. Darby never missed an opportunity to flirt with a woman. Short, tall, fat, skinny, young, old, pretty or ugly, he simply didn't discriminate.

"Avery, I'd like you to meet my brothers, Casey and Darby Sullivan."

Noelle grinned at her disconcerted friend whose head was swinging back and forth like a pendulum between the brothers before she turned a wide-eyed gaze to Noelle.

"All of this hotness in one family? Is that even legal?" Stupefied, Avery shook her head as if to clear it, while Casey and Jack laughed. Darby just continued staring at her fixedly, causing her to blush profusely.

"The pleasure is all mine, Ms. Avery," Darby murmured, and Noelle thought Avery would have an orgasm on the spot. She certainly wouldn't blame her. The Sullivan brothers, with their good looks and southern charm, were detrimental to a girl's libido.

"Jack Sullivan, you are so forgiven for stealing our girl away but not for hiding your handsome brothers," Avery replied flirtatiously, hand pressed to her bosom as she gave a melodramatic sigh. Noelle noticed Darby's eyes followed Avery's hand. She caught Jack's smirk, but before he could tease Darby, Noelle grabbed his hand, leading him away.

"Come on, guys. Let's mingle while the night's still young!"

CHAPTER
Eleven

T HE REST OF THE EVENING progressed smoothly, mainly because Casey and Sidra studiously avoided each other. Thanks to Noelle's expert palate, the group dined on a variety of dishes such as pork vindaloo, curried duck fritters, steamed mussels in lemongrass, and assorted grilled meats with Thai spices. After the meal, there was a performance by traditionally-dressed dancers performing in Lakhon, the graceful, sensual, and fluid dance that portrayed different emotions. Noelle, who was wrapped in Jack's arms, observed Darby's eyes following Avery as she swayed along with the music. She also noticed Sidra glaring at Casey, who was ignoring a group of women attempting to get his attention as he watched the dancers.

"I think one brother likes one of my friends and the other one isn't safe around my other friend. What do you think?" Noelle said wryly, twisting her head back to look up at Jack expectantly. She was waiting for that *voice*. Out of nowhere, his deep baritone had morphed into a panty-ruining southern drawl. Noelle assumed being in his brothers' company brought it out but really didn't give a damn as long as it didn't disappear.

He smiled looking down into her large gray eyes. *I think I could stare at you for the rest of my life, fuck everything else,* he thought, tightening his arms around her while surveying his brothers' and her friends'.

"I think that I'm having the best time that I've had in a long time. I won't worry about them and neither should you. I know it's short notice, but after we get married, I'd like for us to go away for a week. Can you spare a little time off from work? I want to take you to my hometown if you can swing it, okay?" Jack pressed a kiss to the side of her forehead.

He ignored the way his brothers watched him, wondering if Noelle thought he was a creeper because he couldn't stop touching her. Although she always looked beautiful to him, tonight she was glowing, and the men in attendance had definitely taken notice. Several times this evening, he'd stared down men attempting to catch her gaze, ready to beat the shit out of them at a moment's notice. Subconsciously, he pulled her impossibly closer.

Noelle nodded in agreement to his suggestion. Being in Jack's arms, enclosed by his strength and the masculine scent of his cologne, was nothing short of heaven to her, and she would have agreed to anything. Not to mention, he recognized that she was a business owner and as such respected that enough to be considerate to ask, not demand, anything of her.

At the end of the night, everyone received a lantern to write a message on. Noelle quickly wrote her message and noticed Jack appeared to be deep in thought before finally writing on his lantern. Then hand-in-hand, they went to stand with everyone else and released their lanterns into the sky.

SATURDAY MORNING, JACK WAS IN his master bath contemplating whether or not to shave. Last night when they walked the ladies to their cars, he'd pulled Noelle close, nuzzling her neck and breathing her scent in greedily. She'd laughed and wrapped her arms around his neck, at first complaining that his shadow was scratchy. With a sigh, she'd stroked her fingers through the longer hair at his nape, causing bolts of desire to zigzag up and down his spine.

"You don't like it? It'll be gone tomorrow," he promised, dropping a kiss on her nose. Shamelessly Jack glanced down her top to see her amazing breasts cupped by some frilly bra that was the same color as her skin tone. His hands itched to pull the front of her top down and bury his face in her cleavage. "I don't believe I mentioned how beautiful you look." He leaned close to her ear, licking her lobe sensuously and whispered, "You're wearing the hell out of this outfit, darlin'!"

"Well, thank you, and on the contrary, I find this look to be quite sexy on you," Noelle replied, breathless at the hungry look in his eyes that was making her nipples ache to be suckled by his warm, wet mouth. Noelle licked her lips as his heavy-lidded gaze remained on her chest.

"I aim to please, ma'am," he growled, trailing soft kisses along her jawline, causing her fingers to grip his hair more aggressively. Jack felt his eyes roll back in his head with pleasure. Christ, she had him so whipped. It was scary, and didn't his brothers just know it...

"Shit, Jackie, did you just purr like a cat?" Casey guffawed, and Darby joined in.

"Well, butter my butt and call me a biscuit! Our big bro's got it bad, huh, Case?" Darby teased, laughing even

133

harder as an annoyed Jack blushed beet-red and gave him the finger.

Noelle tried to stifle her happiness at the color staining his cheeks. "I think I'll say goodnight now."

Cock aching and frustrated beyond belief, he studied her as she walked to the car, hips swinging enticingly, silently calling his name. Jack shoved his fists in his pocket, willing himself to stay put and not to follow her home.

Casey walked in and sat down on his bed, and Jack shook his head at his brother's perfect appearance. Even as a child, Casey could never look rumpled. He always looked as if he were airbrushed. Only Jack and Darby knew the turmoil his looks caused him. He was bullied first by their prick father, who teased him mercilessly in public, which other kids picked up on. No one dared do it while his brothers were around, but when he was by himself, the other kids teased him cruelly.

It wasn't until Casey was in the seventh grade and shattered a senior named Grady Calhoun's jaw that people stopped fucking with him. Jack could stop bullshit with a look. Darby's size was his weapon. But Casey had a rage that few people could comprehend. It was born from feeling helpless against a parent who loathed him and abandoned by the other whom he loved more than life itself.

"You're up early. Somethin', or should I say, *someone*, on your mind?" With a small smile, Jack met his brother's stormy eyes in the mirror as he plugged in his electric razor.

Casey snorted. "Hell no. I'm just a light sleeper."

He paused, scowling down at his white-knuckled fists.

Wait for it... Jack said to himself. *Ten, nine, eight, seven, six, five...*

"What's her deal anyway? I've only had two conversations with her, and most of it was just helpful advice on how she could improve her job performance," Casey burst out irritably. Although he didn't like the attention his looks brought him, the fact that someone from the opposite sex had been immune enough that she'd told him in no uncertain terms how he could specifically kiss her ass was baffling to him. From the minute Casey laid eyes on the beauty, he knew she was trouble. Her lips were just a little too pouty and her eyes sparkled a little too brightly.

CASEY'S MEETING WAS JUST GETTING underway when she'd sashayed, not walked, into the conference room like she owned the damn place. His cock sprung to life so fast at the sight of her that he'd had to place the presentation papers he was holding in front of his pants. With a deep frown on his face, Casey noticed how every man, young and old, in the conference room followed the high roundness of her ass that was covered in a form-fitting black pencil skirt.

She settled into a chair closest to where he was standing and pulled out a notebook. Casey continued to talk but was acutely aware of the beautiful woman whose cashmere white-V-neck sweater strained against her breasts. And although her hair was pulled back into a polished ponytail, nothing detracted from the subtle blue and purple streaks running through it, which seemed to bring out the richness of her complexion. He watched from the corner of his eye as she appeared to be looking for something.

Dante Johnson, the firm's resident player, leaned in and handed her a pen, and she smiled gorgeously, murmuring thanks in a seductive voice that shot straight to Casey's shaft, making it strain. No woman had ever caused a reaction so visceral in him. When Casey saw Johnson smile at Sidra looking like he was going to get a piece of her, wink and mouth "no problem", the usually unflappable lawyer jumped straight off the deep end.

"Could the two of you flirt on your own time? There are others in here who are taking this meeting seriously and would appreciate not being distracted by idle chitchat. Miss, I suggest you come prepared to my meetings or don't come at all."

The minute he finished his rant, Casey regretted the harsh words. You could hear a pin drop in the conference room. Embarrassed, Johnson quickly mumbled an apology, backing away from the beauty as if she were now contagious. The mystery woman pushed her chair back, majestically rose and gathered her things, her gaze never leaving his. Although her outward expression was serene, her eyes promised Casey a fiery death. Again, all eyes were on her again as she strutted back toward the door. He opened his mouth to say he was sorry, but the words wouldn't come, and then she was gone.

"IT'S NOT YOUR PLACE TO tell her how to do her job. She doesn't work for you. She works for the firm and was there to take notes for Viv. If she knew how you'd spoken to Sidra, she'd rip you a new one. Viv fucking adores her witty personality," Jack taunted, knowing how badly it would get under Casey's skin. Although she was his business partner, Vivienne Romankov was also a mother figure to the brothers, stepping in immediately to help raise them alongside Ian when their dear friend Moira was murdered.

"*Vivienne adores Sidra?* You're fuckin' kiddin' me, right? What's there to adore about her? Pit bulls with menstrual cramps are nicer than she is!" Casey stated derisively.

Jack frowned as he finished lining his jaw up. "That's enough, Case. Not only is Sidra an excellent employee, she also happens to be Noelle's very good friend. Just keep your distance if you can't get along. The last thing I need is for Noelle to think that any group event we have will be stressful and get cold feet about marryin' me."

There was a short silence before Casey changed the subject. "I was thinkin' about goin' to see Dr. Klaus when I get back to D.C."

Their parents' tumultuous marriage, the pain of losing their mother, and rage toward Patrick had left the boys barely able to function. It was Vivienne who introduced them to Dr. Laura Klaus. She explained that after their mother died, she had so many unresolved feelings bottled up inside that she thought she'd go mad if she didn't work them out. Since they were feeling the same way, they agreed to go with her. The first five sessions were brutal and heart-wrenching, but after that, each visit got just a little bit easier.

Dr. Klaus was patient, firm, and blunt as hell. She knew that Jack blamed himself for being the eldest and not being able to take care of their mother; that Darby harbored resentment because Jack hadn't allowed him to go back into the house to protect their mother, and how helpless Casey felt being the smallest and the target of their father's abuse.

Dr. Klaus knew all of that, but she also told them that in the end, they were kids who'd been severely let down by their failing parents. Darby, blinded with fury, had punched a hole in the wall and needed to be sedated when she said that Moira should have left Patrick a long time ago, especially for their safety. She had friends who would've helped her, but all Jack could think was that he'd let all of them down, which pushed him to try harder to make everything perfect for his loved ones.

"Somethin' wrong, lil bro? You can tell me." Already, Jack was thinking of how he could rearrange his schedule to support him. Casey shrugged his shoulders, struggling for words. Finally, he spoke.

"There's this case I'm workin' on...it feels too much like our childhood. I feel like I should recuse myself from it because it's gettin' *too* personal for me. But if I don't do everything in my power to put him away, he *will* kill her, Jack. It's only a matter of *when* if he doesn't go to jail. The signs are all there."

"*Shit!* Case, you're a damn good attorney. If anyone can put the bastard away, it's you. But I don't want you goin' all vigilante on me and takin' matters into your own hands. Let's put a detail on her. I'm sure Darby wouldn't mind," Jack suggested.

"Darby wouldn't mind what?" their middle brother demanded suspiciously from the bedroom doorway before stumbling in and flopping on Jack's bed. "Please tell me what y'all are settin' me up for now? You boys must think I sit around all day just scratchin' my ass waitin' by the phone for your calls."

"I don't think you just scratch your ass all day, D. I'm sure you're a little more productive and manage to get your balls too," Casey deadpanned, and Jack laughed.

Darby slyly rebutted with, "I'll tell you who's got a set of balls — the beautiful Ms. Barton, that's who," he smirked. "I could listen to that woman rip you a new one all day and look fine as hell doing it."

Casey narrowed his eyes at him. "You done? If not, maybe I should just call Ms. Avery over here to shut you up! Good lord, did you get a look at them curves, though? Now, that's an hourglass with more than a few extra minutes!"

Darby sat up and punched Casey's arm twice, causing Casey to wince before slugging him back. Before they could take it further, Jack intervened.

"Y'all are too much for me on an empty stomach. Let's go get some breakfast. We've been invited out again tonight. Avery said they're goin' to some club."

Darby looked up at Jack with speculation in his eyes. "I've been thinkin' about somethin' ever since you told me you were gonna get married. How'd you propose to Noelle? Was it a grand gesture of undying love?"

Jack stiffened, surveying his brother carefully. "As a matter of fact, it was."

"Yeah...bout that," Darby drawled, watching his older brother like a hawk. "I wasn't even aware the two of y'all were seein' each other." His eyes lit up, seeing the tick in Jack's jaw, an indication that he was annoyed with the conversation. "I mean, you never even mentioned her at all like you did with Vaughn or the other chicks you were rumored to be hookin' up with."

Jack struggled to control the telltale twitch. He knew Darby would be all over him like a shark smelling blood if he sensed anything out of the ordinary. "Since when do I ever really go into great detail about any female I'm associated with? With Vaughn, you guys asked who she was, and I told you her name. Everythin' else about her, you found out on your own like the gossip whore you are, dickhead."

Darby leisurely scratched his beard, still eyeing Jack. "Huh...me thinks he doth protest too much." He turned to Casey. "What say you, baby bro?"

"I think that there is definitely a mutual admiration between them, but I am also curious as to know why her name has never been mentioned before," Casey added. "Does this have anything to do with her ex?" he asked Jack curiously. "I mean, does she know what happened to him?"

"She knows what that shithead is capable of," Jack 's short tone warned his brothers to drop the subject. Tension filled the room as Darby and Jack locked eyes.

"I hope you're not playin' some kind of game with her heart, Jackie," Darby cautioned carefully. "That gal looks at you with stars in her eyes. Like you hung the damn moon and shit. If you don't feel the same, you should probably say somethin' before you fuck shit up."

Casey added his two cents. "She seems like a really good girl, Jack. As long as you're marrying her for the right reasons, I'm cool with it. Does Ian know that you're gonna be defilin' his precious goddaughter on the regular?" he joked, trying to lighten the mood, but their older brother needed to let them know how serious he was.

"Noelle Kramer is goin' to be my wife," Jack's voice rang with cold finality. "Anyone who has a problem with that needs to shut the fuck up. Now, let's go get something to eat."

And he would destroy anyone who dared to take her from him, he vowed silently, exiting the bedroom, leaving his confused brothers' staring after him.

CHAPTER
Twelve

$\mathcal{N}$ OELLE PARKED HER SILVER MINI Cooper by the servants' entrance of her parents' home. She was hoping to get in, out, and undetected by her mother's keen radar. This morning, Chef Martin had called hysterically, lamenting that he was having no success recreating her chocolate torte for Alicia's dinner party tonight and that he desperately needed her help.

It was a setup Noelle realized as soon as she walked into the kitchen and spied her mother looking immaculate in tennis whites, calmly sipping a cup of tea at the breakfast nook. She was perusing a newspaper with her reading glasses perched elegantly on her slender nose. A meal of eggs benedict, roasted asparagus, and mixed fruit lay on the table behind her. The table was set for two.

Noelle cut her eyes at the terrified chef who offered her pleading eyes before going back to hastily chopping vegetables at the massive marble island. Quickly, she contemplated backing out of the room before her mother could see her, but today was not her lucky day.

"Oh, don't be mad at him, darling. I think he was just taking pity on an old woman for having to tell a lie to get her own daughter to visit her," Alicia Kramer sweetly explained with a pleasant smile, meeting Noelle's startled gaze as she folded the paper in two. "After all, Martin is a culinary genius. Why would he need *your* input?"

That last remark let the other two people in the room know that Alicia was aware of Noelle secretly cooking for the family and that Martin was getting paid for work he didn't do. *Shit!* Noelle had a sinking feeling that Martin's days were numbered in the Kramer household. Ashamed, he quickly excused himself from the kitchen, and Noelle hoped he was going to go work on updating his resume. If he did get terminated, she would help him find another place of employment.

"Don't just stand there, dear! Come sit down and eat. It isn't every day that I get to see your pretty face, Noelle. Of course, if you still lived here then I wouldn't be experiencing this problem, now would I?" Alicia pouted, tilting her cheek toward her daughter. Noelle kissed the offered cheek before resignedly pulling out the chair across from her mother and sitting down.

Noelle felt her mother's calculated eyes assessing her appearance. After the frantic call this morning, she'd only had time to put on a pair of black leggings and a short-sleeved, fitted denim shirt with black ballet flats. Her hair was pulled back in a tight bun without a curl in sight, and diamond studs were her only accessories.

"Don't you think it's a shame when a mother who spends seventy-two hours in labor with a baby who turns out to be colicky, prone to eczema, and refuses to sleep, hopes to spend time with that child as an adult, only to find that said child has abandoned her?" Alicia continued the guilt trip as she fixed their plates. "At least now, I know who will be the one to sign off on my room at the nursing home in my old age."

"Please stop exaggerating, Mother. I'm sorry that I haven't been by. It's just that I've been really busy with work. How are you and Dad doing?" Noelle politely inquired, accepting the plate of food from her mother, mentally rolling her eyes hard enough to sprain them. A small portion of eggs benedict, asparagus, and a piece of fruit; four ounces exactly she was willing to bet. *Gaaah.* Under her mother's watchful gaze, she picked up her fork and speared an asparagus tip.

"Oh, we're fine, dear. He's actually back in Washington, working on some committee, but I'll be joining him next week. You know that town is just crawling with eligible young men. You should come back with me, and I can introduce you to some of them! Perhaps, you'll find someone you share the same interests with. That way, you can quit your hostess job and focus on being a wife," Alicia suggested in a sickeningly sweet voice.

Noelle set her fork down with a thud. "I'm not interested in being some kept woman, Mother. I like my life the way it is. As for my *career,* I happen to enjoy it very much. I'm sorry it's not mention-worthy at your soirees, but it suits me perfectly," she affirmed, picking her fork back up to spear the cantaloupe viciously. *Relax; don't let her get to you.*

As she chewed, Noelle watched her mother shuffle through a pile of papers next to her plate, and the name of Jack's firm caught her eye. "What are you working on?" Noelle asked casually, not wanting to appear too interested in anything pertaining to Jack. Not much got past Alicia, and if she even suspected there was something going on between her daughter and Jack, she would do everything in her power to sabotage it.

"Oh, nothing; just reviewing our contract with Ian's firm. Lately, I've been dissatisfied with the limited coverage our family has been getting. I think it's time to possibly look elsewhere. I'm finding Jack to be under-qualified in anticipating our needs. Good help is truly hard to find," Alicia sighed heavily before continuing. "Then again, what can you expect from someone with his background?"

Noelle's hackles rose in Jack's defense and a warning bell went off in her head as she met her mother's piercing stare, but she refused to take the bait, forcing herself to appear unaffected. "Well, I'm sure there are plenty of PR firms that will understand your healthy affection for Michelle Obama and find a way to accommodate it," she smiled innocently, finishing the small bite of fruit, aware of her mother's slight stiffening at the subtle dig.

"Hmmmm, I suppose you're right, darling. Well, enough about that. Tell me what's new with you! I ran into Anita Hernandez at the club this morning, and she mentioned that her aide saw you cozied up with some handsome man at an event last night. I told her that such news was rubbish. I would certainly know if my daughter was dating anyone worthy of her time and name," Alicia said pointedly, looking at her daughter over her glasses.

Noelle bristled at the insinuation that Jack wasn't good enough for their family. "It was a work event. I didn't bring a date," she said evenly, which was theoretically true as Jack had met her there. "Besides, even if there was someone, do you really think I'd bring them around to get the 'Kramer Inquisition'?"

"Is it so wrong to want the best for you? We can't help but worry! Don't take this personally, darling, but it just seems as if you're constantly struggling in all aspects of life. All of us are very concerned about you.

You don't date. You're not interested in obtaining a time-worthy degree. You shy away from all family social functions. We've all been wondering...are you a... *lesbian*?" Alicia queried with more than a little concern. "I've heard homosexuality could be hereditary, and while it's not something that we'd be thrilled about, we could certainly turn it into a positive aspect and use it to our advantage in your father's career."

Noelle stared at her mother incredulously. "Are you hearing yourself? Why would you think that? Because I don't bring anyone around you guys? Why? So you and Dad can interrogate them to the point he'd curse the day he met me?! No, I'm not a lesbian, but even if I was, it would *still* be none of your business who I date. This right here...," she gestured between them, "this *orchestrated* event is precisely why I left home. You try to manipulate me, *and* you suffocate me. It makes me absolutely crazy!" She took a deep breath and slowly released it. "On that note, I think I'll head back home."

Noelle stood up and kissed her mother's cheek. When she would have turned away, Alicia's hand shot out to capture her wrist. Surprised, Noelle met her mother's steely gaze. "I'm not sure what's going on with you and Jack Sullivan, but he is *not* for you. His bloodline is tainted, and in the end, he will only hurt you or worse. That's all a Sullivan man is good at. For once, you need to listen to me, little girl."

How did her mother know about her and Jack? And what the hell did she mean tainted blood? Pulling her arm free, Noelle backed away in denial. She wasn't going to let anyone hold her back anymore. Not in life and especially not in love.

"Thank you for breakfast. The next time you want to spend *quality time* with me, just call. Please tell

Daddy I said hi. Goodbye, Mother."

Noelle walked out of the house and immediately felt freer. She got in her car and checked her phone. There were two unread text messages.

AVERY: I HAD A GREAT TIME LAST NIGHT. DON'T FORGET WE'RE MEETING DOWNTOWN. LUXE FIT. 8 P.M. SHARP! TRYING TO CONVINCE PIERCE TO GO. XOXO

SIDRA: YOU'VE BEEN WARNED THAT I ORDERED A BODY BAG IN CASEY SULLIVAN'S SIZE IF HE GETS OUTTA POCKET. THE BONUS IS THAT IT ALSO FITS PIERCE IF HE MAKES AVERY UPSET. SEE YOU TONIGHT. MUAAHH!

Noelle laughed aloud and shook her head. Where would she be without her girls? As she started the car, Noelle noticed her mother at the kitchen window. With a wave, she reversed and drove off. She didn't look back.

There was no point. She wasn't headed in that direction.

THE LINE OUTSIDE OF THE club was ridiculously long. Luckily, Avery had reserved a booth where the guys were already waiting for them inside. As they followed their hostess to it, Noelle felt butterflies fluttering in her stomach in anticipation of seeing Jack again. After leaving her parents' home, she went to see Avery's hairstylist for a blowout. Even though he hadn't said he would, she kept hoping Jack would call just to hear his voice. It was silly because she knew with his brothers in town, they were probably out doing guy things and catching up. She wouldn't sweat it.

When they arrived at the booth, the hostess, scoping out the handsome trio, immediately shifted into man-killer mode, blatantly ignoring the women standing behind her, waiting to be seated.

"Are you gentlemen being taken care of? If not, my name is Sophia, and I'll be happy to see that *all* of your needs are accommodated," she purred, leaning in closer to the table and exposing her cleavage as all three men stood.

Avery rolled her eyes at her boldness. Casey stared at Sophia's cleavage with interest as he sipped his drink. Jack ignored her and walked around her to greet Noelle. He looked dangerously handsome in all black, and her body felt overheated at the intensity blazing from his eyes as they scanned her appreciatively.

Darby grinned devilishly at Sophia and leaned in closer, his head practically resting in her surgically-enhanced bosom. "*All* my needs, Sophia?" he questioned, voice dripping with innuendo. "I don't know. I'm kinda needy, darlin'."

Before she could answer, Sidra stepped to the hostess and tapped her on the shoulder. When Sophia turned to face her, Sidra gave her a brilliant smile. "I hate to fuck your world up with some truth, but your skankiness is showing, and it's extremely overrated. Be a good girl and tuck it back in."

Casey choked and spat his drink out, causing Sofia to jump back from the table. Jack, Darby, and Noelle tried to hide their smiles while Avery lowered her head in disbelief.

"Come on, Sid. Chill, it's not that serious."

Sidra flashed Avery another megawatt smile, deliberately ignoring the outraged hostess's glare. "I disagree. I'll be damned if I'm going to stand here waiting to be seated while she gets her ho' on. If I wanted to wait this long, I would have stood outside in that long ass line."

She turned back to Sophia. "Close your mouth, boo. You know I'm right and just a word of warning: you can't out-bitch me; so don't even try 'cause I got time today."

Jack finally spoke. "We have someone already helping us, Sophia. Besides, you're blocking my *fiancée* from entering."

This last part was accompanied with a stare menacing enough to make the hostess scurry away.

"Well damn, Ms. Sidra...there's never a dull moment with you around," Darby remarked with a rakish grin, looking handsome in a dark purple, button-down dress shirt left open at the collar and tucked into well-fitting gray slacks. He took in her slick, red lips and the black form-fitting leather mini dress with cut-outs at the waist she wore. "Lookin' beautiful as always. Did you have an extra shot of feisty in your coffee today?"

Sidra shrugged prettily at him. "Nope. I was just born with a generous level of hella-awesome-dopeness. What can I say?"

While everyone else laughed, Casey rolled his eyes and snorted, causing Sidra's eyes to narrow evilly, and lean in with a hand on her hip, mouth primed to go *off* on him. Avery quickly shrugged out of her black silk blazer, revealing an oyster-colored, shimmery tube dress that accentuated every voluptuous curve. The neckline was heart-shaped, and she wore a simple diamond pendant nestled in her bosom. Jack noticed Darby's jaw virtually hit the floor.

"Casey, let's dance!"

Fearing for his life, Avery tossed her jacket on the table and yanked him by the arm toward the crowded dance floor. They left a scowling Sidra and Darby glaring in their wake.

Holding Jack's gaze, Noelle removed her black wrap to reveal a bronze-colored, bandage wrap mini-dress. It, too, was form-fitting but had a modest boat neck and ¾" sleeves. She knew that the color against her skin made her look as if she wore nothing at all and laughed to herself watching Jack's eyes darken while a flush crept up his neck. *Bet he wouldn't NOT call her again,* she thought smugly, turning her back to him and revealing the large cutout in the back of the dress that ended at the dip above her ass.

"Feel like dancing?" Noelle glanced over her shoulder at Jack seductively. He was crowding her space in an instant, hands clutching her hips possessively and pulling her back to him.

"That's not all I feel like doin', sugar," he growled in her ear and she shivered with a tiny moan, feeling him pressed against her backside.

"Why do I have the feeling that someone's gonna lose tonight?" Darby groaned, causing Sidra to laugh uproariously as they stepped on to the dance floor with David Guetta's and Nicki Minaj's bass thumping "Hey Mama".

JACK DREW NOELLE INTO HIS arms, and she pressed herself into him. They stared into each other's eyes, moving in perfect precision to the wall-shaking beat. Crooning the lyrics in his ear, Noelle seduced him with her moves. Jack wasn't surprised that his girl had rhythm. Not because she was black but because she was always so graceful in her movements, despite the killer heels she wore.

He made a promise to himself that the next time

they made love, she'd only be wearing those and a satisfied smile. Jack admired the way her hips twisted and dipped to the beat. Her straightened hair swinging like sharp, black blades around her shoulders as he spun her around and pulled her back in, close enough that she could feel his arousal.

"Nice moves, Sullivan," she said admiringly, wrapping her arms around his neck and grinding into him. Sweat touched his forehead and Jack groaned internally. Noelle was so fucking hot, and he was so fucking *hard*. All he wanted to do was back her into a dark corner and slide into her silken heat.

"I aim to please, ma'am."

Noelle's eyes moved to a point beyond his and widened in recognition. Jack felt a tap on his shoulder and turned around. A tall black man, dressed in all white silk and a thick gold chain dangling around his neck stood behind him. His bald head was covered in tattoos, and when he smiled, a big diamond gleamed in his front top tooth. He was flanked by two huge men dressed in all black.

"What it do, Sully! I thought that was you with this fine young thang!"

The man gave Noelle a lecherous once-over that made Jack grit his teeth. Normally, he didn't mind Raymond Sway's (A.K.A. Big Thang in the music industry) behavior, but this time it was directed at his woman, and Jack didn't play that shit.

"What's up, Raymond?" Jack shook the other man's hand while pulling Noelle to his side with the other as Raymond continued to look her up and down.

"Nothing. I was just chillin' in the booth, passing time before the studio was available. You know I do my best work at night, homie," Raymond smiled again, and the gleaming diamond flashed. "Well, aren't you gonna introduce me to yo' friend?"

"Noelle, I'd like you to meet Raymond Sway. Raymond, my fiancée, Noelle." He put heavy emphasis on fiancée as his hand slid down to drape across her stomach. He could feel her gaze on him and wished he knew what she was thinking. *Not tonight motherfucker,* Jack thought, listening as they exchanged greetings and taking note of how the jackass was *still* eating Noelle up with his eyes.

"Hey, Jack, do you mind if I steal Noelle away for a dance?" Raymond licked the lips that made all the girls swoon. Jack opened his mouth to say, "yes he fucking minded", but Noelle, laying her hand on his chest, said to Raymond, "Actually, we were just going to have a seat. Please excuse us."

She grabbed Jack's hand, leading him away and Jack gave Raymond a curt nod as he passed. Behind him, he heard Raymond mutter, "Stuck up bitch."

Jaw locked and nostrils flaring, Jack kept moving forward.

It looked like Darby's premonition would be coming true after all.

———————

AVERY FINISHED HER DANCE WITH Casey and excused herself to go to the ladies' room. She was glad that she decided to go out despite the argument with Pierce earlier. He'd fussed over her dress and refused to be seen in public with her.

"Don't you think you should cover all that up?"

For a brief moment, Avery considered it. Nah, fuck it. Standing proudly, she confronted him.

"Why are you so offended by my body, Pierce? We barely have sex and it's always in the dark with me covered up! And in the same position all the time! Also,

you look positively green during foreplay," she challenged him angrily. *"I'm sorry that I'm not a size two with a stick figure, but there are other men out there who appreciate women with curves. Why don't you find yourself a child-size bride, and I'll find myself a real man? We're done here."*

Soon after Avery left, Pierce was blowing up her phone with calls and apologetic texts, all of which she ignored before deciding to turn her phone off. As she studied herself in the mirror, Avery gave a sad smile. Oh, sure she knew she was attractive enough, but it was times like this that she wished her body wasn't so voluptuous and that the man she was with could look past it. With a sigh, Avery reapplied her lip gloss and left the bathroom only to collide with a hard body.

"Excuse me! Are you okay?" she cautiously asked the man who was staring at her like she was a pork chop, eyeing her up and down, repeatedly licking his lips.

"Oh no, mama, *excuse me!* Damn girl, you're really wearing that dress!"

Avery recognized him as the rapper Big Thang. While he had a large female following that loved him, he did nothing for her personally except give her the creeps as he invaded her personal space. Avery held his gaze but took a wary step back, cursing when she hit the wall.

"You know who I am, right?"

Not trusting herself to speak without cussing his arrogant ass out, Avery simply nodded. "How about you and me get out of here and talk business? I'm shootin' my new video, and I could really use a girl with your...*assets* in it," he finished, staring at her ass, lewdly licking his lips.

Avery's top lip curled in disgust. "I don't think so. Excuse me," she dismissed him firmly.

She pushed past him and felt his hand brush her bottom then squeeze it salaciously. Furious at the violation, Avery whirled around and slapped him upside his big head with her clutch. "Asshole!"

He lunged at her but ran into Darby Sullivan, who quickly wedged himself between them.

"I believe you owe the lady an apology," he said in that southern drawl of his that was normally friendly. Presently, Avery could hear ominous, rumbling undertones in it.

"Ayyye, man, back the fuck off me! You know who the fuck I am? I'm Big Thang, you overgrown country mouse!" the rapper shouted, pushing back at Darby.

It was like pushing against a brick wall; Darby didn't budge. Avery's cough didn't quite conceal her laugh. Darby, being the charming rascal that he was, looked over his shoulder and winked at her. A pleasant warmth spread through her stomach as she smiled up at him. Avery couldn't help but think that if she was with Pierce, he would have been upset with *her* for drawing attention to herself. Immediately, she felt guilty for the comparison.

"Listen here, lil' man. I may be just a country mouse to you, but where I come from, *nobody* disrespects a lady. Now you're either gonna apologize or–"

"What's goin' on here?" Jack's voice boomed down the hallway, interrupting Darby. The unlikely trio turned to him as he strode toward them. Avery could see from his expression that he was pissed and growing more so by the minute. She couldn't blame her friend for falling for him. Jack oozed boss swag and was gorgeous to boot. He gave her a concerned look, and she smiled reassuringly. He turned to the two men.

"Nothin'. Just a country mouse tryna teach a city mouse some manners. This one here was bothering the lovely Ms. Avery. Called himself havin' the right to touch her bottom." Darby's tone was downright deadly now.

"Yo, Jack, you know this freak show?! I was tryna talk with ol' girl, and this giant ass hillbilly got all up in my face! I want him thrown outta here!" Raymond shouted, wiping the sweat from his bald head as he warily side-eyed the size and muscle that defined Darby Sullivan.

Jack coolly assessed him. "This young lady you *assaulted* is a dear friend of mine, and I'm sure my brother was doin' nothin' but defendin' her honor. You're extremely lucky he didn't crack your fuckin' skull open, Raymond. I recommend that you don't try to step to him again."

With an audible gulp, Raymond took four steps back from Darby, keeping him in his sights.

Darby smirked at him sinisterly. "Apologize, sweetheart."

Avery tried her hardest not to laugh when the supposedly hardcore rapper mumbled an apology to her, which she grudgingly acknowledged with a curt nod.

Jack stepped forward smoothly. "One more thing, Raymond. A woman has the right to say *no*, and her choices should always be respected, whether you like them or not."

He sucker-punched the other man in the stomach, knocking the wind out of him. Raymond fell to the floor, gasping and struggling not to vomit. Avery grimaced, and Darby laughed his great, big, booming laugh that echoed down the hallway as Raymond lost the battle and tossed up all the alcohol he'd consumed tonight, soiling his all-white outfit.

"Client or not, if I ever hear you refer to my woman as a stuck-up bitch or any name other than

Mrs. Sullivan, I will *end* you and your career. I'm releasing you from your contract with R.R. & S. I trust there will be no blowback behind my decision, correct?" Jack stared down at him dispassionately as he straightened his jacket.

The ill-feeling rapper was too busy wallowing in his self-created misery to answer him.

"Have a good night."

CHAPTER

Thirteen

*T*HEY WERE MARRIED, AND SHE wanted to shout it from the rooftops – that *she,* Noelle Kramer, was now Noelle Sullivan! She couldn't stop staring at the hammered gold band with the huge diamond in the center that was easily four carats. It had tiny diamonds sprinkled on either side, and the inside was inscribed with their wedding date. The ring, now her most prized possession, was created by an up-and-coming jewelry designer named Vixen. Jack had surprised her with it this morning by placing it on her left ring finger during the brief ceremony witnessed by Avery, Sidra, Casey, and Darby in Jack's good friend, Judge Marcus Harold's private chamber.

When the girls saw the ring, they squealed and jumped with joy, much to the amusement of the Sullivan brothers'. Noelle explained to them that they each had several pieces of Vixen's jewelry, and that the designer's pieces were wildly popular and highly coveted. The ladies rolled their eyes when the brothers grew even more entertained by that statement.

Although it was supposed to be a simple business arrangement, Noelle couldn't help but get caught up in the moment. She'd worn a spaghetti strap, white eyelet dress with a sweetheart neckline. The dress was knee-length with a full skirt and she wore white SJP high-heeled sandals. Her curly hair was left free, with a simple rhinestone barrette pinning the curls off of her forehead. She'd kept her makeup limited to bronzer and coral lip gloss. A waist-length faded denim jacket completed her look. Meanwhile, a scruff-free Jack was handsome in a wheat-colored custom-tailored suit.

After the ceremony, they celebrated with lunch at the River Café in Brooklyn. The gorgeous restaurant sat right on the water, and it was where the women celebrated all special occasions. They gorged themselves on foie gras, Mushroom Wellington, branzino, and strip steak. For dessert, they indulged in the two cakes that Noelle had made from scratch. The first was a small champagne wedding cake with strawberry-mascarpone filling. The second was a decadent chocolate Guinness cake with Bailey's Irish cream frosting, which also was a birthday cake for Jack's birthday, much to his surprise. It was a wonderful meal, and the newly-married couple felt blessed to share it with friends and family.

Now the married couple, along with Casey and Darby, was flying on a private jet to Whiskey Row, but making a pit stop in D.C. first, to drop them off. Jack also needed to do a brief touch base with his other partner, Vivienne. Noelle peeked at him and found Jack staring at his wide gold wedding band, a pleased expression and contented smile on his lips as he rolled it around on his finger. Noelle glanced across the aisle to find Darby and Casey grinning at them with identical proud expressions. She flushed and turned her attention to the window with a satisfied smile of her own.

The plane ride was short and smooth, and they

arrived in the nation's capital in no time. It was a perfect afternoon in D.C., weather-wise, as they drove through the city. Noelle was delighted to see that the infamous cherry blossoms were in full bloom, coloring the streets in gorgeous shades of pink and white. They pulled up to a distinguished-looking six-story building in Georgetown and took the elevator to the top floor, which housed both R. R. & S. Public Relations and the law offices of Sullivan and Associates.

Casey gave Noelle a quick kiss on the cheek, leaping out of the way before Jack could punch him, chuckling at his brother's thunderous scowl. "This is my stop, sis. Feel free to pop in if you get bored over there. Or if Viv scares you, and you need a place to hide, whichever comes first. No pressure. Congratulations again, bro. Comin', Darby?"

"Nah, go ahead. I'm gonna chop it up with the 'Dragon Lady' for a while. I'll catch up with y'all this evenin'," Darby responded, holding the door open for Jack and Noelle.

"Bye, Casey. Thank you for everything." Noelle smiled warmly and waved.

Jack clasped her hand in his when Noelle would have given his little brother a hug. She narrowed her eyes at him, and he responded with a bland smile, motioning her through the door before him. As she passed through the entrance, Noelle heard Darby hiss, "Man, would you do us all a favor and fuckin' relax?"

———————————

INSIDE, THE OFFICE WAS FULL of women in all sizes and ethnicities, wearing harried expressions as they bustled about. Noelle could hear one voice in particular barking orders over everyone, and she suspected it was the reason for the tense environment. The atmosphere shifted as the women gradually noticed the brothers'. Strained expressions relaxed into flirtatious ones. The pretty, dark-haired receptionist whose nameplate read Marcella gave them a frazzled smile while efficiently answering and connecting calls.

As busy as she was, though, Marcella managed to pause long enough to give Darby a sultry look and private smile when he lingered at the desk. Jack just shook his head, placed his arm around Noelle's waist, guiding her down the hallway to where the barking voice was rising. Turning the corner, Noelle braced herself, prepared to meet an ogre of "Lord of the Rings-like" resemblance.

Instead, she saw a petite, black woman with a darkened honey complexion. Her shoulder-length, thick black hair was styled in big curls and waves. She wore a well-cut, short sleeve, hot pink sheath that molded to her slender curves and paired it with pale pink pumps. Her elegantly arched brows, eyes the color of molasses, short, straight nose, and wide yet full mouth epitomized pretty, despite the blistering tongue-lashing she was administering into her Bluetooth.

Vivienne Romankov was absolutely gorgeous, and from what Noelle heard, hell on wheels.

"Go on in," Jack urged softly. "I'm goin' to grab us some coffee."

He placed a brief kiss on the back of her neck before walking toward the coffee station located at the end of the hall. Noelle turned back to the sizzling fireball of energy practically bouncing off the walls of the huge office decorated in varying shades of white and cream. She observed the large, framed pictures of the Sullivan brothers at varying stages in their lives, along with photos of a stunning girl of mixed heritage who resembled Vivienne.

"Well, what the hell are we paying you for if the press junkets are a no-go? You're either going to move forward with them or give us back our damn money plus interest, as you obviously didn't read the contract. Don't screw with me, Marvin," she warned in a softer tone. It was almost seductive, and Noelle found herself leaning forward, captivated as she imagined Marvin on the other end doing the same thing. "Or I will sue your ass for everything you've got!"

And with that, Vivienne disconnected the call.

She caught sight of Noelle in the doorway and raised an eyebrow as she looked her up and down curiously. "Okay... a couple of questions: One, do you always eavesdrop on conversations? Two, how did you get back here? And three, who the hell are *you*? If you're the new receptionist, you obviously didn't get the dress code memo, sweetie."

Noelle's spine stiffened at the woman's blunt approach and decided to meet it head-on. "One, I wasn't eavesdropping. I could hear you as soon as I entered the building. Two, I walked back here with my husband, Jack Sullivan. And three, my name is *Noelle*, not 'sweetie.'"

Vivienne's eyes went wide with her response, and then she went *off*. "You're *married* to Jack?? Oh no, he didn't have a wedding and not invite me! *That little shit!* I helped raise that boy, and this is the thanks I get?! Wait a minute. *Noelle*? As in Kramer? You're Harvey's niece, which makes you Ian's goddaughter! And Alicia...your mother?"

The last was asked with a sour expression before a thought occurred to her. "Wait! Does Ian know you and Jack got married?"

"Ummmm...well, no. The thing is...well ..." Noelle

fumbled over her words, and judging by the humor in Vivienne's eyes, she was enjoying her discomfort. A lot. The tiny dynamo, with her quick wit and 'don't fuck with me' personality, reminded Noelle of Cookie from the hit television show "Empire".

"Cut it out, Viv," Jack ordered pleasantly as he entered the room with a tray of cappuccinos, setting it on the dark wood console and passed Noelle a cup. She breathed a sigh of relief as he grabbed her other hand and held onto it. He walked forward and gave the other woman a brief kiss on the cheek before also handing her a cappuccino. Jack guided Noelle to sit next to him on a baby blue tufted loveseat, his arm stretched out behind her possessively.

Vivienne contemplated the two of them with pursed lips. It was strange to see her normally imperturbable godson being affectionate with a woman. Although he dated, Jack was not one for PDA or bringing anyone around. This pretty young thang had him wrapped around her elegant little finger, and from the looks of it, she was clearly unaware of this fact as she innocently sipped her cappuccino while he played with her curls.

"I never thought I'd see the day...," she murmured gleefully, taking a sip of her own frothy, caffeinated beverage. Jack shot her a warning look, and she found herself wishing her best friend was here to witness this in person. *Oh, Moira, I hope you're watching,* she thought wistfully. *Our little Jackie's got it bad!*

"And I'll do no such thing," she retorted in response to his look. "Not until you admit that taking on Inez Gaines was a mistake! That damn woman could ruin a wet dream! Her ex is having all of his boys come forward to say that she was distributing drugs, Jack. She has a horrible temper and keeps doing crazy things like throwing eggs at reporters who get too close to her. Why is she carrying eggs around in her Gucci bag anyway?! *It's Gucci for Christ's sake!* Bless her heart! She doesn't even *realize* how crazy she is!"

Jack laughed at her horrified face. "I'll admit she may not have been my best idea, but we can still fix it. I'm not leavin' her hangin'."

"Humph! Well, that was Marvin Sinclair with Modern Girl cosmetics. They're trying to break her contract and cancel her press tours. I think I threatened him with enough lawsuits to keep him at bay. If that doesn't work, I want Casey to hand me his balls in a blue and white Tiffany's box after they're transformed into earrings for me," she said with enough enthusiasm to make Jack wince and cross his legs while Noelle laughed. Vivienne winked at her conspiratorially before continuing. "But back to y'all. I'm sure there's a story here that I'm missing. Why don't we go to Public Trust for dinner and you can fill me in? How long are you guys in town?"

"How about Clyde's instead? We're here for the night and then I'm takin' Noelle for a visit to Whiskey Row. Wanna go?" Jack casually asked, even though he knew what the answer would be as his Vivienne's eyes went blank.

"You know damn well I don't," she declined matter-of-factly. "Please send Kat my love and let her know that she can't put off a visit forever. She seems to think that she can hide out there."

Vivienne flatlined her lips in dismay, and Noelle got the feeling that she was extremely agitated. The laughter of several women from the front of the office quickly diverted the older woman's attention. "Is your good-for-nothing womanizing brother out there?"

"I'm sure Darby would be hurt to hear himself described in such a manner, Viv, but yes, he is up front." Jack stood and helped Noelle to her feet, entwining their fingers together.

"Oh Lawd! I should have known since you got your country boy twang going. You left him at the reception desk with Marcella? Do you know I had to threaten to fire her because she wouldn't stop Googling his ass?" Vivienne hurried out of her office and down the hallway.

"Darby Liam Sullivan, stop that flirting right now, or I'm going to smack your big ass silly! Why the hell is everyone gathered around the reception desk? I'm not paying you all to stand around and look pretty! Get back to work!"

———————

DINNER WAS A LIVELY AFFAIR with Vivienne regaling Noelle with stories of the boys and the mischief they'd gotten into growing up. She could see what a close-knit unit they were and found herself enjoying the camaraderie they shared over crab cakes and carbonara pasta. Outside of the restaurant, they exchanged goodbyes with promises to get together soon.

Vivienne pulled Jack to her for a fierce hug, quietly sharing her opinion with him. "Your mama would be so proud of you and your bride. You chose well, Jackie."

She gave Noelle a big hug as well. "It was a pleasure to meet you. You're just like Harvey, and I can see why Jackie is so taken with you! Look after my boy and let's stay in touch."

To Darby, she simply said, "Baby, stay out of trouble and have your sister call me."

Darby responded with a hug that lifted her, spinning her around while she laughed. "Relax, Mama Bear. She's a good girl."

After making sure Vivienne and Casey got into their cars safely, Darby went back into Clyde's to hang out. Noelle noticed the receptionist from Vivienne's office hurrying towards the entrance of the restaurant, smoothing her hair in place as she and Jack got into a cab.

———————————

PER THE ADDRESS JACK GAVE, the cab took them to a small, nondescript hotel that almost looked abandoned. The inside was another story, however, decked out in sleek modern furniture with glass and chrome accents. The lobby and bar vibrated with lively chatter from well-dressed guests waiting to check in or having a nightcap. Jack informed Noelle that it used to be owned by an infamous madam. The elevator ride up to their room was filled with physical awareness as they realized they were alone for the first time today.

Jack thought Noelle had never looked lovelier. Her eyes dancing partly due, he was sure, to the alcohol she'd consumed, and she was glowing. He let his gaze travel down to the swells of her breasts, framed enticingly by wisps of lace, to her long legs, down to the palest pink shimmer on her toes. Jack wanted to pull her close and explore the softness of her sexy mouth, followed by sliding the dainty straps of her dress down, lowering his head, and feasting on her plump breasts. His dick was painfully hard and pulsating in his boxers, dying to be inside of her. He leaned back against the wall, watching her eyes drift down and linger between his legs. Jack smirked as she bit her bottom lip and averted her gaze.

Noelle was feeling some kind of way about her sexy-ass husband. She struggled for composure before glancing his way again, taking in his relaxed pose across from her. He'd loosened his tie, and his black hair was slightly rumpled. She admired the way he filled his suit out before her eyes dropped to the bulge pressing against his zipper. The evidence of his desire started a throbbing between her legs, causing her to press her thighs together to control it. Noelle's eyes caught his, and Jack's intense stare made her stomach flip-flop in response. Inhaling sharply, she blurted out the first thing that came to mind other than sexing him.

"What's the deal with your little sister?"

Jack smiled affectionately.

"Her name is Katerina, and as she likes to tell us, she's not so little anymore," Jack chuckled fondly. "She's actually Vivienne's twenty-one-year-old daughter with her estranged husband, Alexei. We call her Kat for short, and in our opinion, she's growin' up entirely too fast. She divides her time between school and her parents, but from what I gathered, she's been avoidin' her mama. I'm thinking it has somethin' to do with a boy."

His eyes narrowed in displeasure at such an occurrence, making Noelle grin.

"Tell me about Vivienne," she prompted. She was quite curious about his family dynamic. Clearly, his parents weren't in the picture, and she could sense a doozy of a story behind it.

"She's our second mom. We were raised by her, Ian, and Alexei. Growin' up, we divided our time between D.C. and Tennessee." Jack's face and voice were robotic, setting off Noelle's red flags. The elevator reached their floor and opened up to the penthouse. Jack didn't elaborate further. Instead, he made a sweeping motion with his hand for Noelle to precede him.

Well damn.

Confused by his sudden mood change, Noelle stepped into the lavishly decorated scenery with the huge California king bed that dominated the room. Jack brushed by her, and she felt burned by the heat of his brief touch as he pulled the curtains back. The sexual tension was killing her, and it was all she could do to control the urge to rip her clothes off and beg him to take her.

When she opened her eyes, Noelle gasped in delight, for the floor to ceiling window revealed a stunning view of the Washington Monument and Potomac River glowing against the twinkling evening sky. She moved across the room to stand close to Jack, absorbing the view.

"How beautiful," she whispered, amazed by the beauty of D.C. illuminated at night.

"Absolutely stunning," Jack agreed, his hot eyes riveted on her rather than the scenic view outside. Noelle turned to him, and he closed the brief space between them. His arms encircled her waist and slid down slowly to caress her bottom, hiking her dress up while drawing her up against him. Noelle felt his heavy erection imprinting on her belly. His hands cupped her generous lower cheeks that were easily accessible thanks to the thong she wore.

The fullness of her ass in his hands was pure torture for Jack. He had to fight back the growing feral instincts because the need to possess Noelle expanded at an alarming rate every day. Staring into her lovely gray eyes, he slowly lowered his head, giving her time to accept or decline his kiss. Her eyes closed, and her mouth parted in invitation. That was all the encouragement he needed as their lips touched softly. Once. Then twice. And the third time, clinging together.

"I want you so bad that I ache, Noelle," Jack hoarsely confessed against her lips. She could barely hear him over the thunderous beat of her own heart as he pulled her thong to the side. Her lady parts already jumping for joy in anticipation.

Eagerly, Noelle sought more of his addicting kisses as her hands slid up and around his neck to hold him in place. The heat from his hands as they rubbed on her booty was becoming her undoing. With each stroke, his strong fingers slid between her cleft and caressed her forbidden hole while his tongue tangled with hers. The sensations overwhelmed her, and soon, ripples controlled her limbs, then overtook her body. Noelle had to wrench her mouth away for oxygen, trembling uncontrollably. She attempted to clench her thighs together to stop her release from flowing down her legs.

Jack was panting just as hard as he pressed his forehead to hers, turbulent eyes boring into her eyes. "Did you just...?" he started to ask but stopped when she averted her face, head nodding jerkily.

Noelle wanted to die from embarrassment at her body's reaction to Jack's talented ministrations. *She was such a rookie!* More than anything, she wanted to feel him moving inside of her again, making her burn hotter than the sun. She pulled his head back down to hers with one hand and kissed him while the other hand slid down between them to softly stroke his shaft through his trousers. Jack's body jerked in response to her boldness. His hands gripped her thong and yanked it down completely. He smacked an ass cheek sharply, and Noelle moaned into his mouth, raising one of her legs to curl around his muscled thigh. His thick fingers found their way into her wet heat and gently thrust inside of her. Noelle sobbed and bit down on his lip. Jack pulled his fingers out to smack her ass again and then put them back in to feel her fresh arousal as she gushed in response.

"You like this don't you, baby?" Jack grunted as she stroked him feverishly. He was going to come if he didn't get a hold of himself. She nodded her head eagerly, tracing his lips with her tongue, teasingly flicking his lips. Jack repeated the action, and Noelle's legs shook, causing her to let go of his dick and cling to his jacket lapels as she rode his hand as if she were on a mechanical bull. He hooked his fingers against her G-spot and devoured her lips, swallowing her scream as another climax rocked through Noelle's body and over his fingers. Slowly, he withdrew them and put the glistening digits up to his lips. Jack's gaze stayed locked with hers as he opened his mouth and licked them clean. His eyes closed, he groaned his appreciation at the heady taste of his wife. The title only made what they did together even more sacred to him.

The sight of Jack enjoying her so thoroughly was the most erotic thing Noelle had ever seen. She wanted to return the favor and give him the same pleasure he'd just given her. She dropped to her knees and quickly unbuckled his pants. He attempted to stop her and pull her up. "Noelle, you don't have to–"

Noelle gave him a steely look. "Shut up, Jack."

His hands dropped to his sides, and she smiled at the surprised look on his face. And because she was raised to have manners, she sweetly added, "Please."

Hurriedly she pulled his pants down and stared at the lengthy bulge trying to escape from his boxers. Gently, she reached into the opening of his boxers and withdrew his engorged penis. *It was truly a work of art.* Noelle's memory of it did not do justice to the real thing. Thank God she'd done some research on blowjobs last night. She'd read articles and watched YouTube videos. Even though they were very informative, Noelle decided to just go with the flow.

The broad crown was already flowing pre-cum.

Noelle wrapped both hands around the base and boldly stroked him from base to head. Jack's hands clenched her curls to hold her in place as he watched her with pained concentration.

Noelle licked the liquid from the tip, closing her eyes, and savoring the essence of him as the fingers in her hair tightened. "Mmm, that's good, Jack," she said huskily, opening her eyes to meet his hooded gaze again.

"I want more," she whispered naughtily, closing her plump lips over him and gently suctioning the head. Jack muttered a curse and bit his lips as he tried to restrain himself from ramming his dick down her throat. *Noelle literally had him by the balls and it was like heaven with a side of hell*, he thought, feeling her delicate fingers caressing his sac while sliding her mouth up and down on his shaft, deep-throating him as far as she could, her tongue swirling around him. What she couldn't take in, she stroked just the way he liked. He groaned, feeling the pressure soaring inside of him. Jack told himself that he would have to stop soon. But Noelle surprised him by pulling her mouth completely off of him.

"I know you're holding back with me, Jack Sullivan," Noelle informed him defiantly. "Maybe I'm not as experienced as some of the other women you've been with, but I am a big nerd. Nerds like nothing more than doing their homework and studying, especially the art of *fellatio*. So, stop holding back and fuck the hell outta my mouth," she ordered wickedly, taking him in again and sucking with a contradictory tender-vigor as she cupped and lovingly massaged his balls.

Who was he to argue with her?

Jack kept his hold in her hair gentle as he fucked her mouth with increasing speed. Noelle stayed with him, slurping, licking, and fondling him; her eyes zeroed in on his face until he could bear it no more. The combination of the pull of her voluptuous lips, talented tongue, and nimble fingers drove Jack to the brink with embarrassing speed. When that time came, he threw his head back, eyes closed and shouting out hoarsely to the rooftops as his seed exploded into her eager mouth. While Noelle enthusiastically swallowed every drop until he was wrung dry, Jack was thanking the heavens above for studious nerds.

CHAPTER
Fourteen

ELUCTANTLY, JACK PULLED HIS COCK from her mouth, sinking to his knees in front of her. Noelle was radiant with satisfaction, her hair a wild mess, thanks to his frantic fingers. His eyes drifted down to rest between her legs. Though she was covered in layers of tulle, Jack could scent her arousal, making him ravenous for her.

Jack reached up and yanked his tie off. Next, he unbuttoned his shirt and tossed it aside. Through clenched teeth, he ordered, "*Get. On. the. Bed. Noelle.* Grab onto the headboard and don't let go. I told you I wouldn't fuck you again until you came to me and asked for it. And I won't because I like to think that I can keep my word. But tonight, we're going to indulge in 'almost'. Tonight, is about pleasurin' you until your voice is hoarse from screamin', and you pass out," he promised, enjoying the way her eyes ballooned in response to his bold statement.

Jack smirked as Noelle scrambled to her feet, kicked off her shoes, and leaped onto the bed, eager to do his bidding. He stood, kicking off his pants but pulling his boxers back up before walking over to the bed and sliding between her thighs.

———————————

THE FLIGHT TO KNOXVILLE, TENNESSEE was a smooth one. Noelle spent most of the time making notes in her planner for Tarik's party and how she should organize her closets and drawers when she got back home. She did just about anything to avoid looking into the dreamy, hazel eyes of the man sitting next to her.

"Pick up sock clamps? What are sock clamps?" Jack asked in amusement over her shoulder, his cool breath caressing her face. Noelle glanced up and immediately felt her heart flutter in response. Their faces were scant inches apart. He hadn't shaved, and the dark stubble covering the lower part of his face was ruggedly sexy and calling her name.

He'd undergone a one-eighty from the polished businessman she was accustomed to seeing. His hair wasn't perfectly gelled, and he'd exchanged his suits for a pair of dark denim jeans that did wonderful things to his firm ass and thighs. A long-sleeved, plaid shirt that he'd left open at the neck and rolled at the sleeves exposed the muscles on his lightly-tanned arms covered in a dusk of fine, dark hairs.

"They're..." Noelle croaked then stopped at Jack's sinful smile. She could *feel* the smugness radiating from him. After yesterday, he'd definitely earned it and had her nose wide open. Last night, he'd made good on his promise and brought her to multiple orgasms that had her wailing and bawling until the concerned night manager placed a call to their room because they were disturbing other guests.

Exhausted, Noelle almost felt relieved about the call from downstairs until Jack flipped her on her stomach and told her to bite the pillow if she had to. They'd indulged in 'almost' until the wee hours of the morning when she finally passed out. Lord, the things that man could do with just his hands, mouth, and tongue should be illegal. He'd licked, sucked, and nibbled all over her body, rolled Noelle onto her stomach, rocking his cock between her ass cheeks while his fingers played in her pussy, whispering sinfully wicked things in her ear about what he couldn't wait to do to her. When she came, so did he, all over her backside.

Noelle blushed vividly, recalling him straddling her at one point so that she could take him into her mouth as he directed Noelle by grasping her hair. Never in a million years would she ever have dreamed that she would love being so wanton. *She loved how Jack played her body.* He was an adventurous and generous lover who could be rough in the most pleasurable ways possible. There was also a lot of foreplay around her ass. Noelle suspected that if given the chance, he would introduce her to pleasure there as well. Somehow, the thought wasn't as horrifying as she thought it to be when 'Remy the Dickhead' had suggested it.

"Look at me," *Jack ordered thickly, one hand gripping the headboard. His face was a harsh mask of desire as the other hand tangled in her hair while he slowly fed her his cock. Noelle watched him watching her swallowing his thickness inch by inch. It was such a turn-on that when he came, she was surprised to find that she did too. Afterward, he slowly pulled out, lying down and drawing her close as she gave a colossal yawn. With a hoarse chuckle, he informed her,* "We're not done, darlin."

For a big man, he moved fast. A surprised Noelle found herself on her knees with her pussy hovering directly above his face. She bent to look down at him between her thighs, feeling a fresh stream of arousal coating them.

"Feed me, baby," Jack commanded, making her giggle with a renewed burst of energy.

With a whimper of anticipation, Noelle gripped the headboard and lowered her sensitive pussy close to his sinful mouth. Jack's powerful hands clutched her hips, holding her in place. Noelle could feel his breath on her weeping slit, and it made her quiver in anticipation. She convulsed, feeling the barest flick of his silky tongue running along her seam.

"Please stop teasing me!" she begged, reaching a hand down to part her plump, slick lips in invitation. Jack gave a devious chuckle before shoving her down and thrusting his skilled tongue high into her wetness, deliciously alternating between tongue-fucking her and hoovering her clit while a finger slowly teased her puckered star before pushing inside. With a scream, Noelle shattered under his skilled onslaught.

"They keep your socks paired," Noelle muttered. Jack laughed, slinging his arm around her, nuzzling her neck with his whiskers. Laughing, she pulled away. "You're going to give me beard burn, Jack!"

He, too, laughed and pulled her back to him, "At least it'll match all the other places that you have it," he whispered, kissing her cheek.

"How are we doing over here? Can I get you anything else?"

The perky blonde flight attendant was back. *Again.* Although her questions were aimed at both of them, her blue eyes were trained exclusively on Jack. Looking over his shoulder, Noelle's gaze narrowed, noticing another button had come undone on the little hussy's uniform, now exposing an indecent amount of cleavage.

"We're fine, thanks. Just tryin' to enjoy our

privacy," Jack dismissed her, keeping his attention trained on Noelle's irate face. Earlier, as he was leaving the restroom, the attendant was waiting outside, attempting to engage him in flirtatious conversation. It was a complete waste of her time. Jack only had eyes for his wife. *Damn, that sounded real good.* Noelle was finally his wife, and he was going to do everything in his power to keep it that way. An unwanted image of his father's enraged ruddy face popped into his head.

"Yer mine, Moira! Ya hear?? I'll never let you go!!"

He blinked back the unpleasantness when Noelle's soft hand touched his clenched jaw, her pretty face stamped with concern. "You okay, Jack?"

He caught her hand and pressed a quick kiss into the middle of her palm. "I'm fine, darlin'."

AFTER LANDING, THEY PICKED UP their car rental and began the scenic drive to Gatlinburg. Noelle enjoyed the clean, fresh air and the lush, green views of the mountains. They stopped several times for her to take pictures. Jack enjoyed how taken she was being surrounded by nature as she looked highly out of place with her stylish ripped jeans, black crop-top blouse, and high-heeled ankle boots.

The sunlight caught the gleam from her multi-layered gold necklaces and aviator shades hiding most of her face. He watched the other male tourists surreptitiously checking her out and their female companions giving her the side-eye. Jack felt a burst of pride knowing she belonged to him. *My chick's badder than yours,* he smirked to himself. They lunched at the Peddler Steakhouse before hitting the road again.

"So, tell me a little bit about your hometown, Jack,"

Noelle urged, flipping through radio stations. "Oooh, I love this song!" she exclaimed, turning up Otis Redding's "(Sittin' on) The Dock of the Bay".

Jack looked at her in surprise. "What do you know about Otis? He's for grown folks, missy."

Noelle snorted as she snapped her fingers in time to the beat. "Puh-leeez! Ian and my uncle used to have the best barbecues, and they would play the skin off of old albums." She sighed with contentment. "Those were good times! Did you know my uncle?"

Jack shook his head. "Unfortunately, I never had the pleasure. Growin' up, we weren't even aware that Ian was gay until Casey was fourteen, and we were allowed to visit him in New York City. Since we were orphans, our time was divided between two residences after our parents died. Ian would always come for us during the summer, and we'd go off on some cool adventure. School was spent at 'The Row' except for winter and spring breaks, which were spent in D.C."

"D.C. and New York have some of the most prestigious schools in the nation. Why wouldn't you get to go there instead of a school in the mountains?" Noelle asked curiously, and Jack looked at her in amusement. "Damn, that sounded snobby! I'm sorry about that."

"I got a pretty good education in the mountains, Noelle," Jack murmured, switching stations until Kid Rock's "All Summer Long" poured through the speakers. Again, he was surprised when she started singing along. Together, they belted out the words as the vehicle sped toward the Smoky Mountains.

When the song was over, Jack turned down the music. He gave her a brief glance before turning his eyes back to the road. "Can I ask you a question?"

Warily, Noelle nodded. "Ask away."

"Why did you let the chef take credit for your work?" On more than one occasion, he'd been highly annoyed by the way her family lavishly praised the little punk while she sat quietly in the background. "I mean, it's obvious that you're far better at cookin' than him, yet you said nothin'."

Noelle was silent for so long that he thought she'd changed her mind about answering. Finally, she spoke. "I've always loved cooking, but I love my family more, even though they can be a bit critical of me. That's just who they are. Don't get me wrong; at times, it can be highly stressful. After years of seeking their approval, I finally decided I didn't care about it anymore and just wanted to be left alone."

She shrugged carelessly. "When my parents first hired Martin, I could tell he had charmed his way in. There was a lot he didn't know, so I decided to help out. Why not, you know? I had recently graduated from culinary school but wasn't implementing my skills. Why not be of use? He needed help."

Noelle paused to take a sip of her water. "Besides, I liked the challenge of cooking for my family. Their expectations are really high, so if I could please them then I know I could please the POTUS if he ever came to dinner. Anyhow, I don't need them to validate me. Validation is for parking anyway."

Jack glanced over to see Noelle looking out the window, and he wished he could take away the hurt still lingering inside of her that was painfully obvious in her voice. An image of the night he first saw her popped into his mind. "I used to think sometimes that you were bein' smothered alive. You seem like the kind of girl, that if no one was lookin', would slide down that long spiral staircase."

Noelle giggled, and realization dawned on him. "Holy hell, you did it, didn't you?"

The car filled with the sound her musical laughter as she confessed. "*Every* chance I got, I was sliding down that staircase! Until Mother caught me, and I spent a month pruning the garden and polishing all the silverware by myself."

Jack laughed again and silently vowed to get her to loosen up again on this trip.

CHAPTER

Fifteen

*J*ACK'S HOMETOWN WAS NOT THE 'Hicksville' Noelle expected it to be. Nestled in the Smoky Mountains not too far from Gatlinburg, Whiskey Row was a small yet prosperous town, with a population of 10,000 according to the welcome sign. It was founded in the late 1870's by European and Asian immigrants who found the overcrowded, larger cities, such as New York City, Chicago, and Philadelphia, too competitive to thrive in. Because it was at the edge of the mountains, they cleverly called it Mountain's Edge. Blacks eventually moved in, and for a while, racial tensions ran high as the many cultures collided, but eventually, everyone found a way to co-exist. For the most part.

In 1915, a Russian named Petr Romankov, while exploring, discovered an old, abandoned mine further up the mountain. He had a good feeling about the place and convinced his younger brothers Ivan and Sergei to explore it with him. They agreed and down the mine shaft they went, not telling anyone but their wives where they were going. The brothers were gone for three days before only Sergei and Petr were seen again. Ivan had met a terrible fate in the mine when it collapsed. The remaining two brothers were lucky enough to make it out alive.

A week after their return, the brothers left town again. When they came back, much to the astonishment of the townsfolk, they brought with them the deed to the land the town was settled on. The Romankov brothers didn't stop there. They bought up as much of the mountain land as they could and then began to restructure and expand the town by adding a bank, more schools, and other businesses. The year after Prohibition ended, they opened up distilleries, a winery, and a brewery. With all the alcohol now being made and sold, the Romankovs' decided to change the town name to Whiskey Row.

'THE ROW' AS JACK CALLED it, was now a fusion of Aspen, Colorado and Park City, Utah but more ethnically diverse from what Noelle could see. The tree-lined town was filled with specialty boutiques, hotels, and restaurants. Down Main Street was a beauty salon, an old-school type of barbershop, a tattoo parlor, and a dance studio. There was also a livery and a blacksmith. The town was rustic Americana at its hippest, and Noelle instantly fell in love. She was relieved that it was nothing like the movie "Deliverance" or that Animal Planet show "Mountain Monsters".

Driving down Main Street, Noelle noticed people stopping to stare at them. Jack nodded to some, and the greeting was reciprocated. In the rearview mirror, Noelle could see people stepping out into the street to get a better look at their vehicle. Their presence was causing a stir. She glanced at Jack and would have thought he was unaware of the reaction they were creating, but his white-knuckled grip on the steering wheel answered her question

"It's a beautiful place, Jack," Noelle spoke sincerely, and he nodded but didn't flash his signature grin. He seemed contemplative as they continued to drive, and Noelle decided not to push it for now. Instead, she turned her head, continuing to absorb the gorgeous scenery. The diversity in this small space was amazing. She saw people from all walks of life: cowboys, hipsters, rockers, bikers, prepsters, and business geeks.

Jack drove south into what appeared to be the residential area of town. Then he made a right, and they were cruising down a long driveway toward a Chateau-style white mansion, surrounded by a tall, black wrought-iron gate. Outside of the gate was a security booth where they halted, and Jack rolled down his window. A stone-faced behemoth of a security guard stepped out, and Noelle could see the gun holster under the man's suit jacket. The man silently nodded his acknowledgment, pressed a button to open the gates, granting them access.

As they pulled into the huge circular driveway next to a crystal water fountain, Noelle studied the exquisite landscaping of the grounds and the guards with leashed Caucasian Ovcharkas patrolling them. *It was a beautifully designed fortress,* she decided. Jack got out of the driver's side and walked around to open her door. With guarded eyes on the enormous, Russian bear-sized dogs, she slipped her hand into Jack's warm one, warily allowing him to assist her out.

"Ummm...is this your home? And did I see a helicopter landing?" Noelle glanced around suspiciously. "And if you say yes, is public relations really code for something else?"

Jack's broad shoulders shook with silent laughter.

"No this is actually–"

He was interrupted by the front door opening, followed by a loud squeal of excitement. A tiny girl with a huge, reddish-brown curly afro and a peanut butter complexion shot out of the entrance and down the steps. She launched herself at Jack, pushing Noelle out of the way in the process. He caught her, twirling her around as she screeched happily with laughter and he joined in.

WHAT. THE. FUCK.

Noelle went from zero to a hundred *real* quick as she contemplated how she was going to kill Jack and this broad who was content to wrap herself around him like a fucking boa constrictor. Fists curled, she stepped forward. They were too caught up in their moment to realize that imminent death would soon be upon them both, bear dogs present or not. A deep, slightly-accented baritone behind her stopped her in her tracks.

"Please excuse my daughter, Miss. She hasn't seen her favorite brother in months. Don't tell Casey and Darby I said that or I will be forced to deny it."

Noelle swung toward the voice and found herself gawking into a pair of gorgeous, ink- blue eyes. They belonged to a giant god whose wavy, shoulder-length black hair was lightly threaded with silver. He was obviously older, but his face was barely lined. Not an ounce of fat could be found on his insanely fit body from what Noelle could see as he approached her. His looks combined with that voice made him downright lethal.

"It *has* to be the water," she mumbled to herself.

First, the Sullivan brothers, then the girl in front of her, and now, this strapping god. There really could be no other explanation for the freakishly good genes in this town. He reached her and held out his hand. Noelle found herself responding to his warm smile as she took his large hand.

"I'm Alexei Romankov. And that unruly wild child is my daughter Katerina."

"It's a pleasure to meet you, Mr. Romankov. I'm Noelle Kr...er Sullivan." She felt her blood pressure settling now that she knew they were all family, now foolishly recognizing his daughter from the photos in Vivienne's office. *This was Vivienne's husband?* The woman was completely certifiable to have left a man this fine!

"Please, just Alexei or Lex. No need for formalities, eh? May I call you Noelle?" She nodded and attempted to pull her hand back, but he held fast, his brow furrowed in concentration. "Forgive me for staring, but you are a very beautiful woman."

Suddenly, her hand was pulled out of Alexei's grasp as Jack yanked her against him. He gave the older man a sinister stare. "Stop puttin' the moves on my woman, you old commie bastard."

Noelle gaped at Jack's rudeness, but Alexei and his daughter found the hostile comment to be uproariously funny. While they laughed their heads off, she gave her husband *(oh how she loved that title!)* her best bitch face. "Jackson Conall Sullivan! That was completely uncalled for."

With a playful look, Jack pressed a hard kiss to her lips, drawling, "Damn woman, I love it when you full-name me. Do it again. That was hot."

Still chuckling, Alexei rubbed his chin thoughtfully, eyeing Jack with interest. "So, *Yakov*, the rumors are not just rumors, *da*?"

Katerina stepped forward and Noelle was taken aback by her exquisiteness. It made sense that the offspring of two great-looking people would look like this. Her facial features were all fragile and fine-boned with full bow lips. Except for her eyes. They were huge in her heart-shaped face and molasses in color with an exotic tilt, like her mother's. She was a pocket Venus with a petite figure also like Vivienne's, except curvier. Noelle felt like a giant standing next to her.

"Forgive me, Noelle. My Papa is right, and I've been incredibly rude. It's just that Jackie hasn't been home in so long. I couldn't control myself when Mikhail announced that it was him," she confided in a lilting voice. She gave Noelle an impish grin. "My name is Katerina Romankov, but you can call me Kat. It is an absolute pleasure to meet *the* Mrs. Jack Sullivan! I can't believe that I've finally got a sister! Yaaaay!!"

And with that, Katerina launched herself at Noelle, who automatically caught her. *What the hell.* Amidst Jack and Alexei's laughter, she spun Katerina around also.

CHAPTER

Sixteen

*H*E WAS LATE, AND *VIVIENNE was going to kill him,* Casey thought, stepping out of his silver Jaguar XFR and hurrying up the sidewalk to her D.C. townhouse.

His phone vibrated in his pant's pocket, but with his hands full, he ignored it. Casey carefully balanced the bags of wine bottles and cheese in his arms to ring the doorbell. As he waited for the door to open, he heard another car pull up. Then a door opened and slammed with a woman's sultry voice cooing, "Thanks! Keep the change, baby!"

Why did it sound familiar? Casey wondered, turning to look, but the door opened, and he was snatched inside by his irate godmother, who looked madder than a wet hen as she scolded. "You're late! What took you so long?"

"Gee, I don't know. Maybe it was someone's insistence on needing to have a Blonde Lillet! You know Cheesetique is the only place in town that currently has it in stock, right? And I'm also sure you know that it's nowhere near my office?" he retorted, kissing her offered cheek. Casey felt a presence behind him, so he stepped aside only to be enveloped in a cloud of flowers with a hint of apples as Sidra breezed past him to give Vivienne a hug.

"Sidra, I'm so glad you could make it! I hope the flight wasn't too bad?" Vivienne cooed as they exchanged air kisses.

"So, so sorry, Viv! There was a slight delay on the tarmac, but I'm just glad I made it. Fabulous dress! Celine?" Sidra smiled pleasantly, deliberately ignoring Casey.

Casey was in shock to see his nemesis here. He'd spent an insane amount of his free time thinking about her and that smart-ass mouth. His night had officially gone to shit. Reluctantly, Casey admitted to himself that she looked damn good. Her wild, just-got-fucked curls framed her striking face, and the short, clingy black and white geometric patterned dress hugged her in all the right places. Black platform heels almost put her at eye level with him.

"Sidra. I wasn't expecting to see you here."

He would not say it was good to see her or spout some other untruthful bullshit. Although, a certain part of his anatomy proved him to be a liar. With a ferocious scowl, he discreetly shifted the bags in his hand to cover the front of his tented pants.

"Casey. You're looking uptight as usual," Sidra replied in a honeyed voice. *If uptight meant fine as hell*, Sidra thought with dismay. She just couldn't resist needling the self-righteous lawyer. It helped her to combat being one of the thousands of women in his fan club. Although she would never admit it out loud, like even if she was under oath, Casey Sullivan was easily the best-looking man she'd ever seen. She just knew the corny-ass pickup line about heaven missing an angel was inspired by him.

Even now as he eyed her with distaste, Sidra's

reaction to his ire-filled gaze sweeping over her created a party in her lady parts. He lifted a hand to rake through his thick, dark blond hair in frustration, and she longed to replace his fingers with her own. To yank on the silky strands as he pleasured her. Damn! Now the panties were wet also. *It was going to be a long night,* she thought, but not without irritation.

Vivienne's delicate cough did not quite cover her laugh. Slipping her arm through Sidra's, she pulled her along. Viewing them suspiciously, Casey's scowl increased tenfold.

"Why yes, it is Celine, Sidra. And please, children, no bickering tonight. Come on and let's mingle."

Casey had no choice but to follow, ignoring his phone as it vibrated in his pocket once more.

———————————

THE NETWORKING DINNER WAS A great success. After dessert, the guests moved to Vivienne's parlor to socialize. Casey stood in the corner, sipping a vodka tonic, observing the room. Well, he was actually watching one person specifically. She was having the time of her life, wrapping everyone she came into contact with around her itty bitty finger. He was annoyed to see one particular individual brave enough to linger in her presence without fear of his soul being sucked from his body.

Casey's fingers clenched around his glass as Sidra gave a lusty laugh at something Dominick Harris, the lead singer of Bison Blue, was whispering in her ear. The sound alone made Casey's groin tighten with lust. When Sidra laughed, her whole face lit up, making her even lovelier than usual. Entranced, Dominick stepped closer to her, effectively using his body to block any other males from poaching on what he considered to be his territory Casey assumed, as Dominick touched a blue curl by her throat.

Succubus is what she is, Casey thought sourly. He'd seen the lustful looks on the men at the club when Sidra jumped on a low table to dance by herself, her body twisting, bouncing, and turning with the thumping beats. She'd drawn a crowd of admirers who egged her on while he'd watched it all from afar, wishing it was only him she danced for. *Why was he even thinking about her??* He didn't even like the bossy, demanding harpy.

But he did want to fuck her.

Yeah, he really wanted to fuck her, especially her mouth because for once, she'd have to be quiet. Casey shifted his stance to again accommodate his growing hard-on. He was going to have to do something about it. Mentally, he ran down his list of women that he could hook up with on a moment's notice. There were plenty of prospects, but he wasn't keen on fucking a substitute. *What would it take to get Sidra in his bed?* Casey mused. Civility was not their strong point, so a courtship was out of the question.

"Are you enjoying yourself, Mr. Sullivan?"

Casey reluctantly dragged his eyes away from Sidra and met a pair of shy, blue eyes. They belonged to Anna Dayton, a cute pit bull lobbyist who worked on Capitol Hill. In the past, they'd attended many of the same functions, but before tonight had never really interacted. He looked down at her almost empty wine glass then back up to her overly flushed cheeks as she swayed to the music in her head.

"Indeed, I am, Ms. Dayton. How about you?" he inquired politely. She laughed, and the high-pitched sound grated on his ears. Casey wondered what the fuck was so funny, but he forced himself to laugh with her. At least she was laughing, so apparently, he hadn't lost his touch with the opposite sex, just Sidra, whose face looked like she smelled shit whenever she saw him.

"Yes, I am, and *please* call me Anna. Do you mind if I get something off my chest? It's just something that I've been absolutely *dying* to tell you!" At his congenial smile and encouraging nod, she continued. "You are just the most attractive man I've ever laid eyes on, Casey Sullivan. And I can honestly say that if I hadn't had three glasses of this wine for Dutch courage, I doubt I'd be over here talking to you," she finished wistfully, tucking a strand of her long, blonde hair behind her ear.

Great. He *was* losing his touch. Now, women had to drink themselves damn-near silly to talk to him. Casey watched as her face turned red with mortification at her admission. His phone vibrated once, and he pulled it out to read the text.

PLEASE CALL ME! I'M WORRIED ABOUT YOU. I WON'T STOP CALLING UNTIL I KNOW YOU'RE OKAY, CASEY!

"Well, thank you for the compliment, Ms. Anna. It was a pleasure speaking with you, but I'm afraid I have to make a call." Casey excused himself and ran, not walked, away from her.

Cursing to himself, he left the room and stepped out into the garden, closing the French doors behind him quietly. Casey dialed a number, and it rang twice before someone picked up. He didn't give the person on the other end a chance to say anything other than hello.

"Stop callin' me! I have nothin' else to say to you! What happened earlier didn't mean a damn thing! I'm not comin' back, so stop fuckin' beggin' to try again! Do

you get it? The calls stop now!"

His words were low and threatening. There was silence on the other end, so he hung up, knowing that the caller had finally gotten the message. Casey shoved his phone back into his jacket pocket and leaned his head against the stone wall, fighting the urge to smash something. His emotions were on overload, clawing to break free of the compartment he kept a tight lid on. Coming here tonight and attempting to be civilized after his session with Dr. Klaus had been poor judgment on Casey's part.

The case he was working was too close to what he'd experience as a child, and today he'd broken down and cried like a baby. Dr. Klaus insisted that it was the long, overdue breakthrough he needed to move on, but Casey felt too raw and vulnerable to go on with the session. He'd gotten the hell out of there, and she'd been calling him ever since. A tingle at the base of his neck made him realize he wasn't alone. Casey whirled around to find Sidra glaring at him. Slowly, she started clapping. *Very slowly.* Intentionally insulting.

"Wow! You are one cold-hearted bastard. Whoever she is should be lucky that you were heartless enough to end it."

The look of disgust on Sidra's face as she looked him up and down contemptuously before dismissing him broke his restraints. Casey closed the distance between them and grabbed her arm, spinning her around to face him. Shocked, she narrowed her eyes dangerously and yanked back. He refused to let go, jerking her closer. "You don't know a damn thing about me! Do you hear me? Not a damn thing!"

"Get your hand off of me before you draw back a bloody nub, you fucking psycho!" Sidra hissed, venom dripping from each word. What a fool she'd been to be attracted to this cold-blooded son of a bitch. He chewed women up and spit them out like it was nothing and had the nerve to be mad at *her* for calling him on it. *Motherfucker, puhleez.* Casey's hazel eyes were raging with fury and his full lips were pulled into a snarl. Even now, she should be able to resist him but found she had to still her body from swaying towards his.

Casey hated that as angry as she made him, he still noticed shit he had no business noticing. Up close, she was even lovelier – flawless dark skin flushed with anger, eyes glittering like diamonds, and her tempting lips were pursed together like she'd been sucking on lemons. He felt her body shift. Casey knew that she was going to swing, so he moved first. He used both hands to jerk her against him and out of the light, backing her up against the side wall of the house. Sidra opened her mouth to scream bloody murder, and Casey brought his lips crashing down on hers, channeling all of his anger, frustration, and desire into a sizzling kiss.

SIDRA WAS STUNNED AS CASEY'S firm lips covered hers. His tongue invaded her mouth, familiarizing her with his cinnamon taste as he thoroughly dominated her, using tongue and teeth to drive home the fact that he was in control. Then the kiss softened, and Sidra found herself drowning in unfamiliar sensations. What started out as punishment turned into ecstasy, making her helpless to defy him. Stroke for stroke, she met his tongue. *This is really happening,* she thought numbly while Casey expertly caressed her mouth and swallowed up every cry she breathed. Sidra could feel his erection pressing against her, and she pressed back, running her hands through his hair like she'd fantasized about.

Casey groaned into her mouth, wishing he could stop kissing her but he couldn't. Now that he'd tasted Sidra's soft lips, he was officially under her spell. She tasted like ripe berries. The time for sanity had come and gone. He'd rather die than walk away without knowing what her pussy felt like wrapped around his cock.

They continued to exchange ardent kisses as Casey lifted Sidra's dress and yanked her panties down. They fell around her ankles, and the musky scent of her arousal drove him wild. She stepped out of them, and he yanked at his belt then unbuttoned his pants letting them and his boxers fall around his knees. Sidra licked her lips, placing her hand on his dick, causing him to jerk back as if burned.

"No! I won't last if you touch me. *We're fuckin' now, Sidra!* Turn around and put your hands on the wall," he demanded, and she willingly complied, her pussy quivering in response to his authoritative tone.

Casey was hypnotized by her magnificent ass, thinking that it was a true work of art. With Sidra naked from the waist down, he could see how round and firm the satiny, chocolate globes were in the pale moonlight. Her waist was tiny, and her legs long and toned. He stepped up to her, and his dick was cushioned by the cleft of her ass and coated by her arousal. He was so turned on by the sight of his paler skin against her darker skin that more pre-cum oozed out as he rubbed himself against the lips of her soaked pussy. Sidra moaned, her core clenching at the sensations his thickness stirred in her. She clawed at the wall in front of her, arching her ass out, silently begging for him to take her.

"Spread your legs," he growled, torturing them

both by dragging his shaft from her ultra-sensitive clit through her dripping lips. Casey's eyes rolled back in his head, knowing he wasn't going to be able to last. *Shit, he wasn't even in yet, and it was fucking amazing!* He wasn't alone in his conclusion. Sidra was panting heavily and going stir crazy with anticipation.

"Are we gonna fuck or what? Let me know because I have a potential suitor inside who could probably do what you're doing...maybe even better," she taunted, anxious to get more than a 'rise' out of him. If he stopped now, Sidra felt like she would die. Seeing red at the thought of some asshole replacing him, Casey shoved into her with one powerful thrust. She jerked forward onto her tiptoes. "Aaaah!"

Casey allowed her a moment to adjust to his girth, gnashing his teeth at how right it felt to be in her overly-saturated walls. Then he started to move, pulling Sidra to his chest as he thrust deeper and harder into her. Casey pressed her back against the wall, grasping both of her wrists in one hand high above her head and holding them there. His other hand drifted between her legs to massage her tender nub.

"You think that you're gonna get this somewhere else?" When she didn't answer, he thrust even harder and pinched the engorged gem. In response, she coated his dick with fresh juices. The cry Sidra emitted was long, low and steeped in pleasure. "You think he's gonna fuck you like me? No baby; you ain't findin' no one else who's gonna be balls deep in your sweet pussy like this."

Sidra was trembling as she willingly and repeatedly took his dick. Dayyum, the lawyer could fuck. *Who knew all this passion lay beneath the uptight prim and proper esquire?* And the shit he was talking in her ear turned her on even more. Casey's nimble fingers playing her clit was nothing short of sorcery, and Sidra couldn't get enough. She spread her legs, even more, giving him better access to her pussy.

"More! Fuck me harder! I'm almost there!" she demanded breathlessly, clamping down on his shaft as he put the fiercest of dick-downs on her pussy, continuously hitting her g-spot oh so right. Casey dropped her wrists and yanked her head back for a bruising kiss, sucking on her tongue as he fucked and rubbed her. Sidra reached behind to hold his head in place while they exchanged sloppy kisses. Together, they were spiraling out of control and loving it.

Sidra was going to combust; the pleasure was too unbearable. Her legs started to shake harder, and then she was splintering from the inside out as her body exploded and she squirted all over Casey's hand. He was coming too, shoving her right leg upward and holding it in place to delve deeper into her, filling her tunnel up with his cum to the point that it was overflowing and running back down her thigh. Casey loosened his grip and they fell against the wall, gasping for breath.

Reality set in shortly afterward.

Silently, Casey pulled out of her, and they attempted to adjust their clothes. As he buckled his pants, he watched Sidra intently while she attempted to ignore him. She looked beautifully undone to him as she stumbled to pick up her panties. He felt a perverse feeling of satisfaction at the way she tentatively moved around. Just thinking about how her pussy stretched, just for him, made Casey harden again. Idly, he wondered how long they could stay gone before they were missed.

Sidra just wanted to get the fuck out of Casey's presence, still incredulous of the dick- down he'd thoroughly put on her. Her body was aching for a repeat performance, but she wouldn't be the same fool twice, she vowed silently. Avoiding his eyes, she hurriedly bent down to pick up her underwear but paused as something wet trickled down her legs. She stiffened at the same time that Casey also saw the pearl-colored fluid. They looked at it and then each other and simultaneously exclaimed what summed up their situation perfectly.

"*Fuck!!!*"

CHAPTER
Seventeen

*D*INNER WITH THE ROMANKOVS WAS a lively affair. The food was excellent and the wine even better. As the designated driver, Jack limited himself to one glass but encouraged Noelle to enjoy the finest that Romankov Wineries had to offer. Before they left, Alexei promised to pack a crate of wine for them. Jack was glad to be home because it gave him a chance to catch up with his sister who proved to be evasive in answering any of his questions. He planned to get to the bottom of it. Alexei had been oddly quiet during Jack's subtle-as-a-bull-in-a-china-shop interrogation, which Noelle cut short by asking Kat where she got her necklace from.

Grateful for the diversion, Kat proudly confessed, "I made it! I'm going to school for fashion, but I really love making jewelry."

Noelle studied the hammered gold design of Kat's necklace with a sense of déjà vu. She looked up to find all three of them watching her then glanced down at her wedding ring, and it clicked. "Oh, my goodness, are you *Vixen*? You made my ring, didn't you? Kat, my friends and I love your work!"

She raved as Katerina shyly accepted her praise, and Jack and her father looked on with pride. "Yes, I did! I'm very excited to know that you love it. I told Jack that if he didn't drive you crazy enough to leave him, I'd make the matching bracelet for your one-year anniversary."

Noelle glanced at Jack, and he smiled at her enigmatically, knowing what she was already thinking: that they didn't have a year, and their wedding was just a big hoax. She glanced, with a wistful expression, at the ring again, taking in the beautiful design and gorgeous stones.

"It's very beautiful, and I love it. Thank you for taking the time to design it. You're amazingly talented," she simply said, not willing to address the fact that there wouldn't be an anniversary to celebrate. Across from her, Jack shook his head. *Poor Noelle.* She had no idea the lengths that he would go to ensure there would be plenty of anniversaries in their future.

The only awkward moment of the evening was when Vivienne's name was brought up. Katerina went as still as a statue when Jack mentioned that her mother was annoyed that she was avoiding her.

"I'm not avoiding her," she sulked, stuffing food into her mouth, a clear attempt to avoid talking. Alexei focused sharply on his daughter.

"Katya, is this true?"

She shot Jack a mutinous glare, shrugging her shoulders as she met her father's quizzical stare.

"Papa, I'm not avoiding her. She would like for us to take our annual summer trip, but this year, it's not possible for me. I have...things I'm working on. Mom should understand that as a fellow business woman! Did I complain when I spent all my time with her at the office instead of hanging out with my friends? No, I didn't! We can still go, just not this summer. Instead, I would rather be here with you in Whiskey Row."

Alexei was silent for a minute, surveying his daughter who could be just as stubborn as her mother. "If that is your decision, then I will respect it, *milya moya*."

Jack was surprised that the older man did not insist Kat contact Vivienne, but he kept his mouth shut. As Jack and Noelle prepared to leave, Alexei motioned for him to hang back, allowing the women to walk ahead of them.

"How is she?" he inquired in a low voice, the *she* in question being Vivienne. Jack sighed, the feeling of guilt weighing in his chest as it always did whenever he thought of Alexei and Vivienne's estrangement.

"She's good. Busy with work. Or her book club. Or her mentoring program. You know Vivienne; she stays busy," Jack replied neutrally. His heart hurt watching as the big, powerful man he'd looked up to his entire life, allowed his shoulders to sag in defeat for a moment before his gaze hardened.

"I cannot change what happened that night years ago, and for that, I am truly sorry, *Yakov*. It will haunt me until the end of my days. *But enough is enough.* This thing between Vivi and Katya will not be smoothed by me. If Vivienne wants to see her daughter, then she will need to come here. It is time," Alexei declared, his deep voice ringing with finality.

UNDER JACK'S SKILLFUL DRIVING, THE SUV shot smoothly down the two-lane road. In the silver moonlight, shadows cast from the tall trees on either side falling all over the road. It was if every star in the sky had come out to welcome him home. Chase Rice's version of "Ride" played softly on the radio while Jack replayed the evening in his mind. Other than the obvious avoidance that Kat showed toward her mother, something was off. It had something to do with the way that she was overly attentive to her father. Her hovering over Alexei's every move was suspicious to him. Jack made a mental note to ask Darby about it the next time he saw him. Noelle's yawn drew his attention back to her.

"How long before we're there?" she asked sleepily.

"Not long, another ten minutes. Did you have a good time?" Jack asked, thinking how adorable she looked snuggled in his leather jacket. Although it was mid-spring, the temperature was still cooler due to the mountain's higher altitude.

"I did. They're great people, and Katerina is incredibly chill and talented. Jack..." Noelle hesitated, struggling to find the right words without sounding how she felt, which was pathetically grateful. "Thank you very much for the ring. I promise I'll give it back when this is all over with. Words can't express my gratitude to you for helping me out with everything and just being a really good sport about the whole thing."

Jack took his eyes off the road for a moment to look at her. "Noelle, you don't ever have to thank me. I wouldn't have done any of this if I didn't want to. As far as I'm concerned, the ring is yours forever."

They passed a sign that read "Devil's Hill", and Noelle saw Jack's fingers clench around the steering wheel. She reached over and touched his arm and found his muscles were tense. Noelle rubbed in circular motions until she felt the tension leave his body. Jack shot her a tired grin.

Fifteen minutes later, they were pulling up to a

huge, three-story, white rustic farmhouse with modern touches, hidden by huge weeping willow trees. The greenery surrounding the house was lush, overgrown, and wild with azaleas, hydrangeas, gardenias, magnolias, and varying perennials. About half a mile from the house, under the bright moonlight, Noelle saw an industrial-looking wood and steel building. Behind it, the mountains provided an endless backdrop.

This time, Noelle didn't wait for Jack as the car came to a halt. She jumped out, spinning around to take it all in as the heady floral fragrance seduced her nostrils. She felt Jack standing behind her, and his masculine scent blended right in with the rich aromas of nature surrounding them, but she paid him no mind. Noelle was visualizing children, *their children*, running around with wild curls, and the double kitchen windows thrown open with pies cooling on the sill. Lazy weekends filled with family and friends, maybe a pool where Jack would teach their babies how to swim? She wanted that dream so badly, it became hard for her to breathe.

Finally, Jack spoke, "Welcome to my–"

"Home," she finished softly; because Noelle knew in her heart of hearts that was what this was and where she truly belonged.

―――――――――――

THE INSIDE OF THE HOUSE was large and spacious with whitewashed wood floors and lots of windows, allowing natural light in. There were four bathrooms and six bedrooms. It had a dreamy, romantic feeling, and Noelle could easily picture it filled with a mix of feminine and male touches of floral patterns, velvet, leather, and wood. With the exception of a huge dark brown leather sectional sofa and coffee table in the family room, the only other room with furniture was the kitchen with its exquisite teakwood dining set. Noelle spent at least ten minutes oohing and aahing over its detailing.

"This fucking rocks! Look at the colors in the wood and the intricate pattern on the table legs. This is a four thousand dollar set easily! It reminds me of my table and bookcase back home. Is it the same craftsman? How'd you get your hands on it? Uncle Ian said the designer only makes one-of-a-kind pieces." She fired off questions as she walked around the set.

"On top of just being a good guy, I'm pretty well connected, darlin'. Who wouldn't want to be nice to me?" he smiled, blinking at her slowly with those gorgeous hazel eyes. Instantly suspicious that the designer was a woman, Noelle treated him to a skeptical look. As if reading her mind, Jack laughed.

"Relax, Mrs. Sullivan. The person in question is a he, not a she," Jack laughed again as Noelle haughtily turned her nose up at him glancing away to hide her smile at being called his missus.

"What are you going to do about furniture?" she asked, continuing to inspect the kitchen. Jack leaned against the doorway and put an arm around her, effectively trapping Noelle with his body. His nearness made her heartbeat increase while his scent filled her nostrils. His eyes focused on her parted lips, reminiscing on the memories they'd given him, before slowly rising to meet hers. The air between them swirled with awareness and sexual tension.

"Tonight, we can crash on the sofa. It has a pullout bed. I've got some pieces bein' delivered the day after tomorrow, but I was hopin' that we could go to Nashville and pick up some things. I've been meanin' to make it look more like a home but never seemed to have the time. Since you've got excellent taste, maybe you could help me pick some stuff out?"

Select items and stamp her mark all over his home so that he would be reminded of her when she was long gone, and another woman would be made aware of her presence?

"I would love to," Noelle replied sweetly.

Jack kissed her forehead as they walked out. "Why don't you take a shower and relax? I had Kat come over two days ago and fill the master bath with toiletries and towels. There are some sheets and blankets in the closet off the living room. I'll grab the bags from the truck, then make up the bed."

Noelle headed toward the stairs. "Sounds like a plan."

"Oh, and Noelle?" She turned back to him with a questioning look.

"Anythin' Kat might have put in there for you that's small and lacy, please leave outta sight. I don't think my poor heart could take it if it was just for show," Jack said seriously, eyes full of heat. Face burning at the longing his words evoked, Noelle hurried up the stairs for a cold shower, certain it was going to be a *long* night.

JACK COULDN'T SLEEP.

He looked over at Noelle and she was face-down on the pillow, knocked out. Being with her was so easy that he knew bringing her here was the right choice to accomplish his goal. She kept the demons of the past at bay. After bringing their luggage in, he went upstairs to also take a quick shower and spied the La Perla bag in the middle of the master bedroom floor.

"Christ," he muttered, resisting the urge to explore the bag's contents.

When he came back downstairs, they stretched out on the sofa bed and caught up on their respective correspondence. Jack deliberately ignored the emails he received from Ian and Alicia. Instead, he focused on reading the bios Margaret had compiled on two potential clients who were requesting the firm's representation. One prospect was an Italian-French chef with her own cooking show. Jack was convinced that with her ambition, she could be the next Giada De Laurentiis. The other prospect was a young social media tycoon who just wanted to make the world a better place with his oodles of money. Ian voted yes to the tycoon and no to the chef. Vivi wanted both to come on board, except Ian was adamant that the chef would be even more trouble than Inez was already proving to be. Jack had the deciding word and would meet with both candidates when he got back to New York.

Noelle occasionally asked Jack's opinion regarding promoting Tarik's party as she typed away on a new business plan that she was drafting. She confided to him that she and Avery were hoping to expand the business to include a floral and gift arrangement division. She was too cute with her curls pulled into a sloppy bun and large, black-framed glasses that hung on her nose, waving her hands animatedly to get her point across. Finally, the day's events caught up with her. One minute, Noelle was talking about what to put in the baskets, and the next, she was snoring. Unfortunately, gorgeous girl that she was, her snoring was horrifying. She would kill Jack if he ever mentioned that her snores were as loud and grating as a chainsaw.

The night hummed with nature's choir. The frogs croaking, crickets chirping, and occasional bird calls had once soothed Jack to sleep when he was a little boy. Now, all he heard was his last conversation with his mother in his mind. He felt his guilt for not doing more eating away at him, leaving him raw and exposed as a coward. Jack hated this feeling of helplessness, of wishing he'd been bigger and stronger so that he could have taken on Patrick. Countless nights, after putting his brothers to bed, he'd take his shower, allowing his tears of grief to mix with the hot water scalding his skin as if to atone for his sins.

This house was Jack's tribute to his mother. The flowers and trees planted outside were her favorites. She'd often told him and his brothers of the farmhouse that she longed for back in Ireland, describing it in great detail. Jack had implemented some of her descriptions to the best of his abilities and mixed it with his own aesthetic. The barn beam mantle over the stone fireplace had her name, birthday, and zodiac sign elaborately carved into the wood. Moira Sullivan had been truly well-loved by her family.

The only tribute Jack had dedicated to his bastard father was putting the "Devil's Hill" marker by the road that led up the hill where the motherfucker was buried.

Noelle rolled over, and he looked down at his sleeping beauty with concern, watching as a tiny frown marred her lovely features. She snuggled closer, pressing her body to his with her face in the crook of his neck. Her black curls sprawled over them, and the frown disappeared. Jack sighed with contentment and soon drifted off into a peaceful sleep.

CHAPTER
Eighteen

THE NEXT MORNING, NOELLE WOKE to the delicious aroma of bacon tempting her nostrils. She blinked at the bright light filtering through the windows, noticing the now empty spot where Jack slept last night. Being in his strong arms, with his heartbeat as the lullaby beneath her ear, had been nothing short of heaven. She could hear low voices in the kitchen and decided it would be best to go and make herself presentable.

Eager to get the day started, Noelle quickly relieved herself, braided her hair, showered again, and brushed her teeth. After slathering on moisturizer and some mascara, she released the thick braids and applied sea salt spray, shaping them into beach waves. *Now what to wear.* She decided on a white off-shoulder tee with layered gold and silver necklaces and light denim cutoffs. White espadrilles completed the look.

As she headed to the kitchen, Noelle could hear Jack and another man's voice that she didn't recognize. The country drawl was even deeper than Jack's, but there was a hint of something else – Spanish, perhaps? When she entered the room, all conversation stopped.

Both men rose to greet her, but Noelle only had eyes for one.

Jack was dressed in a dark green t-shirt, which clung to his sinewy muscles and made his tan appear deeper, paired with dark distressed jeans. Brown, worn, country boots adorned his feet. His hair was rumpled, and although he hadn't bothered with shaving, the scruff covering the bottom of his face was such a turn-on that Noelle didn't mind one bit. Gone were the tailored suits and gelled hair. The only thing left on him that was city slick was his Hublot watch. He'd turned into a full-fledged country boy overnight, and it just made him even sexier to Noelle. Heaven, help her, but she was loving this look. Jack smiled warmly, his eyes perusing her head to toe.

"Mornin', darlin'. How'd you sleep?"

Slow heat unfurled in her belly, and Noelle felt her body responding to his heightened southern drawl. It amazed her how sexy he sounded dropping his 'g's' and allowing words to meander out of his mouth now. There was none of the hustle and bustle that could be found from living in the Big Apple.

"Morning. Fine, thanks, and you?" she responded huskily and hearing the need in her tone, Jack's hazel eyes clouded with lust.

"Like a baby."

Jack's voice was a low rumble that let her know exactly what was on his mind. Carnal tension filled the air between them. Self-consciously, Noelle licked her lips, and his eyes burned brighter as they keenly tracked the movement. He moved toward her and she to him like magnets, but the spell was broken by someone noisily clearing their throat. Embarrassed that she'd quickly forgotten someone else was there, Noelle glanced to her right and couldn't help but wonder aloud, "What the hell kind of Kool-Aid are the people in this town drinking?"

The stranger arched a perfect black eyebrow, full lips quirking. In a deliciously slightly accented yet southern drawl, he spoke.

"I'm afraid that I have no idea as to what you're talkin' about, Mrs. Sullivan. I'm more of a bourbon and whiskey man, than a Kool-Aid one myself," he finished with a wink.

As far as Noelle was concerned, he could have been telling her to jump off the side of the mountain for all the attention she paid to his words. Standing before her was one of the most gorgeous men she'd ever seen. He was at least at least six-feet-four inches of lean muscle and bore a striking resemblance to the male model Willie Cartier. Where Casey was blonde and angelic, this olive-skinned man, with freckles sprinkled across his nose and high cheekbones, was darkly beautiful and sensual. His straight black hair hung to his elbows. Thick, slashing brows and an aquiline nose dominated an angular-shaped face that managed to be both fragile and masculine at the same time. Sweeping black lashes covered almond-shaped black eyes that burned bright with mischief, and those wickedly sexy lips were framed by a Fu Manchu.

He could have been a poet, renaissance man, vampire, warrior, or the leader of a drug cartel because his look was that versatile. Hollywood would salivate to get their hands on a man who looked like this. Masculine and lithe like the artist Prince, he was a walking contradiction and packaged far too erotically for his own good. Noelle knew she was staring and that her beloved Jack was starting to get antsy, but she couldn't help herself. Then the tables were turned as the stranger subjected her to the same thorough scrutiny, making her blush. *Oh, my.* Jack finally broke the silence by walking over and pulling her close to him possessively, giving the other man a territorial look that made his eyes twinkle.

"Baby, I'm gonna give you a pass because there ain't a woman alive who hasn't had the same reaction when they were introduced to Guiles Keetoowah-Marquez, the handsomest son of a bitch in the state. Guiles, my wife, Noelle," Jack grudgingly introduced, his voice laced with irritation. Apparently, it was too much to ask that Noelle be immune to his friend's good looks, he supposed. Women had been making fools of themselves over the handsome bastard since he was born.

Noelle held her hand out, and the other man reached out to take it with a devastating smile. Jack conveniently chose that moment to direct Noelle toward the table. Gritting his teeth at the knowing chuckle behind him, he pulled out the chair closest to his and pushed it even closer before gesturing for her to sit. Ignoring her look of irritation at his high-handedness, Jack pointed to the plate in front of her. "Are you hungry? I made bacon, eggs, and toast. Let me get you some coffee, too."

Noelle shook her head in exasperation at Jack as he placed a heaping helping in front of her before looking at Guiles. "It's a pleasure to meet you, Guiles."

The other man smiled at her. "My friends call me Guy. Forgive me for starin', but it's a pleasure to meet the beautiful woman that finally captured ol' 'Serious Sullivan's' heart. I wasn't aware such a gem was hidin' in New York."

The last was said in a tone rife with the sensual promise that Noelle instinctively knew was meant to irk his friend. Jack walked back over to the table and placed the steaming mug of coffee in front of Noelle, who murmured "thank you" while cautiously sneaking a peek at him. He didn't even notice as his hard eyes were trained on Guy, who was staring back at him with mirth-filled eyes as he sat down across from Noelle.

"Do you remember when we were kids and we jumped out of that big Oak tree on Huckleberry Lane? And your britches got caught on a branch? How you were stuck cryin' and hollerin' because of that mighty wedgie you got?" Jack smiled pleasantly as Guy's smile flat-lined and his skin flushed with embarrassment. "Who would believe that your lady-catchin' voice could have hit a note so high–"

"Rude, Jack! Rude!" Guy shouted as a laughing Noelle dug into her meal. Jack snatched a piece of bacon from her plate only to have it disappear as she snatched it back twice as fast, putting it on the far side of her plate.

"Do not play with me when it comes to bacon," she said, shaking her head at his gall. Guy laughed at Jack's hangdog expression, and Noelle took pity on him, scooping up some egg and grits and offering him a bite.

"So, tell me about yourself, Noelle," Guy continued in a friendly tone. "Never thought I'd see the day that this one here would settle down. Hell, you're the first girl he's ever brought home! Congratulations on the weddin', by the way. How'd you two meet?"

Noelle blushed, and Guy was enchanted by the heightened color in her cheeks. A sharp pain in his ankle made him wince, breaking his gaze away from her to find his childhood friend mad-dogging him. Leaning down to rub his injured ankle, Guy plotted retribution.

"Well, I co-own an event planning company with one of my best friends. I'm sure you know Jack's partner, Ian?" At Guy's nod, she continued, "I'm his goddaughter, and my family is a client of their firm. We met four years ago at my birthday party."

"Was it love at first sight for you?" Guy teased.

Noelle shifted uneasily in her chair. Now, how exactly was she supposed to answer that? With the truth? Jack would freak and divorce her if he thought she harbored any type of feelings for him. Sensing her discomfort, Jack responded for her.

"What's with the twenty questions? All you need to know is that she is married, married, and *married*. Got it?" He offered the pot of coffee to his friend. Guy shrugged, holding his cup out to be filled.

"I'm just sayin'. How many southern boys do you know, Noelle? We are a unique breed to experience and savor. You can't just up and marry the first one you meet! *Owww shit!*" Guy yelped, yanking his leg out from underneath the table to rub his ankle furiously, scowling at Jack who was innocently eating his breakfast. Noelle managed to hide her grin behind her coffee mug.

"So...how far do you guys think the Grizzlies will get in the playoffs?" Noelle asked, intentionally changing the subject.

The conversation quickly turned to the Grizzlies, then football, and finally hockey. Noelle was surprised to learn that Darby played with the Nashville Predators for four years before a knee injury forced him into early retirement.

"Wow, I didn't know that about him, but I guess I could see it," she said, easily picturing the largest brother causing mayhem on the ice and talking shit to the opposing teams.

"Oh, you shoulda seen "The Blade", Noelle! He was quick on his skates. We used to all go down to his games, and there would be rink bunnies wantin' to party with us. Man, Jack, remember that one girl ..." Guys voice trailed off at Noelle's raised eyebrow and Jack's pointed look. "Of course, that was waaaay before he met someone of your beauty and caliber. Thank you kindly for upgradin' my friend," Guy backtracked with a sweet smile.

"Anyway, it's good to have you home, Jack. Been way too long. When you get a moment, I've got some new wood for you to take a look at. Picked up some sand-blasted Manzanita and Tectona Teak that's amazin' for furniture makin'. People are goin' to go crazy for it," Guy boasted confidently as he finished his breakfast. "The pieces you requested are out on the porch. Coffee table, end tables, and–"

"Wait a minute. Are you a carpenter? Did you design this table?!" Noelle interrupted him, excitedly. Guy looked at Jack in confusion. Jack ignored him and scooped up another forkful of eggs from Noelle's plate for himself.

"I am a carpenter and designer–" Guy spoke slowly, but she interrupted him.

"This table is fantastic! You did the coffee table and bookshelf that my Uncle Ian gave me, didn't you? I'd love to see more of your work! We were just talking about decorating last night and I think–"

"Yeah, I am familiar with the pieces," Guy confirmed, interrupting her as he tried to catch Jack's eye again, but this time, he was busy drinking his orange juice. Noelle looked at Jack who smiled pleasantly at her and then back at Guy whose brow was creased in concentration as if trying to figure something out.

Abruptly, he stood up. "Well, I'd better get going. Thanks for the breakfast, man. Like I said, come and check out that wood. Noelle, it was a pleasure to meet you. See you around."

"Likewise," she murmured with a puzzled look.

Jack also stood. "I'll walk you out."

Hmmm, the townsfolk are as weird as they are good-looking, Noelle thought, reaching for her phone to call the girls. They were coming to visit at the end of the week, and she wanted to reassure them that the people in Whiskey Row weren't like the hillbilly friends from the "Looney Tunes".

OUTSIDE OF THE HOUSE, THE two men walked in silence until they reached Guy's red vintage Chevy pickup. It was a classic that he'd spent many hours restoring and never allowed anyone else to drive it.

"Hey, thanks for not savin' me back there. You were as useful as a trap door on a canoe!" Guy groused. "You wanna tell me why your pretty little wife has no idea that you're the one who made that furniture, includin' hers? That you own a quarter of Americana Traditions?"

"No, I don't. Mind your own business, Pippy," Jack warned, referencing his friend's childhood nickname. Growing up, they occasionally gave Guy shit, calling him Pippy, as in Longstocking, when he wore his long hair in two braids to show pride for his Cherokee ancestry. "I would prefer that it not be disclosed until I'm ready."

"Well, you better get ready, son. We've got orders pourin' in, making us busier than a one-eyed cat watchin' five mouse-holes, so we're gonna need to expand our crew. Holt's not complainin' about the amount of work he's doin', but we're only a six-man team. I've got some interviews lined up this week. Can you do them?"

Holt was their other partner and childhood friend. Where Jack was charming, and Guy was friendly and talkative, Holt was quiet. He never spoke more than necessary. Aside from the three of them, they had one more carpenter that worked for them occasionally and two office staff members.

"Yeah, not a problem. Let's do them in groups at Hooligans."

"Cool. By the way, we've also got a shipment of Blue Mahoe and Golden Spanish Elm comin' in from Jamaica. Thinkin' about makin' a sample modern furniture collection with it," Guy casually mentioned.

"Since when do we buy from Jamaica?"

"Since we can justify it as a buyin' trip with our accountant and write it off," he informed Jack, wiggling his eyebrows deviously

"What were you doin' in Jamaica, bro? You don't even like anythin' remotely tropical."

Guy's face turned serious. "I was chasin' a lead. Supposedly Fern was holed up down there with the kids," he grimaced. "Unfortunately, the trail went cold. Ran into an acquaintance of hers who said she was runnin' a little gift shop. Said she got spooked, took the kids, and ran off again."

Jack was compassionate toward his friend's plight. He clasped his friend's shoulder in support. "Damn, I'm sorry to hear that. Do you think she'll ever stop runnin'? She has to know by now that your brother passed, right?"

A flash of pain crossed Guy's face. "I would think so. I just want her to know that they're safe, but maybe it's just too much for her to deal with right now."

Jack still couldn't imagine Miguel, Guy's easy-going, older brother morphing into the manic-depressive, violent man he'd become since coming back from his tour in Iraq and was diagnosed with PTSD.

"Let us know if you need anythin', man. We're family and will do all we can to help. Don't try to carry all the weight on your shoulders."

Guy raised a sardonic brow at him. "Hi Pot, I'm Kettle, fool. I remember how it was for you after Ma passed, may she rest in peace, and how you refused to break down. You've stayed away from this place because of what happened, but I gotta say, you look really happy right now." He turned to look back at the house and so did Jack. They could see Noelle on her cell phone talking and laughing as she washed dishes. "This girl is really good for you, brother."

Jack smiled, hoping he didn't look as pussy-whupped as his brothers suggested he was. "I've got no complaints, but I did wanna let you know one more thing. Noelle's girlfriends are comin' down this weekend, so be on your best behavior."

Guy's eyes lit up, and he rubbed his hands together gleefully. "Girlfriends? As in plural? Do they look anythin' like her?"

"Down, boy."

CHAPTER
Nineteen

THE DRIVE TO NASHVILLE WAS a smooth one, albeit longer than Noelle expected. Luckily, the gorgeous scenery more than made up for it. They spent the better half of the day shopping at the home décor stores Remix Furniture, Restoration Hardware, Anthropologie, Williams-Sonoma, and Z Gallerie. For lunch, they went to the Firefly Grille. Noelle had the buttermilk battered shrimp po'boy, and Jack ate the grilled flank steak and they split a plate of sweet potato fries.

Afterward, Jack took her to the famous Bluebird Café, and Noelle loved the performances of all the up-and-coming singers. She was awestruck, while Jack chatted up an infamous married country singing couple who popped in. He was so at ease, laughing and joking with them and their daughters. When he introduced her as his wife, they warmly congratulated them, making Noelle glow with pleasure. It was a great day. By the time they started heading back to Whiskey Row, she was exhausted, falling asleep before they even hit the highway.

The next morning, Noelle was busy making

breakfast when Guy showed up with yet another behemoth, muscular man in tow. He matched Darby in height, sported wavy, golden blonde hair and a matching beard that complemented his deeply tanned skin. His eyes were blue as the bottom of the ocean. He nodded at her in a friendly fashion, his lips forming a half-smile of greeting. Noelle just shook her head in disbelief while Guy, knowing what she was thinking, burst out laughing.

"Ms. Noelle, I'd like you to meet another childhood friend of mine and Jack's, Holton Brammer. You can call him Holt." Guy swiped up a sausage patty, biting into it as he gave his friend a contemplative look before his eyes lit up. "Or Thor! Yep, Thor will do also."

Noelle rolled her eyes at him but secretly admitted thought Holt did resemble Chris Hemsworth as the Marvel Comics character. She smiled, extending her hand to him. "It's very nice to meet you, Holt."

"The pleasure is all mine. Congratulations on the weddin'." Holt's southern voice was velvety smooth and his handshake, firm. "Please pay no attention to my demented friend. I'm not sure exactly how many times he was dropped as a baby, but I'm pretty sure it was more than ten."

They all laughed, and Noelle gestured to the table. "Breakfast is just about done. Have a seat, fellas. I'm about to make some coffee or would you prefer cappuccinos?"

Guy said yes to coffee with a shot of espresso, and Holt opted for a cappuccino. Jack came downstairs as Noelle was making his cup. He greeted his friends before coming to kiss Noelle's cheek. "Smells delicious. What are we eatin'?"

"Baked French toast casserole with fried apples, cheese grits, and sausage," Noelle recited, as if a server, resisting the urge to press her hand to her cheek where she could still feel his ice-cold lips, fresh from his shower. This morning, she'd found herself lying on top of him with a raging hard-on pressing into her belly and his hand on her butt to hold her in place. Holding her breath, Noelle slowly raised her head to sneak a peek at Jack, only to find him looking at her from beneath a sexy, heavy-lidded gaze. His black curls, sticking up around his head, and the growing beard were fast becoming her favorite look on him. Noelle hadn't been able to resist lifting her hand and rubbing it across his coarse cheeks. The heat in his hazel eyes should have incinerated her. Grabbing her hand, he kissed the center of her palm.

"Don't start somethin' you can't finish, baby." His voice was low and gravelly from sleep. Jack placed her thumb to his lips, slowly licking it then gently nipping, causing spikes of pleasure in her nether region. She smiled, rubbing her thumb across his lips, teasing him.

With a dizzying quickness, Noelle found herself beneath him with his face nuzzled in her neck, his groin grinding into her sex. His lips trailed kisses up her neck, then her earlobe while his hands slid up her torso to palm her breasts. Noelle caged his head to her neck, rubbing herself against his dick urgently.

"Noelle. God, Noelle. I need you so bad," he bit out, his fingers plucking her rock-hard nipples deliciously through her cami. He bit her shoulder, his hips thrusting his erection against her core suggestively. "Feel what you do to me."

Jack could feel her excitement through the thin cotton of her boy shorts. He knew that he could easily nudge them aside, free his cock through the hole of his boxers and 'accidentally' slide into her. The way Noelle worked her hips was driving him bat-shit crazy, but he couldn't do that to her. Couldn't do that, no matter how bad he desired to be inside of her. It still had to be her choice.

"Shit!"

Frustrated, Jack pressed his face into the mattress next to her face, beating his fist into its softness. Noelle froze beneath him as he fought for control. Suddenly, Jack lifted himself off her completely and left the bed, then the room, mumbling something over his shoulder about needing a cold ass shower.

He grabbed glasses for the orange juice, bringing them to the table where he joined his friends to talk. When Noelle brought the tray of coffee over, they automatically stood, and Jack pulled her chair out. They waited for her to sit down before returning to their seats and conversation. *Man, I love a southern gentleman,* Noelle thought with a pleased smile.

"To what do I owe the pleasure so early this mornin', fellas?" Jack savored his chicory coffee. Damn, add brewing a perfect cup of joe to his woman's endless list of talents.

They glanced at Noelle before Guy replied nonchalantly, "We wanted to know if you could give us your feedback on some applicants. Any chance you could sit in on some interviews? Got two lined up for two and three this afternoon."

"Yeah, I think I can swing it. Me and the missus got plans to go into town anyway and then hikin'. That all right with you, baby?"

Jack took the last sausage and cut it down the middle, placing one half on Noelle's plate. She smiled brightly at him, and he felt it in his soul among other places. Discreetly, he adjusted his lower half underneath the table.

"This right here is serious business!" Guy exclaimed reverently through a mouthful of food, pointing his fork at his plate. The other two men nodded in agreement as they concentrated on their own plates. "I mean, praise-dance worthy! Screw Wheaties, this is the real breakfast of champions."

Perplexed, Noelle watched him make a big show of checking the time and programming his phone. "Thanks, guys. I'm glad you like it. Guy, what are you doing?"

He smiled innocently at her, picked his fork back up, and continued devouring the rest of his food.

Through narrowed eyes, Jack frowned critically at him. "Pippy, I swear to goodness if you set an alarm to be here in time for breakfast, it ain't happenin'."

Holt turned to Guy curiously. "Is that what you were doin'?"

"Maybe," Guy answered noncommittally, looking down at the last of his casserole with great sadness. Holt, too, looked down remorsefully at his own empty plate and empty cappuccino mug.

"Damn. Why didn't I think of that? Pick me up on your way in, okay?" He winked at Noelle who giggled at their silliness. "Do you take requests, Ms. Noelle?"

Jack shook his head in exasperation. "Y'all need Jesus in the fastest way."

"You're more than welcome to stop by the same time tomorrow." Noelle ignored Jack's scowl. With business increasing, she didn't get to cook as often as she'd like, so the more the merrier was A-Okay with her.

WHISKEY ROW WAS HER KIND of place, Noelle thought, walking back to the barbershop. Her first impression when she accepted Jack's invitation to come here was that it would be a mix of a couple of southern reality shows with no color at all, but so far, it was nothing like that. There was a melting pot of cultures. She'd encountered Ethiopian, Ghanaian, Chinese, Japanese, Spanish, Indian, and Native and African-Americans during her walk down Main Street. She also saw a lot of BMWs, Benzes, and Lexuses mixed in among the Toyotas, Nissans, and Chevys.

Noelle stopped in a men's store called Homme. Instinctively, she knew Jack would love anything she got him from there. It was all things manly, from plaid shirts and jeans to three-piece suits. There was a tobacco chew display along with cologne, survival kits with lotions and candles, and ties and suspenders artfully displayed with hunting knives. The shoes were a true lifestyle smorgasbord of Converses, mixed with lumberjack boots and dress shoes. The walls were white and covered with non-exploitive black and white pictures of nude women in tasteful poses.

She couldn't resist picking out an oatmeal-colored cardigan and two ties for Jack. She also picked up a lotion that the sales associate claimed was a best seller. At a little toy boutique called The Rabbit Hole, she bought her nieces and nephews t-shirts and toys. As she strolled back to the barbershop, Noelle heard someone call her name. Turning around, she saw Katerina, strutting down the sidewalk, in four-inch heels toward her. Trailing behind her was the security guard, Mikhail, from the guard gate. Noelle waited patiently for her to catch up.

"Hi, Kat, nice to see you again," Noelle greeted, giving her a hug. She waved at the burly guard, who inclined his head politely before standing sentry and surveying the street.

"You too, babe. How's married life going?" Kat cackled when Noelle blushed furiously. "That good huh?"

"It ain't bad," she murmured evasively. "Where are

you off to?"

"Actually, I was on my way to have lunch with my best friend Autumn." Kat pointed at the tattoo parlor. "She owns the Ink Stain. We're going to Miguel's Cantina. Care to join us?"

Noelle smiled regretfully. "I would love to, but Jack and I already have plans to go to Hooligans after he's done with his cut. He's going to help Guy and Holt with their interview process, and then we're going for a hike."

"Oh well, another time then," Kat suggested with a hopeful smile, and Noelle agreed. Katerina Romankov was a total sweetheart who reminded her a little of Avery.

"I'd love to, Kat."

They both turned toward the Ink Stain as the saloon-style doors swung open and a slender woman, wearing a short-sleeve, fitted white fitted t-shirt, frayed denim cutoffs, and black utility boots stepped out. Her curly hair was short and shaved close on the sides with longer curls on top, tumbling over one eye. It was dyed the color of a sunset and complimented her flawless, golden complexion perfectly. Behind large, round-framed clear glasses, her expressive, dark eyes shone with friendly curiosity, and her pink lips gave her an innocent expression despite the intricate tattoos visible on her arms and sides of her neck.

"Oh, good; you're right on time! Autumn, this is Noelle, my new sister-in-law, and Noelle, this is my bestie, Autumn Brady."

Both ladies exchanged friendly greetings, and Autumn whistled playfully.

"You so know hearts are breakin' all over 'The Row' now that a Sullivan brother has been taken off the market! I bet it's got Darby and Casey quakin' in their boots, knowing the women in this town must be comin' up with new strategies to reel them in."

The women chatted for a few minutes more with a promise to get together before going their separate ways. As Noelle stepped into The Gentlemen's Club, the dry friction of straight razors snapping against leather and shaving brushes sliding through soapy water as men were lathered, filled her ears. A sense of nostalgia swept over her. Instinctively, she knew this was the kind of place that her Uncle Harvey would have loved. It was old-fashioned, designed in reclaimed wood with a black and white tiled flooring. Divided into various sections, there was the main barber shop, a shaving area, a shoe-shining station, and game tables that were occupied with customers playing poker, spades, and dominoes.

She approached Jack, who was conversing with the owner, Antonio Ladeaux, a dark-skinned Adonis who bore a resemblance to a younger Idris Elba, and was just finishing him up. Noelle could tell they had an amicable relationship when they were introduced, and he slyly teased Jack about going over to the dark side. Jack just laughed, taking it in stride.

"Hey, pretty girl. Whatcha got there?"

Jack held his hand out to her. Noelle took it, curling hers around his much larger one reveling in what his touch alone could do to her. She took in the details of his haircut and facial trim. The whiskers around the lower half of his face were now cleaned up and framed his sensual lips and square jaw.

"Nothin'; just a lil sumthin', sumthin'," she teased, loving the way his eyes darkened as they traveled down her body clad in a pilot-style white jumpsuit and nude heels.

Jack smiled at his wife's radiant beauty, sliding an arm around his waist. He'd instantly been aware of her presence when she walked in, and the easy-going atmosphere inside of the shop turned predatory as the men took notice of her.

"Oh yeah? You gonna show me a lil' sumthin' sumthin' when we get home?"

He laughed quietly, loving the way her cheeks flushed, and Antonio joined in. "And on that note, my brotha, I will bid you *adieu*. Mrs. Sullivan, it was a pleasure to meet you."

"It's Noelle, and likewise. You're so bad," she whispered to Jack as they walked away.

"Don't act like you don't know, darlin'," Jack returned with a roguish grin that turned into a laugh at her open-mouthed, wide-eyed look.

CHAPTER
Twenty

*A*VERY STARED BLANKLY AT HER computer screen. She had far more important things to do than waste her time in such a manner. Yet, this was how she'd chosen to spend the last ten minutes. Avery still had to make sure her flower vendor had the product she'd requested for Tarik's party, and that it would arrive on time, or maybe go down to the venue with her checklist and ensure things were progressing smoothly. She also needed to interview the backup deejay in case Sidra couldn't spin that night. Instead, she was wondering what to wear tomorrow night for her first meeting with Pierce's mother.

Ever since she'd finally snapped and given him a piece of her mind, Pierce was falling all over himself to get back into her good graces. Every other day, Avery was the recipient of floral bouquets, baskets of exotic fruit, and courier-read sonnets. *Poems for God's sake!* He called three to four times daily, and tomorrow he was finally bringing her to meet his mother. *His mama.* In all their months of dating, Avery had inquired about meeting Pierce's parents on numerous occasions since he'd already met hers, but he'd always insisted the timing needed to be right. Apparently, her being on the verge of breaking up with him was the perfect time to meet Mother Wesley.

So, everything was going great...except for their sex life. While Avery was not one to base her relationships on what happened between the sheets, she did have needs – needs that had her overworking her B.O.B. and ordering one with more stamina and girth, which she found herself using on a more than regular basis.

The only problem with that was every time she closed her eyes and tried to imagine Pierce, a certain charming redheaded rascal, whispering all the dirty filthy things he'd yet to do to her, always popped into her mind, stimulating the best orgasms Avery had ever experienced.

The phone rang, shaking her out of her reverie, and she answered it without checking since it was probably Pierce with his *third* call of the day.

"Hello?"

She was surprised to hear a deeper voice than Pierce's on the other end. It was smooth with a southern drawl hot enough to singe the tiny hairs on the back of her neck.

"Good afternoon, Ms. Avery. It's Darby Sullivan. I didn't catch you at a bad time, did I?"

Goosebumps spread all over her body, causing her to shiver. His accent had her feeling some kind of way for sure.

"Uh..no..uh..hi," she stammered weakly, slapping her forehead with chagrin. His laugh was low and seductive, almost as if he knew she dreamed about him. "No, you weren't interrupting me, Darby. How have you been?"

"Oh, I can't complain. I was callin' to make sure that you were still comin' down to Tennessee at the end of the week? I'm gettin' all the flights coordinated so that only one trip is needed to pick everyone up in Knoxville. You gonna be able to make it?"

Avery closed her eyes as she fantasized to his drawl. It sounded exactly the same in her dreams. Especially the one where he said things like, *'Spread your legs wider.'* Or *'I'm gonna make you feel real good, Ms. Avery.'*

"Ms. Avery, are you still with me?" Darby's concerned voice startled her out of her reverie once more.

"Yes, I'm still here!" she squeaked. "I was just looking through my schedule to make sure I get everything done before Thursday. Looks like I'll be okay! How about I email you the flight details after I talk to Sidra? What's your email address?"

"It's ringoffire@gmail.com," he drawled, making her laugh knowingly. Of course, he was a Johnny Cash fan.

"I love that song! It's so genuine, and their love was the real deal," she said with a wistful sigh. "Love songs just aren't what they used to be."

"A girl after my own heart. Music nowadays just talks about what someone's gonna do to someone else when they get them alone. No heart, just the physical," Darby scoffed with such disgust that Avery laughed again. "Especially R&B! Old school stuff had you ready to wife somebody, but this new crap gives you specific details on how to cheat and not get caught."

"Exactly! Some people like music because of the beat, but I listen to the *words*. If the beat's great on top of meaningful lyrics, then it's a plus to me," she concurred.

"Amen to that. Listen, when you ladies get down here, you should come check out my bar that I co-own with a buddy of mine," Darby suggested. "After you get settled in, of course. It gets a little wild at times, but there's always a good time to be had at Hooligans."

"*Hooligans?*" Avery repeated dubiously. Although she was down to try it out, the name made her question the type of establishment he owed.

"Yep, when I was growin' up, Sister Mary McCloud used to scold me and call me a little hooligan, sayin' that if I didn't apply myself, I would never amount to anythin'," Darby informed her with great affront. Avery could picture his cocky smile as clear as day. "She's long since retired and wouldn't ya know she's my best customer? Shows up faithfully to participate in the wet t-shirt contest first Saturday of each month to a full house."

Avery exploded into full-fledged laughter, and he joined in with his booming laugh. Talking to Darby was really nice, and despite her kinky dreams, she couldn't believe how at ease she felt with him.

Before she could respond, a woman's voice could be heard screeching in the background.

"*Darby Sullivan! Bring your fine as hell, sorry ass out here, you sexy son-of-a-bitch! How dare you try to sneak back into town and not call me?!*"

Avery sat up, shaken out of her Darby daze. What the hell was she thinking?? She had someone, and apparently, he did too, and a very pissed off someone from the sounds of it.

"Well, it sounds like you need to go. I'll email you that information as soon as I discuss it with Sidra. Bye, Darby." Avery hung up before he could respond. Groaning, she crossed her arms on the desk and dropped her head on top of them.

She was a fool.

A complete and utter fool.

DARBY GLARED AT THE PHONE in his hand, barely resisting the urge to throw it at his best friend Ginger's head as she stood in the doorway of his office at Hooligans, glaring daggers at him. All fucking week, he'd been gathering up the courage to call Avery. Just the sound of her voice had big, bad ass Darby Sullivan's palms sweating. If any of his friends, or *worse*, his brothers knew, they would never let him live the shit down. Downing a shot of whiskey, he'd made the call. *And she'd answered.* The conversation was going great until the hot-headed she-devil standing before him burst in.

"Dammit, G! You've got the worst timin'! What the hell was so almighty important that it couldn't wait? I know Sara told you I didn't want to be disturbed," he sighed irritably.

Unperturbed by his sour mood, Darby's best friend since his junior year of high school, scowled right back at him. Although you'd never know it, to look at her, Ginger Tanner had grown up P.K., a preacher's kid, with a clean, shiny face, glasses, and brown hair, which was now dyed platinum blonde. Her pale skin was heavily tattooed across her shoulders and back, which she displayed with the corsets that were her wardrobe staple. She was the poster girl for 'good girl gone bad', with her full breasts on display and her ass regularly encased in either leather or skintight jeans.

Although she drove the men in town crazy with her come-hither looks, personally, she did nothing for Darby. They were just friends and had been since he beat the shit out of Lance Davis for stealing her asthma inhaler.

He'd gone to the track meet to watch Casey run the 400 relay-race. After cheering his brother on, they'd stayed to watch a couple of more races when he noticed a commotion behind the bleachers. It was the feeble voice that caught his attention, making him get up to investigate with Casey hot on his heels. It was weedy and sounded almost like a mewling kitten.

"Give it back. Please...I really need it. My chest hurts," the pitiful voice sobbed. It was followed by the jeering tone that most of the rich kids in town used. As Darby came around the corner, he saw Lance Davis standing there in his pristine varsity jacket, holding an inhaler over his head, gloating down on the red-faced girl clutching at her chest.

"Why don't you come get it? Poor baby, are you gonna to pass out? Look at you! You were the weak link on the team today, causin' my little sister to place second. My family is second to no one in this town! You hear me, girl? Nobody!"

He bent down, shaking the inhaler in her face, laughing as she tried to grab it. "Not so fast, little girl. Tomorrow, you're goin' to Coach Henderson and quittin' the team. You understand me?"

The poor thing couldn't even answer because she was wheezing so hard. Prickling with rage, Darby charged. His fist slammed into Lance's throat and he dropped the inhaler, gasping for air and grasping at his throat. Next, he sucker-punched him in the stomach, and Lance doubled over into a breathless ball of bitch fighting for oxygen. Then for good measure, Darby socked him in the balls. Lance fell to the ground in agony, desperate for air as his pain-filled face turned blue and tears poured from his eyes.

Enraged, Darby stood over him while Casey helped the girl use her inhaler. He met Darby's turbulent eyes, shaking his head in disgust at Lance. Casey knew Lance wasn't just getting it because of what he did. He knew the rich bastard was getting it for being intentionally cruel like their father.

"What's the matter, motherfucker? Havin' trouble

breathin'? I can't hear you! Get your bitch ass up and take it like a man!" Darby menaced while Lance writhed in agony. He leaned down and covered Lance's nose and mouth, making it impossible for the other boy to breathe. "Breathe, bitch! C'mon, lemme see ya breathe!"

"Please no more, Darby!" the girl begged.

Darby met her pleading gaze, noting she looked better already. With Casey's help, she managed to stand up. Her light blue eyes were huge behind her coke bottle glasses, and she barely came to his brother's shoulder. Darby didn't know who she was, but she seemed to know him.

He jerked his head at Casey, indicating that they should leave him with Lance. He made sure they were out of earshot before leaning down to get in Lance's face. The other boy immediately cowered with his hands over his head. "If you or your homies even look at her, I will come for you, you raggedy piece of shit! I will come for you every day in some way until you can't take it anymore and flee this town. Look. At. Me!"

Fearfully, Lance met his gaze, and although Darby hated saying it, he had to get his point across.

"You know who I am, bitch? I'm a Sullivan, and it's no secret in this town what we're capable of."

IT WAS LATER THAT EVENING as he and Casey were eating dinner with Alexei that the house intercom buzzed. Alexei answered and was notified that there was a Pastor Tanner there to speak to him. Casey and Darby exchanged curious glances that Alexei's shrewd gaze caught as he wiped his mouth, tossed his napkin down, and pushed his chair back.

"I will need to be making a generous donation on

your behalf to the church, da?" he addressed Darby in a dry tone. "Is there something either of you wish to tell me before I meet this man of God?"

Darby quickly shoveled food into his mouth and mumbled, "Yeah...this is some good spaghetti. Cook sure can burn in the kitchen."

Casey and Alexei rolled their eyes before leaving the room to wait for their unexpected guest. With a sigh, Darby reluctantly got up to follow. There was a knock at the door and, Alexei opened it to reveal a middle-aged white couple that Darby had never seen before. The woman was short and round with blonde hair braided in two plaits. She looked at Darby and gave him a smile that made him think of his beloved mama. The man looked older with receding brown hair. He wore glasses and a stern expression. His gaze was penetrating as he surveyed Darby before holding his hand out to Alexei.

"Good evening, Mr. Romankov. My name is Jim Tanner, and this is my wife, Nadine. I'm the new pastor over at First Methodist. We've just moved here from Rock Head, Missouri. We're sorry to disturb you during the dinner hour, but we felt it couldn't wait another day to address the urgent matter at hand."

Alexei grasped the man's hand in a firm handshake before giving his wife a gentler one. "It's a pleasure to meet you both. These are my boys, Darby and Casey. What exactly IS the issue at hand?"

The boys nodded politely, and Darby, fidgeting under the Pastor's and Alexei's astute gazes, stared at the floor.

"Well, sir, as a servant of God, I normally don't condone violence of any kind but...I'm forever in your son's debt and would appreciate it if you would accept our invitation to dinner this Sunday."

Darby's eyes flew up to meet Jim Tanner's tear-filled brown ones.

"Thank you for what you did today, son. Thank you," *the pastor expressed humbly, holding his hand out for* *Darby to shake.*

Not quite sure what to say, Darby nodded his head *and returned the man's handshake, pissed that he was* *blushing like a school girl underneath Alexei and Casey's* *proud gazes.*

———————————

"*HELLOOOO?* EARTH TO DARBY? I apologize for the rude entrance, but I've been emailin' you reminders about our crucial investors meeting all week! You know, the one that I attended in Nashville by myself two hours ago? You swore you wouldn't miss it, but you did!" Ginger pointed her finger at him. "We're partners, Sullivan. Your fuck-up is my fuck-up, and last I checked, I'm not in the business of gettin' fucked without receivin' pleasure, *partner*."

Darby winced, hoping that good Pastor Jim, may he rest in peace, wasn't looking down from Heaven, listening to his little 'Ginny' be so crude. She ignored his pained expression, continuing on with her rant.

"We've been working on this expansion deal for a long time, so I need to know that your head's in the game before we go any further."

And with that, she slammed out of his office.

Darby leaned back in his chair, staring up at the ceiling. Although he came off as a good time guy, he never fucked around when it came to business and making money. He needed to get focused, to stop wasting time thinking about a certain brown-eyed angel with killer curves and a sweet smile.

An angel who belonged to someone else.

CHAPTER
Twenty-One

"FINALLY, A MOMENT ALONE." NOELLE gave a relieved sigh; hearing Jack leave the house.

She was thankful for the solitude. This week was the best and worst of her life. It was the best because she and Jack were having fun hiking, hanging out, and decorating the house. They were instinctively on the same page in deciding what colors and furniture looked great in each room. It was the worst because the days and nights were rife with sexual tension and lustful looks between them. Her nerves were permanently stressed.

Whenever he was in the vicinity, Noelle could feel Jack's smoldering stare on her, and even the most mundane things like watching him drink from a bottle of water or painting the walls turned into some of the most erotic shit she'd ever seen. Two days ago, the sexual tension had finally boiled over. Things had been strained between them ever since.

After doing her nightly yoga routine on the back porch, Noelle went upstairs to take a shower. Miguel's "Adorn" was bumping when she walked into the master bedroom. Jack was just coming out of the bath, fresh from his own shower, wearing only a low-slung towel wrapped around his hips. Frozen at the sight of his near nakedness, Noelle could only stare at all that muscular flesh rippling as he started to apply lotion to his arms. His body was pure perfection- broad shoulders, slim waist with rock hard abs, and thick, muscular thighs and legs.

Jack was speaking but Noelle couldn't answer because she was too busy watching him lengthen beneath his white towel. Just thinking about its thickness moving so deep inside of her was making her sweat, even more, making her sticky workout clothes cling to her even more.

"Noelle? Do you mind?"

She pulled her gaze upward to focus on Jack and the bottle he was holding out to her. "I'm sorry. What were you saying?"

He raised an eyebrow at her, the corner of his lips tilting upwards. 'I know what you want,' his expression taunted. But the real question was could she be bold enough to go and get it? Instead, he repeated himself patiently. "I asked if you could please put some lotion on my back?"

Noelle stared at the bottle of lotion she'd bought for him as if it were a snake. You can do this, she told herself, wordlessly accepting the bottle. Jack turned around and she stared at the wide expanse of golden skin in front of her. Since coming to Tennessee, he'd gotten considerably darker from being outdoors, and brown freckles were starting to appear on his arms, back, and across his nose. Noelle opened the bottle, and the scent of lemon with verbena filled her nostrils.

"Mmmm, that smells really good," she murmured, squirting a generous amount into one hand then tossing the bottle onto the extra-large king bed he'd insisted on buying. Like a brother, she reminded herself as she

240

rubbed her palms together and placed them on Jack's shoulders. Briskly, she started to rub, and he tensed at her touch before giving a guttural groan of pleasure and dropping his head forward, goosebumps breaking out across his skin.

All thoughts of brotherly love vanished as she massaged the smooth liquid into his warm flesh. Her fingers trailed along Jack's skin lovingly, and she watched as the muscles flexed beneath them when she traced his tattoo. The lotion had long absorbed but still, she couldn't resist touching him while he remained silent and still. Noelle's body was aching for this man's touch, and she could tell he was just as affected when she saw his hands clenching and unclenching. His reaction made her feel bolder, and she dared to dip her fingers beneath the top of his towel, grazing his firm ass. The song faded and their jagged breathing filled the room.

"That's enough," Jack's instructed, voice low and rasping. Noelle instinctively dropped her hands, shocked at how harsh and animalistic he sounded. With his fists clenched, he stalked across the room, keeping his back to her.

"I can only take so much, Noelle. You don't have a clue how bad I want to be buried inside of you, do you? That night we slept together and our weddin' night are burned into my mind forever. How good you smelled, felt, and tasted. I need you to do one of two things: You're either gonna get naked for me, or you're gonna walk away. Pick one or the other, but you've got fifteen seconds to decide. Fourteen...thirteen..."

Jack whirled around, and Noelle was shocked at how feral he looked. She lowered her eyes to the bulge straining against the towel as the countdown continued. "Nine...six..."

She yelped as he slowly advanced, a predatory look in his eyes, and ran into the bathroom, quickly locking *the door behind her.*

"Coward," she whispered to her reflection, surprised to see how wild her own eyes looked in her flushed face.

That night, she treated herself to a frigid shower.

NOELLE WANTED TO GIVE IN. Oh, how she wanted to, but there was so much more at stake. He was playing for her body, while she was playing for keeps. When it was all said and done, if it didn't work out, she'd be the one left picking up the pieces...of her broken heart.

So, instead of giving in to temptation, Noelle threw all her sexual frustration into cooking and baking. She'd discovered a love for southern cooking and was addicted, especially to barbeque after Jack decided to order her a plate at Darby's bar, Hooligans. The ribs melted in her mouth, so meaty and tender that she devoured them in record time. Ginger sent her home with a to-go box full of ribs that she held on to protectively as if it were a pot of gold, much to Jack's amusement. Although embarrassed, Noelle practically ran to the car with her bounty, and when Jack found her in the kitchen at one in the morning licking her fingers clean of barbeque sauce, she ordered, "Don't judge."

Since then, she'd been researching cooking techniques and regional styles of the Carolinas, Texas, Memphis, and Mid-South and was currently experimenting with rub and sauce recipes. Every day, Guy, Darby, Alexei, and Holt came over to help with the house, and while the guys worked, Noelle did what she loved to do most – cook.

She made grand, hearty meals, and they all sat in

the backyard, eating under the swaying trees, listening to music, and playing card games. Every meal they ate included sweet tea and something barbequed. They were her guinea pigs and always eager to sample her new recipes. So far, quail wrapped in bacon with Dr. Pepper barbeque sauce was the most popular. They were adamantly opposed to eating the barbequed salt and vinegar pig's feet and teriyaki chitlins.

Noelle was putting the final touches on her baked salmon when she heard a car screech to a stop then doors slamming aggressively. Wiping her hands on the 'Kiss the Cook' apron tied around her waist, she walked toward the front door and opened it in time to see Avery storming towards her, dragging her hot pink roll-on luggage. She was followed by a glamorously sulking Sidra. Behind them, a classic Mustang peeled off down the driveway.

Avery, reeking of liquor, brushed past Noelle and into the house with a mumbled, "Hey girl."

With raised eyebrows, Noelle stared after her. She turned to greet her other bestie, who offered her a wan smile and slid by her as well, leaving Noelle gaping and alone by the open door.

"Well, damn."

NOELLE WALKED BACK INTO THE kitchen to find Avery, nails tapping on the granite, mad-dogging the hell out of Sidra as she leaned against the island and took a bottle of Bud Light she'd found in the fridge to the head. An unusually subdued Sidra avoided eye contact and plucked nervously at her purse strap.

Uh-oh, Noelle thought, eyeing the now empty bottle that Avery had killed in under a minute. Avery was a light drinker. More often than not, she only drank a fourth of whatever alcoholic beverage she ordered. Shit had to have really jumped off for her to down a beer like that.

"Soooo...how was the trip?" she asked brightly, walking back over to the oven to check on lunch. Silence. *Okaaaaay.* Noelle tried again. "I hope you brought your appetites because per your requests, I made my famous baked salmon with a berry salad! I told Jack we'd meet him and the boys in town for a night out after we had a chance to catch up. Sound good?"

Again, silence. She slammed her hand down on the counter. "Alright, heffas! Start talking! I'll be damned if the two of you are going to come up in my space and disrespect it!"

Avery took a deep breath and finally looked away from Sidra. She flashed Noelle an apologetic look. "I'm sorry, babe. You know I'm always happy to see you. Thank you for having us here this weekend."

She turned to Sidra, pointing a perfectly manicured index finger at her. *"But this one...I just can't... with her. Maaaaaan, listen..."* She inhaled a deep breath, eyes crossed in exasperation.

Rolling her own eyes, Sidra defiantly informed Noelle, "It wasn't that bad, I swear! Ave's totally exaggerating."

"I'm exaggerating?!" Avery's shout made the other two women jump. *"Really, Sidra?! I'm exaggerating? Did I or did I not, just spend the last three hours trapped between you and Casey as you two slaughtered each other with insults while Darby tried to play peacemaker? It's a wonder I'm not covered in blood!"*

Avery was the most mild-mannered person Noelle knew. Not one to normally lose her cool, she could be counted on to see the positive side in any situation - except for this one apparently. Sidra's only response was to bare her teeth until, in Noelle's opinion, she resembled Stitch from Disney's "Lilo & Stich". Avery retaliated with two middle fingers. *Oh boy*. For the first time, Noelle really noticed how haphazard Avery's normally impeccable appearance was.

Her thick, shiny hair was pulled to the side in a sloppy ponytail with strands sticking out all over. The collar of her fitted black and white gingham checked shirt was twisted and her full black skirt was severely creased. Noelle looked down at her feet and saw that her open toe black pumps were slightly scuffed and the polish on her big toe was chipped.

With a sympathetic look, Noelle gave Avery a hug before gently steering her toward the doorway. Speaking to her in a soothing tone, she said, "Okay, baby girl. You're no longer a witness to a potential homicide. Why don't you go wash up while I finish with lunch? Afterward, we'll head out, so I can show you guys around."

Noelle gave her a reassuring hug as another shudder wracked the shorter woman's frame.

"I think they were a serial killer couple in another life," a horrified Avery whispered to Noelle, cringing. "You should have seen the joy they took in hurling insults at each other."

She whipped her head around, glaring at Sidra. "If you even *think* of continuing where the two of you left off the next time you see him, you're going to get more of what I gave you in the car! I will be all over you like a freaking spider monkey, Sidra Jane Barton."

The threat was enough to make Sidra clutch at her ear protectively as Avery flounced out of the room, leaving both of her friends staring after her in shock.

DARBY EYED CASEY'S LOCKED JAW as they sped away from Jack's house. The way his baby brother was gripping the steering wheel made him think Casey wished it were Sidra Barton's graceful neck in his hands right about now. Darby was amazed at the change in Casey. He was unused to seeing him this *rattled* by a woman. Even when he was beating aggressive women off with a stick, the youngest Sullivan was charm personified in his rebuff, the perfect freaking gentleman at all times, except when it came to Ms. Sidra Barton.

So, it was no surprise to Darby when Casey, upon seeing Sidra this afternoon as she entered the cabin of the private jet, prickled with animosity. She promptly ignored him, reaching up to kiss Darby's cheek in greeting before mutely sliding into the seat across from Casey.

WITH HER EYES HIDDEN BEHIND oversized dark sunglasses, Sidra pulled out her laptop and proceeded to type away, appearing oblivious to the steam pouring out of Casey's ears.

Darby started to make a joke to ease the tension but immediately forgot about them when Avery Monroe entered the cabin. Just seeing her honeyed smile and radiant brown eyes made his heart pound. She was so pretty and ladylike that she made him sweat.

The goody-two-shoe ones always did, which was exactly why he stayed away from them. Sure, they looked like butter wouldn't melt in their mouth, but he knew firsthand that behind the wide eyes and fluttering lashes lurked scheming brains and hearts made of stone. So instead, Darby went for the wild-as-fuck ones who knew the score. They had a raunchy good time, and nobody was blindsided by pesky things like feelings. He'd made the goody-goody mistake once. It had been a hard lesson learned.

"Well, hey there, Ms. Avery! Aren't you a sight for sore eyes?"

Darby was fascinated by her becoming blush. In the background, he could hear a low-heated exchange escalating between Casey and Sidra.

"Hi, Darby. It's very nice to see you too. Thank you for the ride; it was very nice of you to offer."

After receiving an email from mizzmanners@hotmail.com informing him that she and Sidra couldn't get same day flights and wouldn't be in Whiskey Row until the next day, Darby asked Alexei if he could borrow his private plane.

The Russian agreed on one outrageous condition, which Darby readily accepted but still had no idea how he was going to pull off. All this just to see if what he felt the first time he'd seen the beautiful Avery Monroe was a fluke. Standing in front of her now and hungrily drinking her in, he realized it wasn't and that he was definitely up shit's creek without a paddle. He had a witty reply ready, but it was interrupted by Sidra.

"You asshole!"

Casey maturely replied with, "Takes one to know one."

From there, it was on and poppin' with Sidra and Casey flinging insults at each other the entire flight. Some were subtle, most, harshly direct. Avery tried to distract her friend, and Darby attempted to play peacemaker while the flight staff avoided crazy like it was contagious at all costs. It was only when drinks were served that Avery and Darby thought a peace treaty was possibly in the works.

Unfortunately, it wasn't to be. When Sidra stood up to put her laptop in the storage compartment, Casey muttered something, and Sidra froze before snatching her drink and whirling around. Darby, seeing her intent, lunged forward to grab the glass. He grabbed Sidra's wrist and held it high, which unfortunately led to the drink spilling out over her shoulder and directly onto Avery. For a moment, there was silence as everyone stared at her shocked face and her now liquor-stained outfit.

"Ohmygod, ohmygod…I'm so, so sorry, Avery!" Sidra babbled.

Grabbing some napkins, she attempted to wipe her friend dry. Casey got a towel and also helped. Avery just sat there in shock. Then the bickering started again.

"Are you attempting to cop a feel? Take your hands off of her, pervert!" Sidra hissed, smacking Casey's hands away.

"Me?! This would never have happened if you hadn't been acting like you have no home trainin'," Casey muttered under his breath.

Sidra sucked air viciously through her teeth. "What the hell did you just say?! You–"

Darby was done.

"The both of you shut the fuck up!!!!" he roared, and all three of them jumped at his thunderous command. "Now, let's work together to get her cleaned up! Your silence would be appreciated for the rest of the trip."

But again, it wasn't to be. The drive home was proving to be just as torturous as Casey drove the classic Mustang that he kept at the airport hangar. Sidra sat behind him in the back seat, and he took great pleasure in winding his window all the way down, which caused her to complain about her hairstyle being ruined. Then *she questioned his choice in white devil music and played Kendrick Lamar's "Bitch Don't Kill My Vibe" on her iPad. Casey retaliated by playing Kanye and Rihanna's "4, 5, Seconds".*

Through it all, Avery remained quiet, but Darby saw, in the passenger mirror, that she was on the edge of exploding when her left eyebrow started to twitch uncontrollably.

Sidra was just starting in on Casey's masculinity when all of a sudden she yelped, "Ouch! What the fuck, Avery?! That shit hurt!"

"Shut. It." Avery's ordered in a deadly voice.

Sidra opened her mouth to argue, but the only thing that came out was a high, painful squeak that reminded Darby of a puppy whose tail was stepped on. Casey was grinning gleefully until Avery's hand snaked between the front seats and gave him a pinch to the elbow, making him shout, "Holly hell, Ms. Avery! My arm feels like it's goin' numb!"

"WANNA TALK ABOUT IT?" DARBY asked conversationally, watching as Casey's knuckles turned whiter.

"No," Casey replied in a terse tone, then a moment later, "That woman is goin' to drive the crazy bus 'til the fuckin' wheels fall off!"

"Okay." Darby paused a beat. "When did you finally sleep with her?"

The car almost swerved into the next lane. "What the hell man! Who told you that?!" Casey howled. "That loudmouthed witch," he mumbled before assuming a high falsetto that Darby could only assume was supposed to be Sidra but sounded nothing like her. "'This never happened, Casey Sullivan! If you even fix your mouth to say we slept together, I will deny it, and you'll be hearin' from my lawyer!'"

Darby gave a shout of laughter, realizing what a blow to his brother's ego that must have been. "It wasn't really that hard to deduce if you knew the signs to look for. The way you guys watch each other when you think the other isn't lookin'. Or the way you guys take jabs at each other just to make the other pay attention," Darby remarked mildly. "It was bound to blow up in y'alls faces. The two of you separated are cool as shit. Together, though? I wouldn't wish you on my worst enemy. Y'all are like toddlers without naps."

"Screw you, D!"

Casey could admit to himself that today was certainly one for the books. He planned to apologize to Ms. Avery the first chance he got her away from that loud-mouthed shrew. When Sidra first entered the plane's cabin in her black leather pants and a white tee, his body hummed with pleasure at seeing her again, and he had every intention of being civil until he realized she was going to just pretend he didn't exist, turning her nose snootily in the air. Anger rising, his mind flashed to their last showdown in Vivienne's garden.

AFTER REALIZING THEY HADN'T USED a condom, Sidra shut down completely. Casey offered her the handkerchief that he never left home without. Wordlessly, she'd taken it, turning away to clean herself up, scrambling to rearrange her clothes. She was attempting to smooth down her curls when his calmly asked question gave her pause.

"Are you on the pill?"

Casey felt like his heart would jump out of his mouth at any minute. How could he have done something so irresponsible? And with 'Psychotic Sidra Barton' of all people? One minute, he was thinking about how much he disliked her, and the next, he was convinced her pussy deserved its own gold star on the Hollywood Walk of Fame.

Jerkily, she nodded her confirmation.

"Listen, Sidra, I've never had unprotected sex, and my last physical was eight weeks ago. I came back with a clean bill of health. I'll get your email from Margo and send the report to you."

Still avoiding his eyes, Sidra remained silent and attempted to walk around him. Irritated, Casey latched onto her wrist when she would have walked away altogether. Her reaction was immediate. Jerking away from him as if she'd been scorched.

"Don't ever touch me again."

The words were soaked in conviction. Casey could only surmise that she was just as shaken up about them fucking as he was. Her rejection still stung nonetheless, and he retaliated with words.

"Relax. You don't have to worry about me touchin' you again," he said coldly, shoving his fists into his trouser pockets. "What I would like is reassurance that you're clean. That you don't make a habit of fucking men you barely know in dark corners."

Crack!

His head snapped back, and the side of his face throbbed from the impact of her retaliation and the feeling she'd put into it. Fury roiled through Casey even though he knew he'd deserved it. Grabbing her by the arms, he snatched her flush against his body. Instinctively, his cock hardened again. Casey knew Sidra was aware of his reaction when her eyes widened in response. Inwardly, he cursed her, wishing that even as he fought off the urge to respond in kind, he didn't want to be deep in her voodoo pussy again. Casey saw anger mixed with fear and awareness in her lovely eyes. Sidra licked her lips nervously but defiantly held his gaze.

"I'm clean, and no, I don't randomly hook up with strangers." She pushed at him, and his arms dropped away from her. "This was a mistake, and it'll never happened! If you say that it did, I'll deny it, and then you'll be hearing from my lawyer, do you understand?"

"Like I said, you don't have to worry about me touching you...unless you put your hands on me again. Do YOU understand?" he whispered sinisterly, taking perverse pleasure in her retreat from him. "And the next time, I won't restrain myself, sweetheart."

"Yo, CASE!"

Darby snapped his fingers, pulling him out of his musing. Lips twisted bitterly, Casey snarled at his amused brother.

"Just forget it, man. I plan to."

There was a five-minute pause before Darby spoke again.

"It was really good though, huh, bro?"

Instead of replying, Casey cranked the volume up on the radio.

But even the music blasting through the speakers couldn't drown out Darby's diabolical laugh.

CHAPTER
Twenty-Two

*F*ROM NOELLE'S BACK PORCH, SIDRA sipped her glass of orange blossom iced tea, taking in the scenic view of the Smoky Mountains around her. It was so peaceful here with the birds chirping musically and the gentle breeze blowing that she was surprised at how much she liked it. A city girl, born and bred, Sidra was used to the hustle and bustle of New York with its busy energy.

In the city, you moved at such an incredibly fast pace that there was no time for regrets. But here in the country, the pace was refreshingly slower, giving one time to reflect on ...*things*. Like how a certain anal-retentive jerk managed to get under your skin and fester until you made a complete fool out of yourself and wound up on one of your dearest friend's shit list. Sidra moved to an Adirondack chair, slipping her heels off to tuck her legs under her when she sat down. It was true that she could be bold and outspoken. She wasn't one to hold back, especially when it came to her sistah-girls, work, and family. Her mother's voice rang in her ears.

"Why can't you be better, Sidra Jane? Just try

harder, and he'll come back to us okay, baby?"

It was an outlook her maternal grandmother whole-heartedly disagreed with.

"Baby, you're my little firecracker!" her Granny Evie used to tell her. *"Folks best not stand too close to you, or they gonna feel your spark! Don't let it bother you none though, chile. You sparkle and don't let anyone or anything ever dull that sparkle!"* she'd cackle. *"You don't want no one around you who can't appreciate you for who you is."*

And that's how Sidra tried to live her life – unapologetically and to the fullest. She was passionate in her relationships, believing in giving her all and expecting the same of the other person. If she wasn't getting what she was giving, then it was time to break ties. Loyalty was very important to her and violating her trust was the ultimate no-no. She always went with her gut, and that's where impulsiveness was a problem.

With work and school, going with her gut was always a success and brought Sidra great commissions and straight A's. In her personal life, however, going with her gut led to mandatory anger management classes when an ex found the balls to call her a bitch. Following her gut, Sidra stabbed the foul-mouthed motherfucker in the thigh with her letter opener. And now, this latest thing with Casey Sullivan...

If Sidra hadn't thought about it every single moment since it happened, she would never have believed that she let Casey Sullivan fuck her. Or worse, that she would have enjoyed it so much! Who knew that prissy, uptight, snooty Sullivan could fuck like a roughneck? It made her knees weak just thinking about his powerful thrusts that had her damn near climbing the sidewall of Viv's home.

"You think that you're gonna get this good shit

somewhere else?"

The memory of Casey's hot words in her ear always excited her. It was best to focus on why she didn't like him instead. She could still recall seeing him for the first time and thinking he was the finest man she'd ever seen as he commanded the conference room. Suited up with his hair slicked back, he looked like he just stepped out of a GQ magazine. His hazel eyes were bright with determination and his smile so charismatic, it took Sidra's breath away. Then he'd given her a condescending dress down in front of the 'Boys Club'. Sidra's admiration turned to dust, and she vowed to make his life hell every time she saw him. After today's fiasco, the score in humiliation was 3-0, and not in her favor.

The back door opened, and Noelle slipped out to claim the chair next to Sidra's. Ten minutes passed before she finally spoke, her eyes focused on two birds flitting from tree to tree.

"Please don't kill my husband's brother. I happen to really like him, but I *love* you, Sid. I'll always have your back. Whatever it is that makes Avery and I think we need to keep Gloria Allred on retainer, *please*... don't give in to the urges," Noelle begged.

Sidra rolled her eyes. "I'm fine, Noelle. Again, Avery was grossly exaggerating."

"So, you really didn't say that you wished Casey would step on a hundred Legos, barefooted? Lego threats are pretty dire. And the pain?" Noelle gave a mock shudder. "I've stepped on enough of my nieces' and nephews' Legos to know they're no joke."

"I was just joking! I can control myself. Honest," Sidra insisted as the suspect look in Noelle's eyes called her a liar.

Noelle snorted, "I'm fairly certain Anakin Skywalker said the same thing to Obi-Wan before he got a new name and outlook on life."

"Hey, Anakin was getting pressured left and right to be better. Sometimes, being the better person is overrated and you just need to go uber-ghetto on a mother–"

"Sid," Noelle interrupted firmly. "Listen, I appreciate the dedication you have to your particular brand of crazy, but I'm seriously going to have to ask you to dial it back four hundred notches. Right now, our calm, sweet Avery is upstairs half-drunk off a single bottle of beer! A beer that she needed to down after spending time in the presence of you and Casey. This is supposed to be a *relaxing* weekend. I've got my girls with me, and I just want to enjoy our time together."

"Okay, fine. I give you my word that I will not start any trouble with him," Sidra grouched. "Let's change the subject."

"Thank you, boo," Noelle said sweetly, blowing her a kiss.

"Uh-huh. Now, let's talk about how the honeymoon is going. Have you guys christened every room in this gorgeous house yet? Ewww! On second thought, please say you refrained from doing it in the guest bedroom," Sidra pleaded.

"We haven't actually consummated the marriage," Noelle announced glumly, ignoring Sidra's startled look.

"Damn, girl! What the hell are you waiting on? World Peace? The weapons of mass destruction to be found? If I had a husband who looked at me the way Jack looks at you and puts it down like you say he does, I would never leave the house, much less my bed!" she exclaimed incredulously.

"It's not that I don't want to, Sidra. Believe me, I'm *dying* too. It's just I'm already in too deep, and we're just pretending! I knew the very first time I saw Jack four years ago, that I loved him. The spark was there for me, but he's always been a perfect gentleman who never showed any interest.

He's a good guy who's willing to sacrifice a little of his time and freedom right now so that he doesn't have to work harder later if the shit hits the fan and my dirty secret became public. Why not get some free ass while doing it? He'd be killing two birds with one stone, that's for sure. I just don't want to be the same fool twice, you know? Remy came off as a good guy too and look where that got me," Noelle finished bitterly.

"Noelle, are you *crazy*? I've seen the way Jack is around you! That kind of shit can't be faked," Sidra argued heatedly. "Do you know how many women are dying to be in your position? Or how many interns Margo has replaced because their attention was focused solely on him and not work?" she disputed. "So, Remy was a piece of shit! Do you think he'll be the only one you'll ever come across? If you're worried about something like that, then you're in for a long, lonely life. Stop being such a coward and go for it already!"

"I'm not a coward," Noelle retorted, eyes snapping with irritation. "You don't understand what's at stake, so let's agree to disagree."

"I call bullshit! You are a coward. Up until six months ago, you've spent your life living up to other people's standards. When you decided that you finally had enough of their crap, you made shit happen. Now, look at you. You've got your own place. You're co-owner of a growing business, and you're married to your dream guy! It doesn't matter *how*; you just *are*!" Sidra exclaimed, and Noelle conceded her points reluctantly.

"Now, here the two of you are living alone in this

big beautiful house, and instead of taking every opportunity to enjoy your time with Jack the way you really want to, you're hiding! And for what? Because you're scared the feelings won't be reciprocated? When you look back on your life at these moments, do you really want to say that it was a good thing you played it safe and kept yourself from the man you love? Or that you loved every single second of being with him completely?"

Sidra stood up then gently pulled Noelle up also.

"I may be crazy, but at least I give it my all," she joked, giving Noelle a bear hug. "Don't let that bastard Remy steal all the joy and love that you have to give. Go get your man, girl."

Sidra was absolutely right, Noelle thought, returning the hug.

It was time to get her man.

TAKING A HEALTHY SWIG OF his beer, Jack leaned across Casey to swipe an onion ring from the basket of appetizers in the center of the table. They were sitting at the honorary 'Fab Five' table in Hooligans along with Guy, Darby, and Holt, watching the Boston Red Sox and New York Yankees series. It was nice hanging with the fellas after being gone so long. The afternoon was spent working at the shop, and it felt good to use his hands and work with wood again. Guy wasn't kidding when he said they were getting busy, so Jack quickly dove in to assist with the piling orders. Although his degree was in business, it was woodworking that kept him sane after his Ma was gone, and he loved it.

Americana Traditions was his baby. Jack was a

designer along with Guy, who was also a skilled cabinetmaker and did all the fine and detailed work, specializing in making cabinets from wood as well as wardrobes, dressers, chests and other furniture designed for storage. Holt, like his father before him, was a master carpenter. After graduating from high school, he went to Germany to follow in the family tradition of obtaining his master certification in carpentry. He could make just about anything with wood. On his twenty-second birthday when he came back from Germany, his father graced him with a deed to some land, and Holt bought some wood and built his log cabin.

The last member of their team was one of the most talented, finished carpenters in the country, and they had been lucky to get him. His name was Quaid McKay, and his specialty was cabinetry, furniture making, fine woodworking, model building, and musical instrument making. Scottish and a bit of a daredevil, Quaid roared into town three years ago on his monster Harley and offered up his services, which they quickly accepted. He wasn't as quiet as Holt nor was he as outgoing as Guy, but somewhere in between. Unfortunately, he only worked when he wanted to, almost as if it was an outlet.

Jack suspected he was running from his own demons because he never spoke about his personal life. As far as he was concerned, since Quaid passed both his background check and psych test with flying colors, Jack couldn't care less what the man did as long as he maintained his perfect work ethic.

It was early Saturday evening, and the pub was packed. Lots of folks had stopped by the table to say 'hey', making Jack think that he shouldn't stay away so long. He tapped his foot in time to the country music playing from the jukebox in the corner, waiting impatiently for Noelle and her girls to join them. He'd received a text from her saying they were on their way ten minutes ago.

"Hey, Jackie! Heard you were back in town," a female voice cooed in his ear.

He glanced sideways to see Kara Ann Winter standing next to his chair, looking as if her jeans and tank were spray painted onto her surgically-enhanced form. Her long, blonde hair fell in waves underneath a pink cowboy hat, and he could see that her brown eyes were wolfing him up. At one time, she'd been his high school girlfriend. They'd dated for three months before Jack discovered she created t-shirts that said "Mrs. Sullivan" on the back and told everyone how she was going to have his babies. Jack couldn't break up with her fast enough.

"Kara Ann, how are you?" Jack kept it cordial but didn't attempt to hug her, lest he give her the wrong idea.

"Well, don't just sit there! Gimme a hug!" she pouted, holding out her arms. "I haven't seen you in ages! Maybe we can slip away and... catch up. I can do that one little thing you used to like. You know... make it a proper homecoming," Kara Ann suggested licking her lips.

Jack could see that she'd even had those done. *They looked like someone punched her in the mouth,* he thought distastefully. Immediately, Noelle's plush lips popped into his head. There was nothing in the world that compared to the feel of his woman's all-natural lips.

"I'm afraid that I have to decline your thoughtful offer. I'm a married man now, and my wife wouldn't like me spreadin' my affections around," Jack discouraged her mildly. He waved his ring finger in her face, feeling the usual wealth of satisfaction run through him at being able to say that. Besides, any girl could give a blow job. He was with a woman who beyond blew his damn mind.

Kara Ann's face turned an unbecoming shade of red. "Well, that right there tells me you went and married a damn yank, didn't ya? Southern women are a lot friendlier and would never deny a man a little hospitality. I'm sure you're really enjoying your highfalutin' Yankee, Mr. Hot Shit," she snarked.

"Tell you what, Kara Ann. You'd best run along before my wife shows up. I reckon you'll be in a world of hurt if she hears you runnin' your mouth. She doesn't take too kindly to shit talkers," Jack coolly advised, snatching a buffalo wing and dipping it into the ranch dressing. The other men tried to stifle their chuckles when she left in a huff. The table broke out in laughter, and Jack scoffed in disbelief. *As if he'd go for someone other than his Noelle.*

"So, where *is* your hot wife, Sullivan?" Guy asked, chuckling at Jack's dark look. "What? I can't pay your wife a compliment? Relax man, yeesh."

"No, you can't," Jack answered seriously. "And I'm gonna whup your ass if you 'compliment' her again."

"Do you even hear how *insane* you sound? Damn, man, the next round is on you." Guy pointed at the empty plates on the table. "You damn near ate all the appetizers by yourself."

Jack was surprised to see that the generous portions of wings, onion rings, and mozzarella sticks were just about gone. He didn't recall eating that much, but he supposed it had to do with having Noelle on his brain since the night she'd touched him. Just remembering how her soft hands felt gliding over his flesh was enough to make him shift subtly to avoid the discomfort in his groin.

One touch and he was a goner. He'd wanted to peel

away her workout clothes, which were driving him nuts the way the fabric clung to every curve of her body, and have his way with her. Judging from the way her breathing had changed and how dilated her pupils got, she was just as aroused as him. Jack knew it would have taken minimal effort to take control of the situation and give them both what they wanted. No, *needed*, so desperately, but he wasn't that big of a bastard to do so and have her thinking he couldn't keep his word.

Although the house was fully furnished, by silent mutual agreement, they continued to share a bed. Every night, they went to bed with a respectable distance between them in the huge California King, and every morning, they woke up with Noelle in Jack's arms and his hardness grinding into her bottom. It was the most exquisite agony he'd ever experienced. It was all he could do not to slide down between her legs and put his mouth on her hot spot, to hear her moans of excitement, egging him on as he pleasured her to his heart's content then fucked her deeper into the mattress.

No, Noelle had to come to him. The sooner the better so they could both be put out of their misery. Jack knew it wasn't easy for her because she had trust and confidence issues, but hopefully, he could help her to overcome those fears. Away from all the bullshit in the city, she was a lot more carefree and appeared to be enjoying herself here in 'The Row'. He would definitely have to arrange for them to make more trips here.

"Everythin' okay, Jack?"

Out of all of them, Holt was the most reserved, content to chill and listen. He was also the most perceptive. After their Ma died, Holt would come over and just sit with them for hours on end. He'd bring pocket knives from his uncle's bait shop, and they'd just sit quietly whittling on wood Ian provided, not saying a damn thing. It was what helped Jack get through the first three months after Ma died until Vivienne took them to see the shrink in D.C.

"Yeah, just thinkin' about some stuff I need to rearrange when I get back to New York so that I'm able to spend more time here. The way things are movin' with all the projects we got goin' on, I figure it'd be best for me to start pulling more of my weight around here."

"You're actually gonna divide your time between here and New York? What does the gorgeous Mrs. Sullivan have to say about commutin'?" Guy wondered, deliberately ignoring Jack's dark look of warning.

"Yeah, Jack. What does Noelle have to say about it?" Casey was intently aware that there was something going on in his brother's marriage that the couple wasn't disclosing. Darby, who was busily shoving chili cheese fries into his mouth, also looked up with a raised eyebrow.

Jack narrowed his eyes and threw a French fry at Casey, which he neatly avoided. The sound of loud heels clicking on the wooden flooring shifted their attention to the approaching newcomer who stopped next to their table, plucked a fry out of the basket, and popped it between her cherry-red lips.

"Mmmm, don't mind if I do," Kat smirked, surveying the table.

"Hey, get your own," Casey mock-scowled and Kat stuck her tongue out at him then leaned down to give him a quick kiss on the cheek, leaving a red lipstick stain behind. She ruffled Darby's hair affectionately and winked at Guy who winked back at her. Holt gave her a measured stare that made her blush to her roots and she quickly looked away to address her brothers from another mother with a narrow-eyed stare.

"Is this how brothers are supposed to treat their *only* sister? Leave her to hang out all by her lonesome on a Saturday night?" Kat pouted, and Guy leered at her.

"Well, I don't have any sisters, so I wouldn't know about treating one badly, Kat. But what I *do* have is vast knowledge of what women like, if you're interested," he generously offered with a salacious grin.

Kat rolled her eyes at him, while in unison, every male at the table turned to look at him with the same unblinking stare.

"Whaaaaat?" Guy was innocence personified. "I said *if* she was interested; clearly, she's not interested."

"Stop flirtin' with her," Casey ordered. "Not unless you want us to make you cry again, Pippy. Besides, what all do you know about women, lyin' ass? You'd call an alligator a lizard all day."

Darby frowned censoriously at her. "Why the hell is your skirt so *short*, Kat? Does Lex know you're runnin' around paradin' your hoo-ha? Go grab a damn apron from Ginger and put it on."

Kat shot him a dirty look. "You didn't object when Gabby Ferris was sitting on your lap last week at the Founders Day Parade with a skirt at least two inches shorter than this one, *and* it was paired with a shirt sheer enough to show her religion, Darby Liam Sullivan!" she snorted softly. "And did you really just say *hoo-ha*? No surprise you're still single if you're calling it that. It is a vagina. *Va-giii-naaa.* Or va-jay-jay. My personal favorite is kitty–"

Collectively, the guys groaned and covered their ears except for Holt, who gave her a blistering look that practically set her on fire. Ever since Kat bumped into him two months ago at the gas station, there'd been something brewing between them, something that compelled her every time he was in the vicinity to seek him out, only to find his gaze already on her. This *thing* filled her with a certain kind of feeling. It was the feeling you got as you slowly chugged up a roller coast track, knowing there's a thousand-foot drop on the other side. The kind of feeling that left you exhilarated and drained. Of hating and loving it all at the same time as you were swept away by the force of it.

Indecisively, Kat bit her lip. She had no idea how to even proceed when Holt had yet to verbally acknowledge *it*. Kat glanced toward the door and spied her dear friend James Leighton walking through it. He was Autumn's cousin and was in town to pick up the ring he planned to propose to his girlfriend with. She gave an enthusiastic wave, motioning him over. The men all glanced toward the door to see a medium height, well-dressed black man heading their way.

"Who the fuck is that?" Jack's eyes never left the newcomer. "He looks like a damn gigolo."

The others murmured their agreement, and from the corner of her eye, Kat saw Holt's hand clench around his beer bottle and an idea came to her. She needed to distance herself from Holt because she had a feeling that if she didn't, nothing good would come of it, and James would be the one to help her do it.

Kat strove for being blasé. "Y'all don't know him. He's not from around here. We went to school together."

James was now at their table and confused by her beseeching expression as she reached up and planted a lingering kiss on his smooth cheek. Rapidly, she whispered, *"Please play along!"*

He squeezed her waist to let her know he would and gave them all a Colgate white smile that wasn't reciprocated. He pressed a kiss to Kat's curls, hissing, "You owe me!"

A communal growl from the seated men made

him nervously straighten up.

"Hush, all of you!" Kat scolded. "James, these are my brothers, Jack, Casey, and Darby. Those two are my honorary brothers, Guy and Holt..." she finished softly, meeting Holt's dispassionate stare.

Perhaps, this wasn't such a great idea.

"Hi, fellas; nice to meet you!" James' enthusiasm did not override their displeasure made known by their unsmiling faces. "Kat says the nicest things about you guys. I uh...feel like I already know you all already."

Kat winced, shaking her head slightly, and James damn near swallowed his Adam's apple when the temperature at the table dropped a hundred degrees below zero.

"Fuck what *you* heard. *We* haven't heard shit about you," Jack coldly informed him.

James looked ill as he nervously tugged at his collar. Kat grabbed his hand and pulled it down to intertwine their fingers, holding on tight when he tried to yank away. Holt's gaze lowered, remaining on their locked fingers, and this time, it was Kat who had the urge to pull away.

"If you knew us then you'd know that we despise ass-kissin'," Casey chimed in brusquely.

"You ain't from around here, is ya?" Guy challenged belligerently, pulling a long, wicked-looking knife from underneath the table and placing it on the table next to his drink. The blade gleamed evilly underneath the ceiling lights.

"No...no...sir!" James squeaked, eyes riveted on the knife. Kat wanted to roll her eyes as she felt his hand go clammy in hers. *Ewww.*

"It is my people's belief that if a man is serious about takin' a woman out, then he has to play five-finger roulette for every brother she has. This game is called *'Osiyo'*. To refuse would bring dishonor to the woman as if to say she is unworthy," Guy explained menacingly, giving James a fierce glance that called forth his Native American warrior ancestors. "You ready to play, boy?"

"Ummm, you know Kat, perhaps this wasn't the best idea." Looking at the knife in horror and then the hardened faces around the table, James snatched his hand back. Kat stomped her tiny foot in frustration.

"Cut it out, all of you!" she yelled, causing other patrons to look their way. "Tell him you're not serious!"

Stoic glances met her livid one as the men ignored her, continuing to silently intimidate James. Finally, Holt stood up, and seeing his full height, James took a step back, reached into his jacket, and took two puffs of the inhaler.

"Leave him," Holt's voice simmered with anger. Grabbing his beer, he headed toward the bar, leaving the friends to stare after him in puzzlement, missing Kat's remorseful look as she, too, watched him walk away.

Mission accomplished. But instead of feeling relieved that she'd caused a rift in their unspoken game, why did she feel like shit?

Darby turned back to James. "The Smoky Mountains ain't no joke. It's beautiful but deadly. A man could get lost or die tryin' to find a way outta here. You even think about puttin' your hands on her, and they'll never find your body, ya hear?"

James blanched at his ominous tone. "Yes...s-s-sir."

Kat sucked her teeth at the group and pulled him away. "All y'all need to quit! Let's go, babe."

The group of men waited until they couldn't see the couple in the crowd of people before speaking.

"Isn't *Osiyo* 'how are you' in Cherokee?" Jack asked Guy mildly. "That's the best you got?"

"I was improvisin', man," Guy said defensively.

"Besides, I don't see anybody else at this table that's able to lay claim to a bad ass tribe of people! And would somebody please get this knife away from me? Holt asked me to hold it because my jacket has large pockets, but you know how I feel about knives."

Shuddering, he gingerly pushed the knife toward Casey, who rolled his eyes.

"You're such a big baby! Well, I'm pretty sure we put the fear of God in him, and he'll think twice about puttin' his hands anywhere they're not supposed to be. Besides, thanks to Vivienne, Kat is pretty up there in Krav Maga. She could probably rip his spine out with her dainty little hands," Casey mused, grabbing his beer, bottle poised near his lips he paused. "Holy hell!"

All the men turned towards the door as the noise died down in Hooligans, and everyone turned to watch the trio of black goddesses standing in the doorway, all uniquely different but equally beautiful.

CHAPTER
Twenty-Three

G UY'S WOLF WHISTLE WAS LONG and lusty.

"*Goodness gracious!* I call dibs on either one that's not Mrs. Sullivan!"

Simultaneously, Darby and Casey growled, "She's unavailable."

"*Oh, come on! None are available? Is this true, Jack? Jack?*" Guy whined, valiantly trying to get his friend's attention but getting nowhere.

Jack tried to appear nonchalant, but his attention was held by the second tallest of the trio, wearing a black mini tank dress that clung to her curves and showed a lot of her silky skin. Black gladiator stilettos with gold and silver jewelry completed her look. Her hair was styled in a long braid over one shoulder, and she wore one of those chain headbands that took her already exotic look to another level of mystery.

Noelle searched the bar until she saw Jack and smiled, causing his heart to slam painfully against his ribs. This wasn't her normal sweet smile. It was just as beautiful but filled with seduction and a promise of carnal delights to come. A glance around the bar showed that the women were the center of attention, and the admiring looks Noelle drew stirred jealousy in the pit of his stomach that was quickly spreading. He wasn't sure how it happened, but suddenly, he was on his feet and in front of her, hands cupping her face and laying claim to her silken mouth in front of everyone, leaving no doubt of exactly whom she belonged to.

———————————————

NOELLE CLOSED HER EYES, MELTING under the dizzying onslaught of Jack's territorial kiss. She wrapped her hands around his wrists and returned the kiss with fervor, loving the way his tongue stroked hers and devouring the taste that was uniquely him. On and on it went and she wished they could stay locked like this forever. Eventually, people started clapping and whooping. Only when someone yelled 'Get a room!' and the whole bar erupted in laughter did they separate. She opened her eyes drowsily returning Jack's smile.

"Hey."

"Hey yourself, pretty girl," Jack returned huskily, dropping his forehead to touch hers, his eyes traveling all over her face as if trying to memorize it.

"Something tells me we should make other sleeping arrangements for the night," Avery murmured, fanning herself. *If only Pierce would look at me like that*, she thought, hit directly in her chest by a pang of jealousy watching Noelle and Jack staring at each other like no else in the bar existed. Instead, Pierce looked at her as if she was a 'weighty' burden that he had to deal with, especially when it came to being affectionate. Avery couldn't understand why their relationship was so screwed up.

Pierce and Avery should have been the perfect

couple. Both were twenty-five years old. She attended Spellman College while he went to the neighboring Morehouse, two historically black universities. They liked the preppy modern look and had the same taste in music and wine. According to a palm reader she visited occasionally, a powerhouse match to her Aquarius sign was his Leo.

So, why wasn't it working?

"I think you may be right," Sidra saw Darby from across the room, gesturing toward the empty seats at his head table. "Come on, let's leave the lovebirds alone and go mingle."

Noelle watched them walk away before turning back to Jack. He was still watching her, with that hungry man look in his eye. She glanced around, taking in the rustic decor, big screen televisions, and huge electronic bull in the corner.

"Wow, do people really ride that?"

"Who? Shanna? Occasionally, some poor soul will try it. Mostly it's cowboys who think they have somethin' to prove. Nobody's been able to stay on it for more than fifteen seconds, though," he said, sliding his hand down to curl his fingers around hers.

Noelle spied the empty dance floor and jukebox. "Come on; let's dance."

Jack handed her some quarters, standing to the side as she put the change in and selected a song. Noelle led him to the dance floor, he wrapped his arms around her and they moved to the slow beat of "Fire" by the Pointer Sisters as catcalls and wolf whistles ensued.

I'm ridin' in your car, you turn on the radio
You're pullin' me close, I just say no
I say I don't like it, but you know I'm a liar
'Cause when we kiss, ooh, fire

Late at night, you're takin' me home
You say you wanna stay, I say I wanna be alone
I say I don't love you, but you know I'm a liar
'Cause when we kiss, ooh, fire

Noelle plastered herself to him, and Jack buried his face in her neck, as she swayed seductively singing the lyrics into his ear.

You had a hold on me right from the start
A grip so tight I couldn't tear it apart
My nerves all jumpin', actin' like a fool
Well, your kisses they burn, but my heart stays cool...

Her tongue traced his ear, and her fingers gently raked through the hairs at the base of his neck, causing him to let out a low groan. "Noelle, don't tease me. Darlin', I really don't think I can take any more cold showers. I want you so bad, and I'm all outta control," he whispered starkly. The unadulterated lust and need she heard, primed Noelle's body. He clasped her hand in his, keeping the other on her waist and spun her around before drawing her back in.

"In my arms. My Bed. Anywhere and any way I can get you. I want to hear your cries of passion filling my ears as I make you cum over and over again. Say yes, baby. Think about how good it is between us," Jack crooned, his lips trailing down her neck to her shoulder blade. She gave a deep, wanton moan that almost made him explode on the spot. He was at his wit's end and beyond caring that he sounded like he was begging.

Noelle felt like she couldn't think much less breathe. She was so consumed by Jack. His lips left a trail of fire on her skin while his whiskers brushed erotically against her over-sensitized skin. "Jack?"

"Hmmm?" he murmured and bit gently on her earlobe. Her moan was a little louder, causing Jack to turn his head and silence her lips with his own. His hand slid down to palm her ass while he skillfully explored the recesses of her mouth.

"Jack," she tore her mouth away from his, panting harshly as their eyes met and held.

"Talk fast, darlin'," he urged, kissing the corner of her mouth.

The fall looked so freaking far, predicting a devastating blow if shit didn't pan out.

"Baby? What do you need?" Jack breathed against her lips. "I got you, baby. I promise I won't ever let you fall."

Noelle took a deep breath and leaped, eyes wide open.

"You, Jack. I need you."

ACROSS THE ROOM, THE GROUP watched in rapt fascination.

"I think he's gonna fuck her on the dance floor in front of everybody," Guy speculated.

"They're causin' quite the scene. Someone should tell them to get a room," Casey suggested.

"Someone should," Darby agreed.

They all looked at each other before mutually agreeing, *"Nah."*

Sidra, nibbling on a cheese stick, nudged Avery. "Let's definitely get a hotel room. There are some things you just don't want to know about your boss and BFF."

"We'll be fine. Sex is so overrated. Besides, how

long could it last?" Avery mumbled, eyes still enviously on Jack and Noelle.

Silence filled the table, and she realized that she'd wondered that last part aloud and was now the focus of the group's attention. Their looks ranged from amusement and disbelief to pity and incredulity.

Defensively she demanded, "What?"

"Darlin', that man is a country boy from 'The Row'. We aim to please, go the distance, and don't disappoint," Darby explained as if she were a wayward child.

Avery blushed vividly while the guys chuckled knowingly and clinked their beers together. Sidra grunted but found her eyes inexplicably drawn across the table to Casey, who returned her stare. A vivid memory of him deep inside of her came to mind. As if reading her mind, his hazel eyes darkened to burnished gold, and Sidra squirmed under his intense scrutiny. Yes, sparks were still flying between them, but as long as they weren't knives, she would do her best to behave.

Sidra looked away, raising her glass and finishing off her amaretto sour. Turning her head, she found Avery gaping at Darby in wonder, his words finally hitting rock bottom to her. Her poor friend had obviously never been the recipient of great pipe-laying and never would as long as she kept herself tied to that stick-in-the-mud otherwise known as Pierce. Well, not this weekend. Sidra would be damned if she let Miss Prissy sit around feeling sorry for herself. She managed to catch Darby's eye and jerked her head toward the dance floor. He flashed a smile of understanding.

"Ms. Avery, have you ever done any line dancin'?" he asked smoothly and immediately Avery looked intrigued.

"I can't say that I have. It does sound like fun, though," she mused, tapping her foot in time to the music.

"Oh, it is, and you're about to find out just how fun," Darby announced with a crafty expression.

He rose, clapping his hands and whistling to draw attention to himself. Everyone stopped what they were doing, and Ginger turned off the flat screens.

"Everybody!!! I need your attention, please! Do y'all know what today is?"

The crowd looked at each other curiously then chorused, "NO!"

"Today is......the first time my brothers and I have been back home at the same time in over five fuckin' years!!" he shouted, throwing a fist in the air. On cue, the room exploded with cheers, foot-stomping, hooting, and whistling.

"Now, you can understand why it's pretty special to me. Not just because my brothers are with me but because I also get to introduce y'all to my beautiful sister-in-law Noelle, who Jack has been monopolizin' by suckin' on her face since she walked in the door!"

Laughter broke out as Jack mouthed "fuck you" to him and an embarrassed Noelle shyly waved as people started shouting congratulations to them. Darby raised his hand, and the crowd fell silent again, waiting for his next announcement.

"Now, Noelle didn't come alone, folks. Please give a warm welcome to her dearest friends, which automatically make them an extension of *my* family. Ms. Sidra and Ms. Avery, come on up here!" he bellowed, motioning to them.

As the ladies approached, Darby took a moment to admire how pretty Avery looked in a white, off-shoulder, ruffled eyelet top that showed off her sexy décolletage. Her full denim skirt, with a tan belt encircling her waist, hit modestly above her knees and swayed with each step she took.

The modest outfit only emphasized her bountiful breasts and generously curved hips, which left little to the imagination about how she would look naked. Darby groaned inwardly as she gave him that sweet, shy smile, noticing how other men in the bar were also checking the two ladies out.

"Hey, y'all, Ms. Avery just let me in on a little secret," Darby confided wickedly. "Now, normally I don't kiss and tell..." Loud raucous laughter filled the room, and he gave a look of mock hurt. "A gentleman *never* tells. Anyhoo, she told me that she has NEVER...EVER...in her ENTIRE life...participated in a country dance! I figured that we'd help her cross that off her to-do list. I want everybody who ain't got two left feet to join me on the dance floor, so we can set this shit off right!!!"

The cheering crowd complied and moved to the dance floor. Darby eyed Fyodor, one of Alexei's guards, moving toward Avery, and he maneuvered her closer to him, ignoring her startled look and staked his claim. For a moment, Darby thought the Russian would challenge him as his gaze traveled lustfully over Avery. Darby could understand his reluctance to concede defeat because she was certainly a catch that any man would be lucky to have in his arms.

He held Fyodor's challenging gaze, silently conveying that he would not walk away unscathed if he turned his thoughts into actions. The coconut smell of Avery's hair lured him in, and the feel of her breasts against his side burned through his shirt as Darby waited for the other man to concede defeat. Finally, with a grimace, the bodyguard turned away.

A triumphant Darby caught Ginger's shrewd look but looked the other way, avoiding the questions he saw there that couldn't be answered at this time. He didn't really know what he was doing, but what he did know was that he couldn't stand the glimpses of sadness in Avery's eyes any longer. He planned to do everything in his power to make them go away.

"Alright now! How about we start off with a little bit of line dancin'? Ginger, baby, gimme somethin' funky!" Darby shouted as the men and women lined up in separate rows to face each other.

The Kongo's "Come With Me Now" came on and feet tapped in time to the rhythm.

"Try to keep up with me if you can, sugar," Darby dared, giving her his signature shit-eating grin, and Avery tossed her hair over her shoulder with a smile. You couldn't help but have a good time with Darby. His larger-than-life personality was contagious. He was the life of the party wherever he went.

"I don't think so, slick. Let a city girl show you how we get down."

Avery immediately caught on to the twists and turns. It was very similar to the electric slide. Darby was a great dancer, and although no one else was really touching, he kept his large hand on her waist almost the entire time. Avery saw Jack and Noelle dancing together, as well as Sidra and Guy.

Casey was dancing with a tiny honey-skinned beauty, and Holt was dancing with a platinum-haired woman whom Avery was surprised to find staring daggers at her. *Why would she be looking at her like that?* She was pretty sure that she hadn't done anything to offend anyone in the forty-five minutes they'd been there.

"Drinks are on the house for the rest of the night!!" Darby shouted to an enthused crowd. "As long as you have a designated driver! Keys will be confiscated at the door if you don't! Enjoy!"

CHAPTER
Twenty-Four

T HE SEXUAL TENSION IN THE truck was palpable. Noelle felt like she couldn't breathe without inhaling Jack's lust. He was staring straight ahead, his face a rigid mask of concentration as he drove. Shortly after Darby's free drink announcement, Jack grabbed Noelle's hand and headed toward his middle brother.

"Make sure the girls get home safe, please."

"Aye, aye, Captain."

At Darby's perceptive look, Noelle buried her hot face in Jack's tense back. Before she could respond, Jack was pushing her out the door and into the Range. The anticipation of being intimate with him again was killing her. Nervously, she wiped her hands on her dress. Jack jerked his head away from the road to watch as the black fabric slipped a little higher, exposing more of her thighs. *Jesus.* He pressed down on the gas pedal a little harder as his cock threatened to burst through his jeans.

Noelle gasped as the vehicle shot forward under the sudden burst of speed. Jack's hands were wrapped around the wheel in a stranglehold, his face a mask of taut desperation. "I'm sorry and I apologize if I come off as sounding like a douche, but I need to get you home," he said harshly. "Watching you shake that sexy ass in that next-to-nothin' dress has been driving me crazy all night."

Noelle smiled, heady with her God-given power of womanhood. "Oh, you mean this old thing?" she teased, pulling the dress higher on her lap to expose her black panties.

Jack's eyes were riveted on her flesh, beads of sweat formed on his brow as he gave an appreciative whistle. "You're playin' with fire for sure, baby."

She laughed seductively. "I must be because it's awfully hot in here. Maybe I should cool off?"

The spaghetti straps slid off of her shoulders to reveal the tops of her enticing breasts, bathed in the moonlight. Noelle tilted her seat, so she was half reclining. "Mmmm, that's much better."

Her hand drifted across to his lap, and Jack jerked in response. "Baby, don't play with me. I already feel guilty enough about how deep I'm gonna be in that ass," he growled. "There ain't enough yoga and pilates exercisin' in the world to make you limber enough for what I plan on doin' tonight," he vowed, eyes glowing with sinful intentions.

"Oooh, Jack! You just made me ruin my panties. Guess I'll just have to take them off." Feeling daring, she wiggled out of her panties, twirling them around her finger, releasing her fragrance into their confined space just as they turned onto the private road leading to the house.

Jack stopped the truck, turned off the ignition, and pushed his seat back. "Get your sexy ass over here now, Noelle!"

Pussy clenching in response to his demand, Noelle threw the soaked garment to the floor, scrambled across to his seat as he quickly unbuckled his pants and pulled his jeans and boxers down to his knees, revealing his rigid erection standing straight up and glazed in his excitement. She straddled his lap, sliding her arms around his neck as he grabbed her around the waist to hold her in place. Jack yanked her head down and claimed her lips in a thoroughly dominating kiss that let her know she might be on top, but he was going to be running shit. He bit her lip and sucked away the sting. His hands untangled her braid and shoved into her thick strands, holding her face steady. Against her lips, he murmured, "I can smell you, baby. *Mmmm...*Your sweet, creamy goodness all over my dick."

Noelle whimpered her eagerness, more of her essence coating his swollen shaft. Every time the broad head bumped against her clit, it sent jolts of ecstasy coursing through her body.

"Who makes you this wet?" he whispered as she sucked his neck, yanking at his tee shirt, pulling it over his head.

Noelle trembled as he let go of her hair to reach between them to insert the tip of his dick in then pull out, beating it against her tender clit. Jack yanked her dress and bra down with his other hand, drawing a succulent nipple into his mouth. He sucked hard then switched to slow lazy circles around it with his tongue before treating her other nipple to the same decadent pleasure. Noelle fell back against the steering wheel, clutching his head to her bosom. Her hips lifted in rhythm to his teasing

"Answer me, dammit!"

"You, Jack. Only you!" Noelle was spiraling out of control and loving it. *"Please, don't make me wait any longer."*

"Spread your thighs wider, sugar," he urged, feeling like he was going to come any second as he fed her inch by controlled inch of his dick. Sweet mercy, nothing in this world was as good as Noelle's pussy. *So hot, tight, and juicy.* Jack willed himself to think of the time he saw old man Abner's wilted, veiny balls when he accidentally swam under him at the community center. He remembered coming to the surface and throwing up in the pool, which resulted in the pool closing for the rest of the day. All the kids in town had been upset with him. The image yielded the desired effect, and Jack was able to calm himself somewhat.

Noelle absorbed the fullness that she was impaled upon, tentatively moving up and down, rotating her hips and enjoying the sensations just as much as the expression of pure bliss on her man's face as his eyes drifted closed. She grabbed Jack's face and rained kisses all over it before settling on his lips. He gripped the backs of her thighs, fingers digging into her ass and moved her faster on top of him. Their breathing was ragged, their kisses, hot and sloppy, and the windows were fogged up despite the cool mountain air. Jack tugged the nape of her neck back, running his tongue along the column of her throat while his other hand dipped between her ass cheeks, fingers teasing her forbidden hole.

"Ride your dick," he encouraged his wife, sliding his lips down to alternate sucking between both of her nipples. *"Take all of it, Noelle."*

"Yesss, baby! Yesss!" She praised as she bounced up and down, pushing her ass back to take his finger. *"It's so damn good, Jack!!"* Noelle crooned as his length continuously rubbed against her g-spot. *"Uhhh! Don't stop...so good...Jack..."*

She arched into him, stars exploding behind her eyelids as writhing and twisting on his cock, Noelle came apart.

Watching Noelle cum all over his dick was the most erotic and rewarding thing Jack had ever seen and he memorized every detail of his wife in the throes of passion. She looked like a goddess with her luscious boobs bouncing and jeweled headband atop her wild hair billowing around her shoulders. He continued fucking her, leaning Noelle back against the steering wheel as he bit and licked her breasts. The horn blared, but he didn't stop.

Christ, it was fucking amazing.

Her arousal coated his thighs, making him swell even more inside of her, as pressure in his balls increased and ecstasy shook the base of his spine, intensifying as it vibrated upwards. Jack reached between them, stroking her clit and overloading Noelle's senses. It triggered a second orgasm, and a convulsing Noelle clutched at his hair with a scream as she clamped down around him, milking him. Jack finally peaked, forcefully his hips jerked as he shot streams of his hot load into her welcoming channel.

Spent, they remained clasped to each other until finally Jack reached down and pushed the button to slide the chair back even more. As it reclined, Noelle fell forward against him, and they collapsed onto the seat.

"Noelle?" Jack murmured drowsily.

"Yeah?" she breathed against his throat.

"Don't go to sleep. We're just gettin' started."

THE MUSIC AND DARBY'S MOVES were getting to her.

Avery stepped outside of Hooligans for fresh air after dancing for an hour straight. Goodness, the way he moved had her imagining what he would be like between the sheets with permission to do what he wanted. *Pierce,* she told herself. *Keep your thoughts on Pierce!* That had been so hard to do with Darby's large hands spanning her waist, lifting her like she weighed nothing. Next to him, Avery felt like the tiniest thing ever.

Music poured out as someone else exited the bar. The crisp, fragrant scent of cypress pine and sandalwood teased her nostrils. Instantly, Avery knew it was Darby when he came to stand close behind her as she viewed the starry velvet sky, serving as a backdrop for the stunning mountain range. The heat emanating from his body seeped through her clothes. With any other man, the lack of space between them would be deemed inappropriate, but Avery felt perfectly content being in such close proximity to Darby, with the exception of the achy feeling uncoiling in her stomach and *lower* that she didn't want to label.

"Everythin' alright, Ms. Avery?" Darby quizzed in that lazy inflection that always made her toes curl.

"Yes, I'm just getting some fresh air. I haven't danced that much in...well, forever," she admitted, striving for calm and unaffected, though her heart was racing. *Don't turn around*, she told herself. Avery feared that if she did, she might do something silly like beg Darby to kiss her.

"And why is that? You're a great dancer. Hell, you caught on to the line dance so fast that I didn't have a chance to impress you with my skills." His voice dipped an octave lower, and the sexy tone had her teeth tugging on her bottom lip worrying about how bad she wanted to do that something silly, like *really* bad.

Stepping to the side, Avery laughed breathlessly and faced him. His dark green eyes, locked on her face, were a storm she couldn't withstand in her weakened state. Shyly, Avery lowered her gaze. *Big mistake*, she thought with an audible gulp, taking in the outline of his manhood pressing against the front of his jeans, before averting her gaze to the parking lot. *Holy good wood, Batman!* No wonder he was so confident.

"Well, to be honest with you, my boyfriend feels that when we dance, we, no, *I* draw too much attention to us," Avery amended. "He says that my body is a distraction, that I should lose some weight to try blending in," she finished softly, now embarrassed that she'd admitted such a thing to carefree, zero fucks given, Darby of all people.

There was a heavy silence as he leaned against the rail and frowned down at her disapprovingly, eyes resembling emerald ice.

"Did you ever just tell your boyfriend to go fuck himself?" Darby politely inquired with a pleasantness he wasn't feeling. He was livid that this goddess was being forced to walk with mere mortals when she should be dancing among the clouds in all her curvaceous glory. He wanted to find her prick of a boyfriend and beat the ever-loving shit out of him.

Avery gave a startled laugh. "I've thought about it a couple of times, just haven't gone there yet. Wanted to but haven't."

Darby's face was serious. "You shouldn't be with someone who treats you like you're ordinary or wants you to fit in – unless they're your AA or drug sponsor," he joked.

They shared a laugh, simultaneously marveling at how easy it was to be around each other.

"So, your boyfriend has a problem with your body, huh? How long have you guys been goin' out?" Darby asked curiously, eyes sliding over her again.

Avery was the kind of woman who needed a label stuck on her forehead. One that read: *Warning: If you can't stand the curves, get off the highway.* Numerous times tonight, he'd given his death glare to regulars who couldn't keep their eyeballs in their sockets. It annoyed him, but he understood completely. He was in that percentile that wanted to be the one to mark her knees and leave her lips bruised and swollen in the best ways possible.

"We've been together for over a year and are compatible everywhere except in this area and ..." She trailed off in embarrassment.

"Ahhh," Darby nodded, comprehension dawning. They weren't compatible in the sack because her man didn't know how to handle her sexually. What an asshole. Because he was lacking, he put that shit back on her. Darby decided to go easy on her. Well, as easy as someone like him could go.

"You're not sexually compatible because you have a girlfriend, Ms. Avery," Darby announced bluntly, watching her eyes balloon with indignation.

"What?! That's not true! Pierce is very manly, Darby," Avery insisted while Darby snorted his skepticism. Of course, the douche's name was *Pierce*. The hell kinda name was Pierce?? Maybe she would understand better if he showed her.

"I don't think so, darlin'. Your man is extremely threatened by all you have to offer and the fact that he can't keep up. For instance, can he do this?"

Swiftly, he picked Avery up by her waist, pressing her against the wall. Darby stifled a groan as through the layers of fabric separating them, his hardness found the soft apex between her thighs. Automatically, Avery wound her arms and legs around Darby, holding on for dear life, her large brown eyes alert and wide with disbelief. The weight of her breasts nestled against his chest would be forever imprinted in his mind. Avery smelled so fucking delicious that Darby wanted to rip her clothing aside, cover her lips with his, and fuck her senseless

Instead, he settled for leaning in close to her. He

knew she felt his erection by the way her breath stuttered. Their lips were mere inches apart, and he could count every one of her curly lashes fluttering in the bright moonlight. Gazes locked, Darby held their position effortlessly.

"You are *perfect* just the way you are, Ms. Avery. Don't change for anybody. You're gorgeous, smart, kind, carin', and sexy as hell. Since I'm such a fuckin' gentleman, I'm just gonna leave you with this bit of advice. If your man can't pick you up against the wall and fuck you like this, it's because you really do have a girlfriend. Just sayin'."

Slowly, he slid her down his body, and Avery clutched at his shirt, her dilated eyes trained on him. "I think I understand what you're trying to say. Thank you for the demonstration."

Darby looked up at the moon. Christ, the things she made him *feel. T*he spell was broken when he reluctantly stepped back. "It was my pleasure, Ms. Avery. Somethin' else to think about? Bones are for dogs and meat is for *real* men. Now, how about we get you and Ms. Sidra fed? She's got to keep her strength up for her next rumble with Casey, and you and I need to keep score. This time, no interferin'."

He chuckled at Avery's heartfelt groan, slipping an arm around her shoulders to lead her back into Hooligans, breathing in her scent every step of the way.

SIDRA EXITED THE LADIES ROOM and was surprised to see Casey leaning against the opposite wall in the narrow hallway. He'd obviously been waiting for her. Bracing herself for a battle, she glanced down the empty hallway before warily eyeing him. *It really was a crime for a man to be this good-looking,* she thought ungraciously, drinking in his tall, hard frame encased in a pair of khaki slacks and a worn, dark blue denim shirt with the sleeves rolled up. He looked like a Ralph Lauren model with his streaked, disheveled hair and faint shadow covering his square jaw.

Suddenly parched, Sidra raised her gaze back up to his, now filled with hot turbulence.

"Skulking outside of bathrooms, Sullivan? To what do I owe the pleasure?"

His lips twisted into a wry smile, and Sidra was surprised at the rich southern twang that emerged. It hadn't been that prominent before. She was certain she would have noticed. "No skulkin', Sidra. I just wanted to apologize for my shitty behavior earlier. I was completely outta line. Neither you nor Ms. Avery deserved any of it."

"Ummm...*wow*...okay. I was *not* expecting that. Apology accepted," she said, and then feeling generous, she added, "It wasn't just you. I was completely over the top and should apologize too."

There was a pause and then another as their eyes clashed. Casey raised an expectant eyebrow at her, and Sidra smiled slyly.

"I said I *should,* not that I *would*, Sullivan."

Lips quirking, Casey acknowledged that fact before pushing off the wall. "Fair enough. I'll leave you in peace then. I believe Darby will be bringin' you and Ms. Avery back to Jack's later this evenin'. Enjoy the rest of your night."

Holy. Shit. She'd gotten a small victory! So, why didn't it feel as fantastic as she thought it would? He turned to walk away, and strange as it was, Sidra was reluctant to see him go.

"Wait!"

Casey turned, an inquisitive look on his face.

Feeling foolish, Sidra scrambled for something to say. "Can I ask why you refer to Avery and Noelle with the 'Ms.' title, and I'm just plain, old Sidra? Like I'm not good enough to have a title?"

The last part was just a tad bitter as feelings of childhood inadequacy reared their ugly head.

It happened so fast that Sidra was unsure of how she found herself backed up against the wall, cornered in by Casey. His body leaned into hers, and she was enveloped in his mouth-watering fragrance. Sidra tried to speak, but his smoldering eyes had her ensnared and incapable of speech.

"You wanna know why I address them that way and not you, right?"

His cool breath teased her lips. Casey framed her face with his palms, watching as her beautiful brown eyes burned brightly in response to his touch. *Damn, she took his breath away.* He was so attuned to Sidra that he'd known she was present as soon as she entered the bar. Like a sixth sense, the hair on the back of his neck rose and his dick was on high-alert.

Wearing a dark-gray long muscle tank and a denim cutoff miniskirt, Sidra's sexy legs were on display for every man in the bar checking her out. She wore black ankle boots, a black fedora, perched jauntily, and a stack of silver bangles on her wrists. Just like her laugh, the sound of them jangling had Casey focused like Pavlov's dog. With her heavily made-up eyes and purple and blue highlights, Sidra looked exactly like who she was – a sexy and beautiful woman with an uninhibited streak. Her look screamed she only dated rockers, so staid lawyers need not try to step up, and although he wasn't interested in *dating* Sidra, it still infuriated the hell out of Casey.

Her bumping and grinding on Guy was almost

enough to destroy a lifelong friendship. His good friend's blatant enjoyment as they moved together almost got him knocked smooth the fuck out. Normally, he liked hanging around his friend and couldn't wait to shoot the shit with him, but not tonight. Not when Guy was looking at Sidra like he was going vegan and she would be his last carnivorous meal.

"Because I don't think of doing unladylike things to *them*. I don't dream of being buried so deep inside of *them* that I wake up fucking my own hand, okay? It's *you*. You're the one I want to fuck 'til we're both speaking in tongues. You're the one whose pussy I want to eat like it's my three-square meals a day with snacks in between."

His thumb slowly caressed her bottom lip, and a deep tremble ran through her pliant body. "*This* is the mouth I want swallowing my dick whenever I whip it out. That's why I don't call you *Ms*. You feelin' me now? I don't want to do polite, ladylike things with or to you, Sidra."

It was the longest Sidra had ever gone without having a snappy comeback. For the life of her, she couldn't vocalize a damn thing witty to say, but her body responded to his enticing words. The images they evoked were so bold and erotic that they left her speechless. Casey took advantage of her silence and licked her bottom lip, slowly drawing it between his teeth. Her response was instantaneous. She captured his lips in a hedonistic kiss and his hands slid into her curls, knocking her hat to the floor as he took control, voraciously claiming her mouth.

Casey wedged a muscled thigh between hers and she rode it, her skirt bunching around her waist as he rubbed it between her legs, their kiss turning hotter than the sun. Grasping at the front of his shirt, she sucked on his tongue, so turned on by just kissing him that Sidra could feel an orgasm blooming. She clung tighter to Casey, riding his khaki-clad thigh with abandon, desperate to reach the finish line.

Abruptly, he broke away with a pained expression, leaning his head against the wall next to hers.

"We're not doin' this here. I'll be in New York in two days' time. You have until then to decide if you want this. If you don't, I'll never mention it or come at you like this again. Two days, Sidra."

He sauntered away, leaving a sexually frustrated Sidra, ready to scream and yearning for more of him.

CHAPTER
Twenty-Five

THE NEXT DAY, NOELLE WAS up at the crack of dawn, cracking eggs into a bowl at the kitchen counter. Humming under her breath, she added salt, pepper, and a little half and half to the bowl, whisking the concoction briskly then setting it aside. Next, she moved on to biscuit preparation. She gathered cold butter, shortening, all-purpose flour, salt, and milk. As she prepared the dough, another yawn escaped her. Noelle still couldn't believe that she was up so early after the night of thorough loving she'd partaken in.

She jumped when a large, warm hand covered her belly then smiled as whiskers brushed her neck, causing currents to run through her body in anticipation of Jack's next move.

"Good morning, husband."

"Mmmm...Come back to bed, wife. Can't sleep without you," he informed her, nuzzling her neck. Giving a sigh of pleasure, Noelle backed into him, her head on his shoulder, his arousal against her bottom. "We're lonely."

"Oh, it's a *we* thing now?" Noelle archly queried. "It doesn't sound like I'll be getting much sleep if I get back into bed with the both of you."

Yet she continued to rub back against him, and he placed his arms on the counter effectively caging her as he torturously ground his raging hard-on into her bottom.

"We'll be good for you. Besides, it's a proven fact that everybody needs a daily dose of Vitamin D," Jack persuaded, one hand shifting to untie her robe.

It fell open and his large palm caressed her breasts through the silk of her peignoir, plucking and tweaking the aroused peaks. The other lifted her garments from behind, and his large thigh wedged in between her legs. Noelle braced herself against the counter and willingly spread her legs further as Jack pushed her floral panties to the side and the cool, morning air hit her slick center.

"Well, what do we have here?" he murmured, gleefully admiring her glistening pussy. "I like the flowers, darlin'." He positioned himself at her entry, his lips tickling her ear. "They're definitely brightenin' my day."

He surged into her, and Noelle fell forward from the force, but his arm snaked across her chest to hold her shoulder, keeping her in place.

"Play with your breasts, wife. Touch your nipples like I would," he ordered.

Noelle cupped her aching breasts, imagining it was Jack fondling her, which brought her closer and closer to an orgasm. Desperately she sought his mouth, and he gave her what she needed. Lips clinging together, Jack's fingers slid down to play with her clit, strumming it in time to his rhythm. She exploded, her pussy death gripping his cock until he succumbed to the fiery pleasure as well.

"Now, that is what I call a great way to start the day," he panted.

"I concur." Fatigued, Noelle dropped forward to

rest on the counter, trying to catch her breath. But Jack wasn't done. Tilting her head back, he fed her lazy kisses. Noelle smiled against his lips as she felt him stirring back to life inside of her. She whimpered as his finger slid back down her body to tease her oversensitive bud. "*Again Jack?* Really?"

"I have no willpower when it comes to you and my pussy, baby," he assured her, sucking on her neck as aftershocks ran through her body. "It's perfect and you're fuckin' perfect the way you cum all over my dick."

This time, it was nice and slow, but the quaking orgasms at the end were just as powerful, leaving them both panting and weak-kneed. Suddenly, they stiffened as the sounds of cheerful whistling outside the kitchen door could be heard. They stood frozen for a moment before Jack pulled out of her with a curse. Noelle attempted to cover her breasts but only succeeded in getting flour on her lingerie and chest as they scrambled around.

The door opened but quickly shut again.

"Aaaargh, my eyes! What the hell is wrong with you people?!?! Get a freakin' room already!" Guy shouted in outrage. "Are you guys really doin' that next to the biscuits?! I had my heart set them on them, with lots of honey and strawberry jam! It's the only reason my hungover ass is even up this early!"

Mortified, Noelle allowed Jack to carry her upstairs, her face buried in his chest. She was shaking with laughter as an unremorseful Jack insincerely apologized.

"Sorry, Pippy!"

––––––––––––––––

THANKS TO JACK AND NOELLE'S early morning activities,

breakfast turned into brunch. After a shower, where she had to fight off her horny husband's advances, Noelle threw her hair in a haphazard bun and put on a fitted, gray t-shirt with silk flower-printed track pants. She sent Jack to the store to get the ingredients for drinks, and he dragged a pouting Guy with him, promising to bring his brothers, Holt, and the Romankovs back with them.

Noelle got Sidra and Avery out of bed to help her cook. Instead of the meal she was prepping earlier, she decided to fry the chicken she'd been brining for dinner, with waffles and apple-whiskey syrup, spicy kale-scrambled eggs, and roasted potatoes.

When Sidra spied the chicken frying to a nice golden hue in the huge cast iron skillet, she squealed with delight, rubbing her hands together "Bird Man" style.

"Yasss, honey! Bringing out the big guns for 'Operation Get Yo' Man, are we? I'm so glad I brought my appetite," she added with relish as she set the table.

"Hush, girl, and plate the eggs," Noelle scolded lightly, smiling happily as she set the potatoes in a dish and garnished them with chopped parsley. Playfully, she bumped Sidra's hip as she passed her.

"It was really good, wasn't it?"

Surprised at the question, both women turned to Avery who was polishing glasses at the counter. Chagrined, she elaborated further. "I know it's not something I normally comment on, and you both think I'm prudish, but I couldn't help noticing that you're walking with a little, umm...*caution*...and you have a hickey on the back of your neck."

Going ramrod straight, Noelle grabbed the back of her neck. "I'm not going to say anything about it except that I am extremely happy with the results of our fornication," she stated primly, returning to plating food in dishes.

There was a moment of silence then Avery scoffed, "To coin a phrase from Sidra, 'Bish, please!'"

They fell into peals of laughter and high-fives as the kitchen door opened, and Jack walked in, followed by their guests, laden with bags.

"Smells good in here, baby," Jack dropped a kiss on Noelle's forehead. "Mornin', ladies."

Greetings exchanged, everyone gathered around the counter while Jack and Darby made a production of making Bloody Marys and Mimosas. When everyone had a drink, they gathered around the loaded table to clasp hands in prayer. It was decided that Avery would say grace. Unable to resist teasing, Guy opened his mouth.

"Why are we doin' this?" he asked innocently. "I could swear that the food was already christened this mornin'."

He yelped when Jack slugged his arm. His wife's hung head let everyone in the room know that hanky-panky had ensued bright and early in the Sullivan household, much to Noelle's chagrin and their guests' amusement.

"All right, children. Let's not embarrass the happy couple anymore. How about we bless their union instead?" Alexei suggested with a solemn face, though his eyes twinkled with mirth. All agreed, bowing their heads so that Avery could say grace.

Everyone sat down, and small talk followed until Jack removed the lid of the largest platter containing the buttermilk fried chicken. The delicious aroma filled the air, and conversation trickled off as the men looked at the chicken then each other. Guy, Holt, and Alexei were apprehensive while the brothers' stared at the heaping platter of golden brown chicken with

D. A. YOUNG

something akin to horror. Noelle, Sidra, and Avery were worried while Kat covered her eyes, a gurgled noise escaping her throat. Since she was sitting between Jack and Darby in the corner, she squeezed Jack's hand and gave Darby's shoulder a reassuring rub, making him flinch and lower his head.

Unease filled Noelle as she looked at her husband, standing over the dish and staring with dread as if the chicken would reassemble like a transformer, rise up, and beat his ass.

"Is something wrong, Jack? If you don't want chicken, there's other stuff to eat. Let me make you a plate." Noelle stood up eager to ease the tension in the room that seemed to build by the second. She shot her friends a helpless look, but they were just as in the dark as she was. Still, Jack didn't speak, but surprisingly, Holt did.

"Let it be, love." He smiled kindly at her. "He'll be fine. Won't you, Jackie?"

Jack snapped out of his trance to find all eyes on him in concern, and he knew he had to pull it together. "Yeah, I'm fine. Sorry about that. I was just thinkin' about somethin' I had to do at work. Thank you so much for makin' this food, ladies. Everythin' looks great. Well, c'mon everybody, let's all dig in!"

He winced, hearing his overly enthused tone. Noelle's raised eyebrow let him know he was full of shit. The advice he always gave his clients was coming back to bite him in the ass.

If you aren't sincere, you sound like a complete fucking moron. Don't. Be. A. Fucking. Moron.

Jack tried to convey a message to both of his brothers: *please eat the damned chicken so Noelle's feelings wouldn't be hurt.* He was rewarded with stiff nods that said they understood. He grabbed the biggest piece of chicken and sat down again, giving her

298

a reassuring smile, but she remained unconvinced that all was well. Kat complimented Sidra's blouse, and conversation awkwardly resumed.

He could feel Noelle's suspicious glare as he brought the poultry to his lips. Taking a deep breath, he resolutely bit into it and was pleasantly surprised. Flavor exploded in his mouth. The chicken, while crunchy on the outside, was really juicy, tender, and savory on the inside with a kick of spice. Jack could taste the tang of buttermilk, seasonings, and herbs she'd used. He closed his eyes, savoring the delicious taste of it that conjured up buried memories. It was exactly how his mama used to make it, and because he hadn't been able to get that taste replicated anywhere else, Jack had long given up on eating fried chicken. He opened his eyes to find Darby and Casey waiting cautiously for his verdict.

Tears blurred his vision as he swallowed and took another big bite. To be sitting in this house that was a dedication to his beloved mother with Noelle, close friends, and family, eating chicken that tasted just like Moira's was a true sign. He believed that she was watching from above. *I love you, Ma,* he said silently, continuing to eat until only a picked clean bone remained. Only then did Jack realize that all conversation had ceased, and he was again the center of attention. He cleared his throat, using his wrist to wipe his eyes. "You outdid yourself with the chicken, baby. It's fucking amazin'."

"Thank you," Noelle murmured uncertainly, watching in amazement as all the men reached for pieces of chicken and proceeded to scarf it down quickly. They spoke with full mouths as they laughed and agreed that it was some damn good chicken! Even the refined Alexei had grease-smeared lips as he chowed down. Both Casey and Darby had tear-filled eyes as they grinned like lunatics at Jack and each other.

"Sooo...do you people not have access to fried chicken up here?" Sidra wondered, snagging the last piece of chicken, and holding it out of Holt's reach as he attempted to steal it from her. "Holt, I will smack you so hard into the future, you'll be able to meet your grandkids! Damn, I've never seen chicken disappear that fast. It was easily two birds!"

Across the table, she noticed the depth of undefinable emotion in Casey's face before he lowered his head, swiping his mouth clean with a napkin. He was just as shaken up as Jack but trying to be a badass. She wondered what the story behind their strange behavior was. Across the table, Avery laughed as Darby made a big show of presenting her with a thigh from his full plate.

"Not like this, Sidra," Jack confessed emotionally. "And not for a very long time."

———

AFTER BRUNCH, WHILE EVERYONE ELSE lounged around watching the NBA Finals, Jack took Noelle for a drive. Before leaving, he asked Avery if she could help him cut some flowers and fancy them up. In her element, Avery grabbed the pruning kit that she traveled with at all times because everybody should carry one on their person she insisted when the group looked at her like she was crazy and followed Jack. The arrangement she composed was colorful and stunning.

It was a lovely Sunday afternoon, and the weather was perfect for a drive. *Sundays are definitely for lovers,* Noelle thought, just happy to be with Jack, whose new way to drive was with one hand woven through hers.

She admired the way their complexions seemed to blend together seamlessly.

"Thank you very much for the wonderful meal again."

The lower half of his face was now completely covered in scruff, and his short black hair had transformed into unruly curls all over his head. He was so handsome to Noelle in the late afternoon light that for a moment, she found the simple act of breathing difficult.

"You're not still weirded out about the chicken thing, are you?"

"Ummm...no. Well, yeah, okay that *was* kind of different, but I wasn't thinking about that just now," Noelle admitted, a little flustered to be caught gawking like a groupie. Even though he was hers, for the time being, it was ridiculous how thirsty she still was for him. Jack grinned, and his white teeth were a startling contrast to his dark facial hair. *I want to have babies with this man really bad,* Noelle mused, her heart leaping in agreement with the idea.

"What were you thinking about then? Penny for your thoughts, sugar." Jack brought their linked hands up and kissed her fingers.

"I was just thinking about what a great time I'm having here. I'm really going to miss it when we leave tomorrow."

As Noelle said the words aloud, she realized it was true. She'd really grown to love the mountain town of Whiskey Row, the fresh air, and the nice people she'd met. She wished things were permanent between them, so she could visit more often. But the thought of being in Jack's hometown when they were no longer an item was incredibly painful. When they were done, it was best she walk away and leave everything behind.

"Why'd you stay away so long?"

Jack didn't reply as he made a left turn and pulled the car over. Noelle glanced over to her right and saw a cemetery. "I think it is better I show you so that you have a better understanding."

He got out, grabbed the flowers, and came around to open her door, helping her out as well, and making her smile. His chivalry was just one of the many things Noelle loved about him. Silently, they walked through the cemetery, respectful of those eternally resting. The many cemetery rows were arranged from smallest to largest tombstones. Jack grabbed Noelle's hand as they reached the back row and stood before a large granite heart-shaped tombstone. It read:

Here lies Moira Aileen Sullivan,
Beloved mother of Jackson, Darby, and Casey.
May you rest in eternal peace.
You are gone but never forgotten for
death leaves a heartache no one can heal,
while love leaves a memory no one can steal.

Underneath were her birth and death years, and as Noelle looked at the dates, she realized how young the boys were when they lost their mother. Jack lovingly touched the heart and spoke. Noelle was surprised to hear his southern accent combine with an Irish one.

"Hello, Ma. It's been awhile since I've come to visit ya', and for that I'm sorry, truly I am. I hope yer not that mad 'cause I've brought my beautiful wife Noelle with me. You'd really like her. She's smart, funny, kind, and makes chicken just like ya, Ma. It took me back today. I almost started bawlin' like a babe, and so did the *boyos*. Even Alexei was caught up in the moment. I wish you coulda seen him shoveling it into his mouth! You know me and the other two haven't eaten it since ya' been gone. Could never find it just the way ya made it."

Noelle could hear the thickness of the tears he was trying to hold back. "She made it just right too, so crisp and juicy, my wife did. It's time for me to tell her our story so that she kinna better understand. Dinna fash yourself, Ma, I won't tell her how ye used to twist our ears."

Jack leaned over to kiss the heart, lips lingering. "Well, that's it for now. I just wanted to come pay my respects to my best Galway girl before we leave 'The Row'. I know I was a real shite not to visit sooner. *Mo ghrá, go deo agus i gcónaí ag* *(My love forever and always).* Until next time, Ma."

Tears flowed freely down Jack's face, and he made no effort to wipe them away as he placed the huge bouquet below the headstone. It was a cleansing process for him to be able to talk to her after so many years of silence. For so long, the pain of losing her had been a gaping hole in his chest that all the therapy in the world wouldn't heal. The regrets of not being able to do more to help her made him the man that he was today. Noelle came to rest her head on his shoulder and slip her arm around his waist. Gently, her fingers wiped away his tears. Together, they stood like that under the warm sunshine until he was able to compose himself and lead her away. Before going, she pulled away to kiss the granite heart as well.

"It was a pleasure to meet you, Ma. Don't worry, I'll look after your boys."

CHAPTER
Twenty-Six

THE DRIVE BACK TO THE house was a quiet one. Jack was lost in his thoughts, and Noelle was hesitant to disturb him. They arrived to find a note from Darby. Everyone had gone to Holt's for a game of Bocce, and they were welcome to join them. The silence was driving Noelle crazy, so she kept busy by making them cappuccinos.

When she was done, Noelle brought them to the living room, where Jack was staring aimlessly out of the large bay window. Sensing he needed time to gather his thoughts, Noelle sat down on the sofa, patiently waiting. Finally, he came over and sat next to her on the couch, head bowed and focused on his hands.

"My father, Patrick Sullivan, was nothin' more than a sperm donor. He was a monster that death was too good for. He's buried at the top of Devil's Hill, and I personally named it after him. My mother was a beautiful young woman from Galway, Ireland. She came to the states to attend the Catholic University of America in Washington D.C., where her father's childhood friend was a professor. She lived with him, his wife, and their son Ian while attending classes there. She was at university for two years before she met Patrick, and they hit it off immediately.

Her family disapproved of my mother havin' any male friends, and her guardian gave my mother an ultimatum, which, if you're Irish, you know is the equivalent to raising a flag in front of a bull. The ultimatum was that she discontinued her friendship with her male friend or risk being sent back to Ireland. So, Patrick and Ian helped my mother get financial aid and become a U.S. citizen. He then helped her to get a place to stay. The smooth bastard introduced her to an ex-girlfriend who needed a roommate, and then he charmed himself into Ma's bed." Jack's fists clenched, and the veins strained prominently on his forehead, he was so overcome with emotion.

"My parents were inseparable, and her family desperately tried to get her to go back to her guardian's house, but she wouldn't hear of it. To hear Ian tell it, Patrick wanted to spend all his time with Ma, and his grades suffered." His hard tone turned to one of pride. "Not Ma's, though; she thrived in the academic environment, and her success put a strain on their relationship. When he started lashin' out at her verbally, she decided to distance herself from him by movin' back in with Ian's family.

Patrick got kicked out of school due to his poor grades, so he went home to Whiskey Row and his wealthy grandfather. Four weeks later, Ma found out she was pregnant with me. She went to see him despite her family and Ian's protests, and he promptly proposed despite his grandfather's objections. Determined to do right by her child, she said yes."

Noelle's her heart ached for her husband. He looked physically ill, as he spoke, underneath his tan, he was unnaturally pale, sweat beading his forehead.

"They eloped, and her family disowned her. I was born seven months later. Darby arrived a year and a half after that, and school was now just a memory for her. By then, Patrick started to show his true colors of bein' an angry, abusive piece of shit, and my mother knew the truth about him."

With a bleak expression, Jack looked away, pensively towards the windows, his hands shaking slightly. Noelle grabbed one and held on tight, letting him know she was there for him. He squeezed it and took a steadying breath.

"See, Patrick's parents were killed in a car crash when he was two. He lived with his paternal grandfather, who sent his only grandson away to school because he was such an embarrassment to the family name, just like his older sister who ran off when she was fourteen. Patrick had an alcohol problem that was discovered when he was fifteen, and there were rumors of him sexually assaultin' several girls in Gatlinburg by the time he was seventeen. When he came back home, his grandfather gave him a job in the family mill as an accountant and let him live in the guesthouse. Then my Ma showed up with me in her belly. Old man Sullivan was so livid that he'd gotten some little immigrant pregnant, he immediately disowned Patrick.

He got a job as a bank teller but lost it due to his ill temper. After that, he had trouble keepin' any job. Ma got a job as a waitress and took in miners' laundry when they came down the mountain on the weekends. She supported our family singlehandedly while Patrick drowned his sorrows in bottle after bottle of whatever liquor he could get his hands on, refusin' to help support his family. Ma was too proud to turn to her family or Ian for assistance."

Jack stopped again, and his expression this time

was so enraged, that for a moment, Noelle felt a voltage of alarm run through her body. He looked like he wanted to hurt something or someone, but at the same time, he looked like a scared little boy. Bending his head, he rubbed his face vigorously, frustrated, and trying to control himself. Noelle cupped his face, staring at him until his eyes gradually focused on her.

"Breathe, Jack! It's okay; *I've got you*. We can talk later if you like. You don't have to do this right now."

Jack's smile was ugly and broken, reflecting his past. "No, you need to know. Patrick was such a stellar human being that instead of gettin' sober for his family and helpin' to support us, he accused my Ma of havin' affairs with the men whose laundry she took in. First, the abuse was verbal but escalated quickly into physical where no one could see because even though he'd been disowned, Sullivans didn't do things like that. His moods shifted from blamin' her for the life he had to ragin' possessiveness that she belonged to him. His sick jealousy knew no bounds. Eventually he began to take his abuse out on Darby and me, even though Ma tried to protect us as best as she could.

The first couple of years in public, we were the perfect family – scrubbed clean and attendin' mass on Sunday, but it was a different story behind closed doors. My Ma refused to sleep with Patrick, so he forced himself on her. When she found out she was pregnant again, she went to an OBGYN in Nashville to take care of the problem. It was there that she met Vivienne. They hit it off immediately in the waitin' room, and my mother ended up confidin' to her the real reason that she was there. Then Viv's boyfriend came in to pick her up, and he was none other than Alexei Romankov.

Needless to say, my mother was scared of word getting back to Patrick, so she didn't have an abortion.

Instead, she went to old man Sullivan and blackmailed him. She told him she'd continue to keep quiet about his grandson's behavior if he gave her enough money to open a laundromat. They struck a deal, and it became one of the most successful businesses in town. For once, we didn't have to struggle, and Ma could finally breathe easier. Seein' how much she didn't need Patrick loosened the lock on his ugliness, and he became the town embarrassment, rantin' and ravin' for everyone to see his craziness.

I was thirteen when my mother decided to put her plans to leave him in motion. She started stashin' money away and slowly bringin' our stuff to the laundromat. Viv would box things up for her and pack them away in a truck that she kept at her home, but they had to be very discreet about it because I'm ashamed to say, Patrick was also a big, racist asshole who refused to interact with anyone who wasn't white." Jack felt Noelle's sharp gaze on him but refused to look at her as he revealed his shameful past. "He felt that affirmative action was the reason he couldn't get a job, not because he was a lazy-ass drunk who thought he was better than everybody else."

Briefly, Jack closed his eyes, as one of the many unpleasant childhood memories he tried to suppress assailed him.

He was ten and waiting for his mother to pick him and Darby up from school. As he waited for his brother outside, he talked football with his friends Guy and Charlie. Unbeknownst to him, Patrick was there to pick them up instead. When he finally noticed his father, he grabbed Darby, and they hurried toward the truck, lest he get out and embarrass them. Jack had barely buckled himself into the front seat when...Crack! He reeled back from the slap his father gave him, his head hitting the passenger window as blood pooled in his mouth.

"Stop slummin' with the niggers and that savage, boy! You'll only give 'em ideas that they're as good as you; then they'll try to take your jobs and women!"

Dizzy from the blow, Jack struggled not to throw up from the instant headache he now had. Opening the door, he spat the blood out as his father continued to scream at him. His eyes met those of his sympathetic friends, and he wanted to crawl into a hole, certain they could hear the bastard from across the parking lot. For weeks afterward, he'd been ashamed to look them in the eye.

"Jack!"

At Noelle's voice, Jack blinked away the memory, covering his face with his hands.

"One day, Viv was leavin' the laundromat with a box of our clothes, and she ran into Patrick. The box fell to the ground, and he saw what was inside. He grabbed her arm and accused her of stealin'. As you know, my godmother is not one to mince words, so she slapped him and cussed him out. He shook her, and my mother came running out to help her friend. I'm told she jumped on his back, and he threw Viv to the ground, kicked her in the stomach, and punched my mother in the face. Little did he know that earlier in the day, the Romankovs discovered that they were pregnant.

Witnesses went to get Alexei and the sheriff, and Patrick took off like the snivelin' coward that he was. Alexei was furious at what the two women had been plottin' on their own, and he took his wife to the hospital where he didn't leave her side until the doctor said she was fine. Viv was mad at him for not goin' to check on Ma, but after speakin' to the Sheriff, who said the bastard was nowhere to be found, there was nothin' she could say or do to dissuade Alexei from leavin' her side.

Two deputies were assigned to our house, and Ma pulled us out of school to get the rest of our things. We were upstairs packing when we heard him. We huddled in the master bedroom and shoved a dresser against the door. She spoke calmly but quietly, giving us instructions to go out the window and to our nearest neighbor's home. We begged her to come with us even as the dresser was bein' pushed away from the door. Patrick sounded like an animal, and we were terrified to leave her there with him. Ma wouldn't hear of it, insistin' that everythin' would be okay. We needed to go now and not look back or turn around for anythin'. When we left, we saw both deputies lyin' on the ground with blood gushing from their heads and a pipe lyin' in between them. Both were still alive and later told the sheriff that he'd been hidin' under the porch."

Patrick murdered my mother that night before taking his own life. He forever changed the lives of seven people. My brothers and I were left motherless. Ian and Vivienne were left sister-less. Alexei ...wifeless because as soon as Viv heard what happened to her dearest friend, she moved out of their bedroom into a guest room, remaining there on bed rest until she gave birth to Katerina Moira Romankov. A month after the baby was born, Viv left Alexei and hasn't been back since because she couldn't and *still can't* forgive him for what he didn't do. Kat lost out on growin' up with two dotin' parents who loved one another and lived in the same household. All she's ever known is bein' shuffled around back and forth between here and D.C. That's why every day since that night, I wish that I would've had the balls to kill Patrick Sullivan and protect my family."

CHAPTER
Twenty-Seven

THE SILENCE BETWEEN THEM HUNG heavy. Mind whirling from Jack's family history, Noelle sensed the emotional turmoil weighing him down and wished she could take away his pain. She grasped his hand in one of hers, held it in her lap, and stroked his rigid jaw with the other. Eyes closed, and drained, Jack turned his head into her touch, pressing a kiss to the inside of her palm. Noelle leaned in and gave him a soft lingering kiss. "Jack, I'm so sorry that happened to you and your family. I wish I could take your pain away."

With a heavy sigh, Jack squeezed her hand reassuringly. "It's not somethin' I usually talk about, but today...just seein' that fried chicken and the *taste*... God, it brought it all back for me! I've never allowed myself to grieve or celebrate the time I was blessed to have with her. In the beginnin', there was never time. I had to make sure that my brothers were alright, to be strong for them and Vivienne, and to never show weakness in front of Ian and Alexei. Pretty soon, it just got easier to say and do the things to make everyone around me feel better that I just buried my feelings and concentrated on makin' sure everyone else was all good. I never looked back, just kept putting one foot in front of the other until it didn't hurt to breathe so much.

Durin' our counseling sessions, I'd expose a little bit of myself to get the sessions rollin' for Casey and Darby, but I wouldn't really divulge too much. Livin' with Alexei after Ma's death was tricky for me because he was always studyin' me like I was a bomb just waitin' to go off. I tried my hardest to be good and keep the boys in line so he would keep us together." Jack grimaced, leaning back on the sofa, closing his eyes wearily.

"It just became...too much for me and when it was time to apply for colleges I picked the ones farthest from home, only come home during holidays and to see my siblings graduate from high school. This visit is the longest I've been here since Kat graduated from high school. Usually, we all get together in Nashville, D.C., or they come to New York to see me."

He fell silent, and Noelle leaned back as well, resting her head on his shoulder and rubbing his thigh in a soothing manner. She listened as his jagged breathing gradually returned to its natural rhythm, silently cursing Patrick Sullivan for the all the damage he'd inflicted on these good people. *How much*, she wondered, *would he have hated that they had obviously taken after their mother and grew up to be well-liked, successful businessmen? That a strong, beautiful, black woman had a hand in raising them, and they had a biracial sister? Or that his son was married to a black woman? Oh, how he had to be turning in his grave....*

Suddenly Jack sat up. "C'mon, let's get out of here and get some fresh air."

Noelle accepted his offered hand, and he gently pulled her up and wrapped an arm around her, drawing her to him.

"Are we going to join the others?" she asked.

Jack shook his head and grinned mischievously. "Nah, we're gonna do somethin' that I haven't done in a long time."

Noelle looked at him expectantly. "Okay, I'm game. What do I need to bring?"

He grinned naughtily, leading her toward the front door. "You don't have to bring anything except a willingness to try new things."

***

Noelle craned her neck, gazing up in disbelief at the sixty-foot tall ladder attached to the side of a massive tree. She could make out the large wood platform at the top. Her gaze followed the zip line that stretched from the tree over the huge man-made lake to a tree on the opposite side. "*This* is what you guys did for fun growing up?"

They'd driven into a denser wooded area that made Noelle think of the "Blair Witch Project", before coming to a stop by a clear path that led to a fenced-in lake. According to Jack, Alexei had it built for all the local kids the year he and his brothers came to stay with him.

Laughing, Jack unbuttoned his short-sleeve black shirt, revealing tanned, sinewy muscles that Noelle couldn't help but drool over. "Awww c'mon, baby. Where's your sense of adventure? This is where you could find the gang every summer from noon 'til dinnertime. The water's not that deep, seven feet, tops. Growing up, parents didn't mind because there was safety in numbers and after Alexei hired lifeguards and security to supervise all activity. If you couldn't swim, you weren't allowed in. You *can* swim, right?"

"Yes, but I don't have a swimsuit, Mr. Sullivan. Something I'm very sure you're aware off," she countered dryly. He was now down to his boxer briefs and despite being extremely familiar with his body, Noelle found herself tongue-tied. Under her perusal, she watched his manhood lengthen, stirring an ache between her thighs. *Damn, she couldn't get enough of him.* Noelle pressed her legs together to squelch her ever-growing desire for him.

"Not a problem. It's just us out here. Let's climb to the top, and I'll show you how to use the zip line. It'll drop you anywhere in the lake, but you probably want to drop into the center," he suggested, glancing at her expectantly.

Oh right, he wanted her clothes off. Quickly, she kicked her shoes off, her tee and pants followed.

Jack felt his eyes glaze over at the brown sugared perfection before him, heightened by a lacy, pink satin bra and matching bikini cut panties. "Ladies first, baby. Don't worry, I'm right behind you."

He dropped his head, groaning as the lush roundness of her ass teased him through the delicate lace, begging him to rip the bottoms off, cup the full globes, and explore the sweet goodness between them. Noelle must have read his mind, tossing him a warning look over her shoulder.

"*Don't even think about it.* This is Agent Provocateur, and you'd best believe you'd be replacing it, mister."

Noelle hoisted herself onto the first step, only to find herself pressed back against Jack's warm body, his shaft nestled perfectly between her ass cheeks. His breath tickled her ear as he slid his large hand up her stomach to rest under her breasts.

"It'd be worth it. Just so we're clear…you're sayin' as long as I replace it…"

"Mmmm, you're insatiable," she murmured, leaning back into him. He gave her a kiss on the cheek and gently swatted her behind.

"Up you go, so I can enjoy the view."

At the top of the wooden platform, Noelle was able to take in the breathtaking view of the lake as it sparkled in the late afternoon sun. The air was so crisp and fresh that she wished she could bottle it up and take it back to the city with her.

"Pay attention, baby," Jack instructed; she listened attentively as he explained the mechanics of the zip line bar.

He looks so carefree, Noelle thought. The heavy weight of his confession had been lifted from those burdened shoulders of his. It was a shame he'd carried all that baggage around for so many years as he was clearly relieved to shed it.

"See ya at the bottom." He turned to grab the bar but quickly turned back around and yanked her into his arms. "One for good luck."

His firm lips covered hers in a tender kiss, tongues meeting and sliding against each other in the slowest of dances. Noelle closed her eyes and lost herself in his firm embrace as Jack's arms squeezed her as if he never wanted to let go. It was different from their usual intense kisses but stirred her blood nonetheless. They broke apart, and her hand reached up to caress his cheek. In the late afternoon sun, she could see every green and gold fleck in his eyes and count every freckle on his nose.

He's the reason our babies are going to be so good-looking, she mused.

Jack was thinking the same thing, taking in her lush, pink lips, puffy from their kiss and the exquisite bone structure of her face, her gray eyes filled with happiness. Heaven help him if they had little girls that looked just like her. Jack knew he'd be wrapped around their little fingers too. "Damn, girl. What's my name again?" he murmured.

Flushing, she pushed him away with a laugh and watched as he took the bar confidently and leaped from the platform. His enthusiastic 'Whooooooo!' as he sped down the line, was contagious, and Noelle cheered him on as he let go, diving into the middle of the lake. A minute later, he popped up and gave her the thumbs up, yelling, "Get your ass in here, babe! The water is perfect!"

Per his directions, Noelle operated the panel to bring the bar back to her. Clasping it for dear life, she copied his actions, and soon, she was streaming through the air, laughing and high on exhilaration, screaming, "I'm the queen of the world!"

A couple of feet away from Jack, she let go and dropped into the lake. She was shocked at how icy-cold the water was and quickly swam to the top, breaking the surface with a screech. Treading water, she pushed her hair out of her face and wiped it free of water. "It's cold as shit, you liar!"

Jack laughed as she splashed him. "I did almost freeze my balls off, but sometimes, you just have to go out on a leap of faith, darlin'."

Noelle shivered, rubbing her arms. "Whatever, Mahatma Gandhi. I'm freezing."

Cupping her bottom, Jack pulled her against him, her limbs automatically encircled him. "Your balls don't feel like they're frozen to me, buddy."

He licked water droplets from her neck. "Seein' your sexy ass glidin' through the air in them next-to-nothin' skivvies has got me all hot and bothered, darlin'."

His fingers pulled her panties aside, easing into her ready heat as his lips met hers. Noelle sighed into his mouth, riding his fingers leisurely as they tread water. Jack smiled against her lips. "Let's see how good I am at warming you up."

FIRM LIPS, GHOSTING ALONG HER jawline, woke her up. The feather-light kisses made Noelle smile. She opened her drowsy eyes to find Jack's face hovering above hers.

"Good mornin', beautiful," he greeted her affectionately, "How are you feelin' this mornin'?"

They'd arrived back in New York City last night. Noelle insisted that they go to his place as she'd never been there, and he reluctantly complied. The moment they entered she could see why. Jack's loft was sleek, cold, and impersonal, revealing none of his warm personality. He stood by the door, as she explored all of his top-of-the-line electronic devices and the few pieces of furniture he did have. It was black and white bare minimalism at its best and didn't suit him at all. Finally, Jack came up behind her, wrapping his arms around her. "Let's get outta here."

They went back to her place, and Noelle insisted on making them something to eat. They sat out on the rooftop and dined on prosciutto, melon, and mozzarella skewers drizzled with balsamic vinaigrette, emptying a bottle of white wine before Jack took her to bed and drove her out of her mind. No matter how out of control she spun, Jack refused to speed up, worshiping her body completely at an agonizingly slow pace until she was delirious and begging for him to take her.

"Awww, I'm feeling cheated," Noelle pouted, swinging her legs to the floor, missing his heated stare sweeping over her.

"Oh yeah? And why is that?" Jack wondered if Noelle knew how stunning she was, especially first thing in the morning. Her eyes, slumberous, soft mouth, inviting, curls everywhere, and her body was calling his name. Judging from her peaked nipples, he was willing to bet money that if he slipped his hand between her legs, she would be ready.

"Because all the sexy scruff is gone," she complained, running her fingers over his clean-shaven jawline. "I had my heart set on being beard-burned this morning."

With a quiet laugh, he leaned over her, until they fell back into the pillows, ravishing her mouth. Jack eased a finger into her already moist center, and Noelle clung to him, spreading her legs wider and rotating her hips, silently begging for more. She ran her fingers through his curls, yanking on them as he added a second finger, quickly followed by a third, and his thumb rotating around her clit causing her to clutch at him feverishly.

"The scruff stays on 'The Row'. If you want it, we need to take another trip down there, darlin'," he suggested roughly against her lips, his fingers curling in and teasing her g-spot. In the bright light of day, the colors of their skin melded together, and as always, the beauty of it stole his breath.

"Oh gawd!" Noelle cried, pulling her lips away from his for oxygen. Jack yanked her back and claimed his victory, swallowing every choked cry she emitted. Her muffled pants were music to Jack's ears, and he leaned down, suctioning a plump nipple into his mouth. Noelle's hips shot off the bed, and he swiftly repositioned himself between her thighs as her hands desperately yanked at the navy sweats sitting low on his hips. She pulled them down, and his cock sprang free. Jack grabbed Noelle's wrists, holding them over her head with one hand, using the other to guide himself to her entrance and take the plunge, powerfully drilling into her and rotating between

sucking her nipples.

"I could stay inside you forever," Jack hissed, licking the perspiration gathering in the valley between her breasts as her legs curled around his calves. *"Jesus...this pussy...is... so... fucking... perfect."*

No one compared to him, Noelle thought as he sexed her oh so thoroughly. He was like a pool shark, expertly shooting the balls into each pocket. God, she couldn't get enough of him. Planting her feet on the bed, Noelle thrust her hips up to receive her just rewards. He released her hands, and she slid them downward, gripping his firm buttocks as she licked and sucked his neck. Jack still couldn't believe he was with her. The feeling was almost religious, definitely otherworldly, entirely on a level that he'd never experienced with any other woman. He raised himself up to his knees, pulling her legs onto his shoulders, and when their gazes collided he slid his thumb down to torment her clit. "Play with your nipples, Noelle."

She readily obeyed, loving how heady and carnal their lovemaking was. The bed shook with the savagery of his thrusts. Her nipples were sensitive from her fingers and Jack's teeth. Every squeeze and tug she gave them caused her pussy to clench tighter and tighter around his cock, making his breathing even more ragged as he propelled deeper and harder into her. She was too hypersensitive from his play. With the way Jack's thrusts intensified, Noelle knew that soon he would come, but like a true gentleman, he would make sure she did first. All it took was a gentle strum of his fingers against her tender clit and Noelle came in a fiery burst, clamping down on him so hard that Jack had no choice but to follow. He released her legs to bury his face in her neck as he emptied himself inside of her with an agonized groan.

———————————————

AFTERWARD, THEY WERE IN A mad rush to get to work, and Jack insisted on driving Noelle. Twenty minutes later, he pulled up to the large warehouse where Tarik's party would be held, and they waited for Avery to arrive.

"What time will you be done today? You look really nice by the way."

Noelle looked up from placing a file into her black Kate Spade tote with a smile for him. Today, she was wearing her hair in a side braid that hung over one shoulder. Her black, silk button-down work shirt was tucked into a form-fitting green, black, and white tropical print skirt. Black strappy sandals showed off red-painted toes. His eyes narrowed as they settled on her bare ring finger.

"Baby, where's your ring?"

All week, Jack noticed her staring at it when she thought no one was looking, so he knew her not having it on was a conscientious decision. She bit her top lip, letting Jack know that he wouldn't like her answer. It was one of the many quirks that he loved about her. When she was nervous, she bit her top lip. If she was aroused, it was the bottom one.

"It's at home on the dresser," Noelle answered nervously. This morning, she'd debated putting it on but decided against it, not ready for the twenty questions it would bring. Already, she was regretting the decision. Her finger felt and looked so naked without it.

"What's it doin' there, Noelle?" His southern accent was coming on strong, a tell-tale sign that he was upset along with his flashing eyes.

"Well…I just thought it would be best considering

that our situation isn't really ...well...*real*..." she trailed off as he waved his left hand at her, showing that his band was very much on display.

While Jack took another shower this morning, she'd checked her voicemail. There were eight messages, and five of them were from her mother, each message testier than the last. There was also a text basically stating that the mountain would be coming to Muhammad if she didn't get a call back. Noelle knew it was serious since her mother despised texting. The showdown was imminent, and she just needed a little more time to gather her thoughts. The ring would certainly not escape her mother's hawkeye.

"No, it's not ideal, but our situation works. Nobody's goin' to know we're together, let alone married if you don't advertise it in some way," Jack snapped irritably. "I gave that ring to you on our wedding day, but I also said that it was yours no matter what! Even if it's not on your ring finger, I'd appreciate it if you wore the damn thing."

Noelle bristled at his tone. "And I'd appreciate it if you didn't take that tone with me, Jackson. I'm just not ready for the questions that would come with wearing it *here*."

He gave her a hard look. "You mean *here* because this is where your family lives, correct?"

Noelle stiffened, looking straight ahead as the tension between them rose. The thought of having to deal with her family's questions immediately gave her a raging headache. "Look, does it really matter? I just said I'm not comfortable right now. Besides, you already sent our certificate to your friend, right?"

The temperature in the car turned positively chilly as Jack gave her an icy glare. "I was under the impression that we were in this together, but it's like you would rather keep everything a secret. Are you so terrified of your family's disapproval that you're scared to rock the boat? That's fine. You're absolutely right; it doesn't matter."

Noelle stifled her gasp of pain, watching him yank his ring off and drop it in the cup holder. Her stunned gaze rose to meet his unreadable one. There was a knock on the window, and they turned to see Avery standing on the sidewalk with a bright smile, holding a tray filled with Starbucks cups. Noelle opened the door to greet her.

"Good morning, lovebirds!" Totally unaware of the strain between the couple, she presented the tray. "I brought you guys coffee because something tells me you two were occupied with ...other things this morning," Avery finished delicately, handing them their cups. "Venti Americano for Jack. Venti Caramel latte iced for Bae." She waved her hand at Noelle jokingly. "Besides, this one is a complete brat if caffeine isn't in her system."

"Thank you, Ms. Avery. Well, I better get goin'. I'm sure there's a lot to deal with at the office, especially since I've been out all week." Jack flashed her a quick smile before glancing down at his watch.

"Thanks for the ride, Jack," Noelle said quietly, knowing that it was her fault that he was pissed off. *Damn.* And the morning had started off with such promise. She'd definitely fucked up big time. "No problem. Ladies, have a great day."

His uber politeness grating on her nerves, Noelle grabbed her things, giving him one last hopeful look as he stared fixedly ahead, his mouth compressed into a tight line. She exited the car and closed the door, watching with a sinking heart as he drove off without looking back.

"Everything alright?" Avery asked with concern. "Jack didn't seem like his usual charming self this morning."

"Yeah, everything's fine. Come on. Something tells me we're going to be grinding long after the sun sets," Noelle said taking a sip of her coffee, her mind still on Jack.

"*Giiiiirrrrl,* who you telling? That's exactly why I wore my hardcore primer today," Avery gestured towards her face. "Oh, and I received a call today from a company called Americana Traditions. Their secretary is requesting a meeting. They want to use us for their launch party. Seems we're growing quite popular..."

CHAPTER
Twenty-Eight

*E*VERYTHING WAS NOT OKAY.

Jack thought to himself as he exited the elevator, heading to his office. He smiled, greeting everyone that passed him in the corridor while growing more pissed off by the minute. They hadn't even been in the city for twenty-four hours and already, things were drastically different.

"Good morning, sir! How was your vacation?" Margo chirped, rising to greet him.

"It was good, thanks for askin'. You look great, Margo. I guess me bein' out of your hair agrees with you." Jack kissed her cheek with a loud smack.

"Hardly. But you'll be pleased to know that everything has been running smoothly under Mrs. Romankov's direction."

At his look of surprise, she further elaborated, "She said that you were not to be disturbed under any circumstances. She has been handling the pageant and Ms. Gaines, who has been on her best behavior, I might add. Mr. Rusnik called several times while you were out. I informed him that you would be in today, and he said for you to call him back ASAP," Margo sniffed disdainfully as she added, "Joel and David Rothman have been calling for you nonstop as well."

Jack sighed, knowing he couldn't put off Ian's calls forever. He was certain Ira's sons were calling to harass him about the stipulations placed on the loan for On a Whim, but he didn't give a rat's ass about those spoiled dickheads. His phone beeped, signaling a text. He pulled it out to check, grimacing as he read it. It was from Viv, regarding Ian.

Just got off the phone with Gandalf. Oooh! You in trouble! LMAO!

"Thank you for holding down the fort, Margo. Please hold my calls for the next hour."

Jack walked into his office, closing the door behind him. After sitting down at his desk, he picked up the office phone and dialed Ian's number. He answered on the first ring.

"It's about damn time. I thought I was going to have to take a flight home and put my Gucci loafer up your behind, dear boy," Ian lectured. "I'm hearing things, Jack. Things that have got my blood pressure soaring and my beautiful, silver hair turning *gray*. Talk to me, son."

Anyone else, Jack might have told to kiss his ass, but not the man who helped to raise him and his brothers. "Your hair's been gray since you were born. That blonde was all Miss. Clairol." He grinned at the offended gasp on the other end. "Hello, Ian; how is Greece?"

"Jackson Conall Sullivan, don't think your big, country ass is too heavy to go over my knee!" Ian barked.

Leaning back in his chair, Jack laughed aloud at the image those words created.

"Exactly what have you heard, Ian?" Jack was stalling for time. He heard Ian exhale with exasperation and easily pictured him, with his long, silver hair in a man bun and matching goatee, smoking a cigar as he stood overlooking the Aegean Sea.

"I've heard that you finally grew a pair of balls and married *my* little girl. That's what I've heard," Ian bluntly stated. "And if that's the case, perhaps now you can stop eye-fucking her every time she enters a room."

Wait. What??

Jack straightened up in the chair. "It's true; *Noelle is my wife*."

As if on demand, a wealth of primal satisfaction surged through him. If Jack lived to be a hundred, he would never get tired of saying that. "Are you saying that you've known how I felt about her this whole time?"

"Are you asking me if I knew that you've had a hard-on for my precious baby since the night of her twenty-first birthday party? If so, then yes, and it's a surprise to me that nobody else has come to the same conclusion. It's quite obvious from the way you make it a point to do all business concerning the Kramers' in person and at their home, which is the one place that you were sure to run into her. Alicia Kramer could drive the Pope to drink, yet you grin and bear her, attending all the family events just so you can be near Noelle. In addition, last time I was in your office, I believe I heard you plucking flowers, singing 'she loves me, she loves me not…'"

"Fuck off, Ian," Jack not in the least bit amused as he glared at his ringless finger.

"I wonder what else you aren't telling me, hmmm? The only reason I know is because I called Alexei yesterday, and he commented on the delicious chicken your *wife* made. Naturally, my curiosity was piqued."

"Ian, it was amazin'! I really wish you could have been there," Jack reminisced. "I haven't had chicken that good since Ma died. My wife can definitely burn in the kitchen on top of being a sweetheart and fine as all get out."

"No need to tell me how fabulous Noelle is. Besides, I've had the chicken, lad. It was her uncle who taught your mother and her how to make it. Your Ma and I would sneak out of the house and go to block parties in D.C. It was there that I met Harvey. He was serving his famous fried chicken, and it was calories at first sight," Ian said with equal parts love and sadness, and Jack knew he was thinking of his beloved late partner. "Now, I want you to tell me why no one knows of your marriage? I would have felt the fire and fury of Alicia roasting my arse about how you took advantage of her baby if she knew."

"Actually, I'm helping her out with a situation that has the potential to become a scandal for her and ultimately, her family. After reviewing the clusterfuck from all angles, I felt that marriage was the best way to diffuse it." Jack hoped that his answer would be enough for the shrewd bastard.

There was a long pause before Ian finally growled, "And you thought you'd kill two birds with one stone, eh? Be very careful about the games you play, Jackie. Noelle won't take too kindly to being your pawn and you playing with her heart. If I'm not mistaken, the saying goes, 'One of the cruelest things a person can do is to awaken someone's love without the intention of ever truly loving them.'"

"This isn't a game for me, Ian!" Jack snarled "I married her with the intention of stayin' married, and I don't give a damn what any of you may or may not believe."

"Does she know that or how you feel? I do not doubt your feelings are real. I've seen the way you look at her. All I'm saying is that if you won her heart under false pretenses, that will be how you lose her," Ian warned direly.

"She is *my wife,* and that is how it's going to stay," Jack felt anger and something else trying to claw its way out of the pit of his stomach. *Fear.* The thought of losing his beautiful, sweet wife terrified him. He would scorch the Earth, ridding it of anyone who foolishly tried to interfere in their relationship, including the man on the phone.

"Don't misunderstand me. I'm very happy for you, Jackie. Despite what you may think, you deserve happiness just like everyone else. As do your brothers, although, it should be mandatory that Darby get his with a shot of penicillin the way he spreads himself about," Ian exasperated. "Vivi just gave me an earful about how she's going through receptionists left and right because they're sprung on his 'damned ginger-headed ass.'"

Relaxing again, Jack chuckled. "Y'all need to leave Darby alone. Now, before I dig into the pile of paperwork on my desk, tell me about your vacation."

He listened as Ian launched into the details of his trip, but Jack was only paying half attention because Ian's words were lingering in the back of his mind.

"If you won her heart her under false pretenses that will be how you lose her."

WHAT A DAY.

Noelle waved tiredly at the two security guards on front door duty. "Goodnight, guys."

"Goodnight," they chorused and returned to monitoring, the surveillance cameras of the building.

It was eleven-thirty at night, and the venue was all set for Tarik's party tomorrow. Everything was being organized onsite, and the deliveries were nonstop throughout the day. Noelle's ears were still ringing from the dancers practicing their routine and Avery's scream of rage when she discovered the florist had sent the wrong kind of flowers. This pushed the arrangements that she planned to make back two hours as they waited for the correct ones to arrive.

Four cases of party glasses arrived shattered, so polishing was delayed. They Skyped with Sidra, who was being vague about her whereabouts, regarding the music genre and did a checklist run-through of all the equipment needed for the DJ booth that arrived early that morning. It was one thing after another all day, and the only way she and Avery got through it was by chanting their favorite Nelson Mandela quote to each other when they crossed paths:

"Everything seems impossible until it is done."

Tomorrow would be another long day, and all Noelle wanted was to go home and get something to eat before bed so that she would be well-rested and prepared. Hopefully, it would also take her mind off the fact that she hadn't heard from Jack at all today. As Noelle walked out of the doors and into the late evening, she came to a halt, wondering if her eyes were deceiving her.

Jack was leaning against his Range Rover staring at the entrance, obviously waiting for her. Pleasure swept through Noelle, and she couldn't contain her wide smile, knowing that he cared enough to come pick her up even if he was mad at her. She marveled at how impeccable Jack looked, as handsome and fresh as he had that morning, except for the tie loosened around his neck. Meanwhile, her light makeup had faded away hours ago and tendrils escaped from her braid and curled around her shiny face.

He smiled arms wide open. Despite feeling exhausted, Noelle ran into them. She wrapped her arms around his neck, glowing up at him, offering a tentative smile. "I'm sorry I was a jerk this morning, Jack. Please forgive me."

Unable to resist her, Jack nuzzled his nose with hers. "It's alright. Let's go home."

Unease settled in the pit of Noelle's stomach as he shut the passenger door behind her. She studied his inscrutable expression as he walked around to the driver's seat. Just because he came to pick her up didn't mean all was well between them. His 'It's alright' wasn't exactly an 'I forgive you'.

When they got to the brownstone, the tantalizing aroma of jerk chicken welcomed Noelle home. She followed it to the kitchen and happy-danced upon spying the to-go bags from the Jamaican restaurant around the corner. Jack entered the kitchen, shrugging out of his suit jacket and tie then unbuttoning the first three buttons of his white dress shirt. For the hundredth time today, Noelle wished that she was back in Whiskey Row with 'Scruffy Jack'.

"Hungry, darlin'?"

"Yesss! It's as if you were reading my mind. I'm starved! I haven't eaten anything all day."

Jack frowned his displeasure, moving forward to take her work bag and purse. "That's not healthy, Noelle. Glad I figured you would be too busy to eat. Why don't you take a quick shower, and I'll make our plates?"

She willingly handed over her things and hurried to do just that. That was really nice of him to be thinking of her after she'd been such a bitch this morning. *I'll make it up to him tonight in bed,* she thought, grinning in anticipation as she shed her clothes and stepped into the steaming shower. Twenty minutes later, Noelle found him in the living room watching the evening news with two heaping plates of rice and peas, jerk chicken, and fried plantains on the coffee table in front of him. Two icy bottled beverages were placed beside them.

"That looks good, Jack. I can't wait to dig in! Thanks again," Noelle said as she picked up a plate and spied the label on the bottle. "Orangina! How'd you know I love this combination? I didn't know you even liked Jamaican food." Picking up her fork, she dug in, ravenous after her long day.

Jack picked up his own plate and started eating, feigning a look of surprise. From the private detective's reports, he knew she liked Orangina and that she visited the restaurant whenever she had a long day. He finished chewing. "You're kiddin' me, right? Who doesn't have Jamaican food and Orangina together? They go hand-in-hand."

"Exactly!" Noelle beamed; happy that he got it *and* her. She took a swig of the fizzy, citrus drink and licked her lips clean. "So, how was your day?"

The hooded look Jack gave her from over the bottle let her know what was up. For good measure, she slowly sucked the top between her lips, running her tongue around the rim.

"It was good," he muttered, staring at her glistening lips as his cock surged to life, reminding him of what Noelle's mouth was capable of. "We're taking on a new client, a celebrity chef named Seline Marcuzzo. Familiar with her?"

"Yes, she was really good on that food challenge show. I remember how pissed all the other contestants were with her because she almost always won the challenges." Noelle frowned slightly. She also remembered how beautiful Seline was. Resembling a young Sophia Loren in looks and knock 'em dead curves, the chef was not only smart but cunning, catering to the male judges and audience. The behind-the-scenes footage with the other contestants had not painted her in the most flattering of lights.

"She's quite smart, and during lunch today, she laid out her game plan. It was ambitious as hell. I almost felt like I should warn Martha Stewart that she's about to be dethroned," Jack said half-jokingly. Seline came from humble beginnings but wasn't about to let that stop her from rising to the top. *Even if it meant attempting to seduce him to get it,* Jack thought, recalling their lunch meeting today.

"Monsieur Sullivan, I promise that if you take me on you won't regret it!" Seline insisted dramatically in her charming accent, pressing a hand to her generous cleavage and slightly brushing her blouse to the side to draw his attention. She tossed her long, brown waves over her shoulders, pouting prettily. "I've bent your ear talking about me. Now it's your turn to tell me what you think about me!"

It was a deliberately calculated move that was wasted on him as he was too busy thinking about Ian's words of warning.

"If you won her heart under false pretenses that will be how you lose her."

Ms. Marcuzzo, I think you're very talented, and I like the plans that I've seen so far. You're hungry and that's good because I will get you where you want to be as long as you are willing to work hard and comply with your contract."

Seline smiled flirtatiously, a speculative gleam in her eye as she leaned in closer to reveal more of her breasts. "Monsieur Sullivan, you are just as hungry as I am, perhaps we should be eating together, non?"

Jack stared coldly until the smile faded from her face.

"I only eat with my woman, and she brings the meal AND table to the table, comprenez-vous?"

"It sounds like you have your work cut out for you, and you're both on the same page. I'm glad it worked out well. You're going to be at the party tomorrow night?"

Noelle stole some chicken off his plate and Jack snagged one of her plantains, avoiding looking at her by pretending to be interested in the news. It flashed to world news and images of protestors in France appeared on the screen. Jack quickly changed the channel to HBO, and an image of a woman nursing a dragon appeared.

Tell her; tell her before it is too late, his conscience urged, and Jack ignored the insistent logic of it, keeping his attention on the screen.

"Yes, much later, though. Our other potential client is coming by the office, and then I have a dinner meeting with Seline and some investors. Did you need me to get anything for you? Let me know, and I can have Margo arrange it for you. I promise I will be there as soon as I can."

Noelle watched him carefully, looking for signs of affection but Jack continued to eat, solely focused on the television. There were none. "No, I think I've got everything covered. "I didn't know you were into "Game of Thrones"."

He wasn't and found the little blonde girl with the dragon sucking on her breast to be fucking weird as hell. Jack gathered the remains of their dinner. "Every now and then. I'm going to clean up in the kitchen and lockup. Why don't you get some rest? I'll meet you in the bedroom shortly."

NOELLE LAY IN BED WAITING for Jack to join her, but he took so long that she fell asleep. The next morning, there was a note on his pillow stating that he'd gone in to work early so he could try to be at the party at a decent time. There was no lovemaking and teasing, and Noelle now knew for certain that his feelings had been hurt by her careless words and actions.

Guess the honeymoon was officially over.

CHAPTER
Twenty-Nine

$\mathcal{T}$ ARIK'S PARTY WAS IN FULL swing and packed to capacity. The "Great Gatsby" theme was a hit, and Noelle smiled as she worked the main room, taking in the activity around her. The crowd went bananas when Tarik rolled into the venue, driving an onyx Phantom Drophead Coupe Rolls Royce and surrounded by scantily clad flapper models. The Art Deco features, including the coach style doors perfectly matched the black, gold, and silver Art Deco décor of the venue. Prints of famous artists from that era were blown up and covered oyster silk draped walls. Cocktails named after 1920's musicians like Duke Ellington and Louis Armstrong, among others, were circulating the room, and the dancers mingled with guests, pulling them onto the dance floor as Sidra rocked out in the DJ booth.

The party was a raging success for On a Whim. Tarik introduced Noelle and Avery to the crowd, thanking them profusely for a wonderful party, and they were now networking as they mingled. Jack showed up around eight-thirty and was at the bar speaking with two men. All evening, he'd been in the background, proudly smiling and watching her do her thing. Although, right now, he wasn't smiling. He had a very stern expression on his face as he spoke with the men. Finally, they stormed away, leaving Jack to sip his drink in peace and survey the crowd. He looked appropriately dapper in his tux with his hair slicked back. His model-perfect profile exuded boss sex appeal.

Noelle was about to turn away and check on the appetizer circulation when a blonde woman greeted Jack and gave him a very long hug, which he affectionately returned. Noelle realized it was the woman from her birthday party on the night that they met. She felt her left eye spasm when Jack kept his hand around her waist, listening attentively while she spoke. Occasionally, he smiled and nodded. Noelle felt a stab of pain in her heart when she noticed his bare left hand.

Well, what did you expect, missy? her conscience jeered. *That's what you wanted, right?*

"That's Jack Sullivan, the P.R. guru. Isn't he yummy?" a woman commented behind Noelle. Over her shoulder, she saw two well-dressed partygoers who probably hadn't eaten in years, surveying *her* husband like he was a seven-course meal. She turned back around, seething that her husband was engrossed in such deep conversation with the leech. The handsome husband that she'd let out of the house without the ring he was supposed to be wearing and was surrounded by beautiful women daily. *She was the dumbass of the decade for sure.* Noelle caught Sidra's look and her raised "bitch brow" as her head swiveled between Jack, blondie, and her.

Whatchu wanna do? her look said.

"Yeah, that's him. They say he'll never settle down and commit to one woman. The woman next to him was his on-and-off again love, Vaughn Emerson. She's a shoe designer," Hungry Girl Two confirmed. "They look disgustingly good together."

"Maybe so, but I heard she's married to some asshole banker who runs around on her," Hungry Girl One confided in a gossipy tone.

To hell with this, Noelle had heard enough. Shaking her head no at Sidra, she walked away. Protocol demanded that she give blondie a beat down for touching *her* man, then turn to said man and knee him in the balls for allowing himself to be touched. *Jerk.* Unfortunately, since she was here in a professional capacity, she'd have to take the high road.

For now.

She grabbed a sidecar cocktail from one of the waitresses and crossed the room to stand by the side doors where she could view the entire floor. Downing a big gulp, Noelle grimaced as she thought about her situation with Jack. She didn't like any of this, the no-ring wearing, the distance between them, and the lack of lovemaking. They needed to fix this shit *tonight*. Deep in thought, she didn't even notice that she was no longer alone.

"There was a time when you could drink three of those like they were water," a British accent taunted. "Now, you're barely managing to nurse one." Noelle spun around with a smile to see Theo standing there grinning at her.

"Theo! What are you doing here?!"

They exchanged hugs, and Noelle stiffened as he squeezed her with an unfamiliar, familiarity, bordering on possessive. Pushing away from him, she put distance between them, arms crossed, and eyebrows raised, waiting for an apology.

Boyish smile in place and hands up defensively, he apologized. "Sorry, luv. It's just always a pleasure to see you. I'm actually a plus one to one of Tarik's cousins. This is your shindig, eh? Absolutely done right! Completely spot on, and I'm proud of you and your mate."

"Awww thanks, babe! It's nice to see you too. How's the painting going?"

Now, it was his turn to grimace. "Not well. My best subject seems to be fond of vanishing into thin air. I'll need you to come by the studio sometime this week and see what I've done with your painting. I've been experimenting with shading, and I have to say that I think I'm onto something. Aside from that, I've got a show in London next month."

"Congratulations, Theo! Look at you gettin' all big time! I'm sorry about bailing on you. Give me a call later, and we'll set something up."

"Okay then; it's a date. Looking forward to it. Hey, I ran into an old friend from school earlier. Elizabeth Markel, from Paris. Busty girl with multi-colored braids? Anyway, she wanted to meet me so that we could catch up. Poor thing looked pretty down in the dumps about an old flame being murdered, so I shall do my best to console her," he wagged his brows and kissed her cheek.

"You are absolutely incorrigible. Don't go breaking her heart, Theo." He didn't say anything for a moment as he gave her a head-to-toe appraisal.

"How is it that you get more gorgeous every time I see you?" He mused. "Gotta go, luv! Congrats to you and Avery on a successful party!" And with a wave, he was gone, disappearing into the crowd.

Noelle smiled to herself. Theo would probably gag if she told him the answer to his question was post-coital glow courtesy of her husband.

"I'd like to laugh with a pretty lady. Care to share the joke?" the voice behind her was silky smooth with a Long Island accent.

Men are just popping out of the woodwork tonight, she thought, meeting a pair of ice-blue eyes. They belonged to a man who wasn't handsome, but there was *something* about him, Noelle decided, with his wavy brown hair slicked back, a nose that was a little on the larger side, and lips that were too full for his face. Something that women would like. He licked his lips sensually, his tongue unusually long, and Noelle knew what it was. This man knew how to fuck, and women loved the way he did it. He was one of the men that Jack was speaking to earlier.

"There's no joke. Are you enjoying the party, sir?" Noelle again found herself in the position of escaping intrusiveness by stepping to the side. He grinned, sloping his shoulder against the wall which put him in closer proximity to her than she liked.

"I am. You and your lovely partner are responsible for putting it together, right? Maybe we should get together to discuss an event that my brother and I are considering for the Fourth of July? Pardon me. I just realized that we haven't been properly introduced. I'm Joel Rothman," he said charmingly and held out his hand.

"It's a pleasure to meet you, Mr. Rothman. My name is Noelle...Kramer," she spoke stiffly, realizing that she couldn't give her married name as much as she wanted to. Joel took her hand and held onto it, looking into her eyes.

"No, Noelle, the pleasure is all *mine.*" Reluctantly, he released her hand when she tugged it away. Joel reached into his pocket, extracted a small leather case and pulled out a business card, placing it in her hand. "Please come by so that we can talk about it."

Noelle glanced down at the blue card with silver writing and took it from him and was pleasantly surprised. Joel Rothman, Vice President of Rothman Investments. "Is Ira Rothman your father?"

Joel smiled blandly at her. "Yes, he is. I believe he made the loan for your business. It was the last one he did before semi-retiring. As a matter of fact, you should come by Friday. He'll be in the office and would love to see you again. Especially after I tell him about the success of this event. I'm sure Dad will want to talk to you about expanding.

"Avery and I have been discussing it, and I would love to see your father again."

"I'm sure the feeling is mutual. It's a great party, Noelle. Call me," he murmured persuasively then walked away.

On the other side of the room, Jack watched Joel's interaction with Noelle through narrowed eyes. First that British pussy and now Rothman. Knowing Rothman, he was probably pissed that Vaughn had sought him out. Joel would be even more pissed to find out that it was in regard to retaining Casey as her attorney when she filed for divorce from his sorry ass.

Good for her. Although Jack had a great deal of respect for Ira, his boys could kick fucking rocks as far as he was concerned. They were lazy, privileged motherfuckers who were just waiting for Ira to die so they could fuck up his legacy. A couple of years ago, he and Vaughn had dated on-and-off. She wanted a commitment, but he didn't. They ended things a week after he met Noelle. Now, she wanted to meet with him to brainstorm ideas for her new purse company, she claimed, but Jack knew from the way her brown eyes clung to his face that wasn't all she wanted to do. He firmly reminded her that they would only ever be friends. What he really wanted to say was there wasn't a woman alive that could hold a candle to Noelle, so, no-fucking-thank-you.

Jack was filled with pride as he looked around the beautifully decorated setting. Everyone was having a good time dancing, socializing, and partying with the birthday boy. The food and drinks were amazing as was the music Sid was spinning, and he wished Ronald and Alicia were here to see Noelle in her element. They made eye contact, and her eyes briefly squinted at him, letting him know that she wasn't too pleased about something. He started to walk across the room but was stopped short by Art Sanchez, a reporter with the NY MAG.

"Jack, I think I have enough coverage of Tarik's party. Thanks for getting me in here," Art said sincerely.

"Not a problem, Art. Hey, a friend of mine at Times Now was looking for a great freelance reporter." Jack could see Art was drooling at the thought of getting in good with Times Now, a political newspaper. "Think it's something you might be interested in doing? Nothing really big but some solid pieces to get you in the door. If you'd like, I could put in a good word?"

"Yeah, for sure, man. That would be great! Thanks for looking out!"

Jack clapped him on the back with a friendly smile. "No worries. Listen, is there any way you could get a picture of the event planners and maybe add something on them? I've got a feeling that their business is going to take off after tonight, and they'd be some great people for you to network with. What do you say?" Jack asked, looking Art squarely in the eye.

The other man didn't even blink as he cosigned, "I was thinking the same thing myself."

Jack spied Joel heading out to the terrace for a smoke and shook Art's hand. "Good seeing you, Art. I'll be in touch."

The terrace was empty except for Joel smoking his cigar and talking on his cell phone. Jack quietly shut the doors behind him. "Enjoying the party, Rothman?"

Startled, Rothman whirled around, cursing as some of the ash from his cigar flickered onto his hand. "What the hell, Sullivan?" Taking a quick puff of his cigar, he sneered, "As a matter of fact, I am. How about you? Are you enjoying my soon-to-be-ex whore-wife hanging onto your every word? Just like old times for you, right?"

Jack stepped closer to him, anger vibrating through his body. Although he wasn't the least bit interested in Vaughn and hadn't been in years, she didn't deserve to be talked about like that. Silkily, he replied, "Tell me who the real whore is when you're banging your unsuspecting brother's wife? You or her?"

Joel froze, eyes bugging in shock but quickly recovered, "Who the fuck told you that–"

"No one had to tell me anything. I do my homework. What I've found is that the Ace Hotel is a great place to have some Rothman family fun time on Thursdays between noon and three," Jack smirked nastily at him.

Joel's face was apoplectic with rage. "You bastard! You even attempt to say anything, and I will deny it! You're nothing but white trash aspiring to be better! You're just mad because I stole Vaughn away from you," he finished triumphantly. "It kills you that she didn't want to marry beneath her status."

Jack stared at him for a long moment before bursting out laughing. He laughed long and loud, which angered Joel even more. "Where do you get these stupid-ass ideas from? Shit, no wonder Ira refuses to retire. I'd be scared too of leaving everything I've worked my whole life for to a brainless, conniving, little shit that'd stab his own family in the back and a moron too clueless to know he was being fucked over. I can't do this with you or even stand too close to you because your stupidity might be contagious. Later, Rothman."

Shaking his head and still chuckling, Jack walked back to the terrace doors, but Joel wasn't done yet. From behind him, he heard, "I don't think I'm so brainless that I can't figure out that you're interested in that fine piece of chocolate who's throwing this event. You've been watching her all night," he added spitefully when Jack swung back his way.

"That's your client Senator Kramer's daughter, right? Hell, Jack, I didn't know you liked them like that. Maybe I should just call you Charlie and the Choc–"

Jack's fist smashed into Joel's nose before he could finish, and he felt a vast amount of pleasure as bone crunched underneath it and the bastard landed flat on his ass. Blood spurted from his nose uncontrollably, staining his white dress shirt. He glared up at Jack malevolently. "You son of a bitch! You broke my fucking nose! I'm going to sue you!"

Jack wanted to pick this asshole up and hurl him over the balcony, raising a fucking toast as Rothman plunged to his death. "Keep Ms. Kramer's name out of your mouth. My business relationship with your father has *nothing* to do with you or your brother, and it would behoove you to remember that. See, Rothman, your problem is, you're too arrogant. You want to run with the big dogs, but you're just a fucking chihuahua nipping at our heels, barely keeping up. This is the only warning you'll get from me. Stay your motherfuckin' ass on the porch, and you won't have to find out how hard I bite."

Jack waited to see if the other man would retaliate and was disappointed that he chose to wisely remain silent and on his sorry ass.

"Just as I thought. *Now,* you can have a good night."

THE PARTY WAS OVER, AND the ladies were standing outside, discussing the night's success.

"Ladies, as much as I loved tonight, this might be my last gig for a while," Sidra announced with an excited smile. "I've been chatting with Dominick, and he wants me to be a DJ apprentice on his upcoming world tour!"

Noelle and Avery squealed with excitement, jumping around and hugging their friend. Sidra smiled proudly amidst their congratulations and encouragement.

"Thanks, lovelies! I'm so excited for the opportunity. I'll be shadowing two other guys for the first half of the tour, but then I'll get to spin independently on the last half. It's all-expenses paid, and it will be good to get away for a while," Sidra said with a pensive look in her eyes that had her friends side-eyeing her. Lately, she'd been preoccupied and vague about her activities. When asked if anything was wrong, Sidra waved them off, stating that she had a lot on her mind.

"Are you going to tell us where you were yesterday? We were stressed about your crazy behind," Avery joked, pulling gently on one of Sidra's springy curls.

"I just had to take care of a problem that came up," Sidra evaded. An addictive, Irish problem that showed up on her doorstep the day before yesterday. She still wasn't sure why she let him in, but one look into his lust-filled eyes, and Sidra, strong-willed as she was,

was powerless to resist Casey. He'd stayed until this morning when they had an argument over her poor eating habits. She didn't think she would be seeing him again anytime soon.

The time away would be great for clearing her head. This thing between the two of them was beyond her comprehension. They didn't like each other and were barely civil to each other around other people, but that wasn't enough to stop them from fucking like rabbits every chance they got. "It's taken care of, though. What's up with you and the hubby? You guys were acting like you didn't even know each other tonight, and *don't* get me started on blondie–"

"It's not like we're running around trying to broadcast our relationship," Noelle interrupted. "Besides, I'm here to work, not sit up under my man."

"Well, here comes your man now, and he doesn't look too happy," Avery warned. They watched as Jack strode purposely towards them, his face drawn in angry lines. "Damn girl, Jack is wearing the hell out of that tux."

"Isn't he, though?" Noelle acknowledged with pride. Although, right now, he looked really pissed, which in no way detracted at all from his fineness.

"Ladies, you were amazing tonight," Jack praised them. "I've got to go, baby. There's a big problem with a client, and I need to leave town for a couple of days." Just thinking about the problem made his head ache. Vivienne was never going to let him hear the end of this.

"I'm leaving you the car and catching a cab to my place to pack. I'll call you when I get to my destination." Cupping her nape, Jack slanted his mouth over Noelle's for a sizzling kiss that left her weak and clinging to his jacket lapels.

A bright flash went off in their faces. Noelle

blinked, and Jack cursed but made no attempts to shield them away from the intruder. Sidra and Avery yelled at the photographer, but he was already gone. Worried, Noelle stared helplessly at Jack who, unconcerned, shrugged his shoulders carelessly.

"Guess the cat's out of the bag, darlin'."

CHAPTER
Thirty

$\mathcal{T}$ HE NEWS OF NEW YORK City's most eligible bachelor being off the market was superseded by the national headline of his client, Inez Gaines being arrested for assaulting her ex-boyfriend. Though Noelle's phone was ringing off the hook and she had two photographers camped out on her doorstep, it wasn't as bad as she thought it would be. The only calls she was taking were from Sidra, Avery, and Ian. Currently, she was bracing herself for a visit from her parents after hearing her mother's contemptuous voicemail.

It was 3:00 p.m. the following day, and she'd yet to hear from Jack, although, she did see him on TV as he held a courthouse press conference in the small town of Baymoor, Maryland. Casey was representing the beauty queen, and Darby was on her security detail. Noelle proudly listened to Jack effortlessly control the conference, southern charm pouring out of him. He cut a dashing figure in a navy Armani suit, fielding reporters' questions. Her phone vibrated with a text from Sidra.

Turn the TV to Post-It-Notes! They're talking about you and Jack!

What?! Noelle found the New York gossip show in time to hear the blonde anchorwoman commenting on the big screen picture of her and Jack kissing last night. Although she was horrified to be caught in a PDA moment of such magnitude, Noelle couldn't help but smile because she and Jack looked damned good together. Eyes closed and the way they held and kissed screamed that they were totally into each other. Perversely, Noelle hoped Vaughn was watching.

"Turns out the mystery woman seen in the scorching lip lock with elusive bachelor and PR whiz Jack Sullivan is none other than Noelle Kramer, one half of the company On a Whim, the hottest new event planners in Manhattan, that created Tarik Owens lavish birthday celebration last night. Mr. Owens is a client of Sullivan's firm, and here's another interesting twist about the beautiful Ms. Kramer; she is the youngest daughter of Senator Ronald and Alicia Kramer, who are also represented by Jack's firm. Talk about keeping it all in the family."

She winked at the camera as the screen changed to a picture of her parents smiling faces at her father's election celebration two years ago.

Noelle turned the TV off with a sigh of frustration. She just knew her mother would try to use this against her husband, and if she got her father worked up enough, he would be demanding Jack's head on a platter as well. Her phone rang again, and this time, it was her sister Sloane, who was currently traveling in Europe with her family.

"Hey, Sloane, how are you?" Noelle answered cheerfully. She could hear her niece and twin nephews shouting hello to her in the background. "Tell my babies I said hello."

"It's always the quiet ones you have to watch out for, Ms. Thang," her sister joked. "I should have known from the way he was always ogling you that something was going to happen sooner or later. You should hear Mother ranting and raving about his improper conduct and possibly suing him."

"She'd better not try it. Jack and I are a consensual thing! As in we're in this *together*. Anyone who has anything to say about it can kiss my ass, present company included if you called on Mom and Dad's behalf," Noelle hissed.

"Okay, sis, no need to get riled up," Sloane cautioned. "Am I allowed to ask how long this has been going on? Despite the way it may come off to you, we honestly only have your best interests at heart."

"That's fine if you have my best interest at heart, but I'm a grown-ass woman who's capable of making decisions that don't require any hand-holding from anyone in the Kramer family. And you can certainly ask how long it's been going on, but I'm not telling you. That's mine and Jack's business. All any of you need to know is he makes me happy, so you should support our relationship." Noelle barely resisted the urge to fist pump. Damn, it felt good to take a stand!

"Well, go on then, girl. I'm really proud of you for standing up for yourself and what you believe. Took you long enough. Just know that I'm always here for you if you want to talk. How's your business going? From what I could see of last night's event, you and Avery did an amazing job."

Noelle glowed with the praise. Even though she'd been in business for a couple of months now, it was the first time her sister had ever inquired about it. "Thanks, Sloane, it's going great. There's still a lot to learn, but I love it. I wish you could have been there."

She launched into some details that she was at liberty to disclose, and her sister seemed genuinely happy for her. They talked for about fifteen minutes more before Sloane changed the subject. "By the way, I'm sorry to hear about your friend Remy."

"Remy? What about him?" Noelle demanded, on high-alert. It was sad to say but most of the time, she forgot all about that idiot because she trusted Jack one hundred percent to handle it, and her time was far better spent on growing her business.

"Girl, you don't know? I guess it wouldn't be a big deal in the States because he isn't American. He was murdered in Paris three weeks ago. He got caught in bed with the Ambassador from Cameroon's wife, and the man shot him in the knees before throwing him over the balcony onto a crowded street where he died on impact. The French want justice, but the ambassador is claiming diplomatic immunity. In the meantime, the wife has disappeared and is rumored to be pregnant by Remy. Tensions are escalating daily, and there have been protests and riots for the last couple of weeks. It's a big freaking mess. Andreas feels that we should probably skip Paris, which saddens me because you *know* how I love Paris this time of the year."

Remy, her blackmailing scumbag ex, was dead.

Noelle's grabbed her laptop to look up his first email to her. It was dated three and a half weeks ago. She tried to compile the time frame of events in her head.

"Sissy, are you still there?" Sloane's use of her childhood nickname made her smile.

"Yeah, I'm still here. Listen, I have to go. It's a madhouse outside of my home. I'm somewhat of a celebrity now that Jack's fallen under my spell," she joked. "Give my love to the kiddos and Andreas. Love you, Sloane," Noelle spoke absent-mindedly as she Googled Remy Dumont's death. Her blood froze, realizing Jack's visit to her home was two days later – after he'd supposedly done all his homework on Ratface.

"I love you too, and again, I'm sorry about Remy," Sloan repeated before saying goodbye.

Noelle paced the length of her hallway. Something wasn't right. Jack's words came back to haunt her.

"Your ex is the type who would make a lot of noise if he was threatened. The pics would come out either way. This could have lasting effects on your father's career and your family."

Noelle tried calling him, but it went to voicemail. Instead of leaving a message, she hung up. Suddenly, something from last night clicked, and she quickly scrolled through her contacts until she found the one she was looking for and pressed the call button. As the phone rang, she peeked out of her front window and saw the paparazzi still loitering around. A groggy voice answered, and Noelle rolled her eyes.

"Seriously, Theo? It's after three in the afternoon. I need you up and alert." Noelle waited impatiently as he groaned his protest. "Listen, I'm sorry to bother you, but last night, you mentioned a girl from Paris? I think I might know her friend and need to talk to her about that. Can you help me get in contact with her?"

"I'll do you one better, luv. She's laying bare arse up, right next to me," Theo admitted slyly, and Noelle made a *tsking* noise as Theo murmured sweet words to wake his bedmate up. "Lizzie, could you be a dear and talk to my mate Noelle about your old bloke who passed? Now, don't look at me like that. I'm sorry to be a cad, and I promise I'll do that thing you like with my tongue. 'Ow's that sound?" Theo cajoled with a raunchy laugh. Noelle grimaced at his ridiculousness as she waited for dear, old Lizzie to get it together.

JACK WAS TIRED AND IRRITATED as he slid onto the bench across from Casey at The Comfort Table Café. They were soon joined by his brother's good friend, Maxwell Hayes, a former lawyer turned farmer. He wished he was back home with Noelle to help her weather the crap that she was probably getting from the press and her family. Unfortunately, Inez's ex-boyfriend made the bad decision to harass her, and the ending result of the altercation was him getting his ass handed to him with a deadly combination of a high heel and frying pan. Sheriff Holloway had to take her in on assault charges, not for defending herself, but for the kick to the groin she gave him with her six-inch Halston heels after he was down and out for the count. It was witnessed and recorded by his new girlfriend and her sister.

The video already had five million viewers worldwide on YouTube, three million likes on Facebook, and the memes were out of control. Comedians were having a field day. The pageant was trying to strip Inez of her title, Viv was fighting to save her endorsements, and Ian already had her scheduled for a couple of talk shows. Inez was furious that they had taken her phone and deactivated her social media accounts.

"I WANT TO TELL THE whole world what that asshole and those bitches tried to do to me on my terms, Jack!" she'd

screamed, pacing back and forth furiously, her lovely honey-colored eyes flashing uncontrollably. Inez was out for blood and refused to be denied. "Casey, you'll sue anyone who tries to break my endorsement contracts, right? Jack, I need to be active on–"

"What you will be doing is stayin' put and shuttin' the fuck up, Inez," Jack icily interrupted, southern accent in full effect. He was tired of her drama. Stunned, she sat down, staring up at him wordlessly. When he next spoke to his partners, he would be willing to confess that he may have bitten off more than he could chew with the beauty queen.

"If you recall, I warned you about becoming involved with this guy, but you didn't listen. Your hostility toward the press and egg-throwin' is beyond immature. I told you to stay put and conduct yourself like a Miss World Beauty is supposed to! That means no postin' pics on social media, comparin' the size of your ex's dick to a caterpillar, and initiatin' twitter wars with women you don't know with invitations like 'What's good, bitch? Get at me then'. Do you recall that conversation?"

She had the grace to look ashamed, and a blush stained her bronze skin. Nervously, she ran a hand over her shoulder-length bob. "Okay, I might have gone a little too far."

Jack shook his head wearily. "You think?! I'm goin' to do my job, but you really need to start thinkin' before you act and focus on your priorities. You're a smart girl with the potential to have the world at her feet, yet you seem happiest actin' out, and that shit has already taken a toll on your image. You're the Dennis Rodman of beauty queens and I'm over it! I'll let Casey fill you in on our next course of action."

"Yes, of course," Inez spoke humbly.

Casey cleared his throat and placed a folder in front

of Inez. "This is your contract with R.R. & S. The immediate next course of action is you complyin' with your contract and not creatin' any more waves, or we're going to sue the shit out of you for breach of contract for the two clauses you've already broken. What's it goin' to be?"

———————————

"WADE SAID SHE CAN POST bail in the morning. Thank you, ma'am." Jack stifled a yawn as a waitress set a plate with chicken 'n' dumplings in front of him. Casey ordered Salisbury steak and mashed potatoes while Max chose the gumbo. "Case, what can you do to spin this in her favor legally?"

Casey and Max looked at each other for a long moment before Casey answered Jack. "That dog won't hunt, Jack. Inez kicked that asshole in the nuts so hard that half the teams in the NFL are offerin' her puntin' contracts."

All three men winced and managed to restrain from cupping their own privates.

"There is no 'spinnin' it in her favor'. She'll probably be required to take anger management courses and have to go to therapy. If you make her leave, her reputation will be that she has to be managed all the time. My suggestion is to let her stay here in her hometown. She's surrounded by people she knows and who will rally around her."

Max nodded. "Wade is a good man and a great sheriff. He'll definitely make sure she gets enough protection, and Inez also has another protector."

As if on cue, the door to the café opened, and a tall, muscular man with curly, dark brown hair strode toward them, fire in his green eyes. He stopped at their table and focused on Max. "Seriously, man? My last words to you were 'keep an eye on crazy pants for me'!

I didn't even get to state lines before all hell broke loose! What the fuck happened?"

"'Crazy Pants', huh? I like it. It's catchy and sure as hell suits Inez," Jack murmured to Casey who nodded as he sprinkled salt and pepper on his steak and cut into it.

Max was unrepentant. "Then you should have taken her with you. Space my ass! I don't know who the two of you think you're fooling, playing it cool and shit. Rafe, allow me to introduce the Sullivan brothers. Jack is her PR and Casey is her lawyer. Guys, this is Rafe. He's the contractor who's been working on Inez's new venture." The men nodded their acknowledgment of each other. "They were in the middle of brainstorming a hero to rescue our damsel in distress angle," Max slyly informed him.

"Your first mistake is thinking Inez needs a man. She doesn't need one because she already has one. *Me.* Your second mistake is thinking she needs someone to fight her battles. She just needs someone to have her back, which I do."

"Sorry for the assumption, Rafe. Last time I looked, your back was heading out of town because you were confused about your feelings for her or have you forgotten that?" Max asked in a mildly accusatory tone.

Rafe stiffened. "I'm well aware that I shouldn't have left, and I won't be making that mistake again. Where the fuck is that motherfucker who dared to put his hands on her?"

"I believe he's in the hospital where they're tryin' to surgically remove his balls from the roof of his mouth," Jack answered tiredly. Damn, he couldn't wait to get home to his wife. His phone vibrated, and it was Ronald Kramer's number. "Excuse me while I take this call, fellas."

CHAPTER
Thirty-One

H E LIED TO HER.

Noelle was completely numb, staring out the window of the cab she and Avery were sharing. According to Elizabeth's timeframe, Remy was dead two days *before* Jack came to her with the information he'd 'gathered'. By playing on her fears, he'd gotten her to do exactly as he wanted, but for what? That's what she couldn't figure out.

Twice this morning, Jack called, but she'd responded only with texts saying she was in meetings with potential clients. If she spoke with him, she knew she'd demand answers to her questions and that couldn't happen right now. Noelle really needed to put her game face on because she and Avery were on their way to a meeting at Rothman Investments. The confrontation would come later when they were face-to-face and Noelle could see his reaction.

"I've got our business plan for expansion, and I spoke to my grandmother's realtor regarding the kind of office space we're looking for. She's available after the meeting if you want to meet."

Avery was talking, but Noelle was hardly paying

attention. Her mind was racing a mile a minute, bombarded with memories.

"Maybe you'll like being married to me."

"I can only take so much, Noelle. You don't have a clue about how bad I want to be buried inside of you," his eyes burning hazel fire.

Fingers snapped loudly in Noelle's face, startling her. Avery was staring at her, lips compressed in annoyance.

"I heard you, and yes, I have all of our financial statements," Noelle automatically replied to which Avery rolled her eyes.

"Chile, I was just asking if Mama A had shown up on your doorstep yet! You need to pull it together. We're about to go up here and show how we can hang with the big boys. I can't have you staring off into space," Avery warned, and Noelle gave her a '*B, please*' look as the cab pulled to a stop in front of their destination.

"Bosses don't *hang* with anybody. They work hard and let the results speak for themselves. Thought you knew that." Noelle paid the cab fare and got out of the cab. "Now, get your sexy ass out and let's walk like we've got ten men following behind us, ready to slay on our command."

THE MEETING ROOM OF ROTHMAN Investments was cold and sterile looking. *Kind of like a doctor's office,* Noelle thought as she sat at the large conference table with Avery and Joel and David Rothman. Noelle was surprised that Joel could see the reports. He had two vicious black eyes, and his nose was bandaged up. She didn't know what the hell had happened to him, but she had a feeling he'd probably brought it on himself. All of On a Whim's financial records and business expansion plans had been reviewed, and now, negotiation terms on the interest rate for their refinanced loan would start. The new loan would allow them to get an office space with a kitchen for the catering side of events, instead of cooking in their kitchens.

An hour later, mutual terms were agreed upon, and the only thing needed was the ladies' signatures. As the contracts were being printed, there was a knock on the glass door. Tarik was waving at them enthusiastically and Noelle smiled and waved back, and Joel motioned him in. The men exchanged handshakes, and Tarik kissed both Noelle and Avery on their cheeks.

"Crikey! What in the hell 'appened to your face, mate?" Tarik grimaced, at Joel's injuries. "I was on my way to meet with your dad about an investment when I saw you guys and thought I'd say hi," he finished charmingly. "Ladies, thank you again for the party! I've never gotten laid so much in my life! Women are practically throwing their panties in my path in invitation, and I shall bed them in the order that they come."

The laugh the men shared was crude, making Noelle and Avery's skin crawl, the room's atmosphere now tainted.

"Let's go," Noelle decided. "Having the kitchen would have been nice but being a woman with pride and standards is better."

"Amen; let's do it." Avery got their paperwork together.

"What's the investment, if you don't mind me asking, Tarik?" Joel asked casually, and something in his tone gave Noelle pause. He was watching her like a tiger ready to pounce. The hairs on her nape stirred.

"A horse farm Jack recommended. He said that maybe since I ride horses, I could probably invest in breeding them. He thinks a lot of people would buy them from a well-known polo player. That man is a genius. Bravo on getting your hooks into him, Noelle. He'll do wonders for your career as well."

Tarik said with a cheeky wink. Noelle glared at him as an outraged Avery sucked her teeth at his gall.

"No, this mutha–"

"I got it, Avery. Hard work will do wonders for anyone's career, Tarik!" Noelle snarled, resisting the urge to brain him with her laptop. "I'm not sure what you're trying to insinuate, but I suggest you refrain from saying or implying anything further of that nature before I sue the shit outta you for slander."

Face red with embarrassment, a panicked Tarik backtracked. "Whoa, darling, relax! Relax! I wasn't trying to say anything of the sort. I-er-better go. Don't want to keep Ira waiting." He flew out the door, and the conference room fell silent again.

"Is everything okay, Noelle? Don't be too hard on Tarik. I'm sure he means well." Joel's derisive smile indicated the opposite.

She studied him, certain now more than ever that something was amiss. He was playing a game with her but hadn't revealed the rules, which made him a cheater. On a Whim did not associate or do business with cheaters.

"David, Avery mentioned on the way in how beautiful the atrium on the third floor was. She'd love a tour. Isn't that right, Ave?"

Noelle spoke without taking her eyes off 'Joel the Snake', and he smiled unpleasantly, finally dropping the facade.

"Yes! I did say that. Would you be so kind as to

show it to me, David?"

Avery smoothed her salmon pink dress around her hips, drawing attention to her body. Noelle knew she would owe her big time as David's eyes followed her hands, swallowing hard.

"Yes, of course! This way, Ms. Monroe."

"Oh, please call me Avery. Lead the way, honey," she cooed, sliding her well-manicured hand through the crook of his arm as they left.

The silence in the room was deafening as the two occupants sized each other up. Noelle spoke first. "Please explain your last comment to me, Joel. You seem to think that I should know what you're talking about, and I'm afraid you have me at a disadvantage because I don't."

Joel gave a scathing laugh. "I was making reference to the fact that you got your loan with us because you're fucking Jack Sullivan."

The hell?!

Noelle shook her head. "What does *my* knowing Jack have to do with my loan with your *father's* company?"

Take that asshole, she thought as his eyes narrowed on her reminder of who really owned Rothman Investments.

"It has everything to do with it! Six months ago, Jack made a deal with Ira that he'd bring the bank more business and advertising if a loan was offered to On a Whim at an extremely low interest rate. He certainly kept up his end of the bargain. Jack got Tarik and some other clients to utilize our services. The catch was that we would have to strongly recommend On a Whim for any social events they do. Do you see where I'm going with this?"

Unfortunately, she was starting to. Noelle's felt like she was going to throw up. Jack had orchestrated not only her business but her clientele. She recalled the numerous times that she'd solicited his advice and how eager he was to give it. How Tarik picked her company when he had his choice of more experienced event planning companies, never mind that his event had turned out to be enormously successful. Fury sprinted through Noelle as she registered how badly she'd been deceived.

"Now, I wouldn't give a shit if Ira wanted to run around in a fucking tutu all day and ride a damn tricycle while doing so as long as he stays out of the office. The problem is, all the new business is bringing him out of retirement, and he's putting his nose where it doesn't belong. David and I don't need him here, but thanks to your lover boy, Ira's not going anywhere! I told that bastard to mind his own business, and *this* is what he did to my face! Maybe you could do me a solid since we are giving you this loan on such generous terms and tell Jack to stay out of our lives?"

Noelle gripped the chair handles, forcing herself to remain seated instead of jumping the table and punching Joel's conniving ass in his already broken nose. For the first time, she noticed what appeared to be a family picture next to the door. It was of Ira and an older, silver-haired lady sitting down. They were surrounded by David and Joel with their wives. David's wife was an uptight-looking, plump brunette with glasses. Joel's wife with a forced smile, holding a crying, toddler-aged boy. Noelle's eyes narrowed in recognition.

"Vaughn Emerson. She's married to some asshole banker who runs around on her."

Jack's ex was married to Ira's loser-ass son. That was the real reason Joel had such a hard-on for Jack. His ego couldn't take that his wife had dated someone more good-looking, charming, and smarter than him.

Someone if judging from the looks his wife had given Jack at the party, she still wasn't over. Noelle had heard enough. Her head was spinning from all the little surprises that kept popping up. She stood up, gathered all her documents, and shoved them into her tote, heading for the door.

"Hey, where are you going? Noelle!" he shouted.

Noelle abruptly spun around. *"Our lives."*

"Huh? What did you say?" Joel was confused. "What are you talking about?"

Noelle gave him a withering glare. "You said *our lives*. Not our business, which leads me to believe that this is a little more personal for you. Go fuck yourself, Rothman! We both know there's a little more to this story than your ego is willing to acknowledge. When Jack finds out what you tried to pull here, for your sake, I hope you have plenty of lubricant. You're going to need it when he jams both of his size thirteens up your self-righteous ass."

His face paled and Noelle detected real fear in his eyes. She walked out despite his protests and texted Avery to meet her in the lobby. Noelle pressed the down button on the elevator, waiting impatiently for it to arrive. Her head was pounding, and for once, she was regretting breaking up with Mary Jane. She'd kill for something to relax her right now. When the doors opened, she came face-to-face with none other than Joel's wife. It was hard to say who was more surprised, but Noelle swiftly composed herself and remained silent as the other woman exited the elevator.

"Hello. You're Jack's friend, Noelle, aren't you?"

Noelle cocked her head at her with a warning glare. *Like this heffa didn't know.* She really didn't want to do pleasantries with the woman who'd dated her husband and was married to the man who tried to take his revenge of Jack on her. Not today, not ever. And as mad as she was at Jack, she really wanted to let his former lover know she was more than a *friend*. She was his wife, lover... oh hell, who was she really kidding? She was nothing more than his fucking puppet on a string.

"I am, and you're Joel's wife." Noelle wistfully watched the doors shut and the elevator began the downward descent without her.

"Vaughn Emerson." She held out her well-manicured hand haughtily, and Noelle grudgingly shook it. Up close, Vaughn was even prettier than she'd first thought, but Noelle could see the exhaustion in her expressive brown eyes and suspected it was due to Joel.

"I always knew you and Jack would wind up together," Vaughn conceded with a wry twist to her lips. At Noelle's surprised look, she hunched her shoulders prettily. "It was obvious the way he couldn't stop staring at you the night of your birthday party. I asked him about it afterward, and he just shrugged off my question. A week later, I went to his place, and there was an open folder with a full dossier on you as well as pictures. I knew right then that any hopes of my becoming Mrs. Sullivan were not going to come to fruition."

"Do you still want him? Is that why you're telling me this?" Noelle demanded, pressing the down button for the elevator. Mentally, she moved Vaughn to the top of her shit list and Jack down to second, or should Jack go first and then the Rothmans? Realistically, if it wasn't for Jack, she wouldn't be having all these damn issues to begin with.

Vaughn looked at her seriously. "If I was single and he wanted me, then yes, in the blink of an eye. Unfortunately, he doesn't feel the same way. At Tarik's party, it was déjà vu all over again for me. He's never looked at anyone the way he looks at you, but you can't even see it, can you?"

Noelle gave her a contemplative look as the elevator arrived, and the doors opened. She moved forward, forcing Vaughn to step aside and entered the elevator. Noelle was surprised that she could address her in such a calm manner. "I sincerely hope you listen to what I'm going to say to you, *Mrs. Rothman.* Mind your own damn business and don't ever think you can address personal issues with me again. I don't believe in repeating myself, and you won't like the results should you be stupid enough to try. Are. We. Clear?"

"Crystal," Vaughn replied haughtily. Noelle's stare remained intently locked on her until the doors softly closed.

"Scoops of bullshit on top of bullshit and then even more bullshit sprinkled on the sundae to make it tastier," she snarled, pulling out her phone and calling the one business-minded person that she could trust at this point.

"Hello, my dear."

The dulcet tones immediately soothed her ire.

"Hi, Uncle Ian."

CHAPTER
Thirty-Two

*I*T WAS SEVEN-THIRTY THAT evening when Jack finally got to Noelle's place. He was furious not to have heard from her all day. His repeated calls were sent to voicemail until it was full, and she hadn't responded to any of his texts. He unlocked the door and entered the dark foyer. She wasn't home, and he was now stressed, worrying about her more than ever. What if something happened to her? Digging into his pocket, he pulled his phone out and called his contact at the police department to see if he knew anything about Noelle being injured. There was nothing regarding her in the system, but he would keep an eye out the detective assured Jack.

Where the hell was she?

"THEO, THANKS FOR SEEING ME home," Noelle hiccupped obnoxiously, struggling to get her keys out of her tote bag. After three attempts, she held them up victoriously. "Aha!"

"Not a problem, luv. It's the least I could do so no

other bugger could take advantage of you in your drunken glory." Theo plucked the keys out of her hand, deftly opening the door to her gate.

"Hey! I resent that. I'm not drunk. I'm...I'm... ine-inebriated," she finished triumphantly, then hiccupped again as she threw her arm around him, squinting her eyes. "Slightly."

"Uh-huh, come on then. It's been a helluva day for you, hasn't it?" Theo carefully maneuvered her up the flight of stairs as she lay her head on his shoulder forlornly. Outside of her door, he cautiously propped her up against the wall before inserting the key into the lock of her front door. The day had ended with Noelle having drinks with Theo, Pierce, and Avery at the Blueprint Bar. She was solidly smashed, which was something that normally didn't happen, but it had been necessary to dull the pain of Jack's betrayal.

Noelle giggled hysterically, observing his disheveled, blonde curls and faint facial hair. "Did anyone ever tell you that you look like that Francis character on "Reign"? He drives all the ladies wild just like you do, my friend." She touched his curls. "These curls are *errythang*, boo. Goldilocks is what I shall call you from now on."

Theo rolled his eyes as she gave a dramatic sigh, drunkenly running her hands through his locks. "I've made a deal with the devil and now, he owns me. Did you know that? Why couldn't it have been you and me?" She shook her head pitifully. "Instead, my heart belongs to a demon."

Theo gave her a serious look, pulling the keys out of the now unlocked door. "I've often asked myself that same question, Noelle. If you even knew well...I don't think you quite understand what you mean to me. Maybe when you sober up, we can have that talk I've wanted to have forever with you."

The door swung open, making Noelle yelp, stumbling back in surprise. Her husband stood in the doorway, murderous intent blazing in his eyes as he grabbed Theo by the throat and squeezed.

"Well, why don't you enlighten us, asshole?" Jack hissed. With a savage smile, he greeted a stunned Noelle. "Honey, I'm home."

HE DIDN'T TRUST HIMSELF TO speak. Jack's fury was evident in every line carved into his face and his shaking hands as he poured his silent, sulky wife a cup of black coffee. He pushed it across the kitchen counter to the other side where she sat on a barstool glaring balefully at him.

"Drink it."

Defiantly, Noelle pushed it back toward him, and some of the hot liquid sloshed out of the cup onto the white marble counter. "That's not how I take my coffee! You drink it," she spat mutiny stamped all over her face.

Jack placed his hands on the counter and stretched across it, so Noelle could see just how serious he was because he was out of both patience and fucks to give. *"You don't want to do this with me right now, Noelle.* Quit actin' like a fuckin' spoiled ass brat. Drink the fuckin' coffee, or I'll pour it down your damned throat. Then you can explain exactly what the hell 'Prince Charmin'" was talkin' about out there."

The southern accent was back with a vengeance, making a quickly sobering Noelle aware of how real shit was getting.

Jack would never admit how much her confessions hurt him. After hearing a noise by the door, he walked over and heard their entire conversation. Jack felt completely validated in choking the little playboy out. He knew he'd been right about Theo's feelings toward Noelle, and that made him squeeze tighter and tighter while Noelle screamed and pulled at his arm. Only when the younger man turned blue did Jack finally let go, a visceral rush of adrenaline and satisfaction surging through him as he watched the younger man struggle for air.

Noelle bent to help Theo, and Jack snatched her arm, yanking her back. "Get your ass inside, Noelle."

Head held high, she stuck her nose in the air before staggering through the doorway.

Jack leaned down and got in Theo's face. "Stay away from her. I catch you near her or trying to get next to her again, it will be my hand crushing your balls instead. Got it?"

Wheezing, Theo tried to answer, but Jack pressed his index finger to his lips with a sinister grin.

"Don't speak. I know you understood."

Then he slammed the front door, leaving Theo lying on the floor.

"Well, I won't have to wait long for us to be together, right? You said we'd only need to stay married for a couple of months until everything dies down." Noelle took a small sip of the coffee, watching his eyes flicker in response.

Lying ass bastard.

Jack didn't know what to make of her behavior. There was something very off about Noelle, and he didn't think it had anything to do with him finding her and Theo together, as hurtful as that was. *She was furious,* he mused, noting the storm in her gray eyes and curled lip. And all of it was directed solely at him.

Noelle pressed on as she jumped up, pushed her chair back, and headed down the hall, her words floating over her shoulder. "That is what you said isn't it, Jack? Well, I don't want to wait for the divorce papers to be drawn up. I want it done ASAP, and I want you to move back into your own space. I'll even reimburse you for the time you've spent with me. This thing between us is *done*."

Heart pounding and blood roaring in his ears, Jack exited the kitchen, following her down the hall to the bedroom where she pivoted to confront him.

"We ain't gettin' a divorce, Noelle. I don't know what the fuck happened with you in the time that I've been gone, but divorce is off the table, sugar," he replied, holding onto his control by a thread. "I'll be damned if I let you go so that you can run off with that snivelin' pansy-ass! I'm not goin' anywhere, so quit actin' like a damned child and talk to me! What's got you so riled up?"

"Theo is more of a man than you'll ever be!" Noelle retorted furiously. "At least *he's* honest! Unlike you, who has done nothing but lie to me! Maybe I should stay away from Theo or he might wind up like Joel Rothman, right? Or dead like Remy?" Her anger reached unexplored levels as realization dawned in his eyes that she knew of his deceit. "Yes, I know about that little fact you decided to keep to yourself. When were you going to tell me that Remy was dead? I had to hear it from my sister, and then an associate confirmed it! You fucking lied to me, Jack!"

So, she knew.

Jack watched her helplessly falling apart. The cause of her pain, he was remorseful and felt like shit. Jaw ticking, he ground out, "I never lied to you, Noelle."

She looked at him crazily. "Correct me if I'm wrong, but was it not you who said that Remy would do all sorts of crazy things if he didn't get what he wanted? That was you, right?"

"That was me, but I never said he was dead or alive. I just told you that his threats checked out and relayed worst-case scenarios. Then I offered a solution to avoid those scenarios," Jack calmly explained, even though his stomach was churning, and he could feel sweat forming on his back. He really needed to get a hold of himself. He was a sailor that could navigate the deadliest of waters, but this one woman could capsize him with the gentlest wave. Jack knew it had been a dick move to play on her fears. Now she knew and planned to leave him. *He couldn't let her.* By rights, he should, but in Jack's world, that wasn't a possibility to entertain, now that he knew what happiness felt like. What *they* felt like together.

Noelle paused, and Jack could see she was trying to remember exactly what it was he'd said. Finally, she threw her hands up in exasperation, "It doesn't fucking matter, you manipulative asshole! You already knew what happened to him, and you kept it to yourself on top of arranging my business loan for me and giving me pity clients! What a laugh you must have had at my expense as I discussed my business with you and considered your suggestions. You're no better than my family with their goddamn interfering asses!" she raged, smacking the dresser with her palm.

"You need to calm down, darlin'. It wasn't even like that," Jack uttered slowly. "As far as the business is concerned, yes, I did make a deal with Ira to help you get the fundin' for your company. I only did it because I knew that your parents weren't goin' to give you the advance on your inheritance, and you wouldn't accept a loan from me. Your business, one that can provide food, entertainment, and décor, is solid though, so it's an investment in itself for Rothman because you, Avery, and Sidra all bring something to the table. You didn't have to take that loan, but the businesswoman in you recognized it as an excellent opportunity," he explained earnestly, hoping that she would see his reasoning. Jack was struggling to remain cool, even though the walls were quickly closing in on him.

"In regard to the clients, they only had to *hear* your ideas. No one *made* them hire your company. That was you and Avery's hard work as well as the repeat business! I simply got the ball rollin'. You had a vision that you were trying to achieve, and I had the means to assist you. What's wrong with helping out if I can?" Jack asked reasonably.

Noelle stared at him as if he was Lucifer himself coming to claim her. "Nothing, as long as you were straightforward and direct about it, which you weren't. You created this grand scheme to get what you wanted! Jack did what Jack does best: *You fixed me.* Isn't that what you do? In order to marry me, you had to make me worthy, someone you could be seen with and not just fuck. Poor, pathetic Noelle who still lived at home with her parents just wouldn't do for the great Jack Sullivan! You made it so I'd be good enough to be seen on your arm."

Jack shook his head vehemently, his patience finally lost.

"No, that's bullshit, and you know it, Noelle!" he yelled causing her to jump and retreat at the contorted rage on his face. "You're the one who was so afraid of your own shadow, always scurrying around like a damn mouse! You let everyone put you down and were content to stay in the shadows. I've wanted you forever and just knew if you had the chance–" he trailed off realizing as Noelle looked at him expectantly that she was semi-correct.

"What you did was *despicable*, Jack! From the beginning, you manipulated me to fall in line with your scheme, not giving a damn about how I felt or if my heart could survive it because you have a hero complex. And that's what it all comes down to, doesn't it? You couldn't save your mother, but you could save pathetic Noelle from slowly dying away in her parents' tower like Rapunzel. I'm right, aren't I? Aren't I, Jack?!" Noelle screamed, getting in his face.

She was beyond humiliated and furious, barely able to contain the tears that were trying pour. *She'd be damned if she cried in front of him.* So enamored by his physical appearance, she'd never really known the real Jack Sullivan, to know he was capable of such cruelty took her breath away. *What a complete fool I am,* she despaired.

"Enough!" Jack roared, driving his fist into the bedroom wall, stunning her into silence. He couldn't breathe as he stared at the damage. Suddenly, he was that scared thirteen-year-old boy again, losing the love of his life. Then it had been his mother, but now, it was his wife. Jack knew he would not survive the loss of Noelle if such a thing occurred. Without her, he faced a life of abject misery and darkness just when he was stepping into the sun. He couldn't-no *wouldn't* go back to his life before they happened. To even call it a life was a gross exaggeration.

"The worst part about all this is that you had me thinking this could really work between us," Noelle smiled cynically, raking a hand through her messy curls, her eyes bright with unshed tears, bitterness, and anguish. "That's not your fault, though. Again, you were very careful in what you said or didn't say. But you didn't have to involve me with all the wonderful people in your life and your beautiful hometown. *You made me fall for you and them.* You made me believe that I had a chance with you. You made me...made me...*love you,*" she finished brokenly, turning away from him.

"It can work, Noelle," Jack pleaded desperately. "You just have to want it as badly as I do, baby. *Please don't do this.*" He'd resorted to begging, but he could tell her mind was already made up as she shook her head to and fro, refusing to turn around. "Give us a chance."

"You're off your goddamn rocker! Get out, Jack. You took me for dumb pussy, and that's something I won't tolerate anymore." Noelle was now coldly in control on the outside even though on the inside, her heart was fragmented into pieces so fine that repair was impossible. Self-preservation was finally kicking in, and she would not let him see her fall to pieces. Noelle just wanted him to leave so that she could attempt the healing process. She turned away from him to wipe her eyes. *Damn, this was so hard!*

"This is over. I just want to forget you and this. I'm filing for divorce in the morning."

The finality of her statement was too much for Jack, and refusing to admit defeat, he grabbed her shoulders, pulling her close to him. Noelle struggled to push him away, but he held firmly, turning her around and cupping her face gently. Jack could see her eyes dilate and her breathing quicken in response to his touch. So, she wasn't immune to his touch after all, but still, her mind remained stubborn and unyielding.

"We will never be done, Noelle," Jack vowed. "You belong to me, and I belong to you! That will never change. Clearly, me being away for two days has left you a little confused, so let me refresh your memory."

Jack claimed her mouth in a wildly brutal kiss. She attempted to resist, trying to turn her face away while clawing at his wrists to break free. But Jack kept kissing her, dominating her mouth, tongue teasing at her lips until she stopped fighting it-*him*, and wrapped her hands around his wrists to hold him to her and her mouth opened under his. Instantly, the kiss gentled as he walked her backward to the side of the bed.

Something wet and salty mingled in their kiss. Jack pulled back long enough to see the tears falling from her lovely gray eyes. His heart seared from the pain he was causing her, kept causing her, but Jack couldn't help it. He wasn't strong enough to let her go.

"Stay with me," he begged, too far gone to care how pathetic he might sound. *"Stay."*

"I hate you," Noelle whispered in a subdued voice, and her words were like a knife slicing him wide open, even as she returned his kisses.

"No, you love me, just like I love you," Jack persuaded, following her down onto the bed. Noelle didn't even have time to process his shocking admission as closing her eyes, she was soon swept away by his touch. His lips trailed close to her ear as his warm hands slipped under her blouse to caress her breasts through her bra. Her hoarse moan, a combination of desire and heartache broke Jack, but still, he refused to acknowledge his defeat.

"You're mine, Noelle. Mine! I'll never let you go...."

Jack then proceeded to show her how true his words were.

IT WAS TWO IN THE morning when he finally left the bed. Jack looked down at an exhausted Noelle sleeping as he dressed. Shame and remorse filled him, leaving him feeling sick to his stomach, seeing the love marks he'd left on her body.

He'd taken her repeatedly, driving her body to dizzying heights of ecstasy, only giving her release when Noelle correctly answered his question. Jack refused to let her body come down from one orgasm before he was wringing the next one out of her as she screamed and moaned that she belonged to him while he gorged himself on her sweet pussy. In the end, Noelle begged to be left alone, but still, he couldn't help himself as he gently turned her over onto her stomach and urged her to get on her knees.

It was like a force, stronger than a category five hurricane, that was driving him as he spread her ass cheeks apart and pleasured her pussy and rosette mercilessly with his tongue, taking long, dragging licks and repeatedly plunging into both holes until she was desperately pushing back into his face for more. Driving two fingers into her soaked channel, he scooped the mixture of their generous juices onto his cock and her tight star for lubrication before placing his throbbing member at her ass. Damn, she was so tight, but he knew she was ready for it the way she inched back on to the tip of his cock.

"Do you want it, Noelle?" Jack asked through clenched teeth, fighting for control. He smacked her ass, and she jerked wildly, moaning brokenly with pleasure as he sunk in a little deeper, pushing past her sphincter, allowing Noelle to breathe through the burning pressure. "If you want it, then say it."

"Mmmm, yes there, Jack," Noelle begged helplessly when the pain receded. Jack slid in inch-by-inch until he was seated to the hilt. The feeling was unbelievable and she was so full. Jack withdrew to the head then flexed back in. Noelle winced, and he gave her a moment to adjust as his fingers slid underneath to play with her overly sensitive clit. She shuddered and slowly pulled forward then back to test her limits. Jack was perfectly still, sweat running down his tense body, watching as his dick slid in and out of Noelle's ass.

He needed to move, to punish her for thinking she

could leave him, to savor how exquisite the feeling of being with her like this was. She wiggled her ass, glancing at him expectantly over her shoulder, licking her lips with invitation in her gorgeous eyes. Jack gently nudged her forward, driving her slowly down into the soft mattress. "Lie down flat."

Noelle did and Jack followed, lying on top but favoring his left side. He raised her right leg higher at an angle and braced himself by holding onto the back of her knee. Slowly, he tunneled in and out of her ass, and her breathy sighs turned into deep-throated groans of bliss. Jack fisted her hair, easing her head back, so her face was exposed. "I feel like I'm gonna' explode in your sweetness, darlin'. Do you like how it feels?"

His thrusts became rougher and deeper. Noelle threw her ass back at him, loving the fullness inside of her. Her husband was so thick, so big, so...perfect. Never in a million years would she had ever thought that she'd like anal sex, but the way Jack was doing it had her clawing the sheets, begging for more. "I love it! Please don't stop. Harder... more! Uhhh! Harder!"

Jack stopped, and Noelle whimpered in protest. "Darlin', who do you belong to? Whose pussy is this? This ass that I'm fuckin'?" He his hand snaked under and pinched her clit gently. "Answer the question, Noelle!"

She exploded as she sobbed "You! I belong to you, Jack Sullivan!"

"As I do you, wife," he groaned into her sweaty neck. The pressure of her constricting around his dick was too much for Jack; he shoved her leg higher and fucked her harder, his balls slapping against her ass as he increased his teasing of her clit and Noelle came again. Jack joined her, shooting his hot semen into her with deep shudders before collapsing on top of her. By the time he pulled out, Noelle was beyond exhausted. As he pulled the covers over her, she curled up, whimpering, "No more. Please."

Jack was ashamed of how he'd treated Noelle and used her body against her. All he'd ever wanted to do was love her, but instead, he'd broken her. *Like his father did his mother.* His father's maniacally twisted face flashed in his mind.

"Yer mine, Moira! Ya hear?? I'll never let you go!!"

His guilt was suffocating him. He had to get out of there. Hurriedly, he put on his shoes and grabbed his shit before letting himself out the front door quietly. His conscience taunted him.

Run, you fucking coward! You're just like him! Sullivan men do nothing but hurt those around them! Run!

Jack barely made it out the front door and down the steps before he threw up in the bushes.

CHAPTER
Thirty-Three

FOUR MONTHS LATER

A KNOCK ON THE DOOR made Noelle glance up from the spreadsheet she was examining. Avery stood in the doorway of her office with a binder clasped to her chest.

"Our eleven-a.m. interview, Ella Kemp, is here. You ready?"

Munching on a carrot stick, she stepped further into the office. Noelle leaned back in her chair and smiled, happy at the changes her friend was making that seemed to bring her inner peace.

In the past months, Avery had lost fifteen pounds and was feeling great about it. Sure, she'd always have boobs, behind, and hips, but now, she wasn't so self-conscious about them. She seemed to have embraced it wholeheartedly, a fact that seemed to drive her fiancée Pierce crazy as he tried to keep her covered up and on lockdown. Much to his dismay, Avery wasn't trying to hear anything he was saying.

"Actually, you go ahead. I trust your judgment. I'm going to finish reviewing our budget spreadsheets before heading out to lunch with Uncle Ian. Do you want to join us? If so, I can wait," Noelle offered, pushing her black framed glasses on top of her head.

"Nah, go ahead. Tell him I said hi. We can review my notes when you get back. Don't forget we have that Skype meeting with Cinnamon Farms at 4 p.m., and I can't wait! Honey, have you ever had a conversation with Farmer Hayes?" Avery fanned herself. "Good Lawd, that man's voice alone could impregnate a woman! Toodles!" she waved as she left then popped back in. "Not to dampen your day, but the usual envelope came for you today as well."

Noelle refused to look up from her computer screen. "Put it in the outgoing mail with the usual return to sender label, please and thank you," she managed to politely respond, even though she was screaming on the inside. She could feel Avery staring at her but refused to look up from the papers in front of her.

Avery spoke in a soft voice, "*Noelle*...honey, it's been–"

"Please don't, Avery. Just...*don't,*" Noelle spoke firmly, letting her friend know the conversation was over. Avery left the room without saying another word.

When she was sure the coast was clear, Noelle quickly got up and walked to the bathroom. Quietly, she shut the door and observed herself in the mirror. Her face was thinner, making her large eyes and full mouth more prominent. The look that she dubbed 'Traumatized by Love' was garnering a lot of attention from the media. At first, she was known as Jack Sullivan's love interest. Then she was known as the woman who dumped Jack Sullivan on his ass, causing him to become a recluse. Ian confirmed to her that Jack was the one who leaked this story to the media to make it work in her favor.

How thoughtful of him. Bastard.

Now, she was known as an "IT" girl and successful business owner. She and Avery were in high demand to plan the hottest events in town and constantly photographed for daily fashion and gossip blogs and columns. On a Whim was so successful that they were finally able to purchase a loft in Brooklyn and could afford to hire a full staff of caterers and florists. All of the blessings should have made Noelle feel happy and carefree, but they didn't, and she wasn't.

Jack had left her.

He'd said he loved her and spent the entire night worshipping her body, making her do and say things that still made her blush. And then the next morning, he was gone. She called his cell repeatedly, only to be turned over to voicemail. By noon, he still wasn't back, so she called his office. Margo said that he was in when she got there but left before noon. Noelle stayed in her apartment all day, staring out the window and waiting for him to reach out to her.

SHE DIDN'T BATHE BECAUSE SHE didn't want to wash the scent or feel of him away. Noelle lay in bed, breathing in Jack's scent as the tears rolled down her cheeks, crying into her pillow. The next day, there was a knock on the door, and she opened it, knowing she looked a fright, to accept the envelope from Sullivan and Associates in D.C. A feeling of dread settled in the pit of her stomach as she opened it and read its contents. The first page was a letter stating that Jack Sullivan was requesting that she divorce him on the grounds of irreconcilable differences. He would pay all her legal fees and a generous alimony for the next ten years. Noelle balked at the sum of seven thousand dollars a month. They'd barely been married a month!

The next few pages were divorce papers drawn up by Casey. All she had to do was sign them. Humiliated, and experiencing a new level of heartache, Noelle tore the papers up, called for a courier service, sending the shredded pieces of paper back to Casey and got back in bed. Her world had just ended. Jack didn't want her anymore and was now trying to buy her off to ease his guilty conscience. It was just as she'd thought. She'd been nothing but an expensive piece of ass to him. That first week was the hardest, and she refused to do anything but lie in bed, go to the bathroom, and call his phone. Then Avery came. She banged on the door and wouldn't stop until Noelle threw the door open, yelling, "What?!?!"

Avery shied away from her with a frown, and covering her nose, she redirected Noelle back into her house. Once inside, she led her down the hallway to the bathroom. Noelle scowled, as Avery squirted an obscenely generous amount of toothpaste on her toothbrush and handed it to her. Brushing her teeth, she watched in the mirror as her friend calmly drew her a bubble bath then got her fresh clothing and waited expectantly by the tub. Noelle reluctantly took off her clothes and sank into the warm, fragrant bath surrounded by bubbles. Tears filled her eyes as Avery took her hair out of its ratty bun and gently combed through it then washed and conditioned it.

"How did you know?" Noelle asked quietly, and Avery knew she really meant: how did you know that I was dying? That my heart was gone?

"Darby."

The one-word answer fractured her. Noelle began to cry in earnest. Once she started, she couldn't stop, and by the time Avery dragged her from the water, it was ice cold. Noelle insisted on drying herself and when she came out of the bathroom, Avery had a grilled cheese sandwich and tomato soup waiting for her. She greedily ate the food, not realizing how famished she was until Avery set a second sandwich in front of her, and she devoured it too. Soon, Noelle was sleepy. Avery tucked her between fresh sheets and lay on the other side of the bed, flipping through magazines while she slept.

Avery had Pierce bring her clothes over, and she stayed until Noelle was initiating conversation and eating three meals a day. She was worried about her friend's condition and kept Sidra posted as she was away on the tour but checking in daily. When Sidra confessed to Avery that she'd emailed Jack a very threatening message and would need a solid alibi should something happen to him, she was shocked not to receive a lecture on restraint, but instead, Avery's request.

"Make it hurt twice as much as you originally planned, Sid."

Three weeks later when Noelle asked what their next project would be, Avery knew she was going to be okay. By then, the second package arrived from Sullivan and Associates, and Noelle forgot about being heartbroken and transitioned into Phase 2: State of Fury, where she had since taken up permanent residence.

Noelle opened the envelope and read its contents before sending for the courier service again. If Jack wanted a divorce so badly, he would need to be the one to file. Fuck. Him. She was done letting him pull her strings. She threw herself into her business wholeheartedly. With a loan from Ian, Noelle paid off Rothman Investments and took their business to another bank. Business was booming to the point that they were able to pay Ian back in three months. On a

Whim was in the black and booked solid for the next six months.

No one had seen Jack in months. Alicia was on a mission to sue him for negligence and job abandonment since he'd turned his clientele over to Ian, who was merciless on her. When Noelle spoke to Darby, he said Jack was in Whiskey Row, but he hadn't actually SEEN him, whatever the fuck that meant. The envelope came every week like clockwork, and upon its arrival, she sent it back because deep down, Noelle knew she still loved Jack and always would. She didn't want a divorce. There was no one else for her because his sorry behind was who her traitorous heart wanted more than anything.

A month later, she discovered that there was someone else for her. Someone who would be coming in less than eight months. Noelle received the shock of her life when she went to her doctor's office to see what could be done about her constant state of exhaustion. After running a few tests, her family doctor announced, "At this time, I'm going to prescribe plenty of rest, healthy foods to keep your iron up, along with some pills. Prenatal pills. Congratulations, my dear. You're pregnant."

She'd reminded him of doctor-patient confidentiality, lest he spill the beans to her parents, and for the next week, Noelle's head was in the clouds, trying to get used to the reality of being pregnant. Immediately, she wanted to call Jack and tell him the news, but her pride wouldn't let her. He left her, not the other way around. She kept the news to herself, not even Sidra and Avery knew yet. When nausea kicked in, she tried to work from home as much as possible without alerting Avery, but her overly concerned friend feared that she was becoming suicidal, so Noelle had to drag herself to the office and fake the funk.

Glassy eyes stared back at her from the mirror.

Some days were good, and some were bad. Envelope Day was always a bad day, but the pain had receded slightly due to her little secret. Breathing deeply through her nose, Noelle counted backward from one hundred until she felt calm again. She splashed cool water on her face before looking up at the sign above the mirror.

Make today your bitch!

It always made her smile, and it was a goal she strived to accomplish daily. After making sure the door was locked again, Noelle pushed her flowing, Kelly green kimono to the side and lifted up her white tank top to peer at her small bump covered by her maternity skinny jeans.

"Hi, baby. How's Mommy's angel?" Noelle whispered lovingly to her belly, caressing her bump gently. She was rewarded with flutters for her efforts. _Jack had better come around soon,_ she thought achingly, or he was going to miss all the really good parts.

Noelle straightened her clothes and pulled her gemstone necklace into place. The trick to hiding her baby bump was to have people focus on a statement piece from her wardrobe. Today's piece was a large, gold link necklace with turquoise and peridot stones set in a triangle shaped middle. It was bold and paired with a bright orangey-red lip gloss. The look was stunning and effective, keeping all eyes above her chest.

She missed Jack so much! His smile, his laugh, the feel of his arms wrapped around her, and the way they could just talk about anything. Late at night, she missed the heat of his body moving inside of her and the warmth of just snuggling. When she felt the baby move for the first time, she'd cried all day, wishing Jack could be there to feel it too. Something had to give because although she displayed a cool, calm, and collected demeanor on the outside, on the inside, some days, it still felt like she was barely holding on. A knock on the bathroom door startled her.

"Just a minute!" she called out, hastily checking her appearance one last time.

"Ian's here and-uh...so is your mother!" Avery sing-songed with false gaiety before hurrying away. In the distance, Noelle heard an office door slam shut and knew that Avery had locked herself in the safety of her office, away from Alicia Kramer's acidic tongue. Noelle also knew she would not emerge until the coast was clear.

She groaned.

Perfect.

Abso-fucking-lutely perfect.

CHAPTER
Thirty-Four

DARBY'S HARLEY DAVIDSON ROARED DOWN the long, twisting country road. Normally, he loved the freedom of being on his bike, especially on a cloud-filled day like this, but not today. Today was the day that he and Casey planned to stage an intervention with their normally easy-going and composed older brother. He was a right fucking mess and had been since he'd shown up four months ago. The only time he left the house was when he ran out of liquor according to Mort, owner of the Wishing Well, the local liquor store. He pulled up to Jack's house and saw Casey sitting in his Jaguar, waiting for him. When he saw Darby, he got out with an envelope in his hand that he waved enthusiastically at his brother.

"Mornin'. You ready to do this?"

Darby yanked his helmet off, shrugging vaguely. "I guess, seein' as how you drove all the way here from D.C.. He ain't returnin' Viv's or Ian's calls. Last week, he made Kat cry, and I had to restrain Lex *and* Holt from comin' up here to beat his ass. It's time for him to join the real world again. No more of this hiding bullshit."

Casey frowned. "Why would Holt want to kick his

ass? Lex I can see, but Holt?"

Darby rolled his eyes at his brother as they walked up the front steps. Sometimes, for a whip-smart attorney, Casey was so clueless that he couldn't find his ass if both of his hands were in his back pockets. "You got no clue? Seriously? Never mind. You can't even fix your own shit with a certain sex in her strut, fine ass–"

"Shut it, D," Casey cut him off with a look sour enough to curdle milk as he rang the doorbell obnoxiously over and over again.

"For now. So, how are we doin' this?" Darby peered into a side window for a sign of Jack. "Good cop, bad cop?"

"Nope. Come to Jesus," Casey replied as stomping on the other side of the door could be heard.

"Wait...*come to Jesus*? What does that even–"

The door was forcefully flung open, and they were both taken aback by Jack's appearance. Gone was the meticulously groomed brother they knew, and in his place was a Grizzly Adams-wannabe with red-rimmed eyes.

"Why the hell are you ringin' my doorbell like that?" he snarled ferociously. "Get outta here. I don't wanna be disturbed!"

"Save your 'Fee-Fi-Fo-Fum fuckery' for someone who gives a damn." Darby pushed past him, and Jack stumbled backward into the door.

Casey followed behind Darby whistling cheerily. "Tough shit."

The house was a smelly mess. Empty liquor bottles littered the living room floor, and dirty clothes were strewn everywhere in the darkened room. Dirty dishes covered every flat surface of the kitchen. The sink and stove top were piled high with used pots and pans. Jack pushed past them and threw himself down on the leather sofa, sneering, "I'd tell you guys to make yourselves at home, but since I didn't invite you pricks, feel free to see yourselves out."

Casey went into the kitchen, and soon, the smell of coffee wafted through the house. Darby yanked all the curtains open, pulling the blinds up as well. Then he opened all the windows, ignoring Jack, who roared, *"No bright light!"*

"What are you, a fuckin' gremlin?" Darby retorted, collecting empty bottles from the floor and tossing them into an empty liquor crate on the floor. It was worse than they'd thought. He hadn't seen this many bottles in a home since their sorry ass father was alive.

"Fuck you, man." Jack turned over, burying his face in the cushions. Darby sat down in the armchair across from him, waiting patiently as Casey brought back a tray that held mugs of steaming black coffee and aspirin. He set it on the end table before pulling the large, square paisley-printed ottoman to the side and out of the way of the sofa. Jack kept his back to them, and Casey raised an eyebrow at Darby who nodded.

It was time to begin.

"You want to tell us why you're hidin' out, mopin' like a little bitch caught up in his feelings?" Casey jeered. Darby's eyebrows shot up, and even he felt a twinge of unease at his brother's harsh words. He mouthed, 'What the fuck?', but Casey ignored him.

Jack stiffened but didn't turn around. "Screw you, Case."

"After you, buddy. You're doin' a good job of alienating everyone who cares about you. You made our little sis cry and refuse to talk to any of us! Who knows what the fuck you did to your beautiful wife to be beggin' for a divorce! Now, all you want to do is fuckin' drink your sorrows away. You're a fuckin' waste of space. Or should I just call you *junior*?" Casey finished caustically.

Jack sat up, and slowly faced him.

"Repeat what you just said, little brother." Jack's voice was eerily calm, but his hands twitched as he leaned toward his younger brother, focusing on him intently. Darby stood up, now clear on his part of this so-called intervention.

"What's the matter? Not sober enough to comprehend?" Casey sneered derisively. "Then I'll say it slower for you. You're hurtin' everyone who loves you, breakin' your wife's heart, and drinkin' your sorrows away. Kind of like some other loser we knew."

"You should stop now, Casey," Jack warned, eyes burning, and fists ready.

Casey laughed harshly. "Sorry, I don't understand pathetic drunks when they're slurrin'. That's what you are, isn't it? The apple doesn't fall from the tree does it, *junior*?" he goaded mercilessly.

Jack lunged at Casey who snapped back as Darby stepped forward and rocked Jack in the jaw. He went down in a crumpled heap on the floor, leaving both brothers gawking at him.

Darby turned to look at his little brother in disbelief. "This is your idea of an intervention?! Mentally attackin' a person and then havin' someone knock them out cold?! Pretty sure Dr. Phil never had to cold-cock anybody when he's doin' one of these."

Casey shrugged as he bent to lift Jack up. "I'm sure he's wanted to, though. Besides, he knocks them out mentally. I'm more of a literal guy. Either way, I'm happy with the results. This was my first time doin' an intervention, and it went somewhat as planned. I'm sure I'll get better as time goes by. Now, let's get him up on the sofa."

And they had the nerve to call him the wild and crazy one, Darby snorted. "You pat yourself on the back any harder, and you'll break your arm."

———————————————

LUNCH WAS A DISASTROUS AFFAIR with Alicia and Ian flinging thinly veiled barbs at each other while Noelle struggled to eat avocado toast and keep the nausea at bay. She was barely winning the fight because the sight and smell of her mother's gorgonzola and fig salad was overwhelming her.

Ever since the picture of her and Jack kissing was made public, members of her family made it a point to visit her weekly. The visits were the bane of Noelle's existence as they gently poked and prodded at her. Today was her lucky day as her mother 'just happened' to be in Brooklyn and thought they could have lunch. Ian laughed mockingly while Noelle stared at her like she'd grown a third eye while Alicia flushed at the blatant lie.

"Mother, when have you ever just *happened* to be in Brooklyn?" Noelle's face was set in polite disbelief. Her mother didn't even acknowledge to her friends that Noelle *resided* in Brooklyn. When asked, she responded vaguely with 'the city'.

"Oh pooh, darling! I've been to Brooklyn before. I find it to be quite...*lively*," Alicia murmured, waving her hand dismissively and giving Ian a glare as he doubled over in laughter at her response. They decided to go to Five Leaves in Greenpoint, and Noelle relished watching her mother squirm at the close proximity of the restaurant's tables. As he ate, Ian regaled Noelle with tales of his trip to Europe while Alicia picked at her food.

"It sounds wonderful, Uncle Ian. Sometimes, I think I should go back for a vacation." It wouldn't be a bad idea after the baby was born. The privacy would allow her to relax and enjoy the next chapter in her life, away from prying eyes and inquiring minds.

"I think Europe sounds like an excellent idea! Maybe you should go now, an all-expense paid trip from Daddy and me. Call it an early Christmas gift," Alicia suggested brightly.

"I can't go now, Mother. We're booked solid for the next couple of months. I'd also have to see if Avery has anything planned," Noelle explained, seeing right through her mother's schemes to make her less accessible to Jack. *If* he ever came to his senses.

"Well, my goodness! What's the point in owning a business if you can't do what you want?"

"You poor, delusional thing. I guess that's the kind of mindset one should expect from someone who's never worked a day in her life," Ian mocked.

Alicia bristled. "Ian, contrary to your beliefs, I've built a very fulfilling career as a politician's wife, which has kept me extremely busy. Not to mention, raising children and being extremely active in numerous charities through the Kramer Foundation."

Noelle kept silent, munching on her toast. Despair and anger flooded her at the thought of being a single parent. Although if millions of strong women did it every single day, so could she. *Suck it up, buttercup.*

"Well, it couldn't have kept you too busy. You make time to incessantly meddle in stuff that is none of your concern, and besides, you had four nannies to help you raise the children," Ian jeered as Alicia stabbed viciously at her salad. "If Noelle was going to go anywhere, perhaps she should go to Florida and stay where you did on your recent trips. Those trips did wonders for you as you were practically *glowing* when you came back."

Noelle jerked her head up at her uncle's

venomous tone while Alicia's fork clattered loudly on her plate. The noise caused several other patrons to look over at them curiously.

"How dare you!" Alicia fumed quietly, confronting Ian, who was also vibrating with anger.

"Oh no, it's *you* who dares, Alicia! You dare to put yourself on a pedestal like you're too good for everyone and anything. Unfortunately for you, you are only human, and just like the rest of us common folk, you do...*common* things. Things that eventually... catch up to you," Ian finished in a hard tone.

"Alright, what the hell is going on here? I've never seen the two of you behave this poorly, especially in public!" Noelle offered fake smiles of reassurance to the other diners. She was promptly ignored by the sparring adversaries.

"Did Jack tell you this? It figures. What can you expect from a low-bred hillbilly who thinks he can better himself?" Alicia sneered, throwing her napkin down in disgust, missing Noelle's furious expression.

Noelle's hand smacked the tabletop so hard, everyone around her jumped as the silver and glassware rattled loudly. She looked at her mother, who flushed, hating to be the center of public scrutiny.

Alicia chided her furiously, "Really, Noelle. Everyone is looking!"

Noelle was done with her mother's snobbery. It was one thing for her to be pissed at Jack and call him names, but she would not allow anyone else to do so, especially knowing what she did about his childhood.

"Talk about the man I love again, Mother, and we're *done*. By rights, we should be done anyway, considering how badly you've treated me, but I wanted to give you the opportunity to know your grandbaby who will be arriving in less than six months."

Naturally, they were shocked, but her mother

quickly recovered. "You're pregnant?! I thought you said that the two of you were only *casually* seeing each other!"

"Well, I lied, and obviously we did more than just *see* each other. He wasn't just a casual acquaintance to me and could never be. I've been in love with him for years. This baby was made in love, and if I ever hear you speak disparagingly about its father again, I will move heaven and earth to make your life miserable *and* deny you access to your grandchild," Noelle informed her icily, immune to the crocodile tears filling Alicia's eyes.

"Give it up, Mother. When are you going to understand that I'm not a puppet to be controlled? None of us are! You are so busy interfering in everyone's lives that you don't even notice that you're driving us all away! All my life, I've just wanted you and Daddy to love and accept me. Like a robot, I did everything that you guys thought was best for me, and it still wasn't enough! *It will never be enough.* If I based my happiness on your approval of me, I'd be dying a slow death waiting for it. The only people who have ever loved me unconditionally were Uncle Harvey, Ian, and my friends. They love me without restrictions and, with their love and support, encourage me to be the best I can be."

An image of Jack's tormented face filled her mind.

"As far as the business is concerned, yes I did make a deal with Ira to help you get the funding for your company. I only did it because I knew that your parents weren't going to give you the advance on your inheritance, and you wouldn't accept a loan from me. You didn't have to take that loan, but the businesswoman in you recognized it as an excellent opportunity."

Jack loved her, and maybe she should have done a

better job of hearing him out. Hopefully, it wasn't too late.

"I have to go." Noelle abruptly stood and grabbed her purse. Smiling, she leaned down and kissed Ian's cheek, then her mother's.

"Are you going where I think you are, dear?" Ian eagerly expressed his hopefulness, clapping his hands when Noelle nodded her head determinedly. Smiling his approval, he reached into his leather messenger bag and pulled out a flat package that he handed to Noelle. "Excellent. By the way, this came for Jack at the office this morning. Be a dear and give him that as well as my congratulations on the little one."

"What? You can't just leave! We need to talk about–"

"Mother, I'm not sure exactly sure what Jack has on you, but I'm sure it's nothing you want floating around. He's been nothing but professional to you, and I'm sure you wouldn't want him as an enemy, or me for that matter. I'm going to be with him, and together, we will raise *our* baby. If you can't be happy for me, stay away until you can at least fake it. Last warning, Mother. Stay out of affairs that don't concern you; or you won't like the results."

"Bravo, my girl." Ian watched her leave before turning to an open-mouthed Alicia. "Oh, dear. Looks like someone just discovered that they're not the sun; therefore, we the world, don't revolve around them." He wrapped an arm around her shoulders, giving her a firm squeeze. "Cheer up, old girl! Our baby is going to have a baby!"

CHAPTER
Thirty-Five

NOELLE CALLED AVERY FROM HOME while she was busy packing. "Would you mind me slipping away for a couple of days? I did the payroll this morning and can email you the dishes that catering should be working on in my absence," she detailed, grabbing a handful of socks and tossing them into her suitcase.

"Not a problem. Lunch was so bad that you need to get away, huh?" Avery teased.

Noelle laughed. "Actually, it turned out to be a real eye-opening experience. I got a lot of crap off my chest that I've wanted to say to my mom, and if she doesn't feel the need to speak to me for a while or ever again, I think I'll be okay with that."

"Hallelujah and praise Jesus! Well then, where are you going?" Avery asked curiously.

"Ave, I'm going to get my man," Noelle stated simply, laughing as Avery started shrieking with happiness. She wished her luck and promised she'd find a way to stop Sidra from going through with her plan, whatever that meant, before hanging up.

When Noelle was done packing, she wheeled her

suitcase to the foyer and called for a cab. As she waited, Noelle remembered the flat package Ian had given her at lunch earlier. Walking over to her purse by the door, she pulled it out, studying it before cautiously opening, and peeking inside.

JACK SURVEYED HIS FACE IN the bathroom mirror as he brushed his teeth. Gone was the scruffy, mountain man. The gnarly, long curls had been cut close to his head, and he was clean-shaven once again. He looked like his old self except for the large bruise on his cheek, courtesy of his brother's meaty fist. Jack grimaced, thinking of how badly he'd fucked up. Yeah, he'd needed the sense to be knocked into him, just not so fucking hard.

WHEN HE CAME TO, DARBY and Casey were playing cards. Jack's head felt like it was exploding, and his face felt like someone took a sledgehammer to it. Groaning, he struggled to sit up, but a spell of dizziness had him falling back on the sofa. "Somebody wanna tell me what the hell happened?"

"Oh good, you're up! About time, too. Darby is slower than molasses when it comes to War," Casey spoke cheerfully, handing Jack a cup of lukewarm coffee along with two aspirin.

"Bite me, jerk," Darby grumbled good-naturedly, giving his big brother a guilty look. "How are you feelin', Jackie?"

"Why'd you hit me, D?" Shooting him a dirty look, he carefully touched the injured area of his face. Wincing in pain, he glared at his middle brother, eyes guaranteeing a torturous retribution.

"Because you needed some damn sense knocked into you, that's why! If you were any dumber, you could throw yourself to the ground and miss," Casey responded before Darby could. "You're a grown fuckin' man, poutin' up here like a big-ass baby."

"You're a little shit, Casey. I know this whole thing was your idea, and when I get up, I'm gonna beat the fuck outta you," Jack vowed as he popped the aspirin.

"I'm real scared," Casey dismissed him. "Now that you're finally sober, let's talk. I'm here because Noelle finally decided to give you what you've been asking for."

Jack felt his heart freeze, coffee mug halfway to his lips. "What do you mean?"

"Don't play dumb with me, you heartless son of a bitch! You know exactly what I mean." Casey picked up the envelope that he brought in and tossed it on the sofa next to Jack. "It means she finally saw the light and signed the papers you've been makin' me shove down her throat! In a couple of months, you'll be a free man. Congratulations, asswipe."

Jack's mind was racing while his heart was breaking all over again. This was the moment he'd been dreading. She'd finally realized he wasn't shit and decided to move on. Meanwhile, he was stuck in limbo wracked with guilt and pain. Every time he closed his eyes, Noelle stole into his dreams, making him fall in love with her all over again. But Jack didn't deserve her after he'd hurt and mistreated her so badly.

Darby growled his frustration at his normally intelligent brother's drastic turn into 'Imbecileville'. "C'mon man. What are you doin'?! That little gal looked at you with nothin' but love in her eyes. Everyone could see that! I mean, this was your chance to be happy! You were supposed to break the Sullivan curse and get your happily ever after! You're one of the smartest guys I know. How could you screw this up?!"

"Because I was scared shitless!" Jack yelled, giving a mirthless chuckle at their surprised expressions. "What, I can't be scared?! Well, I was! All anybody wants is someone to look up to and fix their damn problems. I'm supposed to have all the answers and make everythin' better for everyone! Isn't that how y'all see me?

The first time I saw Noelle, I knew she was it for me. She was so fuckin' beautiful and had all these cool quirks that made her perfect, and I wanted her – so badly that I became obsessed with her, and it made me feel sick to my stomach because those feelings reminded me of Patrick. She was all I could think about, but she was too young. What would she want with an older guy like me?" Jack smirked wryly. "I felt like if I did get her, I would keep her under lock and key. Hell, you've seen firsthand how I get about anyone touchin' her, and you're my damn kinfolk! I felt like I didn't deserve her because I wouldn't be able to treat her right.

So, instead of wooing her, I stayed away until the perfect opportunity presented itself, and I just couldn't resist. I selfishly took it and hoped with time that I could make her love me, but the shit backfired. She found out and said she was through with me," Jack finished, his self-loathing evident in his face and words. He tossed back the rest of the coffee. "It made me crazy to think that she would leave, and then stuff got a little out of hand." Shamefaced, he hung his head.

Suddenly, Darby was there in front of him, dragging him up by the front of his shirt and they were nose-to-nose.

"What did you do?"

You could hear a pin drop. The room was so quiet in the wake of his savage growl. Casey stepped up next to him, placing a hand on Darby's shoulder as if to restrain him, but the look he gave Jack let him know that he was seconds away from getting fucked up if they didn't like his answer. The tension in the room suffocated them.

"No, I didn't rape or beat my wife if that's what you're thinking. Despite what Casey said, I'm not as big of a bastard that our father was. Now, release me, before I put you through a fuckin' window, Darby." Jack's chilly eyes and sub-zero tone dared his brother to not obey him.

Darby released him with a ragged sigh and stepped back, raking his hands through his hair. "Hell, Jack, I'm sorry, but you know I had to ask."

"When are you gonna get it through your thick skull that you are nothin' like Patrick?!" Casey shouted. "At thirteen, you were more of a father to us than he ever was! You looked out for us while Ma had to work and disciplined us when it was needed. Even after Lex took us in, you refused to let down your guard and just be a kid! We'll forever be grateful for your love and care. But if YOU, the guy who takes care of all of us, don't think that you deserve happiness, then hell, we're all doomed!"

Darby concurred. "I know you stayed away as long as you did because you still carried pain and guilt over her death, but we could see Noelle helped to ease that. You couldn't save Ma, but she saved us the best she could and gave us the chance to be free. Lettin' Noelle go will be the worst mistake of your life. Ma wouldn't want you losin' out on the opportunity to be happy."

———————————

HIS BROTHER'S WORDS WERE THE ones he'd needed to be free. He'd needed to hear that they didn't harbor feelings of anger and resentment towards him and that they knew he'd done his best.

The first thing he did upon sobering up was send Kat a large apology bouquet of white roses. He also emailed Vivienne and Ian to let them know he was okay, and he'd be coming back soon. His bags were packed, and Darby was giving him a ride to the airport. The signed divorce papers were burning a hole inside of his suit jacket pocket.

Noelle probably hated his guts right now, but he wasn't going to give up without a fight. He was a fool to walk away. But he'd be an even bigger fool if he just let her go and not do anything to prevent it. From the moment he saw her, Jack knew they were meant to be together. Now, it was time to make her see that truth also. He walked out of the bathroom and grabbed his bags from the bedroom before meeting Darby and Casey in the living room.

Darby started humming the "James Bond" theme song. "The name's Sullivan. Jack. Sullivan."

Casey chuckled, and Jack rolled his eyes, "Come on, you clowns! I gotta go get my gal back."

"Yeah about that..." Casey nervously rubbed his neck and avoided Darby's suspicious look.

Jack didn't hear him as he opened the door and peered up at the sky.

"We better get goin'. Judgin' from the look of those clouds over there, it's gonna really start coming down. Lock up, Case!" he shouted over his shoulder, jogging to the car with his suitcases.

Darby confronted Casey as soon as Jack was out of earshot. "Tell me you didn't! Never mind; don't tell me *anythin'*. I refuse to be your accomplice, Mr. Prosecutor. No wonder folks have no faith in our justice system."

"On a scale of one to ten, how mad do you think he'll be?" Beaming with satisfaction, Casey locked the door and followed Darby down the porch stairs.

"Don't ask me. I sure as hell ain't stickin' around to see if he cancels your birth certificate," Darby said cheerfully.

CAUTIOUSLY, NOELLE DROVE TOWARD Gatlinburg, her anxiety building by the millisecond. The rain was a never-ending downpour. The elderly salesman at the car rental place in Knoxville regarded her dubiously when she'd asked for the best way to get to Whiskey Row.

"You sure you want to take that trip right now, Miss? I gotta say, it's startin' to rain here now, and as dark as the clouds are up there, it's surely stormin'! You should probably stay in town tonight and let it slow down a bit," he suggested, even though Noelle was already handing him her credit card.

"Thanks for your concern, but I have to get up there *tonight*." She smiled reassuringly. "I'll be fine; I promise."

Noelle saw the intersection up ahead and slowed the VW Bug down. It rolled to complete stop twenty feet behind the big rig ahead of her. It seemed impossible, but the rain was coming down even harder. Noelle could scarcely see the brake lights in front of her. With a sigh of resignation, she had to admit that the salesman was correct about tonight's weather.

She decided to turn around and head back toward the hotel she'd passed ten minutes ago. Seeing no divider between the lanes, Noelle checked for any oncoming traffic. The opposite lane was clear, so she slowly turned the wheel to the left. A horn cut through the rain, loud and insistent. It startled Noelle, and a chill that had nothing to do with the weather, ran through her. The loud squeal of tires from behind made her jump. In her rearview mirror, there were lights from a larger vehicle swerving on the slick road, hurtling straight at her. Noelle didn't even have time to scream before there was a sickening crunch.

Then everything went black.

CHAPTER

Thirty-Six

Thanks to Darby's expert driving skills, the trip down the mountain wasn't as hard as Jack thought it would be. He looked at his watch. It was only five-thirty in the evening, but the sky was pitch black due to the storm. Prickles of unease slid down his back. Jack felt a little off and chalked it up to them cutting it close for his seven forty-five flight, but he felt confident he'd make it.

"The rain seems to be easin' up as we get closer to Gatlinburg but not by much. It will be much lighter in Knoxville," Casey offered, checking the weather app on his phone from the passenger seat.

"Yeah, hopefully, we'll be there soon. I can't believe that Lex was so pissed at me that he wouldn't let me use his plane." Jack leaned forward between them, shaking his head ruefully. "Kat accepted my apology and said the flowers were great, but obviously, I need to do a little more grovelin'."

Darby shifted uncomfortably in the driver's seat. "Well, it may be a little bit more than that. See uh...in order for the girls to fly in with me and Case for their visit, I asked him for the use of his plane. He said I could use it on one condition. My guess is he's still a little salty that I haven't come through for him yet."

The other two brothers leaned in curiously, waiting to hear the arrangement terms. "He said in his big, scary Russian voice that I had to get Viv to come home. That it was time for them to talk face-to-face."

There was a moment of stunned silence following Darby's confession before Jack spoke. "That's a tall order. Viv will never go for it. How in the hell are you gonna manage that?" He rubbed his tense neck. The feeling of unease was increasing, making him even antsier.

"I know that he's been tryin' to talk to her for a while and that whenever he comes to town, she conveniently happens to be out of town," Casey chimed in. "I've tried talking to her about it, but it's the one thing she actually keeps her mouth shut on, which says a lot 'cause you know she's got an opinion on everythin' under the sun."

"Casey, I need a favor from your private investigator friend. See what he can dig up on Joel Rothman havin' an affair with a stockbroker named Kelly Travers. It's been hot and heavy between them for the last three months, and in that time frame, Rothman has been makin' extremely successful choices with his investments. I'm also gonna need your guy at the Security Exchange Commission," Jack added casually.

Casey side-eyed Jack. "Are you goin' after Rothman because he's Vaughn's husband? Sounds pretty personal. You still harborin' feelings for her?"

Jack smacked the back of his brother's head, making him yelp with pain. "No, jackass. I'm goin' after him because he dared to try and get between Noelle and me. No one and nothing will ever come between us again," he pledged, ignoring the loaded look his brothers exchanged.

Flashing lights ahead caught their attention. Traffic was down to a crawl as passing drivers surveyed the scene. Police and ambulance were everywhere. There was a large semi-truck with its emergency lights on. A Volkswagen Bug was behind it, crushed on its side to while an SUV was smashed into the other side of it. The emergency responders had applied the Jaws of Life system to the small vehicle. It was undoubtedly a gruesome-looking accident.

"Damn, do you think whoever was in that car made it out alive?" Casey was skeptical as he peered through his window. "It'd be a miracle that's for sure. Hey, pull over; I see Henry-Pete's on duty. Let's ask."

"Case, I'm not tryin' to be a dick, but I've got a plane to catch. We really can't afford to stop." The feeling that something was wrong now sat in his gut like a two-ton boulder. If he missed the plane, Casey was going to get it.

"Just hold your horses; it'll take but a minute. What if it was somebody from 'The Row'?" Case said as they stopped by the policeman. "Hey, H.P., can you tell me what happened here?"

The two men shook hands. "Good to see ya, Case! Willard Ross had a heart attack at the wheel and rammed into the car which slammed into the truck. The young woman that was in the car is in serious condition. She had to be pried out and airlifted to the Trauma Center. Damn shame it was. She's not from around here. Her driver's license says New York City, so I gotta locate her next of kin," Harvey said regretfully. "Hopefully she'll pull through."

"New York?" Jack repeated abruptly, a sense of foreboding filling him. "What's her name, H.P.?"

"Well, shut my mouth! That you, Jack?! Long time no see!"

"Good to see you, H. P., can I get the name, please?" He was trying his damnedest to not bite his old classmate's head off.

"Sure thing. The young lady's name is Noelle Kramer. Say, you're livin' there now, ain't ya? You wouldn't happen to know her by chance? I mean I know it's a big city and all...."

Jack couldn't hear anything. His brothers were talking to him, but it was all white noise. He could only hear Henry-Pete's words.

In serious condition. Jaws of Life had to pry her out. The young lady's name is Noelle Kramer.

His love. His world.

What was she doing in Tennessee?

THE HOSPITAL HALLWAY WAS UNNERVINGLY quiet. The only sounds heard were Jack's shoes as he paced up and down the hallway outside of Noelle's room. It was a slow, methodical pace belying the fear that now lived in him as he waited for the doctor to exit her room with a prognosis. The last hour was a blur for him. Jack remembered H.P. arranging a police escort to take them to the hospital and Darby and Casey murmuring words of encouragement as he bent his head and prayed for all that he was worth. The urge to choke the shit out of the slow-moving head nurse upon arrival was strong as she questioned his relationship to Noelle.

"She's my fuckin' life!" Jack shouted, getting in her face, making her flinch. All commotion stopped around them. Although he meant to say "wife", he didn't correct himself because what he said was so true. *Noelle was his lifeline.* He would die if she didn't make it. Darby grabbed him and led him to the elevator as she stammered out the room number and directions. Casey took the forms that needed to be filled out.

Jack yanked on his hair in frustration as he waited for the doctor. Casey asked him questions as he filled out the hospital paperwork while Darby made calls to friends and family. The door opened, and the elderly doctor stepped out. He warily looked for an escape from the three burly men who instantly crowded him, their lethal gazes warning that the news better be good. He addressed the one who stepped forward with the bruised face, unruly hair, and feral eyes. "Mr. Sullivan?"

"Yes, I'm her husband. How is she?" Jack demanded tensely, shoving his clenched hands into his pockets to keep from shaking the man for information.

"She's resting for now. She had a mild concussion on impact but came out of it due to the pain she experienced. Your wife has a cracked collarbone, three broken ribs, and a broken ankle. She's experiencing a higher level of discomfort because we couldn't give her the strongest pain meds possible due to her condition."

"What do you mean *condition*?" Jack barked. *"What fucking condition?"*

"Well, the baby, of course. She's about sixteen weeks." The doctor grew worried when Jack staggered back, stunned by the revelation. "I'm sorry, sir. I thought you knew."

"Can I see her?" Jack was numb. *A baby.* He was going to be a daddy. Joy was a healing balm running through his grief-stricken body. He thanked God, vowing to be the best father possible, to fight even harder for his marriage.

"Yes, but just for a little bit. She really does need her rest," the doctor firmly insisted. "Congratulations," he added scurrying away.

"Congratulations, brother." Grinning widely, Darby clasped his shoulder and shook Jack. Casey chimed in too. "Congrats, bro. Now, pull it together! Don't go in there like a pussy. Make sure you tell her we love her."

"Thanks, guys."

Jack quietly entered the room and was speechless at the number of tubes Noelle was hooked up to. She looked so pale and helpless laying there, her breathing short and shallow. Her lips were dry and cracked and, her eyes swollen black and blue. There was an angry-looking lump on her forehead, and he could see the bruising and swelling above her right collarbone. He pulled back the covers by her feet and saw the cast around her ankle. *The pain she must be in,* he thought, tears filling his eyes. She could have lost their baby., The realization was enough to bring him to his knees next to her hospital bed.

"Don't. Cry."

It was a wispy command yet brought Jack to attention. Noelle's eyes were partially open.

"Noelle... baby, are you okay? Should I get the doctor?" Tears ran unimpeded down his face. He brushed a gentle kiss on her forehead.

"Hurts, Jack," she mumbled, and he clasped her hand gently. Jack wasn't ever planning on letting go. Her eyes closed again, she tried speaking but no words came out.

"What hurts, baby?"

"Heart hurts. See you cry. Don't."

Her fingers curled weakly around his before drifting off to sleep, a content smile on her lips.

CHAPTER
Thirty-Seven

*S*HE AWOKE IN SEVERE AGONY. Eyes wide, her hands flew to her stomach, and she felt on fire everywhere but mainly in her upper chest at her sudden movement. Crying out, and fearing the worse, Noelle tried to feel for the small precious bump of her tummy.

Please be there!

"The baby's fine, Noelle."

She closed her eyes in relief as the warmth of that sweet, southern drawl washed over her. So, it hadn't been a dream. Jack was really here with her. She heard him moving around, but kept her eyes shut.

"Do you need more medicine?"

Noelle opened her eyes at the concern lacing his voice to see Jack hovering above her. His hair looked like it hadn't been combed in a while, his face covered in whiskers, and he was sporting a large bruise on his left cheek. To coin a phrase, he looked like shit, but to Noelle, he was the most beautiful sight in the world.

"What happened? I feel like I went fifty rounds in a fight club," Noelle groaned, licking her chapped lips. She slowly sipped from the cup of water Jack brought to her lips. It was cool and refreshing going down her parched throat. "That's good, thank you."

"You were involved in a bad car accident and sustained some pretty awful injuries, but the important thing is that you and the baby are alive," Jack gravely informed her.

Noelle could see the questions and hurt in his eyes. "I was on my way to tell you about the baby. I didn't think it was something you should say over the phone," she explained quietly, trying to gauge how he felt about the news of impending fatherhood.

"Noelle, you didn't just find out. When were you gonna say somethin'?" Jack tried to keep the censure out of his voice. The relief of having her awake and coherent was great, but so was his anger at her secrecy. He watched as fire flashed in her tired eyes.

"Should I have called you up after your disappearing act?" she retorted angrily. "Or better yet, stick a post-it note on the recurring divorce papers you sent me?"

"You mean the papers you finally *signed*? Yeah, Casey made a special trip to give them to me, and it was the wakeup call I needed to realize how badly I was fuckin' things up," he replied shortly. "I was on my way to the airport to catch a flight to see you and beg for a second chance when we saw the accident. God, darlin', when the deputy said your name, it took about a hundred years off my life!"

Noelle frowned in confusion; what was he talking about? She'd never signed the papers! Comprehension dawned on her that it was Casey who'd forged them for her, knowing it would get his brother moving. "How do you feel about the baby?"

Jack rubbed his hand over his shadowed jaw, a big grin spreading across his face.

"I'm ecstatic about the baby! It's more than I could

have dreamed or hoped for," he replied honestly. "I think you'll make a great mother, Noelle, and I plan to be front and center for every moment in our child's life. I hope co-parenting is somethin' we'll be doing together."

"How do you plan on doing that exactly?" Noelle asked bluntly. "I mean, you said you loved me and then *ran*, not walked, away from me. How do I know that the next time shit gets too real, you won't take off again?"

Jack stiffened. "I fucked up and ran out on you. I can't express how sorry I am for that, Noelle. I did it because I was ashamed of the way I treated you our last night together. All my life, I've been terrified that I would turn out like my father with his violent, dominatin' nature. Our last night together, I...I'd never felt more like him," he explained, cringing in self-disgust.

"When you said we were done, I just lost it. The thought of not havin' you in my life was makin' me crazy. I tried to reach you in the only way that I thought would make you see how good we are together. My perverse need to hear you say you belonged to me was disgustin', but I couldn't stop myself."

"That's why you left? Because you felt like you were turning into your father?" Jack nodded solemnly. "Even though you said you loved me?" Noelle persisted.

"It's the only reason. From the moment I saw you at your birthday party, I fell in love with you. You were the most breathtakin' vision I'd ever seen as you carried on a conversation with yourself and downed a mini bottle of tequila." Jack laughed at her surprised look.

"I happened to be sittin' in the dark corner of the library when you crashed my solo party. I hadn't even planned on goin', but Ian convinced me that I should get to know all the family members since your parents were going to be my new clients. I slipped away for some peace and quiet, and then you drifted into that dark room like the first day of spring. I know I should have said somethin', but I was so tongue-tied. I couldn't even speak and then you were gone. I texted Ian back and told him I was stayin'. The plan was to introduce myself to you and figure out how to court you." He glanced away from her for a moment before continuing on.

"But the intensity of my feelings for you scared the hell outta me. I found I couldn't stop watchin' you, wantin' you, and I wanted to beat the shit out of any man foolish enough to step to you. Then you approached me, and I knew as soon as I touched you that everythin' had changed for me. *I* would never be the same. I spent the next twenty-four hours in a trance. You were all I could think about. I collected every piece of information I could find on you and would just stare at your pictures. The need to have you was so fierce and possessive, it terrified even me."

Noelle recalled what Vaughn Emerson said to her months ago.

"I went to his place and there was an open folder with a full dossier on you as well as pictures."

Jack drew a shaky breath. "I felt like I couldn't pursue you because I didn't trust that I wouldn't consume you with my need and jealousy. So instead, I watched. Why do you think I came out to your house so much? Because I couldn't get enough of your mother and her creepy Michelle Obama obsession?" Jack joked half-heartedly. "Like my obsession with you was any better. Hell, I'm listenin' to myself right now and gettin' creeped out."

"I never knew you felt like that." Noelle looked at him in wonder. "I thought you were this sophisticated guy who had women beating down his door, with no clue your client's gawky daughter even existed! You never gave any indication that you were interested. If anything, you seemed disgusted being in my presence."

The tortured look Jack gave her took her breath away. "Baby, you weren't ready for any of this. It would have overwhelmed you. Hell, my feelings for you sometimes still overwhelm *me*. I was scared that if we did pursue somethin', I would stifle you and you'd eventually leave me." He hung his head, shuddering at the thought. "I wouldn't have been able to bear that. You were so young and still had goals to accomplish. Those looks were intended for your family, for not realizin' how special you are. You can't imagine how many times I wanted to stand up for you and tell them to go fuck themselves," Jack sneered.

"I was there the night you asked your father for an advance on your inheritance. The way you left, with your face full of angry determination, let me know that perhaps you weren't as young and naïve as I kept tellin' myself. I reached out to Ira and you ladies did the rest." He squeezed her hand and Noelle saw the pride in his eyes before they darkened with anger.

"Then the Remy thing happened, and I saw a way to get what I wanted while eliminatin' a problem. I'm sorry you had to suffer under the threat of blackmail. I would have stopped him, but apparently, his knack for pissin' people off finally caught up with him. Though, I did send a man over to clear his hard drive and get rid of any evidence of you in his life. I'm sorry, but I just have to do this. It's been so long for me."

Jack bent down and kissed her tenderly. Noelle closed her eyes, reveling in the love story he'd just told her. She wanted to stay lost in this moment with him forever.

He ended the kiss but remained close to her face. "I was in complete hell after I left you. I hid in my house like a fuckin' coward, drinkin' my sorrows away." Noelle touched the bruised side of his face and he grimaced. "It took gettin' the sense knocked into me and you signin' the divorce papers to make me realize that the best thing that ever happened to me was goin' to be gone. We were headin' to the airport when we came upon the accident. God, to think I could have lost you and the baby forever..." Jack pulled back to sit in the chair beside the hospital bed, putting his hands in his face, attempting to pull himself together.

NOELLE WAS ASTONISHED TO SEE Jack so emotional and open. For years, she'd always known him as being imperturbable. It pained her to see him like this because as much as she wanted to take him in her arms and comfort him, Noelle couldn't until they established some ground rules. Clearing his throat, Jack got up and went to the bathroom without looking at her. She heard water running and then five minutes later, he came out. His red eyes were the only telltale sign that he'd shed some tears. He sat down in the chair next to the bed again, and although she was looking at the ceiling, she could feel his eyes on her.

"You must think my obsession with you is really sickening," he muttered helplessly.

"Not really," Noelle considered, a small smile playing about her lips. "I think it's kinda sweet because I'm just as obsessed with you too."

Jack looked flabbergasted by her declaration. "You are?"

Noelle shot him a 'Duh, how could you not know'

glare. "Jack, I've been in love with you since the moment I laid eyes on you! You've lived in my dreams for the last four years of my life. Never did I imagine that I had any kind of chance with someone like you. I was just the stupid Kramer screw-up–"

"Don't ever say that about yourself, darlin'!" Jack demanded fiercely. "You are so much more than what you think! You're smart, talented, beautiful, and kindhearted and I hope the baby takes after you. Who doesn't adore you? Every time I turn around, you've got some guy fallin' all over you. Whether it's your classmate, a client, or that asshole Rothman; any man would recognize what a catch you are."

"Then why didn't you respect me enough to treat me like one?!" she shouted, wincing at the pain it caused. She tried to snatch her hand away, but he gently held fast. "I wanted to die when you left me! You led me to believe we could have something special and treated me like *I* was, but when the going got tough, Jack Sullivan got going. Do you even know what it felt like to be alone when I found out I was pregnant? You were the only person I wanted to tell, and you made yourself unavailable!" All the hurt and anger of the last few months evident in her furious expression.

"I came down here ready to fight for us, to tell you about the baby, and hope that you would be just as happy as I was. I've fought my mother for you, and by the way, you're going to have to tell me exactly why the hell she has it in for you so badly. I've also told my siblings in no uncertain terms that this is *my* life! Those who are skeptical and negative need not stay in it." Noelle paused, motioning for the cup of water.

Disbelief laced his voice as Jack helped her. *"You took on your mother for me?"*

Noelle sipped most of the water, then nodded her head vigorously. "I did because, to me, *you're worth it.*

423

I'd take on a thousand Alicias' for you," she took a deep breath, it was time to negotiate the biggest deal of her life. *Please let this work,* she thought. "I don't want to be married."

The silence in the room was deafening. Jack slowly straightened, eyes blazing with determination as he pulled his hand back and shoved both of them into his pants pockets. She knew he was resisting the urge to hover over her and be his extra persuasive self, which made her love him even more.

"*Noelle, please don't say that.* Let me prove to you that I'm a better man than the jerk who ran out on you. I'm beggin' you, darlin'. *Don't give up on us.* Let me show you how good–"

Holding up her hand for silence, she interrupted him. "I don't want to be married the way that we are *now*. If we're going to stay married, I have two stipulations and they are non-negotiable. The first one is you have to go to therapy. Until you deal with your parents' issues and deaths, they will always be with us. *You are not and never will be your father,*" Noelle said firmly. "We can't bring a child into our relationship with an issue as crucial and unresolved as this. I'll go with you if you want, but I really think you could benefit from it, whether we stay together or not."

Jack's gaze on her was steady. "I already reached out to Dr. Klaus, the shrink that used to counsel us as kids. My first session is in two weeks. Thank you for offerin' to attend with me, but I think I really need to go it alone for awhile. What's the other stipulation?"

"You have to *date* me. I want and deserve all the wining and dining that I should have gotten! I am never going to love anyone like I love you, Jackson Conall Sullivan, and maybe you *did* have my best interest at heart when you set things in motion, but every girl deserves romance, damn it! I want–"

Her words were smothered under his devastating kiss, and she sighed into his soft lips as he whispered tenderly, "Done."

CHAPTER
Thirty-Eight

ONE YEAR ANNIVERSARY

T HE HUGE RUSTIC BARN WAS packed to capacity for the wedding. The bridesmaids were sheathed in oyster silk dresses designed to complement their body types, and the bouquets they held were an assorted mix of pale pink peonies, white roses, and black dahlias. The groomsmen wore classic, tailored black suits with white dress shirts and black cowboy boots.

Percy Sledge's "When a Man Loves a Woman" filled the room, and all eyes turned to the back of the church as the radiant bride appeared on her proud father's arm. She wore a strapless Vera Wang white satin frock with a V-neck and A-line skirt made of tulle and satin. It was simple and classic, showing off her rich, brown skin and lush figure. The jeweled tiara atop her long, wild curls along with her diamond pendant necklace and matching earrings were created specifically for her by Vixen.

As they started the long walk down the petal-covered aisle, she only had eyes for the handsome groom, decked out in his black, custom-fit Tom Ford tux, and the beautiful baby girl, covered in frothy lace, in his arms. The look of love searing brightly in Jack's eyes was enough to make Noelle's own fill with tears. She had to restrain herself from running down the aisle to her man and their sweet baby girl.

Ruby Aileen Sullivan was three months old and the absolute apple of her parents' eye, as well as her grandparents, uncles, aunts...mailman...random sales clerk...pretty much anyone she came into contact with. Her complexion was the color of creamed coffee, and her big, round eyes were gray just like her mama's, with long, ink-black lashes. The fluffy black curls covering her head were silky soft and striking against her chubby, rosy cheeks. She was named after her late Grandma Moira and Noelle's beloved Uncle Harvey, whose signature color had been Ruby Red.

Finally, Noelle reached her family and was only half-listening as her father announced that he was giving her away. Before stepping aside, he pressed a kiss to her cheek. "Be happy. We're all so proud of you, sweet pea," he said gruffly using his nickname for her, He offered Jack his hand. "Look after my babies, Jackson."

"Yes, sir," he swore solemnly as he shifted his beloved daughter to his other arm and returned his father-in-law's handshake. Noelle handed her bouquet, which was a larger version of the bridesmaids to Sloane, her matron of honor, before intertwining her hand in Jack's larger one. Noelle winked at Jack as she heard her mother sniffle loudly before it turned into full-on bawling from the front row.

After being notified of her accident, the entire Kramer family flew down and took up occupancy in the farmhouse, which drove Jack crazy. It was there that Noelle's parents apologized for their insensitive treatment of her. She was surprised to learn that Jack and her father had engaged in a serious conversation regarding his feelings toward her and that Ronald Kramer had given their relationship his blessing. That was until he found out about the baby and Jack's knowledge of his wife's OxyContin addiction.

Alicia confessed to being so stressed creating the perfect image for herself and family that she just wanted to not feel anything at times. While shopping for a home in Florida, she'd begun to discreetly purchase the pills from a Florida senator's wife. After her third trip down to Florida in less than a month, Jack became concerned and arranged to have her followed. Although he'd been looking into facilities that could discreetly assist her, he admitted to blackmailing her to leave Noelle alone. After Noelle confessed to being pregnant by Jack, Alicia decided it was in her best interests to come clean with her husband.

Ronald Kramer was shocked and saddened that he'd been so clueless, that he hadn't even realized the one person he could always count on hadn't been able to count on him. He was furious that Jack would attempt to blackmail her with the information, and the normally mild-mannered senator punched his much larger son-in-law in the jaw. Jaw clenched, Jack informed Ronald that he deserved that, but there would not be a next time. Their relationships were a constant work in progress, but all parties were committed to making them work, especially for the baby's sake.

As they stood before Pastor Clemmons, he made them man and wife (only their close friends and family knew it was actually a vow renewal ceremony). *It was amazing how far they'd come in such a short time,*

Noelle thought with a grateful heart. True to his word, Jack started his counseling sessions soon after they got back to New York. He also started an all-out dating blitz campaign, wooing Noelle with dinners, brunch dates, and flower deliveries to her home and office. He was there for every doctor's appointment and stocked her fridge and pantry for all her weird food cravings like salami with marshmallows. As her belly grew, he gave her pedicures and treated her to sensual massages. They saw each other every day, and he was the perfect gentleman...much to Noelle's dismay and frustration.

No one told her that pregnancy wreaked havoc with your hormones and ramped up your sex drive. No matter how hot and heavy the petting became, Jack refused to sleep with her. Noelle yelled, begged, cajoled, threatened, and staged seductive scenarios, but he wouldn't budge. He definitely made sure she was always satisfied, but Jack was determined for her to see that his intentions were nothing less than honorable, and reluctantly left every night with a chaste kiss to her cheek and a serious case of blue balls.

When Noelle was seven months pregnant, they decided to live together. Jack sold his loft in Manhattan and officially moved into Noelle's Brooklyn brownstone which they decided to buy. They decorated the baby's room together, and soon, the pale pink nursery with wild, floral wallpaper was their favorite room as they anxiously awaited her arrival. Jack designed and created every single piece of wooden furniture in the room. As beautiful as each item was, none of them were her favorite, despite the time and love Jack put into them. Her favorite item was in a gold frame above the crib. It was Jack's Chinese lantern from the No Child Hungry fundraiser. Sent to

Jack's office, Ian had given it to her the day they went to lunch with her mother. Worn and dirty, the words were still visible and legible in Jack's bold handwriting.

To Whoever Finds This,
Four years ago, I met the most beautiful girl in the world and wished that if I was lucky enough, someway, somehow, I'd be her husband. Fate has smiled upon me because, in three days, my wish will be coming true, so it's time to pay it forward. My wish for you is that you find a love like this if you haven't already been blessed to meet him or her. I love her to the moon and back and want the whole world to know it, starting with you.
Jack C. Sullivan
New York City

Also included in the package was a lovely thank you note from an older, happily married farm couple in Michigan, wishing them a lifetime of happiness.

"I now pronounce you man and wife!"

Heartfelt cheers and whoops of joy rang out as Jack and Noelle kissed sweetly and Ruby cooed excitedly. After they jumped the beautifully-handcrafted broom that was Guy's gift to them, pictures were taken, and cocktail hour began outside under a million twinkling lights threaded among the trees.

While guests feasted on delicious appetizers of shrimp and grits squares, braised short rib and bleu cheese crostini, and chicken salad wonton cups from the bar outside in the cool spring air, Noelle and Avery's team removed all the pews from the barn and transformed it into a beautiful reception area done in rustic elegance. It took ten people to transport the enormous, beautiful seven-tiered, naked sponge cake with fruit, mascarpone and crème brulee cream between the layers. After the transformation, Mr. & Mrs. Jack Sullivan danced their first dance to Whitney Houston's "I Believe in You & Me".

> *I believe in you and me*
> *I believe that we will be*
> *In love eternally*
> *As far as I can see*
> *You will always be*
> *The one for me*
> *Oh yes you will*

"Happy, baby?" Jack drawled huskily. All day long, he could hardly keep his eyes off of her. She was just so damn pretty – and his. *All his.* He didn't know what he'd done right in this lifetime to be blessed with the two beautiful girls that he had, but he would do everything in his power to make sure he stayed in good favor for the rest of his days.

"Unbelievably so, Jack," Noelle assured him reverently as she smoothed short, black curls back from his forehead. Waking up next to him every morning was a dream come true and having Ruby in their lives was the icing on the cake.

"Me too. When do you think we should tell people that we're moving here permanently?" he asked, twirling her around the dance floor. They'd been dividing their time between New York and Tennessee for the last five months as Jack's other business began to expand and he took on more responsibilities. Life in Brooklyn was good, but Whiskey Row just felt like home to them, somewhere that Ruby could grow up running around outside and they opened their home to family and friends.

I believe in you and me
I will never leave your side
I will never hurt your pride
When all the chips are down
I will always be around
Just to be right there where you are my love
Oh I love you boy

"Shhhh! My mother will hear you, and you know how much she loves to spend time with Ruby," Noelle hissed. Alarmed, she searched around for her mother. Thank goodness she was nowhere around. "I think she's transferred her obsession from Mrs. O to our baby girl. Besides, I think you should tell tem that you have other business investments that you need to take care of. You know, the ones you neglected to tell your wife that you're part-owner of, remember?"

Noelle cackled as Jack tipped his head back, groaning up at the ceiling. "You're never gonna let me live that down are you, darlin'? I've said I was sorry a hundred thousand times, and since then I've done all of the furniture for both of our homes like you asked–"

"I know, I know. I just like giving you shit once in a while. Besides, you more than made up for it with your romantic gesture," she said, giggling as he nuzzled her neck.

"Liked that one, did you?" he teased, nipping her earlobe and sending tingles down her body. Jack felt her slight shiver and smiled. *Man, he couldn't wait for their wedding night to start.* To mess up the glossy stuff coating her sexy mouth and turn her curls into the 'just got thoroughly ravished' style he preferred.

"Best. Romantic. Gesture. Ever." Noelle replied lovingly. One day, during the redecorating process for the brownstone, Jack called her into the living room and said he wanted to show her something. Then he flipped the wooden coffee table over and pointed to something written on the inside of one of the legs. When she leaned down to look she had to read it ten times before she could fully comprehend it. Covering her mouth with both hands she raised wide eyes to meet his in disbelief. Solemnly, he nodded his head opening his arms as she waddled over and threw herself at him. It was an inscription that Jack carved in when he was making the table for her. *J.C.S. + N.L.K* with a heart carved around them. Talks of renewing their vows again were back on the table that night.

"Ian looks pretty happy with himself, don't you think?" Noelle asked, catching her godfather's eye and he blew her a kiss. *Happy was an understatement,* Jack thought. The slick bastard radiated smugness as he mouthed the words 'be happy' to them.

"I'll tell you who doesn't look that happy – Viv. Alexei is in hot pursuit of her tonight, and there's nowhere for her to run," Jack chuckled, spying the giant Russian looking at his godmother like she was his favorite snack of beluga caviar and blintzes. Vivienne was doing her best to avoid him by mingling with guests on the opposite side of the room. It was the cat and mouse game they'd played all day.

Darby had found a way to fulfill his part of the bargain with Alexei. It cost him twenty thousand dollars, and that was a deal considering the company he used was family. Darby had offered to pay for the wedding reception as long as they had it here in Whiskey Row, which let him off the hook with Alexei because they all knew Vivienne would come for the wedding of one of her godsons, regardless of where it was held. Yes, his brother seemed genuinely happy with himself as he danced with Ruby in his arms – until his eyes strayed to Avery sitting with her now-fiancé Pierce. Jack wasn't worried. Judging from the way

Avery's gaze drifted longingly to Darby while he played with her goddaughter, it was only a matter of time before his middle brother got what he wanted.

"Are you sure that we have to leave Ruby?" Every time he looked at their daughter, Jack was in awe that he and Noelle had created such a perfect, little human being. He could still hear Noelle's shrieks of laughter when they brought baby girl home from the hospital and she caught him, Casey, and Darby cleaning their guns on the back porch. From the day he found out about Noelle's pregnancy, all of Jack's priorities shifted. He made sure that he worked from home more frequently. And whenever Noelle had to go to the office, he brought Ruby with him, where she had her own space in his office. "It's not too late to change the flight and get a nanny to come–"

"*No.* While I can appreciate the love you have for our baby, this is our wedding night. You will be putting out tonight, Mr. Sullivan. Is that clear?" Noelle replied saucily, planting a slow, sensual kiss on him that had his hands gripping her waist, then sliding down to cup her bottom and pull her closer to let her feel his erection pressing into her stomach.

Jack felt a surge of guilt as all thoughts of his baby girl fled his mind because he couldn't wait to get his wife alone. As much as he loved how beautiful Noelle looked in her wedding dress, he couldn't wait to see her out of it, to be buried between her silken thighs, inhaling every sound he could make her utter. They were going on a three-week tour of Europe for their honeymoon, and he planned to do wild, wicked things to her the entire trip. *I should probably warn her now that she'll be coming back pregnant,* he mused, staring down into her eyes.

"Crystal clear, Mrs. Sullivan," Jack said tenderly against her lips amidst the catcalling.

"Mmmmm...I love you, Mr. Sullivan," Noelle whispered between kisses. "Forever and always."

"I love you too, Mrs. Sullivan," he whispered back, eyes brimming with love. "You're the sweetest obsession ever."

EPILOGUE

 HE LOUD MUSIC FROM THE reception covered the sound of their steps racing up the stairs. Quickly, he pulled her into the nearest room, kicking the door shut behind them. He'd been unable to keep his eyes off of her all night. She was so beautiful in the satin dress that clung to her enticing figure. He was finding it hard to contain his jealousy as she danced with several of the men in attendance.

When he could stand it no longer, he'd snatched her by the wrist and now, here they were, a little intoxicated but by mutual agreement. He pushed her back against the door, hiking the skirt of her dress up before lifting her up, those long sleek legs encircling his waist. She wrapped her arms around his neck, and their lips met in hot desperate kisses as she reached between them to hastily unbuckle his pants and pull him free of his boxers. He used one hand to slide her damp thong to the side, and her arousal was a heady scent that was better than any perfume he'd ever smelled.

Desire raged through them, and the need to come together was so great. They weren't thinking about the consequences of their actions as he lined himself up with her wetness and thrust into her with an unrestrained intensity that made them both growl. *It had been too long.* Hot silk coated his steel rod and the feeling was so intense, his legs almost gave out from beneath him. If there was a feeling better than this, he didn't want to know what it was. She moaned loudly against his lips at the invasion of his thick length but quickly adjusted, eager to be fucked by him repeatedly.

Pulling back slightly, he saw desire warring with defiance on her face. *Lord, she's beautiful,* he thought, a little awestruck to be here with her like this. She raised an eyebrow, smirking as if to say, '*Is that all you got?*' Challenge accepted. He gripped her hips, flexing deep inside of her, and she strived to remain unaffected. Her body called his bluff as his cock was suddenly drenched in a burst of fresh arousal. He groaned, pressing his forehead against hers, resisting the impulse to come right then and there. His eyes drifted down to the swells of her breasts.

"Pull down your dress," he demanded hoarsely, and she quickly obeyed, yanking the bodice of her gown down to reveal two, exquisite, chocolate mounds topped by enlarged, blackberry-colored nipples. His mouth went dry at the thought of her parading around bra-less. He lifted her higher and pulled one of the succulent tips into his mouth. Her head fell back against the door as she shamelessly offered more of herself to him. He switched to the other bud, lavishing it with the same attention.

She tried to draw in a breath as bolts of electricity zigzagged up and down her spine at the feel of his firm lips and warm tongue paying homage to her womanly parts. He was driving her crazy. Grabbing a fistful of his hair, she yanked him off her breasts, imperiously demanding, *"Fuck. Me. Now."*

Now, he was the one smirking as he slowly withdrew to the head then rammed back into her ever-increasing moistness. Once. Twice. She caught his rhythm quickly, and their dance for dominance was on. A fine sheen of perspiration coated her chest and sweat trickled down his neck as the flames of desire burned brightly out of control. Her fingers slid through his hair, and she pulled his lips back to hers, tightening her legs to lock him in while sliding up and down on his engorged cock. She whimpered as he took control, pinning her to the door and got down to the serious business of fucking her. His deep strokes danced the thin line of pleasure and pain, but he didn't stop because he knew she could take it.

This woman was all fire and would die before backing down from a challenge. Over and over they came together against the door, making it rattle and shake beneath their fevered mating. Both were on the verge of an orgasm so powerful, it would change them forever, and yet, even in this very intense moment, their personalities refused to play nice with one another.

"You like this," he stated arrogantly, slowing his thrusts, hips circling achingly slow. Christ, he could feel his balls constricting, but he would not cum. Not until she admitted to him that she was as far gone as he. *He needed to hear her say it, to know he wasn't in this unstoppable madness by himself.* "Say you like the way I fuck you, and you can cum. Don't try to lie to me either. Your pussy's so wet it could flood this room."

She glared at him, working her kegel muscles like crazy, enjoying the way his face contorted uncontrollably. *Like* was too mild a word for the way she felt about his loving, but she'd be damned if she admitted it aloud. *He would break before her*, she vowed, riding him like a jockey in a tie to cross the finish line of the Kentucky Derby.

"You're alright," she taunted breathlessly. Clench. Up. Down. Clench. *Shiiit.* She was so close. "Say my name!" she dictated, and he shook his head no, slamming his mouth down on hers.

Neither would give in, but their sexual release was imminent. Suddenly, it was there, flinging them up at lightning speed to count every star in the sky. His muscles turned to stone, and he slapped at the door behind her as she trembled uncontrollably in his arms. Finally, they broke apart, gasping for breath. "Casey," she sighed raggedly, simultaneously he hoarsely whispered, "Sidra."

———————————————

AVERY FELT GUILTY FOR SEEKING Darby out, but she was just as helplessly drawn to him as she was to the exquisite little girl he was softly serenading. She watched from the lounge doorway as Darby expertly changed Ruby's diaper. His deep, melodic voice crooned Luke Bryan's "Crash My Party" to the gurgling baby who kicked her chubby legs in the air.

It don't matter what plans I got, I can break 'em.
Yeah, I can turn this thing around at the next red light
And I don't mind telling all the guys I can't meet 'em.
Hell, we can all go raise some hell on any other night
Girl, I don't care, oh I just gotta see what you're wearing.
Your hair, is it put up or falling down?
Oh, I just have to see it now.
If you wanna call me, call me, call me you don't have to worry 'bout it, baby.
You can wake me up in the dead of the night, wreck my plans, baby that's alright.
This is a drop everything kind of thing.

The sight of the two of them tugged at her heartstrings. The big, beautiful man caring for his tiny niece filled her with a craving for a family of her own. Avery sighed and saw Darby stiffen. She waited for him to turn around, but he didn't, even though he knew she was there. The silence stretched between them until she spoke. "You're so good with her."

Darby closed his eyes and prayed for the good Lord to give him strength. *Thou shall not covet another man's...*

Silently, he chuckled as he smoothed Ruby's dress back down. He tossed the dirty diaper into a nearby trashcan and applied sanitizer to his hands before picking her up. "Nah, she's good for us. Ain't that right, honey pie?" Darby crooned, bringing the baby close to his face. He was rewarded with her trying to bite his nose. "If you do that, how am I gonna be able to smell your delightful diapers, Ms. Ruby?"

Avery smiled, easily picturing him with his own brood of red-haired kids. Again, silence stretched between them, and she wished she could trade places with Ruby who was now snuggled into her uncle's broad chest, drifting off to sleep contentedly.

"You clean up well," Avery gestured to his tux. During the ceremony, it was all she could do to keep from staring at him outright as he stood across from her. The only one to wear a black cowboy hat, Darby was incredibly handsome. He'd since ditched the hat to one of Noelle's nephews and his slicked back hairstyle made her think of old-school actors like Cary Grant.

"Awww, shucks. I was just tryin' to keep up with the prettiest girl in the room." He flashed a dazzling smile. She blushed, and Darby wondered for the hundredth time how Avery kept getting prettier and prettier every time he saw her. He could tell she'd lost a little bit of weight and wondered if it had to do with the bougie dickweed that was responsible for the ring on her finger. His eyes slid down to the gold band with a two-carat diamond in the center. The ring was too plain for someone as bright and vivacious as Avery. If she were his woman...his jaw clenched as he reminded himself that she wasn't... and it was best he didn't forget it and try to go there.

"Are you excited about the possible pop-up shop this summer in the Hamptons?" Avery asked curiously. Americana Traditions was doing so well that they decided to open shop in East New York. Due to prior commitments, only Guy was available, so Darby decided to tag along. They would reside there this summer, and since they hired On a Whim to plan all their events, Avery would be joining them as soon as her new office manager was trained.

"Now you know schmoozin' with uppity, rich folks ain't my thing! I'd much rather chill on a boat fly fishin' with a six pack of cold beer. When are we supposed to be goin' house huntin'?"

Avery looked at him in surprise. "Oh, I thought you knew that we're all staying together at my parents' house in Southampton. It's close to the beach and shops. There's more than enough room for all of us. You can even bring someone if you'd like."

She blushed furiously at his penetrating stare. Why did she say that?? *Because you're supposedly so happy, and you want everyone you care about to be happy too, her conscience taunted.*

"I can bring someone, huh?" Darby asked casually. His stomach knotted with jealousy as a thought occurred to him. "Is that what you plan on doin'?"

Avery wanted the floor to open up and swallow her right about now. "No! I mean...no. Pierce is actually working on the west coast this summer, and we'll meet up if our schedules permit. We both understand that we have a lot on our plates right now. Understanding is really important in making a relationship work, don't you agree?"

Instead of responding, Darby glanced down at her hands. "I guess congratulations are in order." Staring pointedly look at her left hand and she covered the ring by nervously clasping her hands tightly together.

"Oh, yeah. Thanks." Avery awkwardly crossed her arms. "Guess he finally saw the light."

Darby didn't crack his usual easygoing smile. He just regarded her with some unfathomable emotion in his dark green eyes as he swayed side to side with Ruby sleeping on his shoulder. They smiled at each other as the baby exhaled a gentle snore.

"Why don't I take her?" Avery suggested, coming forward with her arms outstretched. "You haven't eaten a thing all night." At his raised eyebrow, she smiled sheepishly. Damn, now she'd been busted at keeping tabs on him "Go get yourself something to eat, please. It's way too quiet between Casey and Sidra. I'm expecting fireworks at any minute, and I'll need your strength to keep them from ruining this perfect day," she teased.

Darby raised his eyes to the ceiling above them. Earlier, he'd seen Casey take Sidra by the hand and lead her up the stairs. "You don't know the half of it."

He was enveloped in Avery's flowery perfume as he placed Ruby in her arms. Darby smiled as she closed her eyes and held the baby, inhaling her special baby scent with a dreamy smile lighting up her face. *She's a natural*, he thought. Darby could easily see her with a swollen belly, radiating a pregnancy glow. A sense of peace filled the room as they silently enjoyed one another's company.

Avery's biological clock was ticking so loudly, she

was surprised Darby couldn't hear it. *This was heaven on earth: spending time with her precious goddaughter and Darby,* Avery thought. Her eyes flew open, and she took a step back from him. *O.M.G. What was wrong with her?* Her fiancé was right down the hall and could easily have come looking for her. *It was time to go,* she thought with great reluctance. But she couldn't just yet. Although nothing had ever transpired between them, she felt like she owed Darby some sort of explanation.

His calls were the only thing that kept Avery sane during the challenging time of running the business solo and watching over Noelle. He was a breath of fresh air in comparison to Pierce, who called her constantly, whining about when she was coming home or that he couldn't find something. With Darby, it was so different. They'd talked about current events, favorite shows, and their bucket lists. He alternated between laughing with her and cursing his brother on Noelle's behalf as Avery aided her through that dark period.

"Darby, I–" she started to speak but stopped when he raised a hand, also aware that the spell was broken. For a moment, Darby had allowed himself to foolishly believe that she was his girl, and Ruby was *their* baby. *Stupid, stupid, stupid him!* The good girls weren't for him and never would be. *Would he never learn?*

"You don't owe me any explanations. Just be happy, Ms. Avery," he said seriously. "Not everyone gets to be."

Hopelessly she watched him walk toward the door and had to swallow the rising protest in her throat. He paused in the doorway without turning around.

"That song I was singin'?" Darby wouldn't, or couldn't, look back because he knew without a doubt that if he did, he would grab her and kiss her like he'd dreamed of doing since the first time he laid eyes on her.

"Yes, I'm familiar with it," Avery held Ruby tightly to stop herself from running after him. The baby whimpered, and Avery kissed her curls, murmuring soothing sounds to her as she breathlessly waited for Darby to speak.

"Anytime, Ms. Avery. *Anytime*," he offered then walked out, leaving her craving him even more.

VIVIENNE ROMANKOV SIPPED HER CHAMPAGNE, watching as her youngest godson slipped away with Sidra. *Well, I'll be damned,* she thought in amusement. It was about damn time that boy loosened up and had some fun. Ms. Thang would certainly keep him on his toes. She turned away, careful to keep her gaze averted from across the room where she could feel the heat emanating from the laser-like stare *he* had trained on her.

Desire unfurled slowly in her like a dormant genie finally being awakened, proving that after all these years, she still wasn't immune to his virile, Russian ass and probably never would be, damn him. A familiar tinkling laugh caught her attention, and she glanced to the right to see her daughter, who'd avoided her as successfully as she had Alexei all night, laughing with Holton Brammer before going to join all the single women on the floor, dying to catch the bride's bouquet.

Vivienne's lips tightened, recognizing the attraction between the two of them. The last thing she wanted was for her baby to be trapped in this godforsaken town with its deep secrets and evil residents. The laugh came again, and she flinched when Kat caught the bouquet. *No, no, no,* she thought, panicking while everyone cheered. Her daughter brought it up to her face for a sniff, batting her eyelashes at Holt who looked like he wanted to ravish her on the spot. Alarmed, Vivienne instinctively sought Alexei to see what he thought of the whole thing.

But he was no longer there.

Although disappointed, she recognized it for what it was – a sign for her to get the hell up outta Dodge while she still could. He'd toyed with her all day, had her damn nerves straining to the breaking point, but Vivienne would be damned if she let anyone see her sweat. Swiftly, she made her way toward the exit.

"Coast finally cleared, eh?" Ian questioned, blocking her way. His eyes filled were filled with mirth as he nibbled on a canapé. Always flawlessly groomed, he looked quite dashing in his navy-blue suit, his long, silver hair in his signature man bun atop his head. She gave him a look known to make grown men cower, but he appeared unperturbed and offered her a nibble.

"Bite me, Gandalf," Viv retorted affectionately, kissing his offered cheek. "Brunch this Sunday at the usual spot?"

"But of course, my dear," he agreed, squeezing her waist and looking over her shoulder. Vivienne saw that he was focused on Noelle holding Ruby. Jack had his arms wrapped around both of them. They were surrounded by well-wishers, laughing and smiling. For the mother and son dance, he'd spun Vivienne around the dance floor to Ben E. King's "Stand By Me", while Noelle danced with her father and then Ian to The Temptations "My Girl" and Coldplay's "Yellow". Vivienne's heart swelled with love, so happy for her boy and his family. It almost put her in a forgiving mood.

Almost.

"You know that our girl is dancing up in heaven, feeling all the love and joy down here, right?" She was choked-up and blinking back tears.

Ian wanted to say more but feared becoming emotional himself. Instead, he warned, "Better hurry up, Cinderella. Midnight will be upon you soon."

Vivienne swatted his arm with her beaded clutch and continued toward the exit, turning one last time to look at her baby girl dancing in the big Swede's arms. *Oh, how she wanted to snatch Kat away and never let her go!* With a sigh, Vivienne continued on her way. Tomorrow, she would strategize. Tonight, she conceded to cowardice and fleeing.

As she exited the building and hurried down the steps to her black limo, again there was the brief sense of disappointment that she would not be seeing Alexei one last time. *It really was for the best,* she told herself resolutely, smiling at the driver holding the door open for her.

"Thanks. I need to get to the airport, ASAP," Vivienne told him crisply and slid into the car. The faster she could put miles between them the better. Immediately she stiffened in awareness, registering that she was not alone as the scent of expensive cigars, vetiver, citrus, and something woodsy assailed her senses. Seated across from her, oozing more masculinity and sex appeal than any middle-aged man had a right to was her insanely handsome, estranged husband; the man that she'd successfully managed to avoid for what felt like forever.

Alexei Romankov shifted forward in his seat, eyes glowing with victory as he smirked at Vivienne, displaying his brilliant, white teeth. Lustrous black and silver waves fell across his forehead while Alexei surveyed her, stroking his neatly-groomed beard contemplatively. *He was too damn good-looking for his own good and hers,* Vivienne seethed resentfully, allowing herself the pleasure of drinking in the site of him. His tux fit his rugged body exquisitely, and he looked exactly like what he was: a rich as Midas bastard who expected everyone to jump and do his bidding.

"What's your hurry, Vivi?" he inquired in that deep accented baritone that still made her knees weak and her pulse skitter.

Damn, damn, damn!

She was in big trouble.

THE END

ACKNOWLEDGMENTS

THE LAST COUPLE OF YEARS have been such an incredible journey! None of it would be possible without God. He's taken me and my imagination to places I never thought I'd experience and levels I never thought I'd reach. I'm walking in faith, but the encouragement of friends, family, and readers is such a sweet bonus blessing. My heart is full of love and undying gratitude for each and every one of you.

LITTLE PEAR EDITING – Your advice and guidance is invaluable. Thank you for understanding and supporting my vision and my need to constantly hone my craft. Thank you for lending your ear AND shoulder to me, lol. I adore you and absolutely appreciate all you do.

KAREN KUNZ – You've been with me since day one. I appreciate you not running from my crazy, lol. You're simply the best! Thank you so much for your dedication and commitment to your talent.

IDEALITY CONSULTING – Thank you for being an absolute professional. Your feedback, efficiency, and attention to detail make you an invaluable asset that I'm blessed to have.

T.E. BLACK DESIGNS – We haven't worked together for long, but you're amazing! Thank you for understanding my vision.

TO MY FAMILY – Thank you for your endless support, unconditional love, and adapting to this author's hectic schedule. You're my heart and soul, the BEST part of me. My love for you is limitless.

OTHER BOOKS
By D.A. Young

WHISKEY ROW SERIES
Sweet Obsession
New Beginnings
The Pursuit of Happiness
Perfectly Imperfect
No Greater Love

BAYMOOR SERIES
The Farmer & The Belle
Lost & Found
Take A Chance on Me

CIRCLE OF FRIENDS NOVELLA SERIES
Second Chances
Forever Yours

THE TIES THAT BIND SERIES
Book One
Book Two

BAXTER PARK
Winner Takes All (Coming soon)

ABOUT THE
Author

D. A. YOUNG IS A DAUGHTER, mother, Gigi, wife, and work in progress who loves God and the life she's been blessed to create with her family and friends. Food, traveling, reading, and music are her passions. Raised on dramas such as "Dynasty" and "General Hospital", D. A. Young is an author of adventures featuring multiple characters and subplots.

Interested in what I'm doing next?

FOLLOW ME ON FACEBOOK!

https://www.facebook.com/D-A-Young-1695356880704195/

www.ingramcontent.com/pod-product-compliance
Lightning Source LLC
Chambersburg PA
CBHW070831260626
47170CB00007B/2333